The Third Light

The Mad Game
Book Three

Chris Cherry
A Love and War Series Novel

The author and publisher are proud to be working shoulder to shoulder with the Royal British Legion, supporting their valuable work with our Armed Forces, young and old

Published by Trench Publishing, Manchester, UK

ISBN-13: 9780992935122

DEDICATION

This book is dedicated to the men and women, from all nations,
caught up in the tragedies that were
The First and Second World Wars

Also by the Author
Love and War Novels

The Mad Game Series

The Mad Game - William's Story

The Mad Game – Christmas Present 1913
(eBook December 2013)

Odile's War - The Mad Game Book Two

CREDITS
Cover Graphic Design – Mark Bowers at The Devil's Crayon
Cover Photography – Bernadette at Bernadette Delaney
Photography
Copy Editing – Helen Steadman at The Critique Boutique
Cover Costumes - Arranged by Luda Krzak at The Royal
Exchange Theatre Manchester

TEST READERS
Keira Rawden
Barbara Kinsky
Dian Bambaji
Clare Redfern

CHAPTER ONE

Nuremberg The Palace of Justice 1947

The window had a disappointing view. The grey stone and the black painted wood offered a sombre outlook. But beyond, in the wide expanse of the concrete groundworks built by a Germany dominated and ruled by the Nazis, a large crowd was visiting the now infamous rallying stages, the scene of many great oratories from the leaders of a nation. On those heady days, hundreds of thousands clamoured to hear the words of the elite of the party, hanging on every syllable and intonation. Today, it was a few hundred, looking like ants scurrying across the pavements trying to find the shade.

The little room was comfortable enough, containing large and small tables with wooden chairs, providing places to sit and talk, rehearse and discuss, argue and refine. A bustle of junior officers and secretaries, and the constant sound of typewriters and footsteps. This morning, it was quieter and a little tense for today was a first day. On this day would begin another momentous chapter in history, another final act played out to bring the World War finally to an end.

The short walk to the courtroom offered a chance to go over, for one final time, the questions and the arguments for the day. A quick chance to settle, to gather thoughts and to put on the mask, to become the character he would have to be in order to prosecute these cases. At the office door was a short flight of stone steps, then just a few paces in the morning sunshine before entering the sudden darkness at the entrance to the Palace of Justice in Nuremberg.

But today was always going to be different in so many ways. As soon as the little hidden door was opened for him, a heatwave of news-hungry humanity swept over the youngest of the Allied prosecution team. As he looked down to find the first step, he could hear the individual voices and was able to pick out the reporters he knew. There they all were, clamouring for any comment, however brief. He could make out the drawl of the southerner, the rounded vowels of the tall and immaculately dressed *New York Times* reporter and the insistent and clipped typewriter staccato of the bespectacled and moustached British journalist from Cambridge.

He was very good with languages. He had learned English and French of course, as well as German and some Russian. But today, the pack would have to go hungry as he could not, would not, feed them anything out here in the morning sunshine before the trial had even begun. What would happen inside the court in just a few minutes would be enough to satisfy their appetites for news for months to come. But they did not know it yet. Only he really knew what they were going to hear and it was horrific, explosive and shocking. Fine words for the newspapers.

He carried with him an embarrassingly new leather briefcase. Just for this morning, it contained six neatly handwritten sheets of paper. On top of those were six more identical, but perfectly typed, sheets of paper just in case the court needed to see the words. But these few important papers were just the very top of a much bigger pile of papers that he had been reading and digesting, writing and editing, weeping and shouting over for the last nine months. Today, in this now famous room, would be the day that the results of this painstaking and harrowing work would be revealed to the world, released to the stunned and shocked courtroom as a carefully constructed case for the prosecution. Today, the six Nazi officers who were the accused would begin a trial for their lives.

He had now crossed the sunlit walkway and reached the court itself. He tipped his hat to the officer at the door to the palace and he disappeared into the cool darkness of the entrance, breathing out heavily as he did do. The mass of journalists quickly melted away to find their seats in the arena of law, perhaps disappointed for now, but of course they all knew the main event would begin in just a few eagerly anticipated minutes. They could now be seen filing into the cool of the court rooms, wanting to see into the eyes of the accused. They wanted to taste the raw emotion and to see the legal adversaries, the men who would seek to bring the accused to justice, a peace of sorts for those who had suffered and died before them.

At the door to the austere and sparse anteroom, the American chief prosecutor emerged looking pale and grimly determined. He was only twenty-seven years old, but at the pinnacle of the American legal system, which brought with it now the collective weight of expectation from across the world on his broad young shoulders. He took two steps forward, extending his hand.

'How are you feeling? Are you set and ready for this?'

'Good morning, Ben. Yes, I think I am ready. Our first case together then? How about that?'

'I know, a poor boy from Transylvania and the immigrant son of a refugee. Look at the two of us!'

'Yes,' his voice hardened just a little, 'look at us.'

'We had better go in, it is time to begin.'

There was a calm air of expectation in the court. The bench for the judges was empty, but the rest of the court was packed, both the terraces and the ceiling gallery were full of standing and seated people. Once everyone had finally been seated, the two prosecutors stepped forward, sitting together, opening their briefcases at the same time, putting their neat piles of paper in front of them on the large table. The very same table that only a year before had been used during the prosecution of the elite leaders of the Nazi machine whose ministering officers would be on trial today.

Suddenly, the court hushed. All eyes immediately turned to the large door where the accused would enter the court. It had opened just a fraction, but then it moved a little more and someone was clearly holding the handle on the other side. Then, with a quick movement, it opened fully and out of the dark blackness stepped six men to gasps from the public galleries. The men were all dressed in matching dark grey suits, with neatly pressed shirts and ties, and all refused to look up from the floor, except for one of them, the oldest, in his fifties perhaps. He had a handsome, confident, perhaps superior air. He scanned the court room until his eyes fell upon the prosecutors, where they remained fixed and focused. He smiled thinly at them, a smile without humour, a smile meant as the first chess move. He nodded to them, moving his head only slightly, and then took his seat.

Six men would today be charged with terrible crimes committed during the war, offences committed outside even the painful indecency of warfare. Men who had wives and families, eight children between them, shockingly ordinary men of the party. But each possessed a damaged and poisoned soul, holding deep inside the most terrible secrets. Secrets that the court and the prosecutors here would expose to the still-shocked world. Secrets they would prove to the world, which would warrant these men a just death. A death with a dignity not afforded to those humiliated and cleaved in the lands of Eastern Europe.

As the last of the defendants sat, the three judges entered, their gowns billowing just a little behind them, as if there had been a gentle breeze to greet them. As one, the entire court and galleries stood, but the defendants remained defiantly seated in silence, not even acknowledging the judges by looking towards where they had entered. The judges sat and took a moment to compose themselves, also adjusting already perfect piles of papers and folders. The rustle of chairs and the scraping of feet subsided, and collective deep breaths could be heard. The chief judge waited for the perfect moment, looked up and addressed the court.

'Today, we begin the trial of six men accused of some of the most serious crimes against the common decency of mankind, of most grievous, vicious and terrible deeds. That they superintended, directed and actively took part in the murder, on a massive scale, of citizens of Europe. To this aim of prosecuting the accused and to allow justice for those who died outside of the protection of the law to prevail, I call upon you, sir, Mr Deputy Chief Prosecutor, to read and indict the defendants according to the rules agreed for the trials of war criminals before these Nuremberg Military Tribunals.'

The silence was almost tangible and the air thickened to a soup, drying the mouth and bringing perspiration to the palms. Eyes now moved to the young man at the desk. He buttoned his jacket and slid back his chair from under the table.

He slowly stood, now in character, remembering that he had earned his place at the top of the prosecuting team, alongside Ben. This was the biggest and proudest day of his young life. Still only in his early twenties, he took a moment to glance around the court, deliberately scanning the faces of the accused, making his move on the chessboard. He took in the scene; the judges and galleries of newspaper reporters, the snapping cameras, the larger film-reel cameras and the faces of the public, whom he represented. They had brought this trial and he was their voice. He could feel again a collective drawing of breath, the hushed expectation, and now the weight of the case before him gently resting upon his own shoulders, settling onto Ben and himself for the duration of the trial. He was now ready. He had prepared thoroughly, evenings, weekends, late nights – seeing the sun set and the sun rise without sleep. Impeccably dressed, he wore the special cuff weights that his loving mother had given him for this very day. His late father would have been so proud of his boy, and he took a second to think for a moment about his father, imagining his face in the gallery above.

He looked down at the top page, his finger scanning the words, looking for the right paragraph amongst his scribbled speech, with late changes and notes all over, just as he liked, ordered yet fluid, clear and precise, with pencil notes in case he forgot to emphasise a word. He hoped that the most important first word would come out of his dry mouth. For the sound of this first word and the sound of his voice would define his credibility. Now, he too drew a deep breath and looked up slowly and deliberately into the eyes of the six accused. He paid special attention to the older man on the left, who was regarding him with suspicion and superiority, whilst idly dusting off his lapel. He thought of him. He would not get the better of them. Not here and certainly not today. This was his day. This was a battle of wits and words and he was the very best at winning them, just as surely as these accused men had been good at unimaginable acts of extermination.

'War is an unspeakable act, which causes the person to behave in or out of a character shaped by the politics of the age. But an act of war is understood to be necessary where the character of the politicians fails us most decidedly. But where a person, a system, a philosophy acts out of cruelty, revenge or some misinformed sense of superiority to subjugate and to prosecute will and manifest persecution over another, then it is no longer a war. It is a crime of war.'

He paused, just for a second, the words here and now had to be perfect. Give them nothing to build their defence upon and they will hang from a rope for certain.

'The accused sitting here in this court are thus charged and today indicted with the following: crimes against humanity, through persecutions on political, racial, and religious grounds; murder, extermination, imprisonment, and other inhumane acts committed against civilian populations, including German nationals and nationals of other countries. War crimes – that is, murder and extermination of public officials and military persons, outside of the specific provisions customary of war. Furthermore, they are charged with crimes against peace, entailing the pursuit of violence where otherwise a state of legal obedience was observed.'

He sat down, Ben nodded his approval and they both turned towards the accused. His hands were trembling as the first of the accused was asked to stand to answer the charges. The prisoner, impeccably dressed, leaned on the rail as he stood slowly and deliberately, his hand on the front of his suit to keep it neatly against his body. He then let both hands drop to his side as he looked up, now directly and deliberately into the eyes of the much younger prosecutors, perhaps searching for weaknesses in their character. Without flinching or blinking, he spoke, his voice resonating to the very highest part of the public gallery, which ran all around the court room.

'Nicht schuldig.'

CHAPTER TWO

The Western Front 1915

The morning sunshine brought a welcome cheer to the German Army based in Cambrai. The year of fighting had calmed down in this sector of northern France and a routine rhythm of postings to the Front was pleasantly entwined with days like these, safe from the regular shelling of the occupied territories. For Kurt Langer in Cambrai, this posting brought the opportunity to rest and recuperate. For him, as an officer of army transport, visits to the front line were rare and when he did get to the lines, his visits would be brief. His job was to make sure that the lines of ambulances, lorries and supplies were kept open and operating. He did not mind the task, since it was mostly safer than infantry duty, even here in a quiet sector. By chance, he had come upon the civilian camps. These temporary villages of squalor were set up all along the occupied areas when villages were overrun and the citizens did not have the good fortune of escape. For some, the Germans simply moved too quickly and they were captured whilst running from their homes, usually in terror. The German treatment of French citizens was harsh and often brutal, for they had not been recruited and trained to nurse enemy citizens and cared little for their needs. They could be treated badly and no one could make much of a fuss, and if they did, well, they could be removed and silenced easily enough.

For Kurt, today was a day to think about his luck in finding the camps and in meeting a young French girl. It had been a chance meeting since he had not intended getting to know any of the poor wretches living in mud and their own filth. He had eyed them with curiosity, but had soon come to realise that the lines of hungry and dirty faces were simply ordinary people in extraordinary situations, much like his own German family. This girl was not much older than his own sister, Liesel, and had her treatment been like this, then he would have wished to do something about it.

'So, Kurt, you have found yourself a beautiful little French girl then, eh? You are a lucky bastard. When you have finished with her, send her to me, to meet a real man.'

'I will not! You might be a fat and stupid Brandenburger, but you are right about one thing, she is most beautiful. I have a feeling that we will come to know each other really quite well, war or not.'

'So tell me, Langer, how did you meet her again? Tell me, because I want to know your dirty secrets. It can't be because you are a general's son, she cannot possibly know of that?'

'It was the twenty-sixth of April, I—'

'Nonsense! How can you remember it so exactly? You are a damned liar, Langer.'

'Oh no, I remember it perfectly, as if it were just this morning. It was the day I arrived at the holding camps. I was to transport some of the evacuated and the prisoners to another bloody camp. I saw her, something about her I cannot really describe. An inner beauty, and, well a kind of serene peace, even in the dirt of that diseased camp. The dirt we had made them live in. It was also the day that I almost ended up on a charge for feeding her family.'

'What charge?'

'Did I not tell you? I kept the country boys off the father, he is a bloody nuisance and by rights should already be dead. But in all honesty, I could not help but like him, perhaps it is because I was already most likely in love with her.'

Kurt looked at the floor for a moment, to let the wave of feelings for Odile wash over him and subside.

'Anyway, he was fucking around with the lorries and he was due a beating. But I saw her at the pump and we talked, friendly enough I thought, despite the war. I am no fool, I know she felt obliged as I was a German. For me it felt already more than that. But then there was an uproar, it broke the moment and she ran to her father. She was small, fragile against the solid mass of our uniforms. But she was strong and faced them all down. I had to help, but I did not tell her, of course. I ordered them to be starved, as I had been ordered. Then, I took them food later in the evening, hoping to get a second moment of peace with her. It was my own issue of rations but just as well the night-duty Guard did not know that. I must have been seen and I was quite angrily reprimanded.'

'Perhaps you do love her, my friend.'

Kurt smiled, idly kicking a stone across the street. 'I would do anything for her, truly, as if she were a German girl from back home in Dusseldorf.'

'Look, you know you could just, well, have her if you wanted?'

'Yes, well, no! I would not. If we were to, well, to be together, it would have to be something more than just that. It is her and not just a body that I crave and love.'

'Oh yes, Herr stupid Langer, you have the frilly mist floating over your eyes. Best remember you are a soldier first, or you'll do something stupid that you might regret. Doesn't pay to be like this. What happens when we are posted away, hm? You thinking of bringing her along with us? Not very likely, is it?'

Kurt turned away for a moment. He had thought about that already. Perhaps he could find a way. Perhaps the son of a general could use some influence to protect a beautiful girl from the horror of the war. Although she had already suffered much, she was on the wrong side of this particular fight. Perhaps, just perhaps, he could bring her to him, encourage her to see things his way.

Both men finished their coffee and stood at the door to the little café, the warmth inside flowing around them. Outside, little figures scurried and loped through the streets, keeping their eyes down and trying not to be noticed against walls and street corners. Kurt looked at the futility of their movements, and was again reminded of rats. Then he remembered that his Odile was one of them. He had to get her out of here. He loved her already past the point of simple reason. He wanted her in every way. Perhaps he could give her a choice? If she chose him, then that would be enough. He turned back to his companion.

'We should go.'

The coffee had been excellent, imported from Belgium. Cambrai could be a very pleasant place to be, in the warm air. But Kurt's day was probably not going to end as pleasantly as he had hoped. The colonel's aide was pacing down the street looking for someone. Kurt knew instinctively it was him.

'Damn it.'

'Ah, Langer! The colonel wants to see you, and that means now.'

'Did he say what it was about?'

'Yes, but I don't think you want to know.'

'Tell me, although I think I can guess.'

'If you are sure. Of course it's that bloody Lefebvre family and your order that they should be moved here together! Together? Ha! Who do you think you are, Kaiser Kurt? Whoever heard of the women staying here with a man? You have managed to put yourself on the top of the

Eastern Front transport list. General's boy or not, you are a bloody fool.'

'Eat dirt, Hoff, you crawling worm.'

'You'll be eating plenty of that. Can you even spell Carpathians?'

Kurt dismissed Hoff with a shrug, quickly turned, straightened himself up and strode off. It was trouble, but he knew it was coming, he could take the punishment for her, and it was nothing that he was not prepared to face for the beautiful flower that was Odile.

The walk to the colonel's office in the transport quarters was a pleasant one, even if the colonel was angry with him. He could go down by the canal first, past the small German hospital, along by the little row of houses, including the one that he was trying to requisition in order to bring Odile and her mother to Cambrai. He had already secured a valuable job for her father. Had he not been such a talented engineer, Kurt thought to himself, the infuriating man would surely have been shot before now. He might even have been tempted to do it himself. Of course, Odile should now be in Lithuania or some other damned awful place, dead most likely, beaten and taken by someone who did not love her. He shook his head to lose that train of thought. He thought instead of the pleasant reunion with Odile in camp seven, and the lucky, perhaps half-intended duty to care for the Lefebvre family. He smiled to himself that he had managed to get flowers for her – that must have made her very happy, perhaps made her feel above the dirty French around her. He was sure she had liked them, receiving them the way he intended, although thinking about it, she never really made mention of them.

Well, this surprise would top it all, a dry and clean house in Cambrai, and perhaps a job in the factory, but as he passed the hospital he thought perhaps she could train there instead. All of this would ease the possibility of a much greater union, even the notion of marriage to the woman that he craved. She might perhaps soften towards him in the uniform of the enemy. He had a spring in his step as he reached the transport building. The colonel would not really be so bad, it just had to be done, especially since the colonel knew his father. Kurt was no rebel, the colonel knew that well enough. Just routine and some paperwork, nothing to worry about.

The evening was cold and November was drawing to a close. Kurt emerged from the colonel's office suitably chastised, but as expected, nothing further was to be done. He had even been given the house as he had requested. It was supposed to be for Odile's father, but Kurt had grander ideas. He could now return with his transports to camp seven and arrange to move Pierre Lefebvre and his family almost immediately. He could give Odile the pleasant news that for her, the camps would be in the past. She would surely be pleased, grateful even. A lesser man could take advantage of that situation, but Kurt had higher things in mind. He imagined soft days by a stream, arm in arm with his French love. He imagined cool evenings at a fireside, with his beautiful French wife in new fashions from Paris, looking grand and proper against the dark oak panels of his parents' home. He liked that, he wanted that. He wanted Odile Lefebvre to love him.

CHRIS CHERRY

CHAPTER THREE

Verdun September 1918

The trenches were little more than linked holes in the ground. The constant bombardments wore the nerves and stretched men to the point of breaking. To stand in the line was courageous enough. To move out of the relative comfort to attack the enemy was true bravery, which no one outside of this world could possibly comprehend. For Kurt, this was exactly where he now wanted to be. For nearly four years he had been an officer of transport, moving machines and equipment, living in strange envy of the men at the Front. Over time, perhaps perversely, he felt himself less of a man for spending so little time at the Front, for not taking an opportunity to fight in the war. When his friends and comrades sought escape from the terror and tragedy seen daily in the trenches, Kurt had begun to crave the danger and for a brief time lived in a euphoria fuelled by a sense of belonging to a brave brotherhood. But very quickly he had also come to realise that this was dangerous and serious. There were no accounts here of bravery. You were either alive or dead. The dead were now everywhere, unburied and untouched in weeks. The Americans were attacking and did not allow any living thing to exist in the gulf between the lines of men. And they kept on coming.

The late autumn weather was worsening and this particular morning was cool, perhaps even cold. Kurt pulled up the collar of his lighter greatcoat and drew his arms around him. He looked up at the sky, still grey and dark, with a slight hint of the coming dawn over to his left. He had spent the night outside again, because orders had come through that something was going to happen from the enemy trenches two hundred metres away. Many times in the last two hours, he had anxiously paced up and down the trench line that he commanded, looking again at the dugouts, checking that his men were awake and alert. He had come to realise that he much preferred the company of fighting soldiers to the coffee-drinking transport men he had lived amongst up until now. Of course, had he been a Sturmann he would probably already be dead and would never have met his lovely Odile, who was now safe and in his parents' care in Dusseldorf. Today, here and now, he had realised his dream of joining an infantry regiment in the line. He felt immediately at home with weapons, no more timetables, and calculations of weight held no more interest for him. He had finally arrived in the war, and in Verdun as well! Perhaps even now, there was a possibility of the Germans breaking through here, of finally causing France to surrender, finally freeing him to marry his Odile. The thought warmed him slightly and emboldened his step through the soft ground underfoot.

Kurt looked at his own weapons. He carried his trusted Luger pistol and a small knife, which was mostly for freeing himself from debris, but it was a sharp blade, which yet might be needed for a darker purpose. As he turned to go and find something warm to drink, he felt the ground beneath him erupt in an enormous explosion. The earthly bonds seemed to fall away beneath him, as if somehow he could fly. He could not move his arms as wings, but he was watching everything around him in slow motion.

He landed on soft earth, damp and dirty, but still alive. He knew he was dazed but tried to get up, this was no place to have dull wits. He could still feel his legs and arms and saw them move in front of him. He leaned forward, ready to stand, when a second explosion erupted behind him, sending him forcibly forward, with his face pressed hard into the mud. He quickly rolled over and sat up, just as the first enemy soldiers appeared from the smoke. He did not recognise their uniforms at first, they were not French. These soldiers were Americans. There were a great many of them, which disappointed Kurt. The first group of ten or so passed him by, they either did not notice him, or took him for dead. They had appeared as soon as the shelling had started. This time, there was no week-long barrage to prepare a defence. These men wanted this war over. This year it seemed it really would be over by Christmas.

The next group emerged from the mist. There were three bodies moving, crouched with rifles held high. He took aim with his pistol. His eyes were glassy and wet from the pain of his fall, his arm was weakened in the landing, but he held his arm out straight, almost automatically. He fired. The soldier in the middle fell backward, spinning almost right round, reaching up for his head. He was dead. The other two ducked and looked around for the enemy. At that moment, the German machine gun opened fire. The bullets cut the air all around Kurt as he sat on the ground. The two remaining Americans were shot and their bodies, torn and limp, fell to the ground. This now gave Kurt his chance to stand. He needed to find his own trench again and get back below ground. More of the enemy were coming and he needed to defend his position.

Another American soldier came out from the mist. He saw Kurt stumbling and raised his rifle to shoot him, but Kurt was now alert again, enjoying the moment, relishing the sport. Close enough for a pistol to have a devastating effect on a body, he shot the man in his chest as he had been instructed. More soldiers came, but this time, as the smoke cleared, they were too far away to shoot with his pistol. He had also forgotten how many shots he had fired and knew he must only have one or two shots left.

Kurt rolled back the other way to get onto his feet. His legs were still weak and unsteady. Perhaps it was the fall, perhaps it was his nerves. He doubted himself just a little at that moment. But quickly, he tried to get his bearings. Behind him was a large crater from the explosion that had sent him over here, perhaps ten metres or more. Instinctively, he ducked and began to move back. At that moment, six German uniforms rose from the same hole, carrying large tanks and long hoses. He knew what was about to happen and did not want to get in the way or become a victim by accident, so he threw himself back to the ground. This made him a coward perhaps, but it was the only thing he could think to do.

Above him came the searing heat of the Flammenwerfer. The smoke and flame brought agony to the enemy emerging from the shelling. Groups of men were instantly aflame, darting from side to side as they died, burned in pain, and Kurt saw it all, flat on his face in the slimy mud of the battlefield. But it would end quickly. Another shell landed close by, and the lead German and his hose were spun round in the blast. Kurt could see him trying to release the trigger but it was too late, it set ablaze his comrades and the tanks of fuel burned quickly and exploded. In an instant, Kurt saw how a man could be torn apart, split into three pieces, turned into dust, painless and without a hope. He could feel the scream come from deep within him, his eyes widening automatically at the shock. He shouted loudly at the sight, and terror gripped him for a moment. In front were burned bodies, stained red lumps of flesh and uniform where a second ago a man had stood. Clean broken bones were exposed, white and slippery, as if a demonic fist had punched into the bodies of his comrades.

He rose to fall back, but the Germans were now pouring forward, allowing him a little safety in numbers. Now, he wanted to turn and face the still advancing enemy. This was his platoon moving forward, imagining themselves without a leader, and they chose to fight on. They saw Kurt and nodded as they passed, Kurt turning with them, taking charge once again.

They fell forward as a group into a shell hole, Kurt was now able to collect his thoughts and think what should be done next. He had to put the sight of the destruction he had seen out of his mind for now. These men needed him, their movements and lives depended on his clear judgement.

'Kern, Widmer, Opp. Stay with me. We will try to move into that larger hole just ahead to try to stem the attack. Benner, you and Kraus stay here. What weapons do you still have?'

'Just a rifle, sir. One each with about sixty rounds between us.'

'Aim at the gaps in the smoke, at one hundred yards, take them down. The machine gun can do the rest.'

'It's gone, sir, direct hit. The crew are now missing.'

'Well-aimed rifle fire then, don't waste bullets. Mark your targets. Understood?'

'Sir.'

'You three, let's go.'

As one they rose from the hole. No machine-gun fire from behind, shells falling on their left. This was risky and dangerous, but the Americans had to be stopped. Kurt found the larger hole and they all dropped into the new position.

'What bombs do we have?'

'None sir, the sacks were hit when you were blown up. All gone.'

'Rifles then, up on the rim, come on.'

As the three loaded their rifles and took aim at the gaps in the smoke, Kurt sensed that this was rapidly becoming a hopeless situation. They would be overrun and most likely killed. The rifles began to crack as the men found bodies to aim at. Opp fell back into the trench. He was dead. A small piece of hot metal had passed through his helmet and his skull, lodging in his ear. The other two did not look and continued to fight.

Kurt checked his pistol. He had four rounds left. Enough to make a stand, then fall back to the trench. By now, surely, a new machine gun position had been prepared? As he dug his foot into the hole to lift himself to the edge, he was hit flush in the face by a helmet containing the head of the now dead Opp, lifted off by an explosion right on the rim of the crater. Kurt could sense the death of his men above him as all now went suddenly dark, the world pressing hard on his chest, pushing the life and air out of him.

The sucking wetness of the earth oozed foul water into his face. Water that was dirty and tainted with years of fighting. The lifeless face of

Opp was immovably pressed against his own, as Kurt could not move, or even look away. His arms were now useless to him. His right arm was behind him and twisted, the pain from that position was almost unbearable, it was not injured, but it was pulling almost out of the shoulder. His left arm was directly out in front of him with Opp's head resting on it, his glazed and lifeless eyes staring at him. He could move it slightly, but the weight of the soil and debris was great and pressing ever more forcefully, sapping his energy. Now he felt himself being sucked down and knew he had been completely buried. He thought he was going to die and began to reconcile himself to it consciously, whilst he still could. Terror rose in him, his body reacting even when his brain wanted calm.

His body began to convulse slightly, he knew he was cursing repeatedly as the oxygen was used, the air deserting him. None of this was helping his ability to think. He was buried deep in a shell hole that had once been part of the German trenches, and he must have been at least a metre below the surface, since he was standing in the crater. Too far to dig even if he could move, which he couldn't. He now felt strangely hot, then cold. His arms became numb and he could not free them. To move at all would simply exhaust him and he would die faster. Perhaps that would be a relief. His mind sought to protect him, overriding his conscious brain, which was weakening.

Instead, he tried to think of Odile. He realised that it was not a true loving relationship yet, perhaps now it never would be, but he could make her happy. He imagined her now in his mind. There they were, the two of them, strolling happily arm in arm around Dusseldorf. She, wearing a fancy dress and hat. He, smart in a morning suit for church, or an appointment with his family. They strolled the streets and busy squares. Yes, life with Odile, it would have been so sweet. And her beautiful face came closer and kissed him. He felt at rest, at a final peace. A serene blanket covering him, the light darkening to black, warm beneath his blanket. He was not ready to die, but death had come for him nevertheless.

'Sir? Hauptmann Langer? Langer? Opp? Are you there?'

Kurt smiled to himself. He was dreaming of rescue. That was funny now. Imagine that, all too late. The delirium was upon him and he could feel his body mercifully sag, which relieved the awful pressure. His arm did not hurt, all was calm, and the dull sounds of shelling beat a drum for his final passing.

'Here! Quickly. Dig with your hands, you might injure one of them. Fuck, who was that?'

'It's Widmer. Was. His face is gone. I can see his brain. Mein Gott!'

'Oh no! Never mind for now, dig. Our commander is in there, he might be alive, and I did not see him come out.'

Kurt felt a strange heat on his neck, as if he had the sun on his back in high summer. He did not mind the sun, but remembered how quickly it could burn the skin. This did not burn, it was just a pleasant white heat. Almost cold. He could not remember the last time that he drew a breath but he felt no urge to breathe.

'He is here, look. But I think he is already dead. He is as white as milk and his body is all twisted. Where are the stretchers? Where are the medics? Shell! Get down.'

A shell landed nearby and exploded. One of the water bottles was hit and splashed apart. Each man checked his arms and legs.

'I think he is gone, sir. He isn't breathing. I can't see a wound. He looks, well, all there and not injured. But he isn't breathing.'

At that moment, another shell landed with a hard dull thud right beside Widmer's dead body. The hot metal and the shock of a shell landing so near caused Kraus to recoil and lose his footing. He fell on top of Kurt.

Kurt could feel his neck grow hotter, if that were possible. The sensation spread all over his head and down his spine. It was not at all unpleasant. There was a snake, or something hot and dry crawling down his back. Then everything suddenly turned ice cold.

'He is alive! Let's pull him up and out, quickly.'

Kurt was pulled, limp and unconscious from the hole. Around them, the battle was moving on. No more soldiers came past for the moment, but it would not be long until they did. The enemy meant to drive them back from Avocourt village and this was not going to stop now.

'Mein Gott! Did you see it? A bloody dud. A shell, between my fucking feet. Fuck, it should have killed me. I was to die today, I am dead now. Everything else is a lucky life for me.'

'Hauptmann Langer? Can you hear me? Herr Hauptmann?'

Kurt's back was cold. He would have to turn over to pull the blanket back over him. His arm moved. It moved to his face. He wanted to look at it, but he could not remember how to look at something. He had eyes. How did they work? Then he remembered.

'Sir, you are alive! Here, take your hand from your face, it's bleeding a bit. Let me clean that wound. It isn't so bad. You had us worried for a moment.'

A great door opened in front of Kurt. On the other side was the battlefield and the face of his men, those that were still alive. Kurt remembered how to sit up. Then he remembered more.

'The Americans? Are they still coming?'

'Yes sir, the first wave is in our trench. We can't return for a little while. Just give our men a little time to counterattack. We can stay here for now. There are no more coming at this very moment, but they will.'

'We have lost men?'

'Yes, sir. Eight so far. Oh, and the Flammenwerfer crews of course. Nasty death.'

'This is no time to sit here, we must go back.'

'Very good, sir.' Kraus took Kurt by the arm and they crawled towards their lines. For now, the Americans were kept quiet. There were some dead around the trench and some others were prisoners. More were coming now. They would not wait and could not be halted. The German position was hopeless and they would lose this position today. The shelling started again. This time, it did not stop. Perhaps this was not yet even the attack. Perhaps this was just a lost patrol or a raid.

'Sir? Are you injured?'

'I am quite well, thank you.'

Kurt could feel the little blanket returning to cover him. It felt safe and comfortable, clean and warm. He was drawn to it. He was ready.

'Benner, we have to get Hauptmann Langer to a dressing post. He is unconscious again. I think it is his head.'

'Then he is fucking lucky. Look, the Americans are coming again and they will soon be all over us.'

CHRIS CHERRY

CHAPTER FOUR

Dusseldorf October 1918

Kurt was alive, awake amongst the endless men moving to and from the fast-moving front lines of 1918, amongst them, but not a true part of the jostling, grim and damp world around him. The memory of the trench made him afraid. Each time he felt a thought build in his mind, he fought it, lashing out in his head with imaginary clubs and sticks. He could recall completely the smell of the soil, the helpless sensation of sinking into the horrible infected and forsaken earth, the wetness sucking him down, drawing his life away as it did so. His arms were still numb and heavy by his sides because of damage to the nerves from the weight of soil above him and the lack of clean air to breathe. By all reasonable means, he should be dead but he was still counted amongst the living, a cursed life, wandering from street to street in a dream filled with flame and bomb. Punishment for defying the black shroud that had so nearly covered him.

The train from the Koln railhead was even slower and more laboured than usual. Fewer troops were going to the front, but many thousands were returning. Some looked as he did, gaunt and quiet. He was not due to have home leave as he had only been at the very front line a few days. But he was in no state to fight, so he was sent home for eight days to recover. Perhaps by then he would have recovered enough to return, to try and drive the enemy away from his beloved Germany. He felt violated and insulted that his body should be so invaded when his country was in danger of being overrun by the enemy. The little anger he felt remained deep inside him, a fire burning slowly but inevitably, consuming the boy that was Kurt Langer. It was possible that he was imagining all of this, for the world of the real and the imagined was, for Kurt, almost indistinguishable. For him, the real world and the imagined were both at the end of a long corridor, dim lights in the distance, almost out of reach. As he breathed in, he could smell so vividly the foul rotten wetness of the shell hole and the constant smell of burning on his body, as if he were actually on fire, a smouldering ember.

But then there were thoughts within him for his beloved Odile, who was now safe at his home and protected from this war. Kurt was sure that safety had given her comfort and would surely warm her to him. A life in Dusseldorf was not so bad, and an improvement on cow country, anyway. In time she would see that. He would soon be married and that would finally settle the issue. Her love and devotion, he craved them, and now needed them more than ever. Perhaps in time these might be earned, if not given so willingly. But it did not matter. She was there waiting for him. He wanted her softness, but not at any cost. It had not been easy, but behind the big front door of his home, was the daughter of France. He could not think clearly, his head ached and thoughts did not come easily, nor the words to express them. The trench had taken something unexpected from him, something he would not have been willing to give. In fact, had his father asked him how he truly felt, he might have said that he was afraid.

When he stepped off the train he had to think exactly how to walk to his home. He had to remember each turn and step, one foot in front of the other. As he did so, he felt the fog lift a little with the increasingly familiar surroundings. This was home, he was a boy again and he was safe. Around him, people in the street recognised him and grabbed his arm to speak to him, but he heard no words. He wanted his mother, the safety of his father's study, and Odile. Kurt was not sure how to greet her, remembering the harshness of their last time together, but he needed her now more than ever. He loved her, he knew that, but it was a love hard won across the gulf of conflict. The war had brought them together and yet the war was holding them apart. He did not feel strong enough to confront the reality of love and war, but he had to find the strength to try. It might take time and it would take what strength he had.

At the front door, he gently pulled the bell and his mother was at the door in an instant. She looked upon him and immediately drew him to her. The scene was visible from the street, but he cared not that he was resting on his mother's apron.

'Oh my boy, my beautiful man! Look at you! Inside, my love, let me make you something to eat, you look starved. We do not have much, your father is not here just now. Well, more a little later perhaps. Come in and let us get you warm, you are so very cold, my love.'

'Thank you, Mother. I am sorry to return home so quickly and unannounced, but I have had a little trouble at the Front. Nothing to worry about, just, well, just... never mind.'

She held her hands to his face.

'No, I do not need to hear that. I can imagine well enough. Your father tells me about what must be happening. You are here and that is good.'

Kurt was almost too afraid to go upstairs and greet Odile, and his feelings filled his chest to the point of physical pain. He was fearful of her rejection, when he felt so weak and empty inside and did not think he could face that just now. Inside, he was truly hurt and wounded, nothing anyone could see, but a wound just the same, a hard steel ball, filling his body, pushing the boy Kurt aside. He did not want to be a patient, but a strong husband. That is what Odile must see, not weakness, for he was not one of the tortured souls from the Kaiserswerth.

After eating barely enough to keep away hunger and silence his fretting mother, Kurt felt compelled to go to find his Odile. It was pulling his soul to be so near and yet so far. He remembered as he went up the stairs that she was behind a locked door. This saddened him a little, perhaps he had not been so wise in the care of his love. The door lock was stuck to his touch and the key would not turn. Then he realised that the door was not locked at all. This was not how he expected it to be. He entered the room, breathing in deeply. If only she knew that it took all of his courage to turn the corner and come around the door to see her by the window. She was thin, as sick as he, also pulled apart from within by the war that had taken them all as nourishment.

In his mind, he must become now the strong man once again, to remind her of the care and love he had given her, along with protection and security. To remind Odile that her very existence in Dusseldorf, and the comfort and safety she enjoyed, were at his grace. Without it, she would have been broken and abused, like the girls who had provided comfort for his men. He felt a little energising anger rise in him again.

'Odile! I have not seen your face in many weeks. You are thin and weak again, I remember that look on you. You remember me? The man who rescued you from the rapists and the murderers? Have I yet earned my reward? What do you say?'

'Kurt, how can you keep me here like this, a cold and hungry prisoner? This is not love, it is cruelty. I have seen enough of that in my lifetime already.'

'Perhaps it was love, Odile, once in Cambrai. It could be so again, but if it is not, then we must accept it. Perhaps in time you will love me again. The kind man who rescued the wretched girl from the sewer of the camps.'

'This is not a rescue, Kurt. Surely you must see this for yourself?'

'Without me, without my help then, you would all be dead. Your damned father was taking you by the hand into the arms of the ignorant peasant fool soldiers guarding the camp. They cared not a bit for your virtue or your dignity. With me, you were safe. You were loved Odile, believe me when I say this. Somewhere deep within us, you must see this for a fact.' Odile looked to the floor, she had nothing left to say that could make any difference to Kurt.

To Kurt, Odile seemed cold and harsh. It did not matter. It was simply a distraction. They would marry, love or not. She would have to put up with this life. Although she was bitter towards him, she was alive. In time, she would come to love him for that very fact. She would be grateful for the generosity of the Langers. No longer would he try to win her love, for now he had seen men burn to death before his eyes, torn apart and gone forever. He had been buried, flanked by dud shells, and in truth he was himself already dead, so he could behave outside of the rules of the living, they did not apply to him. Now he realised that he was alive for a greater purpose. A divinity without a God surrounded him and Odile would have to respect that he was now a superior soul. She would have to accommodate him and he would have her as his wife. He could not imagine taking her against her will, but he would accept unwilling. To do anything else would shame them all. Here and now in Germany, weakness was the new enemy.

So Kurt turned his confusion of thoughts towards marriage in order to hold onto a little of what he had left – the streets and people that the soldiers in the trenches had died to protect. The women here were grateful and willing to show devotion to such bravery, imagine what they might show to one with the courage to rise from the ground. But the little French one he had saved seemed unmoved by his care and it made him angry. He was not strong enough to bring matters to a conclusion now, and he had to return to the army again soon so it would have to wait. The open sore of his love for Odile would heal a little each day, but it would not be today.

When he left his home, without looking in again on Odile, he saw now more clearly in the street fear and alarm, worry and desolation on the faces of the people. He found it odd, strange. He himself felt nothing at all for he was a vast shell, an empty and broken soul. But he did not care, so what did it matter to anyone else? From now, it would all be for Kurt, nothing and certainly no one, would intrude on his desire to take as he pleased. He had the right, earned from his burial in Avocourt.

CHAPTER FIVE

Dusseldorf February 1919

It would be the last time that Kurt would board a train from Koln to Dusseldorf as Hauptmann Langer of the German Infantry Reserve. For him, the war was at last over. He had been finally discharged from the army, with honour, on the first day of February 1919. The transport column that he had commanded was no longer needed, and the last equipment had been transported a month ago. There was a possibility that he could apply to remain in the army, but for now, he was looking forward to returning home and wearing new clothes because he did not have any that fitted properly.

He desperately wanted to see his loving mother, his beloved, if distant, father and his silly sister. He also finally wanted to conclude his business with Odile. Now, he felt stronger, his mind clearer, the road ahead visible and fully emerged from the fog. He felt more able to assert himself with her, to finally reconcile her to the marriage he had planned, and he would discuss the issue no further. She could scream and spit and hiss and kick, but it would be of no use. He had won, although to his angry shame, Germany had lost. But to Kurt, his devotion to the French girl and his protection of her meant he had won the right to her, the right to have her for himself.

As the carriage rumbled on, so much quicker than the last terrible time, he took a moment to gaze over the fields and plains of western Germany. Once more at peace, of a sort. The war was not quite over yet. The guns had stopped, certainly, the bullets no longer cutting the air and bringing death, but peace was not at all assured. Germany would be blamed for all of it, from the start, for the millions of men dead and the millions still missing. He knew Germany would have to take responsibility for it all and be grateful to be allowed to exist. Kurt knew that a reckoning would come, he could hear it in the voices of his comrades. This was not over. For him, it would be a new beginning, not the end of the war. The fool politicians last November had let Germany fall, to tumble unwanted into an abyss.

As the wet fields turned to wet streets, he knew that he was coming to the station at Dusseldorf. The rain on the windows obscured the moving shapes, but it was not long until the train finally arrived. The platforms no longer awash with grey uniforms and helmets bobbing to the rhythm of the trains. Kurt felt that now he had to temper himself for the meeting with Odile. This would be the last time that he must feel this way. He must take control and be strong to leave Odile in no doubt as to the duties that she must accept. He said it over and over, but he was not able to convince himself.

'Enough, Kurt.'

At the door to his home, he gently pulled the bell. To his surprise, Liesel opened the door herself, which was most unusual. She was in her starched white nurse's uniform, just that hour returned from the hospital. She was thin and tired, her bright young face was a little drawn and she had black marks under her eyes. Kurt had almost forgotten that his sister was now a woman and perhaps he should acknowledge that fact, no longer treating her as just a little servant to fetch him something whenever he desired.

'Liesel, beloved sister. I am now home for the very last time.'

But Liesel seemed somewhat distant and distracted, avoiding his gaze. It was hard to detect, but her head was bowed just a little and she was already backing away from Kurt.

'I am pleased you are home, Kurt. Come, Mother is in the day room. She has been a little unwell this week. Come inside for the cold air might give her a chill.'

'Where is Father?'

'He is with the alderman. Much has changed here. With the Kaiser, well, perhaps he can explain. It is not as you left it.'

'Mother!'

'Kurt, my son. You do not know how glad my heart is to see you here alive and quite well. Too many of the families in Dusseldorf have been broken by death, but we are lucky. You are saved and delivered to us. That must be the most important thing.'

'Yes, Mother, but what did Liesel mean?'

'You are alive and here again with us. Do not be upset, please know that all is well here and your return will please your father. He knows you are to arrive today and will be home presently. But much has changed here.'

'Mother? What are you saying? You are not making sense.'

'You must let him explain what has happened to him and to us. Let him explain, Kurt, and accept the new world that we live in. Do you understand?'

'No, Mother, I do not. What is troubling you so?'

'Sit, Kurt, you should perhaps have something warm to eat. Liesel, please go and ask Frau Lamm to prepare a little supper for your brother.'

'No, Liesel. Wait. Nothing yet. You seem distracted, Mother? Are you so unwell?'

'It is something on my chest, Kurt, a little chill perhaps, but otherwise I am well. Please sit. You should eat.'

'Why are you so agitated, Mother? Why do you insist that I sit? I should go and visit Odile. It is time to put to rest the differences between us and to start our peaceful life together.'

'Please, Kurt, perhaps wait until you father returns and greet him first.'

'Mother? Something is troubling you beyond your chill. I am going upstairs immediately.'

'Kurt, please! Liesel!'

Kurt was at the stairs in an instant. At the top of the stairs, he saw immediately that the door to Odile's room was open wide and empty. The bed had been made and clearly the room was not in use, a film of dust visible on the low shelving. Liesel was now also at the top of the stairs.

'Liesel?' Kurt's voice demanded an answer. 'Where is Odile?'

'Kurt, please understand. We had nothing to do with it, but—'

'But what? Where is she?'

'I… I do not know. Perhaps she has returned to France?'

'What? France? No, it cannot be! How could she do that? She has no papers or identity in Germany.'

'I do not know.' Liesel shifted uneasily on her feet and gripped the rail on the stairs. 'Perhaps she found a sympathetic guard at the border.'

'Sympathetic guard? Why would she need a sympathetic guard? She was in no danger here. We are to be married! I love her and I have protected her. Why would she need to do that?'

'I don't know, Kurt. But she left some months ago, in fact just after you left in October.'

'October? Why was I not informed? I must find her.'

'Father thought it best. You should really speak with him. I do not think you should go chasing her.'

'October! Where is she now?'

'I really do not know, Kurt. You are frightening me. Please, come downstairs and be with Mother.'

Kurt thrust his hand at the wall and then went into Odile's room. He threw open the doors to each wall cupboard, jarring the hinges. Each was empty. The large trunk was still there and he opened the lid slowly. It contained only one item that could have belonged to Odile. A little square handkerchief, which he picked up and drew to his face. He breathed the scent. It was indeed his Odile. Kurt turned and sat on the bed, his face in his hands, weeping gently into the little cloth as if it were the only thing left in the world.

His life again felt shattered, the hopes of a loving reconciliation with Odile now clearly gone. He knew now that he had not won her love, that her time with him was perhaps a device for her safety and that she had always intended to return to France without him, without desiring the life he had wanted for them both. He put the handkerchief into his pocket.

'Curse you! Curse that I ever met you in that filthy camp. You would be dead, Odile, you and your idiot of a father. How could you? After all the protection that I offered, willingly given to one who could not deserve it. How dare you defy me? How dare you leave like a rat out of a sewer, after all that I have done for you?'

Liesel shifted again on her feet.

'Kurt, you are frightening me, I am not used to seeing you so upset and angry.'

'What are you saying, Liesel, that you do not like this new brother? That Kurt is not a man who could be loved by a woman like Odile?'

He thumped his fist on the window ledge and a little ceramic pot spun around and fell, smashing into pieces with a loud crash. Kurt looked down.

'What the fuck?'

'Kurt!'

He snapped out of his anger. This voice demanded obedience.

'Father, I am sorry. I have returned home.'

'So I see. Come downstairs, we have much to talk about, not just your French girl and this bloody business.'

Kurt's father waved his arm dismissively around the room as he spoke. His voice contained just a hint of alarm and worry. Kurt suspected that the politics of Germany were yet to become ever more complicated.

'My son, your little French adventure is over. She is gone. We do not know how. Enquiries have proven unsuccessful. Most likely she is dead, shot somewhere. Perhaps she even made it to France. But this is unlikely. Without a good name or a document, she cannot be found.'

Liesel shifted uneasily again. Kurt tapped the floor for a moment, as if in internal conversation with himself. Then he suddenly lifted his head, turned about and left the room without another word. He bowed his head slightly to his father and left, but glared at Liesel. He stamped downstairs and the front door slammed heavily. At the gate, he looked left and right and walked straight ahead.

--oOo--

Liesel watched him go. At each gate post he slammed his hand furiously on the rail. She knew that this would not be the end of it, not at all. Whatever Kurt was to do, it would not be good for the Langer family. She closed her eyes, glad that Kurt did not know her role in Odile's departure in October, using a permit from the hospital. Since Odile had not been brought back or arrested and there had been no scandal, Liesel knew that Odile had at least made it to the Koln railhead.

Kurt was gone for two hours. When he returned, he was holding a sheaf of papers and notes. Liesel went to the door of his room to ask if he needed anything, but she really wanted to see what he was trying to do.

'Kurt, may I fetch you some water?'

'No, go away, Liesel. Can you not see that I am working?'

'Working on what?'

'It is not your concern, leave me now.'

'But Kurt, I am only concerned for you.'

Kurt got up from the bed, slapped the little pile of papers down and then pushed his sister backward until she stumbled, slamming the door as she fell.

Liesel was a little shocked, but she was also getting used to this type of treatment and knew that whatever had happened to her brother in that trench was responsible for this behaviour. She knew he was suffering the effects of being buried and forgave him for that. What she could not and would not forgive, was his behaviour towards Odile. That would create a distance between them for now and all time. This made her a little sad, but she was stronger for it.

For the next week, Kurt left early each morning and returned late at night, long after dark. The little pile of papers grew steadily larger. Liesel wanted to see what he was doing. She took courage one day when she saw him leave in a hurry, almost running across the road. It would only take a minute. Quickly, she entered his room. It was immaculate and the pile of papers was neatly ordered on his little writing desk. His handwritten notes lying on top meant that she could not disturb the pile too much, for fear of his noticing and becoming suspicious.

The top sheet was a railway timetable for September to December 1918. It was the same timetable she had used to help Odile. Why might

Kurt need this in February 1919? The sheet underneath was the record of troop train movements to Koln in October, with a little underline marking on each one that had carried either nurses or civilians with permits. Four had also been circled. With horror, she saw that one of them must have been the train that Odile had taken. She recognised the date immediately as it was the date of the big parade. Here it was, a train number circled. Kurt had not let go and was planning something. Liesel began to shake. Her brother was truly vicious. The pages below were notes taken from the guards at Dusseldorf and Koln. Kurt knew them all and would have no difficulty obtaining the records as he had been the transport officer there for a little time before his posting to France. One of them stood out and made Liesel gasp with horror.

Kurt,

I have found what you are looking for, although I still know not why? The train left DDF 8 minutes late, Koln only. Troops 440, civ. 46, 1 nurse (Koln permit issued in DDF). For the nurse question – the only reason it was noted was the fact that no more patient transits were run after 25 Sep. V. unusual, but not impossible. At Koln, 14 trains in next 30 hours to Switzerland (Basel), Munich (via), Stuttgart (via) and two trains to Liege (relatives of war dead). From your description, would expect Basel to be likeliest.

Josef

The two pages underneath were maps of Northern Switzerland. Kurt clearly thought that Odile had run to Switzerland. It seemed the most likely route and the one requiring the least amount of administration. If she had gone there, she would have been and gone by now, most likely safe and home again. Kurt could do nothing more to her. But her brother was never to be underestimated.

That evening, Kurt returned in a foul temper, opening and closing the door roughly. His mother avoided him completely, and Liesel supposed it was perhaps because she no longer had any influence on him. Even his father appeared cautious, for a man who had commanded soldiers, he seemed at a loss when it came to dealing with his soldier son with the clearly troubled mind. Liesel could see that it hurt her father to see Kurt like this. She supposed that these experiences were unknown to his father, just as they were frightening and unsettling to all around, and not just to the one suffering.

Liesel felt a little ashamed that she, of all those around Kurt, understood completely what was happening to him, but she felt compelled to restrain herself from offering help. It would surely be rejected, for he was being eaten from the inside by the experiences of the trench. If they were not careful, then the boy who was Kurt Langer with a beautiful open face and a smile that melted the heart, would forever be lost, consumed by a revenge fuelled by a lost hope of normality, a love he had believed won in the war to end all wars.

That evening, whilst Kurt was downstairs reading more maps and notes, Liesel took the opportunity to look in his room again. She had to know what had upset Kurt so much that day. The door was open and on his bed she saw one small scrap of paper, one that had been torn and crumpled, then unfolded again.

Kurt,

Have traced your nurse to Basel. Name listed as Heike Hoth. Departed Koln 3 days after your DDF train (no record of hospital accommodations). At Basel, she was escorted to collect medical supplies to return next day. Contracted SIF and died in Basel Hospital district 12 on 3 November 18. Cremated same day. No next of kin, aged about 20 according to the escorts. No photograph, sorry. Said she was from DDF.

Liesel wondered about this. She knew that Odile had travelled as Liesel Langer so Kurt was on the wrong trail. All of this just gave Odile more time, if she was alive and not already home. But if Kurt discovered that Liesel had apparently travelled to Koln using a hospital permit, then she was in trouble. She had never been to Koln and would crumble at the slightest question, as Kurt knew Koln all too well. On the day she had declared her papers missing, she had left a false trail in the hospital to confuse an investigation. But she had not counted on her brother being the investigator. She was both relieved and afraid. Odile was surely now safe if she was alive. In either case, her dear friend was clear of Kurt. But Liesel was far from clear of Kurt and he was now unpredictable, violent and obsessed. He was as dangerous to her now as the war had been to them all. She would have to be so careful in her own home.

But the time had come to get ready to see Karl. In Doctor Eisner, Liesel saw salvation. In his caring love she saw an escape from this house that felt no more home to her than a faceless hotel by the sea. His touch was never harsh, and his devotion to medicine was charming and powerfully intoxicating. No longer needed as a nurse in the hospital, she only saw him outside of the grounds, although she was always welcome inside. In his arms she felt safe, loved and protected. In him she saw the life that Odile had craved and Liesel loved her all the more for holding out for it.

CHAPTER SIX

Dusseldorf 1920

Kurt sat at the window of his home in Dusseldorf. Outside, a crowd was forming, moving swiftly along towards the old parliament building. He was reading the newspaper, of the violent backlash to the announcement of the *Treaty of Versailles*, whose first instruments had just begun to take effect. All over Germany there were calls for a communist government, or even for the restoration of the monarchy, or investment in industry to help a crippled Germany renew itself, to become once more the power it had been before the war. The news pages were full of large print headlines telling the population what was wrong. Kurt concluded that this was all very well, but it seemed that no one had thought what they might do about it.

'You know, Hans, we may well end up in another war again, if we do not do something about this. Fucking communists? Who the Hell do they think they are? What did we fight for? What was I buried in the filthy dirt for? It is not right. We should not put up with this.'

'We should be careful though, Kurt, the communists really have control of Dusseldorf.'

'Well, not for much longer. I received our orders this morning. We move on the Red Ruhr Army this afternoon, at their meeting in the Latterhausen Rooms.'

'Well, that is good. What are we waiting for here, then?'

'The Freikorps do not run in to battle, Hans, you know that!'

'Well, do we just sit here and wait?'

Kurt took out a cigarette and passed one to Hans. 'That is exactly what we do.'

'Why?'

'Because this uprising is temporary. The people are frightened, Hans, look at them. Each of them wears a face of pain, it is just like eighteen all over again. Only this time, the enemy is a neighbour, or even a friend. That is worse, you know.'

'So you think the politicians will solve our problems?'

'No, they may just change them into new ones.'

'Make you afraid of it and tell you who to blame for it, eh?'

'Exactly.'

'Kurt, do you think we will have to kill German citizens?' Hans frowned, and looked back at the people hurrying past.

'Hans, I know this to be a certainty and it will start today.'

The two men were dressed in the uniform of the Freikorps, the new voluntary military unit, made up of many soldiers from the war. They took a seat at the window, watching Dusseldorf tear itself apart again. They had orders to move on the Red Ruhr Army. The communist uprising to seize the industrial heartland of Germany had risen quickly and burned brightly, but was now doomed to fail. Kurt and Hans smoked quietly until the front bell rang. It was a young Freikorps driver.

'Hans, now it is time, let us go and settle this little matter.'

On the journey, Kurt read the orders again. His unit of Freikorps, under overall leadership of the Reichswehr, was to move on the miners' union, who were meeting at the beer hall in the Latterhausen Rooms on the outskirts of the city in the industrial district. He was given an open order, he was expecting trouble and he was given the weapons to suppress the union at all costs. The challenge excited him.

The car stopped a few hundred metres from the Latterhausenstrasse. Already the Freikorps uniforms were moving along the road as the Reichswehr units were directing the advance. As Kurt got out, a young member of his Freikorps ran to him, shouting that the miners had guns and some munitions used for mining. They were waving them from the windows and threatening to blow up the building.

'Herr Langer, the army are hesitant to move on the miners. They want to speak with you.'

'Major Gruber! How good to see you again. Still playing cards with your men, I see. What of these miners, then?'

'Langer, why am I not surprised it is you? The miners have weapons, I think they may use them. We do not have the authority and orders to end this situation. What are your orders?'

'All means necessary. Will you turn over your men to the Freikorps?'

'I certainly will not.'

'Then step aside, Herr Major, and let me be about my business.'

'What will you do?'

'End this nonsense now, of course.'

'How? They may have guns.'

'I will simply use all means necessary. Will you be courteous enough to stand your men aside, whist we execute our orders?'

Gruber looked shocked.

'What is wrong, Herr Major? You do not like the tone in my voice, perhaps? You wish to avoid danger? You will need to witness it whether you assist or not.'

'We will retreat to form a defensive cordon for you, but I am not sure this is the right course of action, Langer. I want that noted.'

'It is noted, and thank you for your offer of cover for my men. You go and stand behind us now, sir.'

Major Gruber looked worried and doubtful.

'Wait! I have orders to use all means necessary. It had occurred to me that we should not confront the miners directly. Starve them, threaten them, and bully them, yes. But this will end in bloodshed.'

'Herr Major, your orders are clear. All means necessary.'

The major paused for a moment. 'Then we must assist the Freikorps.'

'Good. Secretly, you must be keen to see the communist uprising over. It does no one good to have such an extreme view of politics. Such things are bad for Germany, no?'

Kurt's unit moved along the street of small shops, most of which were already empty. One or two had been owned by communist families and these were marked with red paint and their windows had been smashed. No repairs had been carried out here, and new tenants were awaiting the permissions necessary to move in. He felt a surge of energy in his body. At the entrance to the Latterhausen Rooms, he saw a group of miners at a window, brandishing what looked like sticks. Were they wood? Or dynamite? It was hard to tell. He advanced further, now standing at the front of his group.

'Miners! Will you disperse and end this foolish strike? Will you disband and end the uprising? Will you abandon in favour of the legitimate government?'

Initially, there was silence and then a ripple of sarcastic laughter moved through the group, echoing loudly. Kurt was angered by this, especially in front of his men.

'Fuck off! Who do you think you are, prancing around in a children's theatre costume? You look like a peacock, Hansel! What authority do you have over us, eh? Will you dig the coal that powers Germany? Will you fuel the rise of the German nation? Of course you will not, you dog. You will sit around drinking little sips of pink champagne with your little peacock friends, fucking us over. I spit on you, you ignorant ass.'

That was the answer Kurt craved. He required no further authority. He had now had enough of these fools.

'Drop your weapons, now!'

There was no answer.

'Drop your weapons, or we will be forced to disperse you!'

There were more loud howls of laughter from inside. Large half-empty glasses were thrown through the windows, landing among the Freikorps – some smashing on the stones, others finding their targets and causing injuries. One of them splashed stale beer on Kurt. He looked at his wet uniform and sighed, annoyed that he would now smell of cheap beer.

'Fire!'

The Freikorps ranks simply opened fire through the windows. None of them showed the slightest hesitation. Kurt had ensured that they were well aware of their orders. They were briefed that enemies from within were still enemies, and that was how they must rationalise their actions. After twenty seconds, which was long enough for each man to empty a magazine and reload, he looked up again.

'Cease firing.'

Kurt stepped to the door. He took a deep breath, shielding his face from his men as he looked in. There were bodies littering the floor, some living and some dead. At the back of the room, under cover of a large oak table were the remaining unhurt miners. Kurt saw them, terrified and unarmed.

'I told you to disperse. Now your lives are forfeit. Meier, a rifle, if you please.'

Kurt took the rifle and pointed it at the first man at the table.

'What is your name? Do not lie.'

'Sepp Eber.'

'Goodbye, Sepp Eber.' Kurt shot the man, who slumped back.

'Mein Gott, man! He had a family, a wife and children. He was a worker, like you should be!'

'And you are?'

The man sat up, stiffened and looked Kurt in the eye. For a moment, Kurt wished this man had been on his side of the fence.

'I am the man whose face will haunt you forever, you pig.'

'I doubt it.'

Kurt fired. He had grown bored of the conversation. These two-hundred men would bring him glory. Their deaths might bring an end to the uprising and accolades would be showered on his little Langer band. None of the men left injured and dying could escape. They were weakened, pinned down by their dead and dying comrades. Kurt took one last look around, taking a mental note of the numbers and seeing they were indeed only armed with wooden sticks and rudimentary clubs. But he had one name. That was enough to identify the group, all he would need as corroboration for his report. The report that would seal Kurt Langer in the new order of Germany. He stepped outside into the air again, taking a deep breath. His men's nerve had held, which was most pleasing, but these men would now need strong leadership for their bloody purpose.

'Burn the building, Hans.'

CHAPTER SEVEN

Dusseldorf 1923

The café was quiet tonight. It had been raining heavily and the evening regulars had clearly thought better of it and hurried home to their families. Kurt was sitting alone for now, looking out over the darkening walkways of a damp Dusseldorf. Tonight was the fifth anniversary of the armistice, a night when his country quietly remembered the sacrifice of fallen comrades, but also the torment of a Germany unsure of its future, the political turbulence of a generation of men lost in the fields of the west and the east.

The meeting of the Sturmabteilung that night had been cancelled. Kurt was annoyed with the SA as it made them look amateurish and half-hearted, particularly when compared to their comrades in the east. The Dusseldorf Standarten was still forming and the commander was known to be a fool who just wanted power and influence and was going to change nothing. Kurt knew they should be better, he was manacled to a dead horse and hated the fools. The men who had arrested his own father for failing to immediately denounce the Kaiser in 1918 were still in power. Kurt thought that somewhere, someone knew more than they were telling. Even thinking of the small men in charge of this city angered him. Tonight, his anger was compounded by the weather.

'It rained in the trenches and we did not just cancel attacks. Have these fools forgotten that? Half of the bastards never stood a watch in the line anyway, cowardly...'

Behind Kurt came the scraping of a chair and another man seated himself, sheltering from the rain.

'Still talking to yourself, Langer?'

'That way I am assured of a sensible and intelligent audience.'

'Ha, but you bore yourself too, you brown-shirted pig!'

'Fraulein, two coffees please!'

'And Schnapps.'

'Just bring the bottle.'

The two men laughed and shook hands in the gloom of the corner.

'You know, Kurt, you should make it known that you would like to be the leader of the SA here. I think you would find some allies in the ranks. They respect your single-mindedness and drive.'

'Ha! That is because they have never seen someone so single-minded and driven.'

'Whatever it is that fires your belly, they want more of it. The incident in the old Latterhausen Rooms with the miners, Mein Gott, that was cold.'

'The leadership of the SA is not for me, at least not here. Dusseldorf is a dead city politically. The real movements are in Bavaria, Munich. Look, did you read the paper?'

'I did. Do you think this fellow Hitler can pull it off?'

'Not with that ass Ludendorff weighing him down. It isn't credibility they need, it's money and power. By-the-book politics, not getting drunk in a bloody beer hall and waving a fucking flag. If Hitler isn't in prison by the end of the month then I'm Hindenburg's boot cleaner.'

'Come on, Kurt, think of the future. A new Germany, imagine that.'

'I do. I also remember the past, Hans, I remember all too well. The bloody November Criminals left our army exposed and weak, stabbed in the back by our own fucking people. Germany can rise again. *Will* rise again.'

'So, if not here, then where will you go? Munich?'

'Yes, I feel strongly drawn to it and I think I must go there. I have no connections, but it is where the new Germany will rise. I can sense it. If not Hitler or Göring, then someone else will bring power and influence back for Germany. But it will be there.'

The coffee and schnapps arrived. Both men looked at one another and smiled before downing the first schnapps with a flourish.

'I think I can help you, Kurt. My brother is a member of the organising council for the public meetings of the party in Stuttgart. He has probably got enough connections to set you up in Munich. Go, my friend, if it drives you. Don't be constrained by the rain in Dusseldorf. I have a feeling you will do well. Let us drink to that.'

'I should not drink this much schnapps.'

'Well that does not sound like a man who will help Germany to rise again.'

After the fourth schnapps, Kurt rose to leave. As he passed Hans, his arm was tugged back by his friend.

'But seriously, Kurt, watch yourself. You know what comes with power and influence? Corruption, back-stabbing and politicking. You need to be smart to make it. Smart, wise and fast on your feet. If you want me to, I will telephone my brother tonight.'

Kurt nodded slowly and left. As he walked the short distance home he decided once and for all to make a move to Munich. The struggle for power and new political influence he had tasted had now numbed him to the loss of the Great War. But Odile was forever in his mind and nothing dulled that pain.

CHRIS CHERRY

CHAPTER EIGHT

Bazentin-Le-Petit 1922

William had been looking forward to showing his twins their new baby brother. By the looks of them, they did not quite know how to react to the little body wrapped in a soft blanket, but they seemed to know that it was delicate. Armandine stood gazing at him with her finger in her mouth and Arthur swished his hands almost in embarrassment, perhaps unsure how to react.

'Armandine and Arthur, meet Henri Pierre Collins, your new baby brother.'

Armandine peered again at the baby and smiled. Arthur must have seen enough as he climbed onto the bed next to his sleeping mother, poked her face until she opened her eyes and then smiled at her, falling into her arms.

'Odile, my love, we seem to have a slightly bigger family!'

'Well, William darling, you will need to build some more cars then, Henri seems like a very hungry boy.'

William looked out the window, it was getting dark. Odile's mother was to return later to help with the house and to make dinner for the rest of the family. Odile and William had not slept in two days and neither could even think about the days ahead. As William stepped downstairs to open the door for Madame Lefebvre, a wide grin spread across his face when he saw Marie-Louise carrying a basket of bread and meat for them.

'Bon soir, William. I have brought you something nice for supper. Pierre and I are so excited. Have you and Odile decided on a name?'

'Yes, Mother, we have. Perhaps you should come upstairs and we will tell you together.'

'Oh no, William, you have not called him after her Uncle Olivier? The poor boy would never survive that!'

She laughed, and William took her arm to help her up the stairs.

'No, we have not called him Olivier. We have thought of something very special.'

Marie-Louise took a deep breath. 'Oh, my daughter, how are you feeling? A new mother again?'

'Oh, Maman. I am tired and my back hurts, but otherwise I am quite well. I am so happy that we have another baby and he is so beautiful.'

'So he is, my loves, I cannot wait another second to see him again. May I?'

'Yes, he is awake.'

'Look at you, our beautiful little boy without a name. When are your Maman and Papa going to tell us then, young man?'

She looked at Odile and smiled. It was a smile with a hint of expectation. Odile looked at William and he nodded conspiratorially to her.

'Maman, we have called him Henri Pierre.'

Marie-Louise grasped the baby tighter to her and looked down, with the palm of her hand on his chest.

'Oh, Odile, my darling. Your little brother.'

William knew it would please Odile's mother and sadden her in equal measure. Marie-Louise sat on the bed, a little tear had formed in her eye.

'Both of you, you have honoured Pierre and me with his name. We loved your little brother, Odile, for the few minutes that he lived in our lives. He is such a handsome baby, he will be a fine and strong boy.'

William moved towards Marie-Louise. She lifted her hand to his, grasping his fingers.

'Thank you, William, thank you for this gift to us. I must go and fetch Pierre.'

'No, stay with Odile. I will go and find him.'

'Well if you do, you will be there until dark helping him. I know you both.'

William laughed and left, turning back to see little Henri's grandmother rocking him gently, calling his name over and over. He knew she was thinking back twenty-four years to when she gave birth to Odile and her twin brother who had lived for just a few minutes.

As he walked down the hill towards Odile's family home, he glanced over to the military cemetery, which contained the graves of four men that he knew well. He always bowed his head as he passed, he would perhaps do it every single day. It would soon be time to plant the spring flowers and tend the little brick memorial on the corner of the street opposite his new house. He stepped almost automatically in tune with a march.

William found it hard to be alive when so many others had perished and were buried or lost in the ground around the village. Each and every one of the returning villagers lived knowing that beneath their feet lay the bones and guns of thousands of soldiers from all around the world, from Britain, Germany, France, South Africa, Canada, Australia, New Zealand and India. Men who had lives to live and who gave them so that William could love his wife and cherish each dawn light and every sunset. He knew he had a responsibility and so each time he bowed his head, he remembered.

'William! Where are you going?'

'Ah, Alain. How are you and little Yvette today? She is such a big girl now! How is being an uncle and a father today?'

'Ha, William! I tell you, nobody gives you a book on raising a girl! If they did, I would burn it because it would be wrong. She is so full of energy, William, she will make an old man of me before my time!'

William laughed and walked on. Alain had his hands full, he knew that. But he now had three little ones. Three people now on earth looking up to him as their father. For a moment, he thought of his own parents. He would make plans to see them this coming year.

'Pierre? Papa? Are you there?'

'Ah, Colonel! How are you, and how is that beautiful boy without a name?'

'He is sleeping, thankfully. We have chosen a name, Papa. We are going to call him Henri Pierre. In honour of his—'

'Oh, William!' Pierre grasped his hand, beaming.

He disappeared into the house and brought out a bottle of cognac.

'But Papa, is it not a little early?'

'Ha! Perhaps, but today we celebrate.'

Marie-Louise was right. William was helping Pierre, but not with a car.

CHRIS CHERRY

CHAPTER NINE

Munich 1928

The day dawned bright and clear, the sunshine heralding a day of triumph and celebration. Kurt was looking forward to it enormously as this was the day he would receive his promotion to Sturmbannführer in the SA, in front of the massed audience at the party rally in Nuremberg. Not just a rank in name only, as it had been for the last two years, but a formal rank in the German party and military system. It had taken time as he had to find his family history and prove his Aryan roots for six generations. He had managed to complete the task last month, opening the door to his much-wanted promotion. Although he had been unknown in Munich, with few friends, he had still found ways to use his influence for his own good. He knew he had been spied on with suspicion, but now he was going to be one of them. An officer in the Sturmabteilung, the glorious SA. Today, he would be presented to Göring himself, to receive the pips of rank, it would be his first handshake with the Nazi elite. This was the vision of Kurt that he had craved on that dark night when the rain fell and the Freikorps stayed indoors.

Kurt dressed quickly in his immaculate uniform, his hair short and neat. He knew that the ladies liked his uniform, he had heard enough of their silly chatter to know it, but this was different, for now he was noticed by his own. Finally, he was now part of the story, part of the resurgence of Germany and that made him happy, it gave him a purpose.

At noon, the car came for him. A reward for his promotion. It would only be today that he was to be afforded the luxury of an escorted car, but that only made him want it all the more. One day, this would be his right. For now and for the rest of the rally, he would have to walk or take a transport, like the other keen and excited delegates at this first rally of the year. The driver saluted smartly, his arm arrow straight. Kurt liked that. This was not the weak and defeated Germany of the armistice. This was a strong and powerful Germany, such as the world order craved. When the job was done, they would be strong enough to do whatever they pleased.

He got out of the car into the bright glare of the day. A carpet led up the white stone bank to the steps, the way to the leadership and into the heady air of the Nazi elite. He stepped forward, to the applause of the crowd nearby. Some knew him by reputation. He knew that some feared him. Kurt Langer had come home. He took in the applause and strode up the steps as if this was his right. Even Göring raised an eyebrow.

'Wilhelm, who the fuck is this?'

'Sturmbannführer Langer, sir. The one who shot the miners in Dusseldorf, you remember?'

'Ah yes, Langer. He looks the right sort of officer for this, do you not think?'

'Yes sir. His father was a general. I suppose he thinks it is his birth right.'

Göring chuckled to himself and stepped forward to greet the first officer to be promoted today.

By nightfall, Kurt was ready for a drink. The day had passed in a whirl of salutes, slaps, jokes and formality. But Kurt felt let down by Göring. A fighter pilot from the last war, but now a self-important fool of a man, suckling at the breast of Hitler. But he was at Hitler's side. Kurt had wanted his father there. General Langer would surely have been proud of his son. He had invited his father, but he had declined to come, citing ill-health. That was odd for him, but Kurt paid it no more attention. This was still his day, father or not.

In the dark and anonymous bar, the two other recipients of rank left early so Kurt was left alone in the bar, drinking free schnapps and even a small champagne, courtesy of a loyal Nazi bartender. Kurt was so self-absorbed with the ceremony earlier that day that he did not notice a man enter the bar and seat himself just across from his table.

He had been too nervous to eat earlier and now he was very hungry, but eating in uniform here was not considered appropriate. So he sat drinking and glancing at the papers that had been delivered from the party printers just along the row in Nuremberg. The content was predictably tiresome, plenty of ranting and finger waving in large print. This wasn't the power Kurt wanted for Germany, but this was the party to get it. He knew he could help with that later. For now, he was more concerned with sobriety and reflection. He looked up and saw a man lean towards him. Kurt did not like his attitude and he was intent on snapping him back.

'May I sit here, Sturmbannführer Langer?'

'Why? Who are you?'

'Have you given much thought to what you will do with your new rank, hm?'

'What? Who are you?'

'Trust me, Langer, you will get to know us very well indeed.'

'Whoever you think you are, you are interrupting my evening. What gives you the right to come in here and address me in such familiar tones? You know that I am—'

The man held up a calming hand and eased Kurt back into his seat.

'You certainly are a fireball, Herr Langer. A fireball indeed. Good.'

'Look, I still don't know who you think you are com—'

'We know who we are, Langer. The question is, do *you* know who you really are? What do you want from this? You joined the SA willingly. You left Dusseldorf because you could not stand the weakness of the Freikorps. You came here in search of something. Now tell me, what is it? I, for one, am very keen to hear it.'

'In search of something? Look I'm not telling you anything until you tell me what right you have coming here, interrogating me about my motives.'

'It is clear that you are amongst friends here, Sturmbannführer Langer, be assured of that. Just tell me one thing. Do you think that Herr Hitler will deliver the Germany that you want? Do you think he can command power and influence in the world? Power so that the other countries have to sit up and listen to the German people? How about that? If you are suspicious of me, then I will tell you this. It is exactly what I want for Germany.'

Kurt eased back in his seat a little. A confidence shared was a confidence revealed.

'That is exactly the Germany that I want to see. Strong, powerful, avenging the weakness of the Versailles fiasco. Perhaps even exacting a little revenge on our enemy yet.'

Kurt had not told anyone but Hans about his deeper need for Germany to be strong. He felt a weight lift as he said it.

'Are you a deep thinker, Langer?'

'A what?'

'It's a simple question. Do you think about the future – not content to be just a follower of what is happening?'

'I think a lot, what of it?'

'Well, I am a sinister thinker, second guessing the weaker in our Country. Imagine that and you may do well in our organisation. Is that for you?'

'What are you offering?'

'Just a chance, no more than that yet. A chance to make something of yourself and to put behind us the misery of the last ten years of weakness in leadership.'

'What if I refuse?'

'We don't take no for an answer. Look, you came to Munich of your own free will, and nobody made you seek out power. You want this, you *need* this. I have a feeling you will do very well. Let's go, leave the drink. We have no time to lose.'

Kurt felt all eyes upon him as he got up to leave. He was being wound into the circle of the inner Nazi Party and he was quite willing to go. At each step, he felt a little of his pain subside. A little of the war lifted from him, leaving behind the memories of Odile, who now stood a little further away in his mind. He could look upon her and be strong, not weak and thin, transparent to the light.

Outside, was a long black car with an open top. It was much bigger than the car he had travelled in today for the ceremony. But there was no ceremony here. Already inside, the man in the bar beckoned him to join him on the back seat. Kurt thought for a moment, looked around and then got in. The car moved away slowly at first, east out of Nuremberg and into the coolness of the evening.

'You perhaps ought to know a few more truthful things about the SA before we go any further, Herr Langer. The Führer is not exactly enthralled by their claims of independence from the party. It is felt that they are growing a little too wild, too big for the little boots that they really have. You know it is believed that their usefulness is now exhausted as an instrument of the party? Too much foolish boot polishing and marching around in brown shirts to be of any real use to us. For us, loyalty to Adolf Hitler himself is the central purpose of our existence. It is to him that we pledge our loyalty and it is to him that we look for protection and the opportunity of expansion within the new Germany. Do you see?'

'I see. I don't know if that is for me. Are we not seeking light from the darkness? Is that not what the Führer said today?'

'Understood. So, let me tell you this. There is no other political party that will be allowed to have such influence as our own. The politics of Germany will, shall we say, be *encouraged* to coalesce around one man, one party. Do you see now?'

'Encouraged?'

'I wondered if you would alight there. Yes, encouraged. And that is where we come in.'

'We being?'

'Just call us a little bit of the Schutzstaffel. The bit of the SS with the power and influence, which will hasten the downfall of your SA. If you stay there, you will lose any hope of power and glory.'

'Why is the SA considered a problem?'

'It is not as close to the party as it could be. Its downfall may be some time, but we are certain it is coming.'

Kurt sat forward and turned his body towards the stranger. He tried to place him, but he had never seen him before in his life.

'But why should I now join the SS?'

The stranger lifted his arm and swept it around the inside of the car.

'You like this car?'

'Yes, but what does that have to do with anything?'

'What does this car tell you?'

'Someone has money to spend on cars.'

'So, if we have money for cars perhaps there is money for the more important things? You ever have a car with the SA? You ever have a meeting cancelled, perhaps just because it was raining?'

'How could you possibly—'

'It is not so shocking. Your friend Hans is my friend Hans as well. He just happened to mention it. Think about it, Kurt. Think about making a real difference. Get us back on our feet and remove the filth that is choking our country, your country, our Fatherland.'

The car stopped at the party accommodation that Kurt had been given for today's ceremony. As he got out, a little blue book was pressed into his hand. He recognised the book, but had not read it, thinking it was a stream of nonsense that revealed more of a weak mind than a strong leader. But perhaps he might need to read it now.

'Read it. If you can see the sense in it, then we should meet again. Perhaps tomorrow, in the same place and at the same time. Goodnight.'

The car drove off. Kurt was now entering a deeper part of the party. He wanted to be sure. He was sure. This was his time. He could live in this place knowing he was doing all that he could for his beloved Germany. The little transport officer could now become a major in the SS. A major with a chance of glory. He would become the man that he could be. He smiled to himself.

The next morning was a stark contrast to the one that had heralded the ceremony yesterday. At eleven today, the speeches would start, and everyone here was expected to attend. The meetings on the side were usually quite dull and the level of political detail was stifling. Kurt ached for the main events, the speeches by the leaders of his party. These would prove inspiring and emboldening, with hope for the future.

By the end of the first series, Kurt was hungry and went to a little stall on the road back to his quarters. How he wished for a car today so he could avoid the rain. At the stall he chose a little bread and some blood sausage, washed down with milk. As he watched the comings and goings of the party, he began to notice differences in the attitudes of the different groups. He had never even considered that there could be an insecurity in the SA, or a superiority in the SS. He had never felt any urgency or alarm. But here and now he suddenly saw the divisions, the factions and the clashes of ideology. He only knew SA and the Frontbann it had become in Bavaria. He was thinking and he now knew the answer he would give that evening.

In the bar, the little table he had taken last night was occupied by another group of junior officers of the SA. He could have had them moved, but did not feel inclined to move them just for his convenience. But as he approached, he noticed the man from last night waving discreetly to him. He sat down, placing his wet cap on the empty seat next to him.

'You came and so it is a yes, Sturmbannführer Langer?'

'It is a yes, willingly and wholeheartedly.'

'Good. Each member of the SS is carefully selected. Do you know why?'

'Do I need to know?'

'No.'

'Then do not tell me. I may not like the answer.'

'The SA is dead, you can see it. You will do well in the SS. I can see that. It will give you the chance to flex your talents and stretch you to extremes that you may not have realised you could reach.'

'What do I do now?'

'Return to Munich and report to the SS Southern Command. You will have to go through some processing first.'

'SS Southern Command? I did not know there was such a thing.'

'There is a great deal you have yet to learn. For now, just assume that the SS is a part of the SA. Looks better that way. But remember that we recruited you from the SA. That's where we are going, don't forget that.'

--oOo--

The train rattled towards Munich and the journey seemed endless, hot and tiring. There were a great many members from the party travelling home again. Kurt had no interest in the mechanics of the party. He wanted the bigger rewards. A strong Germany, a powerful Germany, an opportunity to flex new muscles in a new world. That was the medicine that he wanted for his soul.

At the railway station, he got directions to the quarters of the SS office responsible for the Munich and Eastern Bavaria regions. The new department of administration was shielded by a large oak door. He knocked and entered immediately. Behind it were four desks and a row of typing machines. This was certainly administration. Of what, he did not yet know.

The young officer at the first desk barely looked up from his notepad as Kurt approached. This seemed an odd start, but Kurt was more interested in the group of older officers engaged in animated discussion around a large planning table. This seemed more military and in keeping with his ambitions.

'Herr Sturmbannführer Langer, reporting as ordered. Are you expecting me?'

'Indeed sir. Please come this way.'

Kurt was led into a small windowless room and made to wait for nearly two hours. By the end of that time, he was extremely hot, agitated, angry, thirsty and indignant that he should be treated in such a manner. He was ready to explode at whoever walked through the door. But he was a loyal officer and remained seated, angry only on the inside. When the door finally opened, Kurt sprang to his feet. The officer who entered held the rank of a full colonel. Kurt knew that discipline must prevail.

'Langer, hm, Langer. Son of General Manfred Langer?'

'Yes, sir.'

'Good, he was my old commanding officer. A hard man to please, eh?'

'Yes sir. I am pleased that you know my father.'

'Do you know why you have been left alone for two hours?'

'No, sir, I was beginning to wonder.'

'I was waiting to observe you. To see how you respond to such treatment. It was good. You are no doubt angry and uncomfortable in this miserable hot room. But one would not have noticed. Good. There is much you should know and understand. Your education begins today. Formally, you will be retrained as an officer in the SS. I have hopes for you, Sturmbannführer Langer. I am sure that I will not be disappointed.'

CHAPTER TEN

Bazentin-Le-Petit 1937

As Odile's eyes opened, a warm breeze sailed through the window, carrying with it the sounds of a struggle with a stubborn wooden fence. She listened to the rhythmical hammering and some occasional swearing, in English of course, so as not to upset the residents in Bazentin-Le-Petit – that peaceful village, which sits quietly on top of the sweeping ridge from Pozieres to Longueval in northern France.

Odile smiled to herself, hearing the exasperated efforts of her husband to repair the fence again. She rose slowly this morning, allowing herself a rest in bed after the two-week long journey to and from England visiting their children and her beloved English family. Arthur was now studying for his final-year examinations in Hampshire at a private school, thanks to the money left by William's commanding officer and friend, General Cowling. Armandine was spending a year in England to improve her English so that she could follow her dream of being a teacher of French, perhaps one day in America.

Odile had also managed to make the short trip north to Arthur's school. It was the start of term for him and so it was a last chance to spend time with her eldest son for some time. Saying goodbye was always an emotional moment, but she knew that he must have this opportunity for he was so bright and intelligent. Her boy was so full of ideas, and my goodness, he would let you know all about them!

As she reached the window, Odile could not help but laugh. William was surrounded by a pile of wood shavings from the fence building, and Henri was racing around him, throwing handfuls of these shavings at his father. She only now noticed from up above them both that Henri was easily as tall as his father, every bit as strong and athletic as he had been, with the same kindness and loyalty as her beloved husband. But in Henri, she saw something else, something she recognised in herself and her own mother. He could read people, see their true intentions and know how to move amongst them, almost unseen and with a knack of appearing when least expected. Yes, Henri was a clever boy as well, not with books like the twins, but with a charm and spirit all of his own. He also had inherited the engineering gene from both their families and she was sorry for that. He would be condemned to a life of greasy spanners and dirty overalls for sure. As she turned away from the window, she smiled to herself at the memory of the funny motor car from her own childhood.

'Ah yes, that car, I wonder where that old car is now?'

'What was that, Mother?'

Henri was standing at the door, still covered in wood shavings. At least he didn't have dirty hands and overalls. Odile went to him and embraced him gently, picking bits of wood out of his hair.

'Henri, speak in French inside the house, you remember your father's rules?'

'Oh yes, sorry, Maman. What were you saying?'

'Oh nothing, just remembering that funny motor car that Grandpere built with Grandpa Collins.'

'Oh yes, I often wonder where it is, it was so important to our family.'

'Well, I am certainly pleased we built it. Otherwise, your father and I would never have met.'

'Well, perhaps one day soon, I can go to England and see if I can find it, if it still exists. It was an odd car, so possibly it has survived.'

'Well, your father might have to let you go, his father had to let him go didn't he? Let's ask him at supper.'

'Good. Mother, Thierry and I want to go to the Bois de Forcaux this afternoon to help replant the horse chestnuts, next to the ones that the Londoners planted. But Father wanted me to ask you first. I do wish that he would come with me, but you know he won't and he will not tell me properly why.'

Odile took his beautiful face into her hands.

'You surely must know why, my love?'

'Well yes, the war and all that. I know he was fighting here and that must be really strange, but it was years ago now, the wood is beautiful and shady, safe and all of that. I do wish he would come. We never seem to do anything outside. You told me of all your days on a motorcycle, picnics and things. He just won't do that with me. My goodness, I would absolutely love to ride a motorcycle. It isn't any fun.'

Odile sat down, and a little tear had come to her eye. She was torn between them both. She knew the horrors that had been visited here in the Great War, she knew that William had lived the very battle on this hill.

Henri knew of Horace Watkins and the Indians, but how could he imagine it in this place? He could see the crosses and stones but he had not seen his village as it was then, a torn and brutal battlefield. That bitter, torn, bleeding wound of shelling and death. She was pleased he was spared it.

'Henri, your father lived a lifetime of pain here. He came back because it is our home and he loves us. The very ground you walk on is full of terrible memories for him, his comrades are torn and shrouded beneath us. For him even to exist here, in peace, is a triumph over the evil that lived in our village. You already know that. But there is something else.'

Odile put her hand to her mouth, she had not meant to open that memory to her youngest child.

'What, Mother?'

'Sorry, Henri, it is nothing. Just that your father really does want to do those things with you, but we need to help him find his way. Come on, let us go and throw some more wood over him!'

Henri smiled, leapt up and ran down the stairs. Odile knew full well that Henri was right. Arthur and Armandine had been content with books and quiet evenings in, perhaps a cycle ride to Martinpuich or Pozieres, or a stroll to the Tabac for ice cream in Longueval, but Henri had too much of his parents in him. He wanted to take life by the reins and take risks, but William had lost that joy after the Great War. Odile would never stop loving him, but he could never again be like the boy who had jumped out of the bushes just along the street in 1912. Still, she was pleased that William was very busy with his work. He had a little engineering company in Bazentin and was considering a larger workshop in Albert. He had been offered premises in Bapaume, but he had turned them down politely. William never went to Bapaume. Outside, Henri was ducking from a handful of scratchy wood shavings. William had already got a second handful and was bearing down on him.

'Save me from him, Mother! Save me from Colonel Collins and the marauding willow-logs!'

'I certainly will not, you picked on him. You finish it.'

'Very well, prepare to be buried! Father?'

William had slumped to the ground. He raised his hand towards his son, who held onto his fistful of shavings.

'Father! I am so sorry, what did I say?'

'Nothing, Henri. Really, it is all well. Just give me a moment.'

'Mother, what did I do?'

'Nothing, Henri. Go inside and fetch your father some water. Perhaps make some English tea for him.'

'Yes Mother.' Henri dropped the wood, his face instantly pale and worried, his energy drained in an instant. He rushed inside to fetch water and some tea for his father.

'William, what is it? Not again?'

'Ah, Odile. It will always be there. Sometimes it will be expected, like that service at Thiepval, or as now, just the words... I can't know how or why or when. It is fine. Help me up, my darling. I am pleased you are awake and looking so refreshed. I have missed your beautiful face. Let me look at you, it always makes me feel better.'

William placed his hands on his wife's flushed cheeks, stroking her gently. Her finger just brushed his hand. He leaned forward and gently kissed Odile, drawing her to him. Henri returned as his parents embraced.

'I bring water and tea, Father. The tea is soupy, how you like it. Why you like it mashed up, I will never understand.'

The three laughed. William opened his arms wide, his wife and youngest son fell into them, and he kissed them both.

'Henri, I do believe we have some unfinished business. Mother, my love, hold this.'

William passed the cup of steaming tea to his wife. He grabbed Henri, spun him upside down and dropped him in the pile of logs and wood chips. He then jumped in after him. Odile looked at them both, laughing loudly at the faces that Henri was pulling as his father tickled him mercilessly. She was going to get them to stop, but Henri was right, William needed to *live* here, not just to *be* here.

The motorcycle that they had in 1913 was long gone, but she knew how to find one. In Albert was Monsieur Quentin, the cousin of the Guillaume brothers, who made motorcycles in Clermont-Ferrand. She would buy a new one and surprise them both. Henri deserved a father like his good friends had. Everyone knew what William had been through and everyone loved him all the more for staying here. There were favours to call in and she would call one in for a motorcycle.

Odile guessed it would take a month to arrive, which would take the year to September. Cooler and shorter days, but still warm enough to get a little riding in. William could show Henri how to control the machine and the boy could then do deliveries, just like his father used to do. Yes, just like his father. His father could find a life again. She had sent a telegram to Monsieur Quentin, who replied that the new motorcycle would arrive in two weeks. Odile was delighted and could hardly bear the wait until it arrived.

The day the motorcycle arrived was clear, if a little misty. But it would certainly be warm enough to ride. Odile had left strict instructions for delivery. The motorcycle was to be delivered oiled and with fuel, ready to ride. If it wasn't, then William would simply spend the daylight fiddling and tinkering and she wanted him and Henri on it before nightfall. The lorry arrived from Pozieres and stopped by their house on the corner of the village on top of the hill. As the driver stepped out, Odile watched him look down at the small brick memorial by the roadside.

'Madame... Collins?'

'Yes, that is me.'

'That the memorial to the nine men?'

'Yes, the nine brave men.'

'It was right here, wasn't it?'

'Yes it was. They were Royal Engineers, like my husband.'

'English, is he?'

'Yes, he is.'

The driver chuckled. 'So that's why you have a funny spelling to your name. We thought it was a mistake.'

'Many do. So is it all ready?'

'Yes, Madame, exactly as you requested. I started it up just as we left Albert, all is in perfect working order.'

'Quickly, please, they will be here in half an hour.'

'Ha, it will be a very great surprise.'

The motorcycle was moved to the rear, onto a little stretch of path that was out of sight. The path stretched away towards Mametz Wood, the very line that those engineers had been constructing when they were trapped and killed. Every time Odile walked this path, she remembered, just for a moment.

Odile had sent William and Henri to the bottom of the hill to pick up some vegetables. Normally, they were delivered almost to the doorstep, but not today. Her husband and son had looked puzzled, but they had shrugged and gone down the hill, talking about their plans for the business in the future. Now that the motorcycle was in place, Odile went to the gate and waved frantically to hurry them back. They quickened their pace and William was almost out of breath when they arrived at the gate.

'What is it Odile? What is the matter? Are you unwell?'

'Ha ha! No, William, imbecile! I have a little something for both of you. Henri, go inside and pick up the items on the table. Don't ask questions, just bring them.'

Henri rushed inside and quickly reappeared carrying two pairs of gloves, two scarves and a leather cap and goggles. He looked puzzled, but

William immediately burst out laughing.

'A motorcycle? Where is it, my love, in a little tool shed in Martinpuich?'

Odile had to put her hand to her chest at that memory. She remembered the little 1908 Peugeot and the bargain with the owner.

'No, my love, follow me.'

They rounded the corner of the house to where the new motorcycle was waiting. William hesitated just for a second, then made a lunge for it, rubbing his hands all over the new metal and smiling broadly at Odile.

'It is the most beautiful machine I have ever laid eyes on, my love. Thank you, thank you, my beautiful wife.'

'William?'

'Yes, my darling?'

'It belongs to Henri.'

William smiled and looked to Henri, but did not take his hands off the machine.

Henri jumped on the motorcycle and playfully pushed his father away. William pretended to fall and be injured, but then he climbed up behind his son and showed him how to start the motor and how to use the controls. Very slowly, Henri moved forward, wobbling a little. Odile watched as they rode up and down the short stretch of road to Martinpuich and the junction to Pozieres.

'Father, can we ride to Martinpuich, turn right to the wood and then right again along the valley to Longueval? How about that?'

'Perhaps another time, Henri. I am a little tired.'

'Please Father, Papa?'

'Really, Henri, perhaps this is enough for one day.'

Odile rested her hand on William's arm and squeezed gently.

But William looked at his youngest son for a long time.

'Very well, Henri, but you must lead the way.'

Henri smiled broadly, took his father by the arm and then stole the cap from the top of his head.

'Hey, Henri, that's mine!'

'Come and get it.'

CHAPTER ELEVEN

Dusseldorf 1938

The envelope fell onto the new prickly woollen doormat. It was wet from the rain. Liesel liked the idea of letters falling through the new slot in the door. It was always a nice surprise, full of mystery and opportunity. Besides, Herr Lamm looked a fool in his stupid Nazi uniform – and that ridiculous salute every time she opened the door! She too wanted a strong Germany, but did not want the fascist means to this end. Liesel was frightened of the national socialist movement and the monster it had spawned, Herr Hitler. She did enjoy his speeches, could understand the sentiments and could easily be swept up in the seductive, persuasive and energising words. But there was something underneath, something that an intelligent woman could sense. She dare not speak the words of course, for fear of arrest or even death. She knew her husband also felt it.

There was no use Liesel talking politics with her mother and father. Her mother brushed such things aside as unimportant to a strong German woman. She would point out that her daughter's duty was loyalty to the Fatherland and that whatever the Führer said must be right, for the people had put him there, a divinity that could not and should not be questioned. Her father appeared less convinced, perhaps because of his military past. He often mentioned that Hitler had been a brave corporal on the Western Front, but that he had no place among the elite of German political society. Of course, her father had been arrested once, for supporting the Kaiser. His detention by his own people seemed to have shocked and frightened him to eternal silence on the issue. But in a quiet moment, he would squeeze her arm and ask that they silently prayed for a better Germany. The look they shared was the same one every time. May God protect Kurt, for he might already be in the darkness with no light to guide him.

As she reached for the envelope, Liesel knew already who it was from. Her heart leapt and her thoughts, as always, went back to the wonderful day that Odile had disappeared, gambling her life in a brave run for home. She now knew exactly how Odile had done it – Liesel Langer's identity, her pass, the permit and the Koln railhead. Liesel had never discussed it or disclosed the truth to Kurt. Even now, the memory was too painful for him and she did not particularly want to speak with him these days. At the time, she knew he had felt utterly rejected, when he was vulnerable and suffering from Kriegsneurose. Sister Langer had seen her fair share of dying soldiers, particularly those dying on the inside, eaten by an unseen terror.

In the years since leaving nursing, as a newly married woman, Liesel often thought of the men in the wards and what had become of them and their insulted, broken and hurt minds. She also thought how badly Germany had repaid their sacrifice, this man with a swastika and words of venom. But she had to put those thoughts to the back of her mind, for even a hint of distaste for the Führer could end her life and those of her beloved family.

Every time she saw Kurt, which was not often nowadays, she felt a little sick seeing his black uniform and the shocking red and black insignia of the Nazi Party proudly displayed for all to see. She saw how people looked at him with respect, with some people's respect borne from patriotic feelings of national pride, others simply from fear and intimidation. Kurt intimidated. His whole body, held upright and arrogant, radiated a presumed authority. To Liesel, this authority was unearned and tainted irrevocably by the actions of his comrades. Respect was earned, not demanded at the point of a pistol.

Liesel took the envelope into the cool parlour, closed the door and inspected the envelope to see if it had been opened and resealed. She was content that it had not, but Odile did not understand Germany and her language could easily cause offence to someone, which meant that Liesel and her husband could be put in danger. Perhaps she should ask Odile to stop writing to her, at least for the time being, until things improved in Germany. Perhaps it could be hoped that Herr Hitler would fall down the steps at one of those ridiculous rallies in Bavaria, or even fall on the head of her delusional brother, who no doubt was on his knees like a dog, lapping up the titbits of bile dropped by the Führer.

As she opened the letter, Liesel could almost smell France. Of course, the envelope and paper were dry, but there was something inside that made her think her mind must be playing tricks. A smell of new wood. Only wishful thinking but it did make her smile to herself. The letter was shorter than usual, but in Odile's beautiful handwriting. It was, as always, lovingly written with her whole heart pouring into the few brief words, some in French and some honouring Liesel in German.

My beloved sister, my beautiful Liesel

Where do I start? It has been nearly a year since I have been able to write to you! Well, William is as busy as ever, but his wounds take their toll on him. He is always tired in the evening, but tries to cover it up as our men do. I am well. I am busy on our farm and workshop, Father and Mother are very well and Father is still working and earning a living from his farm machines. Mother asked after you, so when you write back, I will tell her your news, if that is agreeable to you. She often asks about you.

So, to our children. The twins are nearly eighteen now. Arthur is in England studying as hard as ever. I am not exactly sure what he is studying at the moment, but he was thinking of changing his studies from Engineering. I did not tell his father! Armandine decided to stay in England to learn to be a teacher of French. Naturally, she is studying hard and succeeding. I think she has found a nice young man to court. William's family think that there may well be a proposal soon, so we are quietly excited.

So to Henri, now sixteen and with the soul of a butterfly. He detests study, adores his father and is in love with machines. I cannot imagine him a son of ours! William has now taken him on as an employee in 'Collins and Son'. The sign is wonderful and so we are all very pleased. I wonder how long before he wants to fly away. His grandmother spoils him completely, of course.

Do write to me with your news, dearest sister. I read that things are not easy for you all in Germany. We worry every day, we see the weakening of the politicians and dread the sea of grey returning over the horizon once again.

With love to you and your family

Your eternal sister, Odile
(Mme Collins)

Liesel read the words again, always so pleased to hear the news of her unseen family in France. She knew that her part in their very existence was small, but she felt a tiny thread of gold reaching out to them, stretching over the distance to Bazentin. She was certain the children knew nothing of her, but she felt as a parent would towards them and yearned for a day when she could embrace them and meet the man who had Odile's heart.

She kept Odile's letters in a velvet-lined box on the dressing table in her private room. Her husband, Herr Doctor Karl Eisner of the

Kaiserswerth, knew all about Odile, having first met her at the military hospital in Dusseldorf. Liesel and he often laughed at the little deception made in his name that helped Odile to escape and the resulting dressing down his own father gave Liesel. If only his own father had known the truth, she was certain that it would have made him chuckle. But he did not live to see his son marry the silly girl who had apparently lost her identification in the laundry. He was taken by the Spanish influenza in early 1919. Before he died, he had told his son to be a good man, to follow his heart, and to have a little fun each day. Her husband held on to those words and Liesel was determined to keep him youthful and free in spirit. As if her thoughts had summoned him, the door opened a fraction and Karl appeared, smiling at his wife.

'Oh, Karl, do stop skulking behind the door. You know I have been waiting for you to come home.'

'Well good evening to my beautiful wife, why are *you* skulking in the gloom?'

'I am reading a letter. Odile has finally written to me, to us. Here read it, I will translate for you if you do not understand.'

'I can understand German perfectly well, Frau Eisner.'

They both laughed. Karl read the letter, smiling at the good news from Odile and her family.

'She certainly was a singular young lady. She won't know this, but she was deeply missed when she… well, when she stopped coming to the wards. Perhaps you should tell her when you reply, it might make her feel better.'

'Yes, Karl, I will do that. Odile will appreciate it very much.'

'I would invite her to come to Germany, given that your brother is now deep in the party in Munich. But I fear the country is sliding into the ocean. There is something strange going on that I cannot put my hand on. Anyway, why don't you write to her now and I will see when supper might be ready, hm?'

'Yes, I will tell her our news and see if we might arrange to meet them soon. It might be wishful thinking, but it makes me happy to think it a plan.'

Karl stepped up to his wife, kissed her and went in search of supper.

Liesel, content now that her husband was back in the house and the evening was set to be cool, sat down at her little writing desk to write her return letter to Odile. How she loved writing to her sister, but what small opportunity she now had in a darkening Germany. She looked out of the window. The first sentence was easy. The second was harder.

My beloved sister, my beautiful Odile,

Thank you so much for my letter. I received it today and thought only of you here in Germany and how it was back then, but how much it has changed since you left all those years ago. Still, I will tell you our news.

Franz and Monika are growing up so fast! Franz is now ten and Monika twelve. We were to have another only last year, but the baby was lost to us. We were very upset but now realise how fortunate we are to have two perfect children. Franz has just changed to a new school, the one he was at became a little overprotective of him, and he was expected to attend extra classes in German citizenship. Karl was unsure of this, so we decided to move him to a new school. Monika now attends a special school for German girls in Dusseldorf. Her studies seem to be a little basic and unimportant, more about making a good home, rather than studying. She is only twelve years old! Neither of them seem to be allowed much time to play. How education has changed since we were young!

It would be great fun if we were able to visit you in France and to meet your beloved family. I fear that it might not be possible just yet, Germany is not yet the country it might have been. It isn't so bad here, not really. I hope that the coming season is a good one for you and if it were ever possible to send me a new photograph, it would be gladly received. I attach one of us, taken in Karl's office at the Kaiserswerth. You will remember it as it was Matron's office in the Kriegsneurose ward. It is now a teaching ward full of diseases that have not yet been fully investigated. How I would have loved to go back to nursing, but such is the world we live in.

All love from Dusseldorf

Your eternal sister, Liesel
(Frau Eisner)

When she had finished the letter, Liesel read it again in case it said anything that a prying eye might find offensive. When she was sure that the words were innocent enough, she placed the letter in a crisp envelope. She imagined the hands that the letter would pass through from now until it reached Odile in France. The post boy, the awful Nazi postmaster, the post office full of socialist fools, the train journey, the French postal officers, the boy walking up the hill to Odile's house. She tried to imagine it. The photographs she had been sent by Odile showed a lovely wood and brick house on the hill. Odile did not want for very much, and how she deserved a life filled with love. The little room she had been locked in at her own parent's home across the city was now never used, cold and a little damp. It was as if the little life it had contained had travelled back with Odile, unwilling to stay in a house of torment, leaving a ghost behind that forbade entry. A house of ill fortune that even Kurt was reluctant to stay in. Kurt, her wonderful older brother, the light of her young life.

Whatever had happened to him, had taken him completely. If she were capable of any feeling, then it would be shame and disgust. But it was really pity that she felt. Pity that the trenches had taken him from boyish kindness and devotion, perhaps a little misguided and immature, to a bitter, angry and resentful man. He was now consumed by an inner drive for something, but what it was Liesel had long ago stopped caring to know. Her brother was as nothing to her now, she was not sure that any of her feelings for him could be described as love.

Karl now returned, having left her to write the letter in peace. He was excited about something.

'Liesel, we must eat supper quickly! We have just been invited to the theatre tonight by Doctor Brunner. *Olympia* is being shown and I have been looking forward to seeing it enormously.'

'But isn't it going to be all about, well the…'

'Yes, but it is also about Germany. We could do with a bit of cheering up, couldn't we?'

Liesel knew that cheering up was the last thing Germany needed. She looked out of the window, then at the large clock in the corner of the room. The rain was harder now, set for the evening. Reluctantly, she rose from the chair and stepped into the hallway. The children were due home now, although they might be late because of the rain. She would wait in here until they were home. Suddenly, she wanted them home more than anything. Writing to Odile was always a pleasure she looked forward to, but it always unlocked the memories, the silent, unsaid knowing between them all. The truth from which she had always tried to protect the children. She longed for them to be home now, to hold them. Her hands ached for them. They would be surprised at such a longing embrace, but they loved their mother.

Almost an hour had passed before the windows of the front door darkened and her children bobbed in, casting aside their wet coats on the floor before falling into the warmth of the waiting arms of their mother. With their wet hair, they seemed not to notice the tears flowing down their mother's cheeks as she wept for their future, as uncertain now as it had been for Odile in 1918.

CHAPTER TWELVE

Germany November 1938

Kurt enjoyed the warm spell, an unseasonably dry period in late October. It was a period of calm that allowed him to attend a number of meetings and preparations for operations that the SS would undertake in the coming two weeks within Germany. He constantly moved from place to place, his excitement building with every discussion and conversation over schnapps at the officers' tables. Standartenführer Langer was very soon going to be able to make a permanent name for himself, to associate with the Nazi machine in a way that could carry him all the way to Berlin and the glory he wanted. Nothing would get in his way, not even the hundreds of Jews whose names he now carried in his green notebook. He did not know them, would never know them and he cared for them not one bit, for these names stood in his way. To him, they were mere obstacles, faceless as cattle and of no value to the effort of hard-pressed Germans. Trained to despise and resent, he followed his orders and despised and resented them with gladness.

'Herr Standartenführer? Herr Oberführer Altmann wishes to see you immediately. By that, I mean he actually said immediately.'

'Why? What the fuck does he want now? I am already on with this damned list. Not more of them surely? We only have two nights for this and it will take two nights to find these bloody rats.'

'Sir, I don't think it is actually to do with the operation at all. It is personal, he has a letter for you from Dusseldorf – marked secret.'

'A what? From Dusseldorf? It must be my father. Mein Gott, he might be dead and I had no idea!'

Kurt ran, despite his rank, to the office of his superior. Altmann was already waiting for him, the envelope from Herr Gauleiter Florian from Dusseldorf unopened but marked *Urgent – Secret – Only*.

'Langer, we do not know what this is, but it was brought by a motorcycle dispatch personally from Herr Gauleiter himself. You must open it immediately. We have been ordered to be present when you read it.'

Kurt was deeply worried. This sounded less like a family illness and more like a serious investigation into his conduct. He felt sure he had done nothing wrong, not in the eyes of the Nazis anyway.

'Yes sir, of course.'

Kurt had not trembled or been fearful since October 1918 on the approaches to Avocourt, near Verdun. The letter was marked secret, so it was certainly not about his father. It must mean something else entirely, but he could not guess what. He opened the envelope. Inside was a single crisp sheet, neatly typed and personally signed by the Gauleiter. The Dusseldorf Gauleiter ruled the city with a zeal that Kurt reluctantly admired. His authority was almost absolute, being the eyes and voice of the Führer in his home city. It was obvious that a copy of this letter had been made as there were imprints from the copying process. This was important and not to be ignored.

SS-Standartenführer Kurt Langer (SS-EzgMME)

My office has received certain intelligence that has caused distress to the Gestapo and regional office of the SS. The intelligence relates to information received regarding the possibility of Jewish involvement in your family, in the name of a Karl Eisner. Eisner has been temporarily classified as a Jew by this office, but in so doing, I felt it important to inform you and to brief you on the information we hold and also on the actions we are taking as it irrevocably affects your sister, Liesel Langer.

On 14 October 1938, we received information (I am verifying the source presently) that Karl Eisner is the son of J. A. Eisner who was, in fact, the son of Jews. J. A. Eisner was the son of Otto and Margareth Eisner, formerly of Vienna, having escaped from Chernigov in Russia in 1903 or 1904. Otto and Margareth died in 1911 and J. A. Eisner of influenza in 1918 or 1919. We are therefore certain, according to our Jewish factors test, that Margareth and therefore J. A. Eisner were Jews. The wife of J. A. Eisner is now assumed Jewish, which categorises Karl Eisner as a Jew.

I thought it important that I inform you personally of our investigations. The outcome is that I am confirming the above as of 1 January 1939. At this time, party decrees will be rigorously enforced on surviving Jews and spouses. In this case, Karl Eisner will be prevented from practising medicine and earning an income from non-Jewish patients. He will be required to carry a Jewish identification card (and will append 'Israel' to his name). However, as the spouse of a non-Jew from the blood-pure Langer family, he will be exempt from interrogation, imprisonment and deportation for twelve months in the first instance. That I am able to guarantee by way of letter to your father as sponsor for your sister. However, this office recognises him as a Jew for all purposes of census and reporting to Berlin.

You are ordered to destroy this letter immediately, I will require evidence of destruction from your superior officer, Herr Altmann, in writing immediately by return.

Obergruppenführer Friedrich Karl Florian
(Gauleiter SA – Dusseldorf)

Kurt read the words in total disbelief. His world of glory and achievement were now tumbling around him as if an earthquake had struck his foundations. His stupid sister had married a fucking Jew! Of all the disrespectful ways to repay his love and devotion – he would have to find a way for this to disappear, or for the Jew to disappear. He would have the marriage declared illegal, perhaps show Eisner to have raped her, anything to rid her of him. She was race-pure and their children could be shown to be pure enough. If not, well, he would have to think of something for them. He could not think, and his mind raced through a fog of desperate anger and worry for his own future. It was vital not to act rashly, or to make a stupid mistake that he would have to live with. Of course, he could just have Eisner killed, but this would not go away just because he was dead. This had to be an administrative task, perhaps even involving the assassination of the Gauleiter, perhaps he would have to do this himself.

'Langer? Are you finished reading?'

'Sir? Yes, sir. I am required to destroy the letter.'

'Give it to me, we will see to it.'

'NO! I will do it.'

'Langer? How dare you raise your voice to your superior officer! Give me the paper and get out.'

Kurt could see events unravelling in front of him. This could be the very end of his army career. He had to be careful. He had to rely on his training. Cool and calculating. It had to be so from this very moment.

'Sir, I am sorry. But this note contains explicit instructions. I am merely following Herr Gauleiter's orders. Sorry sir, but I am a loyal officer.'

Altmann's irritation appeared to subside. He seemed still unconvinced, but the Gauleiter was everyone's superior officer in this matter.

'Very well. Burn it quickly. I will inform the Gauleiter that the letter is destroyed. Do you require any assistance? Are you able to share the contents with us?'

'Thank you sir, and no, I am not able to share the contents. It relates to SS activity in Dusseldorf. I will need to return for one week.'

'But the operation?'

'One week after the operation, sir, if that is agreeable to you.'

'Go Langer, we are mystified that a Gauleiter should be troubled with a rat-catcher like you, but very well. I will give you ten days and then you are needed in final preparations for the East.'

'Thank you, sir.'

Kurt placed the remains of the charred letter in the ashtray. It was completely destroyed, but the contents were in his head, burned onto his brain like a brand. His head was devoted to the Führer, but now there was a stain, an indelible mark that would prevent his rise to Berlin and the glory he needed. A note on his records that would forever distance him from the centre of his beloved world.

There were two things that he must do. First, arrest or kill those on his list. His personal honour would depend on the list being completed. Secondly, and more distastefully, he must deal with Karl Eisner. He could just kill him, but it would do no good. He must clear his own name by clearing the name of a man he now distrusted and despised. A man who he had once embraced as a brother, gladly offering his best wishes for his sister's marriage. A sister he now suspected knew more about the disappearance of Odile than she was prepared to admit. He had been lied to by his sister, his own Aryan blood! Now she had allowed a filthy rat Jew into her bed, to put his dirty crawling hands over her pure German flesh.

No, whatever the administrative outcome, Eisner was a dead man, he was already dead in Kurt's mind. He would go for Eisner, but for now there were two-hundred others who would first see Kurt coming in the night, an unexpected shadow from the dark streets, as their lives drew to an end at the hands of the SS-Standartenführer.

CHAPTER THIRTEEN
Kristallnacht 1938

Kurt looked at his list. Munich was a big city and the district to which he had been assigned contained hundreds of shabby and cramped houses full of Jews. It was unlikely that he could positively identify all of the names and ensure that they were all removed onto the waiting cattle trucks at the railway station three or four kilometres from where he was standing. He noted the order that foreign nationals must not be touched, Jewish or not. Perhaps he would worry about that later. Get them out and away and he might get some sleep and some schnapps tonight.

Now standing in front of him were about twenty Sturmabteilung thugs. To Kurt they were little more than uneducated peasants and he was almost embarrassed to remember once being in the shambolic SA. But they would be the blunt tool that Kurt would use to smash the houses and property of those on his list, and no doubt a few others as well. In his mind, each one of them was somehow family to Karl Eisner. Even thinking the name made his grip tighten on his club, the club he dearly wanted to use on the fat, smug faces of the names on his list and on the head of the bastard who was between him now and Berlin. The grinning fucking doctor who took his sister to bed, who sat laughing in Dusseldorf, laughing at Kurt behind his back, probably encouraging his sister to laugh at him as well. He would go for him and it would be soon.

Kurt's eyes were wide and he took out the little green book, opening it to the first names on the list. A list that would take him one step closer to Berlin, if the problem of Eisner could only be resolved. He was expected to arrest them. But Kurt was angry and now impatient. Timing was important for this operation. The Munich Gauleiter was to send his men into the streets at eleven and the SA men were to go at just before midnight. Kurt and his group of SS would then round up the people, casually ticking them off in his notebook. He looked at his watch. They were already late. Kurt wanted an assurance from the Gauleiter that this delay was temporary, but the telephone would not pick up, and the offices were already empty. In the absence of an order, Kurt decided to move anyway. He was impatient to move on his list. He tapped the book on his leg, turning his head to his left.

'Let us move forward, men. There are only two rules, touch no foreigners at all and no damage to German property, or you answer to me personally. If Jewish-only property is nearby, smash it and burn it down. Move out!'

In his SS uniform, Kurt walked behind men in civilian clothes. He felt his uniform was more intimidating and he wanted those on his list to know who had come in the night for them. He was coming for them, they would remember him, his face reflecting in their eyes as they were taken away.

As he turned into the first street, he was shocked at how shabby and broken the houses were. The windows were already broken, the frames yielding easily to the power of hammers and sticks. The cries of women could already be heard and the grunt of men under arrest reverberated around the small streets. Kurt enjoyed the crisp tap of boots on the cobbles, a frightening sound even knowing that it was his own men. The first house was set ablaze and this brought out some twenty men and women into the street. They were all in a state of undress, faces bewildered and disorientated. As soon as they were outside, the men were pinned to the ground, the women were pushed roughly away and the children were left open-mouthed, looking for a parent, relative or anyone with a kindly face. The SA were unsure what to do with the children, but Kurt would not have his time wasted.

As each man was taken past him, Kurt looked in their eyes. These men were already broken, their eyes filled with humiliation and terror. He wanted to smile at them, to remind them who had won, who had finally exacted revenge on them for years of secret treachery. But the final walk to the lorry was enough, with no hope of escape, or of ultimate survival. The women looked down, barely able to stand and once they could no longer see their children, they seemed to give up hope. Kurt made sure that the children were quickly taken away to subdue the women. The men he could deal with himself and he stepped forward, taking a mental count of the faces. He reached into his pocket and took out the little white handkerchief that had belonged to Odile. It was a little grey from resting permanently in his pocket. He turned it over in his hands once or twice then replaced it in his pocket, along with the little green book. He was no longer concerned with ticking off names. They were all here, and more.

The officer on the train could reconcile this list. He just wanted to clear them all, to sweep the street clean. For a moment, he turned away and looked at his watch, it was getting late and he had only visited one street. He had run out of patience now, and the crying of children was slowing the clearance of the adults.

'Just load them onto the lorry, we will deal with them later. I don't care who or where their mothers are, just get them off my street immediately.'

Within just a few minutes of the children leaving, the street was finally cleared. Kurt saw that there were no non-Jewish properties here and turned to move away. As he turned, he felt a painful blow to his face. One of the men had escaped his captor by shedding his jacket and ran towards Kurt in his SS uniform. Kurt was spun around and almost fell to the floor, open-mouthed. He felt an arm steady him as one of his men came to his aid.

'Sir, are you injured?'

'No, thank you. Where is the fucking dead Jew that did this?'

'I don't know, he ran into that group over there, he will be among them, one without a jacket probably.'

'Hold the lorry, have all the men taken off and lined up here on this wall.'

The SA men roughly pulled the terrified men back from the lorry, almost throwing them down onto the street again. Their faces were resigned to their fate. Hope had already left them. There were nine men, three of whom were too old to be the assailant. Kurt took out an everyday handkerchief and wiped the blood that was streaming from his broken nose.

'One of you filth has just attacked an officer of the SS. Admit the offence now and you can all be on your way. What say you?'

The group was unmoved. Two younger men looked to step forward, but their arms were pulled back by others who grasped their shoulders to calm their anger.

'No one? Well, the assailant did not have a jacket. Of course, in the time since the attack he could quite easily have put one back on, so I shall assume that any one of you attacked me. What say you now?'

The group were as still as the night. This time, no one dared to make eye contact. Kurt let them wait a little longer, he felt this now a game despite the pain of his broken face. He thought the suspense might make one of the men crack and come forward. But they remained still, so he decided to act. He paced up and down the line, perhaps the sound of his boots rapping on the stones might provoke a reaction. The two younger men without jackets were his quarry and he would have his sport tonight.

He approached the first man on the right, an elderly man, who was only partly dressed. Kurt knew that this old man would never have been able to reach up to him. He took out his pistol and shot him in the chest. The shot made them all jolt upright, Germans included. The sound of the cartridge on the floor and the percussion of the shot in the narrow brick-lined streets would surely flush out the assailant. As the old man fell, the others gasped. One of the younger men without a jacket was sick on the cobbles.

'Still silence? So, that means it must have been the old man and I was right first time. That is good. No one attacks an officer of the SS and runs away like a rat into a sewer. But what is worse is that not one of you informed me that he was my assailant. That is not acceptable. Not at all. When I ask a question, I expect an answer. You, boy. Give me a number from one to eight. Quickly.'

'Two sir, two.'

'That is the wrong number, you should have said eight.'

Kurt raised his hand and two stormtroopers stepped forward with machine guns and raked the wall. All eight men fell to the floor. Kurt stepped up to the boy and saw he was still alive. Kurt upturned his face with the tip of his boot.

'I know it was you, the last thing you will see, you fucking Jew, is the boot of the SS crush the life from you. As you die, think of this. You have personally killed two hundred of your fellows with your one stupid act of angering me.'

Kurt watched the light fading from the boy's eyes, then stepped towards the empty car that had come to take him to the next street. At the door, he leaned down and wiped his boot with the bloody handkerchief, tossing it into the growing fire. He had not planned on killing anyone tonight, he only wanted to know that the boy was a German Jew, otherwise he would have to answer for it. He cared not for the others. Without looking back, he moved away to the next street on his list. He could check the names later.

'Clear up this mess and put the bodies on the fires. Do it now.'

'Yes sir, immediately.'

--oOo--

Liesel wondered what the terrible noises coming from the street might be. Over the last year, the Sturmabteilung thugs had begun to intimidate and threaten some of their neighbours and friends. It was most distressing to watch, but Karl had advised against saying or doing anything that might bring them to their door. Karl had seen this in other parts of the city and imagined that it was the Jewish people who were the targets for these attacks, given all of the new laws and practices issued almost daily by the Gauleiter.

'The Rosemanns have had their windows smashed. The poor children, look, there they are now in the street, in their night things, they must be frozen, God bless them. Come on, let us take them a blanket, it is only a little thing to do that no one will notice.'

'No, Liesel! We go nowhere tonight. Something is going on and we cannot become involved. We must do nothing. Whatever it is that is happening, we must not be thought part of it, or become involved. The Rosemanns' children will be just fine, you see. It is probably just something going on in that street. Perhaps you should come away from the window.'

'It is absolutely not fine, Karl. Look Herr Rosemann is being dragged out by his— Oh my goodness, that man just hit him! And look! They are now being taken away in that dirty lorry. Why? See, there are others as well. What is going on in our city, Karl? Has everyone lost their civility? What on earth have the poor Rosemanns done? I'm going out to them.'

She turned to move to the big front door.

'You will not!'

Karl leapt to his wife, gently but firmly holding her, turning her to face towards him, moving her away from the door. She slapped his face, which shocked her, but then immediately and instinctively she put her hand to her own face. Karl drew her close and held her gently. She was shaking and fearful. He kissed her forehead even though his cheek must burn like fire. Liesel was afraid. But not of Karl.

'We cannot do anything, Liesel. Whatever is going on is beyond our powers to help.'

'Oh Karl, those poor people. Who is taking them? We must at least try to stop it. There must be something we can do.'

'Well, it certainly is the Jews, Liesel. Look, Herr Dietrich is there in his ridiculous uniform, strutting around like a devil. Curse the damned fool. Someone, somewhere has given him power over them, perhaps even us. Do you think the Gauleiter could help? Herr Florian knows your father doesn't he? Perhaps I will go to his office tomorrow and see if I can find some answers to this. There might be an announcement on the radio, amongst all of the shouting. Let me see.'

Liesel sat on the little window ledge looking at the two houses opposite. The windows were broken and the glass was all over the floor inside and out. Dark shadows were moving around the house, the owners now gone in a cloud of smoky fumes in the filthy lorry. Nothing was being taken, but men were scurrying around looking for something quite specific. Perhaps they were simply looking for more people.

The next morning was dark and full of a grey foreboding that matched Liesel's mood. She rose early, having spent the entire night holding her husband as tightly as she could, shaking and weeping, not just for the Rosemanns, but in fear for their own safety. Nothing seemed safe or secure anymore, whatever side anyone might be on. Neither she nor Karl had slept very well. What worried her was the uncertainty of who the thugs might attack next. So far, it seemed that it was the more affluent Jews in the city, but who knew what was being said. Fear bred suspicion, and suspicion meant a visit from the sinister thinkers of the Gestapo.

Liesel knew that Karl was resolved to speak to the Gauleiter, being certain that a relative of General Langer would get an audience. Her husband had dressed smartly and left for the official office of the Gauleiter in the old parliament building. He had explained to Liesel that he did not expect to speak directly to Herr Florian himself, but that a message to and from him was almost a certainty. Liesel hoped that he would not have to engage the man. Herr Florian was not known for his sympathetic demeanour. In fact, it was well known that Florian despised almost everyone now that he was a member of the Reich leadership. His position of authority over Dusseldorf was now absolute and unquestioned, answerable only to the Führer himself. Attracting interest from Herr Gauleiter was usually a disadvantage.

--o0o--

As Karl reached the steps, he hesitated. Would turning the gaze of the Gauleiter upon him be a mistake? Perhaps he would go home after all, and keep the incident quiet and away from the light of day. But he had once been interviewed for the job of personal physician to the Gauleiter. Perhaps he would remember Karl as he had instructed him to act as his doctor were he ever to need treatment. But he had never seen him as a patient, nor had he ever received a call from his office. The Gauleiter had either never been ill or had forgotten his requirement of Doctor Eisner.

He took courage and stepped inside where a little attendant wore circular wire-rimmed glasses in an attempt to look more like Himmler. Karl could not help but think that so much of this Nazi machine was paper-thin showmanship, rather than an ideology to run the country. But he would have to deal with the machine if he was to get any answers.

'Good morning. I am Doctor Karl Eisner of the Kaiserswerth Institute and I wish to speak with the Gauleiter.'

'You would? Did you bother to seek an appointment? I doubt it for if you had, you would have discovered that he does not see individuals such as yourself for any issue. You will have to submit your question in writing and I will decide whether the Gauleiter can attend to any aspect of it. Good day, sir.'

'But I am one of the Gauleiter's personal physicians.'

At this, the attendant took off his glasses and stared directly at Karl.

'Now listen to me, Doctor Eisner. The Gauleiter has many physicians. He needs a number of them so that he can call on any one of them discreetly, without delay. You are not the only one and it affords you no special privilege.'

'Well, please find me a time. It is quite pressing.'

'Very well, if only to get you to leave my office, I will look for an opportunity to present your issue. Might you tell me what it is?'

The attendant opened a large leather-bound ledger, with black and red writing on the front. He looked into it, frowned, and then looked up again at Karl.

'Doctor Karl Eisner of Landstrasse?'

Karl was taken aback by the entry in the ledger naming him so directly.

'Er, yes. Son of Professor Eisner, late of the same hospital. He was Professor of Surgery.'

'I see. Well, you had better wait here.'

With that, the attendant stood and disappeared into a darkened corridor. Karl heard a distant rap on a door. Within a few seconds the man had returned.

'Come with me, the Gauleiter will see you personally.'

--o0o--

Liesel busied herself about the house whilst she waited for Karl's return. She was worried, but not just over the events of last night. Having already had two children, she knew the signs. But she could not be sure. The upset over the last year and the last week must have had an effect, and she hoped her sickness was simply that and not the alternative. At nearly forty years of age! And it was almost unthinkable to bring a baby into this world, despite the requirement for blood-pure children repeated endlessly by the Nazis to strong Aryan women every day.

But their world was now so uncertain. Karl had an excellent income from his practice at the Kaiserswerth and his clinic in the district hospital. He was often sought by the well-to-do people of Dusseldorf, including politicians and the Nazi elite. He had inherited his father's house close to the Rhine, complete with its secret basement surgery where his father had once held discreet appointments with those in danger and trouble. But despite this wealth, it was clear that Germany was not stable. The War had shown what could happen to cities and society and how easily it could happen again. With money came the fear that it would become worthless overnight, overrun by an economy that was on fire.

Looking out over the smashed shell of the Rosemanns' house, Liesel saw the children's toys lying about in pieces, perhaps torn from their little fingers by the merciless men of the party. She was thinking a little of her own situation and her demonic brother, the unpredictability and the immorality of his conduct. At that moment, the heavy front door opened. Karl had returned and the door was slammed violently shut, alarming her immediately. She could hear her husband fumbling in the hall, shedding his overcoat, the rain dripping onto the floor.

'Liesel, Liesel! My darling, I must see you now!'

'Karl, whatever is it? Why all this shouting and commotion? Is it happening again outside?'

'No, well, yes. Look I must speak with you. Into the drawing room, quickly now. You must hear what I have to say.'

'Oh Karl, this sounds terrible, whatever has happened?'

'Just sit and listen.'

Outside the shut door, the day maid strained her ears, then broke into sobs, dropping a cup to the floor, where it smashed. The noise attracted the housekeeper, Marthe Weir, who ushered away the day maid, scolding her for her impertinence. But Frau Weir then stood at the door for a moment, rubbed the doorknob clean of finger marks almost absent-mindedly and then stepped away quickly, muttering softly as she went.

'Mein Gott, Mein Gott, das ist ganz schlimm!'

CHAPTER FOURTEEN

Dusseldorf December 1938

Liesel could hardly bear the light coming in through the open curtains. She had barely slept in three weeks, and each morning her breakfast was hardly touched. Her stomach ached with a pain that was real and almost unbearable, moving in waves up and down her body. Worse, as each day dawned, the dreams of bright blue skies and a breeze over meadows was replaced by the sickening reminder that her husband had been torn from German society, declared an outcast in the very streets he called home. The news was not yet public, but the Gauleiter himself had told one of his many personal doctors that Karl was to be classed as a Jew, and thus forbidden from his clinic and practice, instructed to withdraw from the very society that his family had helped to create. Liesel had nothing but sympathy for the Jews, she held no ill-feeling, why would she? They had done her no harm.

Karl was already out trying to find some answers. Liesel knew that he had questions, for he was desperate to see where this information had possibly come from, or even whether it could possibly be true. The day maid had left suddenly, without a note or an explanation, taking with her some gold jewellery. Her poor husband, loving but now powerless, stateless and drifting towards destruction. She could not for a moment think of leaving him, but feared that he would be torn from her, perhaps at the point of a gun, or worse, at the point of a gun held by her brother.

Frau Weir stayed on as housekeeper. She had told Liesel that she cared not whether Karl was Jewish, but if he was, then Dusseldorf was not safe for anyone. While she was allowed to remain and wanted by the family, then she would stay. She had stressed that she especially wanted to stay and care for Liesel, who was so obviously pregnant. By now, Liesel knew she was in danger of losing the baby and she would be in desperate need of care if Karl had to leave. She wondered whether the baby would choose not to stay, choose not to be born into a Germany unworthy of such a gift.

--oOo--

Karl returned a little before eleven, clearly agitated and upset. He saw his wife, and even after years of medical practice, the sight of his beautiful Liesel in pain troubled him, especially in his already disturbed state. She was pale, worn and in need of something for the pain. He was able to help her a little, but without access to medicines, it would be difficult. It felt as though his hands were now tied and his knowledge was worthless. All the young German doctors he had helped to teach, to nurture and to encourage, would simply now turn their backs in anger and shun Karl Israel Eisner.

The morning had been distressing and ultimately frustrating, and it was terrifying to imagine the implications. Nobody knew anything – or more likely, no one was talking. The central office for the administration of citizens in Dusseldorf was open, but it might as well have been closed. He had waited at an empty desk for an hour, to be told again that they only had an identification card for him, temporary of course, until the Gauleiter's office had informed them otherwise. He was not required to attend again, nor to wear any clothing identifying him as a Jew. But he must not attend the Kaiserswerth, his private clinic on the corner of Landstrasse, or issue any prescriptions for the time being. If he breached any of these conditions, he would be arrested, and whether or not he was married to a pure German woman, he would be deemed to have broken the law.

Karl noted the acidity in the words 'married to a pure German woman' as if he had committed a crime. And what crime could an upstanding, dedicated and loyal citizen of Germany possibly commit by falling in love and marrying Dusseldorf's most beautiful flower and having two wonderful children with her? As it was, he knew their two children caused the authorities some particular problems. Liesel was clearly Aryan, with generations of pure blood from the heart of the eastern Rhineland. But Karl's family history was now in public doubt. The school had already decided on a cautious course of action, to keep the children away for now, until the Gauleiter's office set the record straight one way or another.

--oOo--

At home, it was getting worse for Liesel. She was now bleeding. If she had been pregnant, then the pain and suffering of the news of her husband had hastened a miscarriage. Deep in her heart she was glad this had happened. It would be impossible to have another child now, and the two she had would need all of her caring love just to survive. She knew that Karl had also realised this, but he could only help with her pain, her distress and with the suffering of her body. It seemed his sharp mind was numbed by recent events, for he appeared unable to think clearly and struggled to understand what was happening and what to do about it. Even their comfortable surroundings offered them little comfort. Whatever had value would now have to be sold just to keep the four of them alive.

Liesel tried to speak with her father. He seemed sympathetic, on their side of the divide, at least for now. He was worried for her and each day wrote to the authorities demanding answers to his questions. His letters pointed out that it was absurd to think Doctor Eisner a Jew, that there was little evidence of anything of the sort and what there was could be questioned by any reasonable person. He was never sent a reply, but he had told Liesel of the curt telephone call he had received from the office of Nazi affairs at the Gestapo office in Dusseldorf. He had been informed that there had been no decision on Karl as yet, since he was one of many thousands of questionable cases and they would attend to the details in due course.

After five days of anguish and worry, Liesel had at last stopped bleeding, but was still in her bed. She knew she had to get well, as Karl could not afford more time sitting and sleeping at her bedside. Already, they were feeling the effects of his exile from society. Their own friends, as well as friends of the Langer family, chose not to pay visits, finding convenient excuses to avoid seeing them at home or even in the street. The tradesmen who had always visited and offered a little extra to the hard-working doctor in return for medical advice stopped calling completely. Food became a daily effort to find, something that other German families on the street would never be able to understand. Liesel and Karl had no experience of scavenging, but they would have to learn quickly, or find someone friendly who did know.

--oOo--

Karl had tried to open the secret surgery that his father had once used in the lower basement of their house. But without the necessary supplies and without having any proper Jewish connections, he could not find enough equipment to risk treating patients, whoever came through the door. It seemed hopeless. Karl stood in the little bare basement room, staring at the brick walls and empty shelves. He only knew medicine, his life was medicine, but with the world again turning to darkness, the light had gone out on Karl's career and the family he loved and cherished might suffer the consequences of the Nazi dream. As he looked to the floor, casually kicking aside some fallen plaster, he decided that they must take positive action to end this madness. He would ask Liesel to arrange an audience with her brother.

'Liesel, I know you are still weak, but please don't get upset when you hear what I have to say. Please, my love, let me finish before you tell me that I am a fool for thinking of this. I think we, well you, must speak with your brother at the earliest opportunity. Surely he will be able to reason with these Nazi fools and end this ridiculous situation with the Gauleiter.'

'My darling, I have already thought the same thing, but there is one problem.'

'Problem? Do you think he will not receive you, perhaps refuse to help for fear of the consequences for him?'

'He will receive me. In fact, I have just had word that he is coming here tomorrow.'

'Then that is excellent, perhaps he has heard and wants to help us. You are his sister, his... well, his Aryan blood.'

'Oh, my darling husband, I am quite sure it is not like that.'

'How can you possibly know?'

'He has sent word that you must be out of the house when he attends at noon.'

Liesel tried to rise and embrace her husband. Karl leaned to her, kissing her hand as she sat up.

'Liesel, not that it ought to matter for a moment, but I am not a Jew. The life of Judaism is entirely alien to me. I have no Jewish blood. If the authorities investigate, they will see that my mother is an Austrian German, if that makes sense, we are a Viennese family, with good connections in Munich and even Berlin.'

'I know, my darling, but these investigations are not scientific like your brain, they are influenced by rumour, fear and intimidation and now it seems also by the ambition of my brother. You have seen what those fools in brown shirts have done? Where is the intelligence in that? If there was intelligence at work, then none of this would have happened.'

'Quite honestly, I am more German than you are, my darling.'

Karl broke the thinnest of smiles.

'And that is what they will discover when they investigate. My love, I am sorry for all of this, for the work of my brother, for the awfulness of the Nazis and the loss of our... well the chance of another baby.'

'It is strange, Liesel. I feel that I should grieve, but I feel nothing. I am empty of emotion, devoid of a connection with what is happening. The world is in a fog that I cannot see through.'

'In time, we will look back on this with different eyes, when Germany awakens from this nightmare.'

Karl held Liesel close, pulling more pillows behind her. He indicated a small red mark on her breast.

'What is that?'

'What is what?'

'That mark on you?'

'I do not know, but there are more on my back. What can it be?'

'My love, lie back and let me examine you.'

Karl looked at Liesel's back, running his hand over her skin.

'My love, your skin is as rough as felt. Liesel, you must remain in bed and rest. Keep warm and don't do anything until I return.'

'What is it? Is it serious?'

'It is scarlet fever, Liesel. There were some cases in the hospital last month, before… before I had to stop working, so it is in the city. With care, you will be well, but this will not go away without treatment.'

'What about my meeting with Kurt?'

'You might be too unwell to meet him.'

'This will be our only chance, I cannot lose this opportunity. I cannot afford to condemn my family just because of a little fever that I do not even have yet.'

'You will develop a fever, a certainty I am afraid. Now I am going out, and I will be back with something that might help. I am very sorry, my love, but you will need to stay away from the children. Frau Weir will care for them.'

'But Kurt?'

'We can manage, Liesel, he is not coming to offer his help. Perhaps you should now refuse to see him. He is not looking to improve our situation, is he?'

'He is my brother, Karl. I will look him in the eye and ask for his assistance. Let us see if he is the man the Langer family deserves.'

--oOo--

Karl left. He had hoped that Liesel did not see how worried he was. Scarlet fever was serious and infected almost everyone it met. The fever could take days to break and if it didn't, he might lose a baby and a wife in the same week. He must ensure that Monika and Franz did not become infected, or he would also risk losing them. The risks to his family were greatly increased now that he was an outcast without access to medicine or even proper food. But he had one chance, so he was going to take a calculated risk. Liesel was a German, and not everyone had yet learned of the problems he faced. He might just have time to visit an old friend at the hospital in the city. The Kaiserswerth was no use, for they knew, but

Liesel's former hospital in the city had to be worth a chance. His wife was too important to him, she was his life. He treasured her and his children more than anything. He loved Liesel more than that stupid prancing fool Kurt with his ridiculous SS pomposity.

At the hospital, he quickly moved to the mortuary entrance. It was rarely used by non-hospital staff and was often unlocked, for who would come here willingly? He saw the open door and went in. He had no identification, but many knew him by sight so he might be lucky. Once through the two sets of doors, he was into the main hospital wing. The refrigerated units were downstairs.

The tissue dispensary was dark and no one was around. He immediately found the boxes for the various serum samples kept to treat diseases known to be spreading in the city. He left the light off, moving by the little light that the open door allowed through. The boxes were all logically labelled. He opened the convalescent serum box for scarlet fever, his heart racing at finding what he wanted so easily. But the box was empty, a devastating discovery. He had no other ideas. All was lost. The room began to spin as the realisation of his efforts reached his brain. There was no other plan. He stood, only now able to walk home and tend his wife, who would be developing a fever with every hour that passed.

At the door he heard a sound, a conversation perhaps. He was trapped. With horror, he watched a figure darken the door. A light was turned on, the brightness burning him. The shapeless entity in the bright light came into focus, it was a young nurse. She would not know him. That might be good. He could follow her out and ask her about the serum stock. There might yet be a chance. She took two bottles from another box and left, leaving the light on. He followed her out, until they were in an open corridor where his appearance would not be immediately alarming.

'Nurse?'

'Yes, who is it. Doctor? Sorry, I am quite new. Doctor, er?'

'Eisner, Karl Eisner. I am also new here. Tell me, where are the scarlet fever serum samples kept? I cannot get an answer from anyone here today, ha!'

'There is a bit of scarlet fever and scarletina around at the moment isn't there, Doctor Eisner? The new boxes were, I think, taken up to the ward immediately when they came in. We have some more patients giving serum this afternoon, the clinic is preparing them now actually.'

'Thank you. I can find my way to the clinic.'

The clinic was the last place that Karl wanted to go to. It would be full of sick people, tired and irritable staff where almost no one felt responsible for the running of the surgeries. Getting answers would be hard and serum harder still. But he had to try, his wife would be gradually worsening as he stood there. She could even die. This was not the time to worry about himself. He walked as fast as he could to the clinic.

'Nurse, could you— Oh, how are you, Nurse Dressler?'

'Oh, my goodness, Dr Eisner. I am… quite well thank you.'

Nurse Dressler placed her hand on her neck when she saw him. Karl detected no panic on her face and no urgent need to report a rabid Jew to the authorities.

'Good, good. I am looking for some convalescent serum for scarlet fever, I have a private patient with a developing fever and I am hoping to calm it down quickly.'

'It is all over the city. Have you read the order from the administrator about preventing the spread?'

'Yes, yes I have. In fact I helped to draft it last month.'

'Oh, of course, I am sorry.'

'The serum, Nurse? I am in a hurry.'

'Of course, I will find you the new batch. It was being prepared this morning. I am sure it is ready now. It might not yet have been chilled down, you know we cannot use it until it has cooled sufficiently.'

'Yes, yes.' Karl shifted uneasily. He would have to move fast to get out and away. His nerve was failing with every minute that passed, with so many staff coming and going.

'Here, I have a little. You should take a week's worth. I will give you some spare in case of a second case. Will you sign for it here?'

'Yes, of course.'

Karl knew that if he was investigated and the trail led here, he would be arrested on the spot for breaking the Gauleiter's order, husband to an Aryan or not. He had to try and bluff the authorities.

'Oh, I have no pen, I am in a little bit of a hurry, Nurse Dressler. Would you just sign?'

Nurse Dressler seemed to baulk at the request.

'But this is not at all permissible in the procedures.'

Karl gave her his kindest smile.

'Oh… very well, Doctor Eisner, if it saves your valuable time.'

'Thank you.'

Karl took the bottles and turned to leave. He wanted to run as fast as he could and not stop until he reached his home, but calmness would keep him anonymous. He must not seem agitated. He turned at the door.

'By the way, Nurse Dressler, how is your mother? I was delighted to see her back on the wards at the institute after Christmas, but sorry to see her leave so soon after. Her poor leg again, wasn't it?'

'Thank you for asking. She is much better. She can come back to work for you in a couple of months. Splints, I think it was in the end, annoying all the same.'

'Well give her my best, I always enjoyed working with Sister Dressler.'

Nurse Dressler gave the doctor a wide grin and blushed a little. Karl knew that there was not the slightest suspicion anywhere in her face. If he could get away now, he would be free to help his wife.

At the gate to the front entrance, there were two doctors discussing a sheaf of notes. Karl knew them both, and they would ask why he was here. Unlike the nurses, the doctors had a better idea of what doctors should be doing. He was in the same line of work, but had no place being here, certainly not grabbing convalescent serum for scarlet fever. He put the bottles in his pocket.

'Helmut, how are you today?'

'Eh? Oh *Eisner*? What brings you here today?'

'I am planning a lecture actually. For next month. I'm publishing a paper on the lessons learned from the Spanish influenza outbreak. It might help us to contain the spread of scarlet fever. Why are you two loitering here?'

'Ah, well, we were just doing our rounds and came upon an interesting case. Well, why not give us your opinion? It's a strange reaction to prontosil. He is thirty and has a urinary tract infection. Here are his notes. What do you think?'

For the next five minutes, Karl felt a renewed and liberated man, his soul soared to the sky as he conversed with his two colleagues. He was a doctor again, not a skulking rat, stripped of his dignity. He gave his opinion and the two doctors seemed filled with a renewed enthusiasm for the case and some new ideas to try. They could not possibly have known what good they had done for a poor man in a desperate situation. Karl shook hands warmly as he turned to leave, his pace quickening rapidly as he went. He could not afford to wait another minute for fear of detection and the deteriorating health of his wife.

When he finally arrived home, he saw that the door was already open. Panic swept his body for a moment, but there was no sound. At that moment Frau Weir came to the door to shut it.

'The children are home, Doctor. But I have arranged for them to stay with my sister tonight, what with the fever in the house. I thought it best not to go to the Langer house, what with all the troubles.'

'That is very kind and sensitive, thank you. You should take three days away, in case you get the fever as well. I will still pay you, of course.'

'I will not! Besides, I have had it already, probably twice, after all these years ministering to children.'

'Very well. Once again, thank you.'

'Frau Eisner is in her bed still, the children know that they cannot disturb their mother, so they call through the door and their mother tells them that they are loved and that they should not worry. But she seems very worried, and I don't think it's just about scarlet fever.'

Karl went straight in to see her. The serum was taken from patients who had recovered from the disease. Something in their serum helped, but no one knew what it was and it did not matter if it could make her better. He administered the first small dose and laid her head down again. She was hot and getting hotter. He bathed her in cool water, taking care not to inflame the rash that covered her arms and her chest. It was coming on quickly now. The night was long, and they barely spoke, the clock in the room ticking mercilessly, as if trying its hardest to prevent them sleeping. The morning light came late in December, and it was nearly nine before the room was light enough to move around. Karl dared not put on a light, for bright light hurt his wife.

'I will have to speak with Kurt today, Karl. I will have to ask him for help. It is our last and only hope of this being resolved quickly. This could drag on for years otherwise. It is no use. I feel much better. The serum has helped.'

Karl was doubtful, Liesel looked pale in the areas that were not covered in a rash and she was hot everywhere. The serum was certainly helping, but it would be days before she would return to normal. He would have to confront Kurt, it was his house, and it did not belong to Kurt or the bloody SS. If it gave him distress to enter the house of a proclaimed Jew, then that was Kurt's problem to resolve. But Liesel would have none of it and told Karl to wait upstairs. Despite her miscarriage and scarlet fever, Liesel would confront the awful reality of the SS in the form of her lost brother, a meeting in the parlour of a proclaimed Jew.

--o0o--

Kurt arrived at four minutes to noon. He rang the bell loudly and repeatedly. Frau Weir opened the door.

'He still has a housekeeper? Are you a Jew as well, woman?'

'No, sir. I am not. I am a German patriot, just like yourself. I work for a German family, this being a German family. You would know, it is your... your sister, sir.'

'I very much doubt you are anything at all like me. Where is my sister? Are we to meet on the threshold or are you to step aside and let me enter?

Of course, this house is now technically under the protection of the Gauleiter, property seized from the illegal hands of the Jewish infiltrators and I need no invitation whatsoever. The Jew Eisner, I assume he is not present as instructed?'

'He is not here, sir, your sister awaits your presence in the parlour, sir.'

Liesel had risen at ten, bathed in cool water and taken more serum. She did feel better, but knew that the fever was still coming on, not going away. She could last in that room for no more than thirty minutes. By the time Kurt arrived, she had been in there for fifteen. Frau Weir had helped her to dress and she had prepared her face to look as normal as possible. She would give no hint to Kurt that she was unwell. No advantage would be given to the man from the SS, even one in the shape of family. She was hot and tired, but offered no water. Nothing for the brute she had shared her life with for eighteen years, hanging on his every word. In those days, the very ground he stood upon was her kingdom and she had adored him. Now, to her sadness, he was something quite different.

'Liesel, sister. Does your brother not warrant an embrace?'

'Of course, brother. Here. I am a little warm, the fires were lit early this morning awaiting your visit.'

'Well sit, sit girl. No need to stand for me. I will sit here next to you whilst I tell you what will now happen in this household.'

'You will? Tell me brother, whose house is this? A Jew's perhaps? Or a German's? The victim of a terrible mistake.'

Liesel hated this idea. Why would being a Jew be a mistake anyway? Only in this country at this time could it be considered so by these awful and ignorant thugs in power.

'That is the question, Liesel, indeed, that is the question. A question that obsesses me deeply, my only sister. My sister, married… well we will come to that in a moment… associated with a man whose parents have been proclaimed Jews, whose mother and grandmother can be clearly identified as poor immigrants from Russia. Did you know that? Did you know that before allowing this man to impregnate you?'

'Kurt, how could you be so cold and cruel. You embraced him as a brother, you even said so.'

'We were both deceived, sister. A deception that these people are so skilled in playing out. He wanted the most beautiful girl in Dusseldorf to carry on his line of corruption. You were taken in, we were all taken in. Look what he has done to you. Look at you. Pale and thin, the evil has entered your soul and consumed you. He must not be allowed to return. I shall take steps to see that he is banished. No more will his dark arts poison your blood. No more will he look upon you with lust and a black purpose. Look at you, Liesel, you are a sick woman. Can you not see it? It is him. Now that the secret is out, he is bent upon destroying you in the quickest time possible. If he were here, I should strangle the life from his grinning face.'

Liesel could hardly believe what she was hearing. This was her brother. The boy who had playfully allowed her to pull his nose and flick his ears and steal his socks so that he would chase her giggling around the house. The boy who had stood at her bedside when she was ill at ten years old. The boy who held her in his arms and sang her gentle songs until she fell asleep, cooling her brow with a cold towel. How she longed for him to be so again. But here he was, a stranger walking in the house. A vile beast, spitting forth poisoned malice that would get so very many killed. There would be no salvation here, she had invited the wolf into her home and he was now on the loose.

'You must not see him again. I have seen the documents in the office of the Gauleiter. I understand he went there seeking an audience to lie his way out of this. But he has failed. Only this morning, the Gauleiter has confirmed him as an undesirable person. The sadness is that your pure blood protects him. He cannot be arrested and sent to the residential camp. But that does not mean he is to stay here and cast his lustful gaze on your fair skin, Liesel. He will need to leave, or you will need to come home. Today.'

'You are asking me to forsake the man that I love and married for love? The father of my children, your niece and nephew? Your flesh and blood? You surely cannot expect me to do that. I am a mother.'

'The Gauleiter has confirmed that as you are pure German blood and they are your children, then they are unaffected by the proclamation.'

'That is kind of the Gauleiter. Have you any thoughts of your own, Kurt?'

Kurt stood immediately, his face darkening.

'Now look here, Liesel, I have been quite patient enough. I am an officer in the SS, a legal representative of the German people. You defy me, you defy the German nation. Think on that. I was already of this opinion, the Gauleiter simply took an objective look at the evidence. As a daughter of the Fatherland, you should denounce this man. Your illegal marriage has been dissolved. He coerced you into his bed, the filthy swine.'

'Mein Gott! Kurt, how could you? And what if I refuse to denounce him? What then for you and your precious Nazi Party?'

'I am sorry, perhaps I was not being clear.'

Kurt stood, put on his cap and made for the door. He opened it quickly, with his back to his sister, and stepped into the hallway.

'I was not offering a choice. If this is not so today, Karl may find himself the victim of some unfortunate occurrence. That would be a shame now, would it not?'

The front door clicked shut. Liesel collapsed on the floor, the room spinning around her. The fever had gripped her, and now her demon brother had been unleashed in her home. Her husband had been denounced as an undesirable, if protected, person and her marriage had been dissolved as if it did not matter. The world fell about her in broken shards.

--o0o--

Frau Weir checked that Kurt was gone and called Karl to attend his wife. He leapt down the flight of stairs to reach her side. She was burning hot and covered in an oily perspiration. Liesel was now gravely ill, he was close to losing her and her brother had scarcely noticed, the fool, the disgusting fool of a man, wrapped up in the crazy ideology of his new friends.

Karl lifted her up the stairs and ordered a cool bath. He gave her more serum immediately. Her chest was bright red and her legs a mass of lumpy spots, merged into a rash rough enough to strike a match. He wanted to call the Langers to have them come here. Liesel might not live and could quite possibly die tonight. They were Aryan Germans, they had access to the very best doctors. For Liesel, Karl would have to do this. Herr General Langer was not a Nazi and nor was Frau Langer. But they were accepted citizens who could and would help their daughter. He cursed himself for not acting on this conclusion earlier. Perhaps Kurt had not influenced the Langers too greatly just yet and they would still accept their daughter.

Karl packed a small case of clothes and a little bread. Then he wrote two letters. One was the plan for Liesel's care that the Langers' doctor could follow. The second was a note to Liesel, to be given to her only when her fever had broken, if it ever did. Karl doubted it as he saw his wife for the last time that night. He bowed politely to the housekeeper as he left, thanking her for her devotion.

Now, he was desolate. Every cell in his body told him to stay, to tend to his sick patient, never mind that the patient was his wife, his lover, and mother to his beautiful children. The children! To stay meant she would most likely die. To go, well that would give her a chance to live. He had heard the SS officer in the front room and so he had to leave tonight.

At the little table in the hallway, he picked up the telephone and called the Langers' physician, Professor Scheckter. The professor was eating his dinner at the time of the call, but when told it was Eisner, he came immediately to the telephone.

'Eisner, my boy. I have heard. I am so terribly sorry to hear the news of… well it is a nonsense that anyone with an ounce of education would put down as—'

'Herr Professor, sorry. First thank you, but I ask that you come at once, if it is not an imposition, to care for my wife. I am unable to, for the reasons you now seem to know. Her temperature is very high and scarlet fever has developed very suddenly. She is already weakened from a… miscarriage last week. I cannot treat her as I have no access to medicines in the manner that you do. She now needs a – it seems ridiculous to say it – a more German doctor.'

'Karl, I understand. Complete rubbish of course, but I do see. I am sorry about the miscarried child. I will come at once. What have you been able to do for her? Any treatment at all?'

'Serum and temperature reduction. That's all I could do.'

'Serum? Well done, young sir! I will not ask how you came by it, but I will make sure she keeps it up. How much do you have?'

'Enough for a week.'

'Oh? Splendid, yes, you are a resourceful man. You know, you are one to watch, Eisner. Never forget that. Right, you get off, I will be there in fifteen minutes. Housekeeper still there? Not left you in a mess? The same woman you always had?'

'Yes, she is here. She has been a blessing.'

'Why are you still talking to me, then?'

'Very well. Goodbye Professor.'

'Goodbye *Doctor* Eisner. Oh, do find time to walk by Kleinstrasse on your travels. Number forty is about where you need to be, the lights on the water are wonderful at this time of year, and you will be quite overwhelmed.'

The phone clicked and Karl left, closing the door gently, leaving the lock undone for the professor. He waited in the darkness of the trees opposite to see the professor arriving less than fifteen minutes later. With him was a junior doctor who Karl had also taught at the institute. An unfamiliar senior nurse followed five minutes later. So, the Germans, if that is what they now were to him, had the matter in hand as he had hoped. As he turned to go into the night, a small black car arrived in front of the house. Out of it came a man in a leather overcoat and a wide-brimmed hat. He opened the door to General Langer and then Frau Langer. They shuffled up the steps into the Eisner family home.

The man in the coat got back into the car. The faint red glow of a cigarette could be seen through the glass and a spiral of smoke came out of the window on this still and windless night.

Gestapo. Kurt had meant what he said and he had the authority to do it. Karl turned to leave, now skulking in the shadows. He would go in search of the mysteriously cryptic Kleinstrasse. He had not planned on obeying Kurt's orders, but found himself a rat in the night all the same.

CHAPTER FIFTEEN

Bazentin-Le-Petit 1938

Henri had fallen off the motorcycle again. His father saw him racing back from Martinpuich, going around the little tractor and turning into the bend. Once again he was going far too fast, with too little road to make the turn safely. The fields were always soft landings and Henri was never much concerned for himself, but he never liked to damage his much-loved motorcycle.

'Henri, how many times do I have to tell you? Do this again and I will take it from you, do you understand? You fool of a boy!'

'Yes, sir. I am so sorry. But I wanted to feel the wind in my hair again. It is so much fun. I just wanted to see if the adjustments that we made to it have improved the handling. They have.'

'Have they? Then why is your motorcycle upside down in what was a bush?'

'Oh, that was my fault. I was waving to Yvette.'

'Yvette? Really? So you were taking care to watch where you were going, eh? To top it all, she is three years older than you and the daughter of one of my oldest friends! I hope you see what I am saying, my boy?'

Henri smiled and tried to lift the motorcycle, but it was too heavy to budge by himself.

'She still waves to me, even if I am only a *boy*!'

'A sixteen-year-old idiot. Look, you have a puncture as well. I suppose you are going to say that was to blame?'

'Well it did not help. I have done the Longueval circuit in six minutes, Papa. Six minutes. It shows that the changes we have made have much improved the handling.'

'And softened your brain. Your mother will—'

'Never know, Papa?'

William shrugged.

'Very well, idiotic boy.'

Henri flashed his father a wide and charming grin. William laughed as some grass and a lump of mud fell out of Henri's hair.

'Idiotic scarecrow. You are not going to be able to explain away the torn trousers, Henri. Your mother is going to *know*.'

'How, if we do not tell her?'

'Your mother has had to repair many pairs of my trousers that looked just like that over the years. Trust me, she is too intelligent for your charm, Henri. Save it for Yvette.'

Henri smiled again. At that moment, Yvette and Alain passed on the tractor that had helped Henri into the bush. Yvette was very red-faced, but she looked pleased to see Henri up and about.

'Oh, Henri, I was so worried. But I see you are alive and breathing. Perhaps you might like to walk with me this afternoon? I am finished with my chores. Is that agreeable, Uncle Alain?'

'Yes, my darling. But let me tell you one thing.'

'Yes, Uncle?'

'You are not going near that damned motorcycle.'

The four of them laughed and Henri and Yvette quickly walked off together, leaving the motorcycle in a heap by the roadside. Alain and William picked it up and placed it on the tractor.

'Nice to see Henri clearing up his mess again. Good job you are here, Alain.'

'Ha! I think our young man is distracted by some local red-haired charm.'

Alain then took William by the arm and whispered, perhaps to make sure Henri and Yvette were out of earshot.

'You know, my friend, we could do worse than seeing them married. Yvette is the kindest girl, so like her mother and with the intelligence of her father.' Alain crossed himself. 'How he would have loved to have seen his daughter grow into the beautiful fireball that she is.'

'I agree, Alain. But Henri has the better part of it. My boy may well spend his life with broken bones and a sore head if he carries on like this.'

'I think he has half his mother and half his father, eh?'

'Well, perhaps. I can't scold him for that.'

'Then Yvette's father can rest knowing his daughter is in good hands,' Alain kicked the stones on the roadside, 'except when they are holding onto a motorcycle.'

'Come on, it is getting late. Perhaps we should go and see Jean-Phillippe's grave again in Rancourt?'

'Yes, I think we should do that.'

The tractor lumbered slowly, William for a moment casting his mind back to 1916 and to the tanks that came to his rescue in Courcelette, just over the hill behind the ridge. He remembered those awful terrifying weeks of living in the undamaged house in the little cupboard. His life had changed but the daily reminder of his wounded body brought back the reality of the trenches to him. Alain and his brother had also served in France, but Jean-Phillippe was killed in late 1918 when Yvette was yet to be born. When Yvette's mother died of influenza with a tiny infant by her side, Alain had to become an uncle and a father immediately. William instinctively placed an arm around Alain's shoulder, and not just to help him hold onto the tractor.

At the junction with the old road, Alain let William down from the machine. They unloaded the motorcycle. It was scratched a little, but only really with a puncture to repair and it was easily pushed into the garden. Henri was absent and Yvette was also nowhere to be seen. Perhaps young love was blossoming again in the Collins family. Alain waved and drove away, William noting that the tractor could do with a little mechanical help. At dusk, Henri returned, red-faced and out of breath.

'Ah, so you have come home, then?'

Henri grinned. 'I am in enough trouble over the motorcycle, I do not want a second helping for arriving home late.'

William smiled, seeing himself reflected in his son's face, a face that also held the shape of his wife. Although she was also a mother and one who seemed less in the mood for forgiveness this evening.

'Henri Collins! What have you done to this motorcycle again? I have half a mind to take it from you to teach you a lesson. You won't earn any money and you will be in trouble with all of the village for missing your rounds. Serve you right, you fool of a boy. Look at it!'

'Maman, I am sorry, but the road was wet and muddy and the tyre went flat. Papa, you saw didn't you?'

The last thing William wanted was to become involved, or for there to be a scene over Henri again.

'It's possible, the tyre might have made him fall off, Odile. You were going a bit too fast, but you are the son of your mother. Well, er, father.'

Odile looked at William and shook her head.

'My men are all imbeciles.'

'Henri will mend the tyre and polish out the scratches before he is allowed supper.'

All would be well for Henri if he marked his father's words and took more care in future. Henri flashed his father a knowing and conspiratorial smile and set about the polishing of his treasured motorcycle.

In the evening, William had decided to sit in the porch with a blanket until it was time for bed. That day, his mind had become full of the familiar images of the War and he could not get them out of his head. So he decided to let them free, to see them, to confront them and to accept them. They were, after all, almost companions to him.

As always, he saw Fixer Cowling. His bluntness and certainty in engineering reassured him. Fixer had died dragging an unconscious William from the mine in Wijtschaete. William still remembered nothing except a blur of limbs, an intense heat, the sounds of guns perhaps and the smell of sweat. Perhaps it was a blessing that he remembered so little. Next came General Cowling, in the early days in Poperinghe, a Colonel. Grim and determined, loyal and driven, he took care of William in ways that William could never truly knew. William rubbed his eyes and his knee, a constant reminder of the German with the bald head. He always appeared from a shell hole, but no longer carrying the pistol that he had carried on the day that William had killed him. He waved and spoke, but William could not imagine the words. The German would step out and shake hands, before turning away and disappearing. William knew what was coming next. This evening, with his mind alive to the memories, he rose and without a word, started to walk down the hill from the village to the Contalmaison Road. This was the ridge up which he had come that morning in July 1916, with Horace Watkins, the man who had accompanied him on the ultimately disastrous operation. He stopped at the top of the ridge, where it dropped steeply to the road, and fell to his knees, brushing his hands over the damp road, feeling the dirt and sand through his fingers.

He picked up a handful and turned his palms upward. The little grains clumped together on the damp road and formed shapes in his mind. His companions, now dead of course, rolled along his hands and before they fell through his fingers, each one turned to him and smiled. As the shapes fell into the blackness, he felt a touch on his soul, a warmth in his heart. They were here with him. Foolish, he thought, it cannot be and yet here they were, companions still on the slope of the ridge. To his left, he saw the little wooden cross that he had laid on the very spot where Watkins had died saving his friend and his comrades. He straightened its slightly sloped angle and tapped it in a little with his fist, wiping the tiny name plaque clean of dirt.

Sergeant HORACE JOHN WATKINS VC DCM
12 FIELD OPERATIONS (RE)
14 July 1916 Age 31

An Old Contemptible Still Holds This Ridge

William sat on the road as the memory of his run up this hill came to him. Softer now, without the edge of danger, softened by the years to an ache in his stomach. He heard footsteps to his right. It was Henri with a cardigan and a small cognac for him. William felt the cardigan around his shoulders and the glass pressed into his dirty hands. He looked down at the glass and then at the ground. He felt a tear form, blurring the sight of his son, strong and tall kneeling down beside him.

'Henri, without him, we would not be here and your mother would, well, who could know? Thank you for the cognac. Henri, it is most welcome.'

'Yes, Papa.'

William was turning the almost empty glass around in his hand, looking at it intently.

'I had poured more cognac than that into the glass.'

William smiled and drew his son to him. 'It must have splashed out running to bring it to your papa.'

--oOo--

Odile saw that her men were out of the house and she stepped outside into the cool of the evening. She looked out of the garden towards what the British had called High Wood. The gentle slope rising towards the front of the trees, the little copse that marked the cemetery to the Londoners and the marks on the ground all reminded her of the War. She too had suffered and fought for her life and the lives of her parents. Odile wondered how many others she should also thank for her salvation. She remembered Madame from the hospital, Madame Collart and darling Liesel who was like a sister. Clever Liesel, never showing any sign of interest or suspicion in anything Odile was planning. But she watched, she observed and she learned. A warm feeling ran over her. Perhaps it was time to write to her again, but she had a feeling, strange though it was, that Liesel had already written first.

For a second, Kurt's face flashed to her. At first, his smile, charming and gentle. She had hoped that he would be a saviour to her family, delivering them from the horror of deportation. But his face then changed to the grey-ravaged ghost from the trenches. Cruel and unsmiling, cold and distant. She quickly shook his memory from her mind, it did no one any good to remember. The only link to his evil was beloved Liesel. Sharing a sister was the only link she felt to Kurt and his brutality. She counted herself lucky that she had escaped alive.

With a shudder, she turned back to see her husband and son

returning. She imagined that William might be quiet this evening, it would be one of those nights that happened from time to time. Henri, though, was poking him and running around him, saying something that she could not hear. It did William good to have Henri around. Something about him kept William alive, allowing his mind space and time to heal. She thought of her two older children, safely in England, and the times they had spent together when they were growing up. The two of them, in tune with each other, knowing where they both were even when out of sight, sharing jokes and teasing their father whenever they could. Arthur, happy in his studies, reading a book up a tree, or wandering obliviously into the path of carts. Armandine, the little English Rose as her father called her, never getting her hands dirty, spending the days with her mother. First school, chores and then reading the most beautiful French and English poetry. William and Henri were now at the gate. Henri brought in some wood, his cheeks flushed.

'My goodness, you are either cold or exhausted. What have you been doing?'

'He has been running, Odile, although his cheeks may give away something else.'

'What's that, William?'

'A taste for my bloody cognac!'

William smiled. Odile saw that Henri, even though he was in trouble, had stopped his father hurting too much this evening. Odile grabbed her son, drawing him towards her. She squeezed his nose and kissed his forehead.

'Off to bed with you, you old drunk.'

Henri pretended to stagger up the small stairs, singing a little French drinking tune as he went.

'William, come to bed now, I want to be close to you tonight.'

'Yes of course, I want nothing but to hold my wife close to me.'

William stood silently for a second or two, wiping his nose with his dirty hand.

'I miss them, Odile. By all that is holy – and for me it isn't that much – but I miss them all.'

Odile closed the door to the Collins home and took her husband's hand. As she moved up each of the steps she thought of the men and women lost to them in the Great War. At the top of the stairs, she heard Henri in his room putting out the lamp.

'Each day, William, each day I awake grateful for our very existence.'

William leaned into his wife, cupping her head to his shoulder, and Odile breathed him in. There were thankfully fewer of these nights than there used to be, but sometimes the memories overtook them both. They would look at each other and simply know that one of them was somewhere else. It was now unsaid, always, having promised that their children would never know what had happened to them twenty years ago.

CHAPTER SIXTEEN
Dusseldorf February 1939

The winter had been cruel to Karl. The night he had left his own home in the centre of Dusseldorf was cool, but not cold. He detested leaving his gravely ill wife, even in the loving and caring hands of Frau Weir, whose loyalty he knew was in no doubt. The sinister black Gestapo car that had arrived bringing the elderly Langers had visited the house many more times since and Karl knew his house was being keenly watched by unsympathetic eyes. Each time he went back to look, he knew he risked arrest. Even if he was Jewish, as the husband of a notable Aryan woman, he was supposedly protected in law, but that was without taking into account the wrath of Kurt. He now realised that Liesel's brother was cruel, his soul destroyed by the Western Front but then rebuilt by the Nazi machine to create an evil man who would forsake his sister to further his own deluded aims. He remembered him as a younger man, always polite and courteous, preferring books and games to the rough and tumble of games in the squares.

If Karl was spotted and arrested, then the news would find its way to Kurt and whatever the provisions of law, Herr Gauleiter and Kurt were not going to allow justice to get in the way of their personal plans for advancement. Karl knew he was alone but his wife would be better provided for without him. But he wanted to know, he needed to hold on to his love for her and his children a little longer. So he went back to see his home often. He had long ago stopped resenting having to skulk in the cold shadows whilst others made his home theirs, people who would care not for the small items of no value, but which meant everything to him. He cared not for the cigars and pots. But his mother's birth-stone vase and his father's watch collection were no doubt being handled and pawed by unworthy men. At times, he thought they knew he was there and perhaps through a perverted kindness let him be, looking upon his windows from a distance. Then he remembered the Rosemanns and thought no such kindness was possible from these men, the Gestapo officers chief amongst them.

By the end of December, snow was on the ground and Karl had not had time in his hastened departure to prepare for a winter out of doors. January was icy and few souls ventured onto the streets, except through necessity. Even then, they were wrapped up with their heads down, focused only on their destination. Karl reasoned that the weather would be both an enemy and a friend. He could disguise himself more easily, with extra layers adding a greater disguise to hide his form from the Gestapo, whose eyes would most decidedly not be cast down, but would be up and scanning around for the forlorn and broken doctor.

Each day that he felt able to move about and watch his own front door from a safe distance, he bore witness to the same routines. He would see the black car arrive and figures coming and going almost constantly in the evenings. He never saw his beloved Liesel outside, but it was cold and she had been ill. She was never at the window but he reasoned she was alive for nothing gave the slightest image of distress. Occasionally, the professor would call there so she must be alive, or why the movements? He was desperate for news but he did not worry for Liesel for he knew she could be strong, was strong.

What hurt him the most was that he never once saw his growing children, for they were not at home with their loving mother. That was a bad sign for Karl. Either Liesel was still very ill or they had been taken away to live with their grandparents as precious children of Aryan Germany. What he would have given for one glance at their beautiful faces, seeing his much-missed wife reflected back in their bright eyes and charming smiles.

But Karl was to be disappointed daily in his vigil. As each cold day passed, he started to worry more for them and for the health of his wife. Today, he watched for an hour before his nerve failed him, as it usually did. There were hunched and foreboding figures on the street. He could not identify them for their shapes were indistinct and he could trust no one. Although he had tried to find allies on the street, he had found no help – not even from the owner of the house on Kleinstrasse who had answered his desperate knock on that terrible first evening. Karl had feared discovery at that spot, so went instead to walk the streets by the river, cutting down the number of places he had to scan constantly. He was reasonably sure that even the Gestapo did not have boats on the river looking out for fugitives.

As he walked to the river, he remembered that first night away from his home. In his haste, he had simply picked up a bag and left. He wished he had taken an extra coat, he could have worn two, a hat and scarves. But it was done now and too late. As he reached the Rhine, he looked towards the city he had been forced to leave, grieving for his life, which not yet over. His future held nothing but anguish and pain. Dignity lost, little more than a body wandering aimlessly, he wanted to sit down and disappear beneath the cold waters of the river. He wondered where his children were and when he might see them again, and he mourned the loss of his wife, feeling real grief. She was there but lost to him, so near and yet unreachable. To risk Liesel's life for a touch of her warm hand on his face was out of the question. It was unbearable having to be separated only for the sake of Kurt's insipid vanity and a deceitful order from the delusional Gauleiter.

His hands were cold, the Rhine was cold, and the wind rolling off the water and up and over Karl's head was cold. It blew clouds of fresh snow, which fell on his exposed skin, cooling him to the point of exhaustion. The meals he managed were little more than scraps, the merest morsels to stave off starvation, scraped from the alleys of restaurants and cafes that had once welcomed his patronage. If he walked in now, he would be beaten and arrested. He felt detached from Germany, a relationship once forged from nurturing love and respect now turned to ashes.

During the walk to Kleinstrasse on that first evening, he had fought back a desire to run away, or to run home to his wife, to heal her, to calm her fever, to love her at any cost. In any case, he was unsure whether the professor was telling him something, warning him or just sharing a pleasantry. He did not know whether he would find a trap or a welcome. But he had little option as he had not planned for anything, as if anyone could plan to run from home like that. Nothing then had made sense, except that his absence might help Liesel to live.

Karl had found the little door to number forty, exactly where Herr Professor had told him on the night he left Landstrasse. Its entrance was brightly lit so no one was hiding away. He had knocked anxiously, perhaps too eagerly, for the occupants seemed frightened and the figures in shadow danced around the frosted window of the door. A light was extinguished somewhere inside before the wooden door was slowly opened.

'Who is it making a commotion at this time of night? Oh, Doctor Eisner! Doctor Eisner? What brings you here? You are not—'

'My goodness, Herr Doctor Leewitz, I did not know that, well... this is very difficult.'

'Yes, Eisner, we are Jewish you must have known that, so what of it?

What brings *you* here?'

'The Gauleiter has issued me with a new identification card with Israel written on it. You understand?'

'Has he? I see. But your wife, Eisner, she is certainly not Jewish. She is General Langer's daughter I seem to remember. So that makes you one of them, does it not?'

'No, it doesn't. Her brother is in the SS.'

Leewitz raised his eyebrows and stepped back. Karl realised that he was only one step removed from the wolf and Leewitz could not even consider it. The professor had thought this a place of understanding and comfort, but in reality it was a slap in the face.

'Sorry, please go immediately. Never return. Ever.'

The door slammed shut. Karl could hear bolts hurriedly closing, fingers fumbling and voices scolding one another for opening the door to one of them. The light outside was extinguished suddenly, plunging his eyes into temporary darkness. The professor had meant well, of course, perhaps was even now telling Liesel with a conspiratorial smile, that Karl was safe and being cared for.

Karl thought again about the river, cold and deadly. Liesel would marry again, some suitable officer in one of Germany's many ruling organisations, who would gather to her for connections as well as affection. The Langers had been unlucky with Karl, but next time Liesel would doubtless marry some ass from one of the constantly saluting boys' clubs that paced the streets with shirts and boots too bloody big for them. The fools. He looked up at the sky. It was angry, grey and filled with more snow so he moved to a more sheltered doorway. Cold was a constant but he would be out of the merciless wind.

When the wind changed direction, it blew fresh drifts into Karl's face and he turned to the shelter of a network of small passages that he now called home. Here, footsteps could be heard long before a shadow appeared and he could hide unnoticed. And it was only a few minutes from here to get to his vantage point in the bushes near his home. The warm loving home that his mother and father had left for him. He felt bitter, a sick feeling in his mouth and stomach. Nothing tasted fresh to him, even drinking water made him feel like he was drinking bile. He thought again of the river, knowing that he would be dead in a few minutes and it would not hurt any more. With nowhere to go and nothing to occupy his active mind, he wrapped his blankets around him and settled down to sleep. If sleep came, it would pass the time. Perhaps if he was lucky, he would not wake up.

But sleep would not be possible tonight as he heard footsteps, sharp taps on the stones. Purposeful steps, like those of a soldier. They stopped but then there came a scraping noise as if someone were searching around. Then came quicker, lighter taps, perhaps someone running away. But the taps returned and now there were voices and another sound. A woman's heels perhaps. Two voices, but light and amused. Whoever it was, whatever their purpose, they were not searching for Karl Eisner.

Then he saw them, an officer, clearly SS. His heart almost jumped out of his mouth. From where he was hiding he must be partially visible and he had no other route to escape since this was a closed alley. He was trapped. Perhaps discovery would not be so bad. They surely could not just kill him. But this officer had his mind on other things. He saw the woman. Curls of silky brown hair over a large overcoat, a small hat with a feather. At any other time, he might have thought her most attractive. Karl just hoped she would distract the officer. But he need not have worried as the SS man did not take his eyes from her for a moment as he stepped backward, leading her into the alley.

'But you know that I love you, Renate. If it was not for your husband, I would marry you tomorrow. But he would have me arrested and shot. He may still do that if he finds out I am here with you tonight.'

'But he won't, will he, Dieter? I am here alone with you, my darling young man. Now kiss me, you fool.'

'Yes of course, my secret love.'

They kissed. Karl moved towards the shadow of the wall but he still had no way past without them noticing. He hoped that whatever was to happen would be brief, the night was cold after all.

'Do you have a cigarette, Dieter?'

'Of course. A cigarette? Don't you want er...?'

'Oh, you are a pushy young boy, Dieter. It is far too cold and besides, my hair will look a mess. You never do as I say and keep your hands on my body.'

'But I thought...?'

'You can wait until tomorrow, darling. I will be all yours, all night and in a warm bed, undisturbed.'

'Perhaps just a little to keep me keen?'

'Well, a little something to be getting on with then.'

She smiled and took his hand, drawing him to her, then she placed her hand gently on top of his head. Dieter dropped to his knees, Karl did not really want to know what was to happen next. Dieter's boot was now also dangerously close to his own. He dared not move it. The woman's coat opened a fraction, shadowing him slightly. He felt able to gently slide back into the shadows just a fraction, whilst Dieter was distracted. As he began to move, the woman's foot moved, her slim heel now pinning his trouser leg to the ground. His leg was clearly in plain sight. But her leg bent a fraction, the coat dropping to the floor, enough to cover the scene. For five minutes, Karl was petrified, almost daring not to breathe. Dieter's boot moved closer to his own and the coat moved over and down his own leg. Surely he must be spotted. The woman's head was in the air, her hand on Dieter's head and she was asking him for more of whatever he was doing. As long as Dieter did not look down to his boots he might not be spotted, he might be lucky. Dieter was most certainly distracted. Renate's body began to move more rhythmically and she shuddered with a loud moan from deep within her body. Suddenly, the coat was pulled closed and Dieter was lifted by his chin and stood again. As before, he simply looked into the eyes of the woman, Renate.

'Dieter, Mein Gott! I am going to miss you when you go to Berlin. Youthful passion, I had forgotten how raw it can be.'

'Now do you want a cigarette?'

'Oh yes, my love, more than anything.'

They stood facing each other. Slowly Karl drew his boot towards him, out of the light. The couple smoked and kissed and talked idly about Renate's husband. Dieter was clearly keen to have more of Renate tonight, but she needed to go home. Renate dropped her cigarette end on the floor, looked at Dieter and slid her slim leg from under her coat, crushing it on the pavement.

'My legs will still be here tomorrow, my darling.'

Dieter stared down at her legs. Just behind them, just out of sight was Karl, frightened and in an agony of anxiety at the risk of discovery. He wished only for them to go and leave him in peace. If Dieter's gaze moved a fraction from Renate's, he would be spotted. Then Dieter flicked his own cigarette into the corner, right onto Karl's shoulder. The hot, stinking ember rolled along to his neck, settling on his scarf. He could smell it catching fire from the residual heat of the lit cigarette. They had to go now.

'Come on, you naughty young man, take me home.'

'With pleasure, Renate von Adelsdorf.'

With a flourish, Dieter held out his arm, bowing towards the woman.

'The most beautiful angel of Bavaria.'

The tapping of boots and heels ceased and they were gone. Karl flicked away the cigarette. It had burned a hole in his scarf and had burned his shoulder. A little icy snow numbed the pain and he repeated the rudimentary treatment through the night. Although the scene he had witnessed was cheap and lustful, he could not help but think of his own angel of Dusseldorf. He hoped she was still alive and that the serum had worked in time.

--oOo--

The next morning was dark, but the scene from the previous night had roused a desire in Karl to see his wife, to be with her in warmth and safety. But this time he was resolved to get close enough to find out if she was alive and recovered. By this time it would be known one way or the other.

He made his way slowly through the early-morning streets, deserted and quiet. Nowhere did he see a suspicious movement, or a car's tracks in the frost. The road was covered in snow, so it was likely that any visitor must come on foot, making it easier to stay safe. The snow outside his house was undisturbed and it looked as if no one was home. He crept around the side, risking a trail of unguarded footprints to his garden wall, then climbed up and over where it was lowest. To make his movements less noticeable, he brushed off the snow all along the wall. He jumped down on the other side where the garden level was higher.

The first window was Liesel's day room where she spent time with the children and had written her letters to Odile and her family in France. What he would have given to be visiting them now with his own family. Anything was better than this horror of a home destroyed and torn apart. He moved to the edge of the garden so that he could see in the window without being seen. Near the wall, Karl was practically invisible from the house and if the room was lit he could see inside safely.

It felt that an age had passed in the freezing gloom and he felt himself begin to drift away. But then the room was suddenly brightly lit against the dark of the morning. Frau Weir appeared in the room to light a fire. Karl's heart jumped. If this room was being used, it could only mean one thing – that Liesel was alive, at home and well enough to sit in her day room. He wanted to jump out, call to her and wave, but then his heart sank as if a gigantic stone had been dropped on it. His eyes dropped to the ground at the awful sight.

Kurt and another SS officer entered and sat in opposing armchairs by the window looking out over the garden. He had willingly wandered into the mouth of the Nazi lion. Karl suddenly preferred to be back at the sordid scene of Dieter and Renate than to bear witness to this. These men were infinitely more dangerous to Karl than foolish young Dieter. He was certainly no nearer to Liesel, even here in his own garden, but most decidedly closer to danger. Idly, he noticed that the roses had not been cut back yet. This was a job that he had loved and now it reminded him of his forced absence and the distance from his old life, a life where he had been able to think about cutting roses.

Eventually, he looked back at Kurt and the other man laughing in his home, helping themselves to his possessions. Karl wondered if this other man was being encouraged to court his own wife. He was devastated, and he sank into his garden wall, looking at his dirty hands and clothes. Karl wished to freeze time to allow him to weep for his wife. But whilst that might make him feel better, danger still lurked at every corner. Other SS or Gestapo officers could not be far away with these men here.

For an hour, the two men conversed, drinking hot coffee and ordering around his own housekeeper. Frau Weir was the Eisners' friend, not a servant of the SS, how dare they! Kurt rose and looked briefly out of the window. Karl nearly gasped as Kurt had looked directly at him. For a second, he remained staring straight at Karl, still speaking silently to his companion who was now laughing. Had he been spotted? No, for it was still dark outside and the light inside must have prevented Kurt seeing him. Then the light was extinguished and the door was firmly closed. There was still no sign of Liesel. Their own bedroom room overlooked the front of the house, so he would have to go round to the front to see. He wanted to see her more than ever.

The snow gave up the secret of his visit with his footprints clearly visible from the road to the wall. They were deep scores in the snow, but they would only be visible from the side of the house. Karl fervently hoped that no one would inspect the house too closely for the next few hours. The Gestapo might, but Kurt would not, for he would have no reason to do so. But why was he even there, and why with this other unknown officer? There was really only one explanation. Kurt was indeed trying to wean his sister onto this Aryan subject, charmless no doubt, but with a uniform that the current Dusseldorf society accepted.

Karl heard the crunch of snow and the sound of an engine. The two officers were joking about the weather all the way down the path to the car. The heavy door closed and the car immediately moved off, leaving the street in silence once again. The predator was gone. Karl was afraid to look, in case the sounds had also hidden the arrival of the Gestapo or a second unseen car. He waited until dusk, hungry, thirsty and chilled to the bone, before moving to the wall and climbing up and over. The street was deserted still, with nothing nearby that he could see. One clean set of car tracks were present, along with a small number of footprints on the path and some disturbed snow where the two men had entered the car. There had been no one else, no second car and no other visitors. The hall light was on but the front rooms were in darkness. A dim light was visible from the front window, as if the room behind had a light. There was no sign of his family and he would leave more desperate than ever and now with more questions. He would find his alley to sleep in again, this time pleased that Dieter and Renate had already planned alternative accommodation for the night.

CHRIS CHERRY

CHAPTER SEVENTEEN

Bazentin-Le-Petit March 1939

'Where is that boy? He is late again!'

'Oh, don't be so harsh with him. He was off on his motorcycle, which, by the way, you bought for him. Once again, just like every other day, he went off with Yvette. Yvette, you remember, is the daughter of one of my oldest friends. You have done this to him, Odile!'

They both laughed in the half-light of the kitchen. William looked down the road to Martinpuich, along which he expected the adventurous and in-love couple to emerge at full speed with Yvette's red hair blowing behind them. Tonight was to be a very special meal as Odile's parents were visiting in order to celebrate Pierre's seventieth birthday. Pierre wasn't very well but his health had improved enough to get around the village. He had finally stopped telling his daughter how dreadful it was to send their children away to school, even if it was in the care of William's parents. He queried constantly whatever was so wrong with French schools that an English one could do so much better. But William knew, he absolutely *knew*, how incredibly clever his eldest son was, and the language he needed to work on the hardest was English. And Armandine? Just as clever, with a deep desire to be a teacher of her beloved French. So where better to do it than in her father's native country? Odile often teased Pierre that Armandine could have gone to Spain, which always silenced him and made him frown.

William could see the elderly couple slowly walking the short distance up the hill from their farm near the church. He scanned the horizon for his son, listening for the sound of the motorcycle, but all was silent. In time, he heard the rhythmical tapping of his father-in-law's stepping cane and the gentle music of his conversation with Marie-Louise.

'The evenings are cold again, my love. Times were, these fields would have an inch of winter bean growth by now. Before all this iron poisoned the soil.'

'Oh Pierre, listen to you, what do you know about farming, hm? You would think you even knew something about the subject!'

'Well I do! Seventy years in Bazentin must count for something. Besides, we had some wonderful men to help us, didn't we?'

Marie-Louise looked down and signed deeply.

'We did, my darling. It is still an awful thought for their families. To lose so many men, well, the world lost its head, did it not?'

'Most certainly, but more than that, we live still with the loss in our hearts. Look there, the gate that I broke on the day that Odile and...'

Pierre stopped and hesitated, squeezing his wife's hand a little harder, resting on his forearm as he looked at the gate.

'Little Henri, Pierre, we can say his name.'

'Little Henri would be forty-one now.'

'Hmm, don't say that so loudly in Odile's hearing, remember you old fool that is her age as well!'

Pierre smiled a little. 'Yes, the little girl who wanted to live.'

'Look at William, Pierre. He looks our age. I am worried. Do you think I should say anything to Odile?'

'No, I am certain that she knows full well. We all know what is wrong. Let us just take care of him. Look, he might well be able to hear us. Let us talk of birthdays, it is mine after all.'

'Of course. Darling William? Come and take my arm will you. This old man is walking far too slowly for me.'

'Ah, of course, Maman. Here, come with me. Good evening, Papa Pierre.'

'That makes me sound like something from a Mozart opera, English boy.'

'Boy? That makes me feel like I should be leaping from a bush to frighten you all.'

'What on earth is that awful buzzing?'

'Ah. That Papa, is your grandson Henri, with poor Yvette. I think our youngest has taken on a little more than he can handle.'

'Yes, it looks like it.'

Yvette was on the bars of the motorcycle, with her arms locked around Henri's neck. He was riding with his head tilted and his hands barely in control. As he rode by, he slowed just a fraction and shouted over the engine noise.

'Good evening, Grandpere, happy birthday! Grandmere, I will be home in five minutes. I am just seeing Yvette to the gate.'

There was no time for anyone reply for they were gone. When they arrived at Alain's cottage, Yvette jumped off the motorcycle, turned and kissed Henri goodnight more than once. Pierre smiled while Marie-Louise shook her head.

'When is Henri going to start working with you, William?'

'I rather think he already has, apart from when he is with Yvette. He is a very clever boy, but if I am truthful, he is better at the charm. Look at them.'

Once Yvette had gone inside, Henri glanced down the road, waved at his family, turned around and came back.

'That's my last delivery made. Home now, the party can begin!'

'You know it is not your birthday don't you, Henri?'

'Yes, Papa.'

'Well, Henri', declared his grandfather, 'I think you are going to need to work hard to make our Yvette happy.'

'Ha! I think I can manage that. Maman? Is supper ready? I'm so hungry.'

William stared at his son.

'As I said, Henri, it is not your birthday.'

Henri looked towards Yvette's house.

'Feels like it, Papa.'

Pierre pretended to throw his cap at his son. Henri went to his grandfather and took his arm.

'It is very pleasing to see you up and about, Grandpere.'

William thought he had found a politician in young Henri. He looked once over the ridge towards High Wood and went inside, closing the door for the feast.

'Please, Papa, sit down over here for the fire has been made up. William-not-the-Conqueror is good at fires. Here, drink this.'

'Odile, do not fuss. I may be old, but I do still run our home perfectly well.'

Marie Louise raised her eyebrows but said nothing.

'I know, Papa but you are—'

There was a loud rap at the door, which shook the handle. William jumped up, startled, and swore in English. It was an unexpected legacy of army life. Only Odile winced. William thought that even though they all knew the words, somehow it did not seem the same in another language.

'Who is it?'

'It is Thierry, Monsieur Collins, young Thierry. I have a telegram for Madame Collins. It is marked as urgent. It is from, well, it is from Germany. Most unusual.'

'A telegram? From Germany?' William turned to Odile, puzzled.

'Liesel writes to you. Why would she send a telegram?'

'Open the door and let us find out.'

'Sorry, yes. Hello Thierry. Thank you. Here, take this.'

William placed a coin in the boy's hand. It was cold tonight and it was late to be out with telegrams, even those marked as urgent. Thierry nodded and ran back to his bicycle and William closed the door.

'Here, Odile. Should you wait until after supper?'

'No, darling. Papa, Maman. Excuse me. This looks like it is important.'

--oOo--

Odile went into the cool darkness of the front room. She lit a lamp and sat down, opening the single sheet that had been folded and sealed with a little dab of wax. Thierry's father was still a traditionalist and everyone respected him for his discretion.

ODILE. CANNOT WRITE SO SORRY. AM DESPERATE KARLMISSING I THINKK IS INVOLVED. CHILDREN TAKEN BY LANGERS=HAVE BEEN ILL SF AND M/C. MUST ASK SISTER FOR HELP. R/AML.SARAH EISNER

She had to read the telegram over and over for it to make any sense as it was littered with errors. The cost of sending, the language and the notation had all conspired to make the note brief and practically in code. All seemed as Thierry had said, most unusual. Odile's head was full of her father's birthday meal. She felt it would be unfair to send them home so early so she decided to leave the message for an hour. She returned to her family

'It is not a problem. Liesel wanted to inform me of a pregnancy.'

Marie-Louise looked closely at her daughter, then she looked down at her plate and stood up.

'Pierre, my love, I am feeling very tired. Will you escort me home?'

Her voice was harsher than usual and Pierre looked a little bemused.

'But I have not—'

'I know, but my back is hurting me and I need to go to bed.'

'Very well. William, will you walk us home? I do not see too well in the dark.'

'Yes, of course.'

When the kitchen was empty, Odile took out the telegram again. William soon returned from walking Pierre and Marie-Louise to their door. Judging by his panting, he must have run home despite his injuries. He looked worried. Clearly, her husband and her mother could both see through her very easily.

'So, what is it really? Is Liesel pregnant or was that a story for your parents?'

'I think she was, but isn't now. Karl is missing, but I can't imagine why, and if I've read things correctly, Liesel has suffered a miscarriage and has also been ill with scarlet fever. Poor Liesel! And this extra K, that's Kurt. He must have done something to Karl. I do not know what. Kidnapped perhaps, or murdered him. He is quite capable and has perhaps joined one of the Nazi organisations. Perhaps something has dishonoured the family. What, I cannot know.'

'Oh, Odile. Are you perhaps being a little fanciful?'

'I don't know what to think! What can be happening? She needs my help. But what help?

'I doubt it could be money since they have plenty. What help can we possibly be to Dusseldorf socialites? And what is R/AML? Is that a medical term?'

Odile nodded. 'If it were, then it would be to issue a repeating dose. Or she might mean report in the morning. She will write again?'

'Then yes, that is sensible.'

'But why has she signed it Sarah? Perhaps two telegrams got mixed up by mistake? That makes the least sense of all.'

They both sat at the table. William took Odile's hand and gently held it. She stroked his hand, the same touch she had administered to him at the Cambrai hospital.

'I have never met Liesel, but I know how important she is to you and to our family. I know how much she helped you and I want to help her in whatever way I can. But help with what?'

Odile shook her head. 'I am none the wiser.'

'Then let us go to bed and wake tomorrow with fresh eyes. I am sure it will make more sense in the morning.'

The night was very cold but Odile felt hot and uncomfortable, as if the bed had nails and needles to keep her awake. Her mind raced. Sleep would not come easily. She imagined her beloved sister in Germany, for Liesel was a sister to her in every way that really mattered. They had a connection that even William and Karl could not understand. She rose, opened the little jewellery box and took out a single hair pin. It was ornate, but not overly valuable. Neat, not excessive. But this little pin had helped to seal a deception. Odile felt that touching it might bring Liesel closer. She turned it over and over and it warmed in her hand. How she wanted her sister here tonight, safe in France with her children. What had happened to Karl? Should she feel sorrow or anger? Then there was Kurt, the permanent memory of that awful man. Liesel only ever referred to him indirectly, sometimes just... she looked at her reflection in the mirror and saw Liesel, with Kurt grinning behind, slowly reaching for her throat.

She shivered and climbed back into bed, placing her head on William's chest. She could hear his heartbeat, but she could also hear the dull rattle of his chest. As her hands slid down his side to hold him, she felt the deep scar on his side. She wondered if they would ever be celebrating William's seventieth birthday.

--oOo--

The heavy rain on the little window woke Henri from his dream of being in a summer meadow, hand in hand with Yvette. He was just reaching the interesting part when the sound grew loud enough to rouse him. He too had learned to curse in English. It was at least morning, but it was still quite dark, the heavy clouds and fog delaying the start of the day. He was unhappy because it was actually a busy day for him. And he would not be seeing Yvette today either, making his misery complete. Still, he had to get up for the deliveries would not make themselves and he was due in Longueval at the small bakery in an hour or so. He had promised to deliver today before the bread became cold or stale in the pouring rain so at least he would earn extra for delivering in the morning and extra for doing it in the cold and wet. The extra coins would be handy for his plans.

He dressed quickly and went downstairs. The house was too quiet and his mother and father were not at home. The door to their room was open and no one was present. His good morning wishes went unanswered. This made Henri feel strangely uncomfortable. Perhaps it was because they did not usually leave early and never without waking him first as he would probably oversleep without a call. He went to his little covered motorcycle house, but noticed that the little family car was missing. Perhaps his father had taken it for an errand. But what errand? Then he heard the sound, the engine clatter. His father was coming up the hill, the dim little lights at the front shining in the rain.

'Ah, Henri. Good morning! Sorry to leave you asleep but I had to find something out quickly. A bit wet today, eh? Are you late?'

'No Papa. But I will be in three minutes.'

Henri moved the motorcycle out of its little house, dreading the rain to come for he would be soaked in no time. All for a few extra coins. He rode off, straight into a howling gale, smiling to himself for at least he was on his beloved motorcycle.

--oOo--

William quickly went inside, holding a little piece of paper in his hand. It held the answers to the riddles of the telegram, but the solution would be a devastating shock to Odile and he dreaded her finding out any other way. He warmed a pot on the small fire he had lit and sat down to wait until Odile came back from her parents' house. He made some English tea the way he liked it, strong and sweet. Not the watery offering that his French family preferred, if they had tea at all. Army tea would always revive even the most desperate soul.

Odile was gone until just after nine. Henri and his mother arrived together. She scolded him for getting up late and for being late home from his rounds. Henri managed to look suitably sheepish and went to change into dry clothes. Poor boy must be wondering what was upsetting his mother and what was sending his father out so early in the morning.

'Oh, William! You were out early, was something wrong?'

'No Odile, but I could not let the telegram rest. So I drove to Longueval and placed a telephone call to London to ask for help with the message. It took nearly an hour to make all the connections and for the telephone to be answered. The office does not open until seven in England. The day is almost over, it wasn't like it was—'

'What did you find?'

'Well, it is not definitely solved but—'

'William! Just tell me, my love, I am shaking.'

'It seems that the Nazi government makes Jewish people change their names so that they are always recognisable. Women who are Jewish have to add the name Sarah to their identity and identification cards. Men have to add the name Israel.'

'But Liesel is as German as Dusseldorf Cathedral!'

'Yes, but the name Eisner is more complicated. It comes from Austria and it is possible that it has Jewish beginnings. I have been told that if Karl's mother or grandmother are Jewish, then the Germans might simply make him a Jew, even if he is not. That means all the dreadful laws that they have passed might apply to him. Probably to Liesel now as well. Perhaps your theory about Kurt becoming a Nazi was not so fanciful.'

'Oh my goodness! William, that surely means Kurt is behind the disappearance of Karl!'

Odile put her hand to her mouth.

'Kurt is capable of anything. If he is anything important in the Nazi Party then a Jewish brother-in-law would be a dangerous embarrassment. I fear my sister may already be lost to us.'

'I am sorry, Odile, truly. I have asked London to telephone again tomorrow at the same time.'

William put his hand on Odile's back. Her skin was cold and she was shaking. He leaned forward and embraced her. She grabbed him tightly, pushing her head into his shoulder and William sat with her in silence until the fire had died down. Henri came in without a word, simply putting some more wood on the fire and topping up the pot before leaving again.

CHAPTER EIGHTEEN

Dusseldorf April 1939

Liesel rose late on the orders of her doctor, the kind and protective Professor Scheckter. He had ordered rest for her ever since her grave illness in December, some four months previously. Her physical strength was slowly returning but she was desolate, distraught and without her husband and children. She felt there was little reason to rise from her bed. Perhaps out of concern, but perhaps more out of a little Kurt-laden spite, General Langer had stated that until Liesel was strong enough to receive them, then the children were best to remain in the care of their grandparents. But the kind Professor Scheckter had promised to discuss the matter of the children with the Langers.

'Frau Eisner, dear Liesel, I am going to recommend that your children stay with the Langers for one more week. I want to see you able to care for yourself first. With all my power, I will urge their return shortly. What do you say to that?'

'Professor, your kindness has been without end. But it would hasten my recovery to have the children, surely you can see that?'

'Yes, of course, that is why I want their return to be permanent and not to risk having you relapse. Scarlet fever is most serious. If Doctor Eisner had not administered the serum to you in those early hours, you would not have survived the next days.'

'Where *is* my husband, Professor? I hear this and that. But I want a truthful answer. Is he dead?'

'My dear, no. But I suspect the Langers have a way into the heart of this and you know what that means...'

'Has my brother fulfilled his threats?'

'I cannot say, I do not know, but Doctor Eisner did not go of his own free will.'

'Can you help me to think why, if he lives, he has not been here or tried to contact me?'

'That may have something to do with your brother and the Gestapo prowling around inside and out.'

'Are they? I have never seen them!'

'You have barely been out of this room in months.'

'But I would hear them moving downstairs?'

'Your brother is most clever at withholding details from you and clearly intends to control your destiny. I must not speak out of turn, but I do not entirely trust what your brother tells you. That officer he visits with, well, something is happening and I do not think it will be well for Germany. I am no traitor, but nor am I a patriot to this government and the Fatherland that we now live in.'

Liesel put her hand on the professor's arm.

'You do not speak out of turn, it is refreshing to have the truth for once. Kurt has fed us the most dreadful lies about the world outside. Karl has not absconded, nor fled like a rat in the night. He has been taken, stolen from me. Do you think that?'

'Well, he is not here and he did not go willingly. I will see what I can find out. I will see if there is any news. Forgive my indelicacy, but there have been no reports of any bodies recently appearing. My student in the mortuary has already been told to alert me to any… bodies fitting the description of your husband. None so far. That must be a good thing.'

'Yes it must. I wish I could understand what has happened and why.'

'Look, Liesel, you should not worry more than you do already. You are as German as the oak tree in your garden. Its roots are deep and the acorn grew from the soil of Germany. For Doctor Eisner, well it is more complicated. His seed grew somewhere else and landed in Germany. Do you see? The only difference is perspective. You and I both know that he and his family were true German patriots. It is the warped looking glass of Nazism that shows them to be otherwise. The truth is undeniable, whereas opinion is more flexible. I will try to find out what I can.'

The professor tapped his nose and nodded to Liesel. He rose and held Frau Weir's hands.

'Let us make her strong enough to receive her children, for that is the best medicine. It is not right for a mother and her babies to be separated, whatever their age. Keep her warm and fed. I want to see a chin on that beautiful face when I return in four days.'

He stared over his glasses and Frau Weir blushed and nodded.

'She will be as fat as a pig when you come back, bouncing down the stairs, Professor.'

The professor roared with laughter, his hair streaming behind him as he left. Even Liesel managed to laugh at her new physician as he made his grand exit.

'Frau Eisner, your brother was here again today with that horrible officer. They are due to go away soon. You know, I think it might be to start a war. They were talking about room to live in Poland. Land to farm and such things. That cannot be right. I can scarcely believe it, but it is true. Something about white and Danzig? It might be a code, but they are very excited by it.'

'Why do you think my brother comes here but does not come to see me?'

'I suppose he is a dog in a manger. If he is here, your husband cannot be. He uses his house to taunt him.'

'But Karl is not here!'

'Your husband is a clever man. He may not be so very far away.'

'Then I wish he would show himself to me. Perhaps I should show myself to him. Now that the weather is turning, I could go out. This house, loving though it was, is now eternally empty to me and I want to escape.'

'Then that is settled. If you eat everything that I give you, let us go outside to take the air.'

--oOo--

Karl was forced once again to move from his private alleyway. It turned out that it was convenient for many illicit meetings, being so close to the door of an officers' club frequented by the army and the SS on alternate evenings. Thankfully, the Gestapo did not entertain themselves in this way and so the normal clientele were low-ranking SS and officers of the army. Only on the night of the incident with Dieter and Frau von Adelsdorf had he been close to discovery or close to the Dusseldorf elite. Of course, he was married to the sister of one of those very elite, for all the good it did him. Here he was, scrabbling in the dark and unlucky enough to discover his one safe space to sleep was anything but. Instead, it was a hunting ground for the Nazis, with women happy to entertain them for the good of the Fatherland and the reflected glory and security of status it offered them.

For Karl, who was now thin, worn and sick, sleeping and hiding were his daily routine. He probably bore little resemblance to the old Doctor Eisner. No longer was he the tall and strong doctor who drew attention wherever he went. If he were to attempt to get serum from the hospital now, he would not even make it through the grounds without arrest. Now he was always tired, sick and deeply unhappy. He recognised the signs well enough, and said it to himself quite bluntly, he was on the point of suicide. Had any one of the men in the alley dropped a pistol when they dropped their trousers, he would probably have shot himself instead of them.

Today was bright. It was a day to be outside as spring began to warm the streets. His last hot meal had been weeks ago, and his last food had been a plate of dried cheese and meat from the officers' club two days before. He fancied that the lips on the food had belonged to the very men who would come for the former doctor, now Karl Israel Eisner. He had not bothered to keep the identity card. With it, he would be arrested. Without it, he would be arrested. What was the difference? Carrying it sickened him, because it was all just a sham, a farce in order to preserve the rank and reputation of an evil man in an evil regime.

Karl approached his house. There was no snow on the ground to help him judge the danger. The walls were bathed in pale green light and the sun shining through the blossoming trees was as beautiful as ever, the very sight that had made his father fall in love with this house. He stood at the end of the path, no one arrested him and no one took him inside a black car. No men with hats shadowed him. He walked to the door. Should he ring or knock? It seemed quite strange, this was his house after all. But he rang anyway. The large bell, a present from his grandfather to his father, clanked loudly. The sound was unmistakable. But there was no answer. It was the daytime so Frau Weir would be home. No answer.

On impulse, he ran to the first window and looked in, his hands leaving a greasy smudge and his breath a circle of mist on the glass. Nothing, as if the room were a museum. He ran round to the side. The wall was more difficult to climb now, he noted, perhaps a sign of his weakening health. The back windows revealed the same empty rooms, which were tidy to the point of obsession. Nothing. No hint of life or laughter or children. It was clear that no one was home, perhaps nobody lived here anymore. He banged the pane in frustration, cracking the glass and cutting open his hand.

'You bastard, Langer! You fucking bastard, Langer!'

Five months of frustration and pain erupted in this moment from the once calm and considered doctor. Five months of sickness, grief, loss and humiliation poured from him. This was his home. He loved it here, but it was as if he were seeing his home through a frosted looking glass. Unreal and altered in some indeterminate way. Convinced that the house was empty, he walked away, turning only once to look back, to remember his house for the very last time.

Only able to shuffle these days, he felt old before his time, with the last spark of life gone from his body. He was drawn inexorably back to the river. Its blue-grey sheen welcomed him, its arms could cover him, comfort him and take him. At the Jan-Wellem Bridge, he looked over at the flowing Rhine, its rhythm mesmerising and enchanting. Perhaps he could even see maidens below, welcoming him in. A promise of relief, of finding Liesel and the children on the other side, well and happy to greet him. There was no Kurt, which made him smile. He felt a tooth loosen against his tightening lips as he did so. A smile was something he had not managed for some time.

He stepped up on the parapet and felt suddenly years younger, seeming taller and more energised. He leaned his body forward, waiting for that point when his body would have to fall and there would be no chance to return. The sun was on his filthy face, the wind in his matted hair. He looked up to the sky, down to the water, closed his eyes, spread his arms wide and rocked forward, waiting for the hammer blow of the water.

CHAPTER NINETEEN
Dusseldorf April 1939

Rottmeister Bauer was looking forward to a quiet evening. Twice today the police officer had been called to attend incidents in the streets of Dusseldorf, both involving the arrests of Jewish families. He was just there to keep the citizens away whilst the other organisations did their terrible work. Bauer disliked this way of doing his job, he disliked the new order of things. But he was a lowly foot patrol officer, a team master, but of a team serving an administration that told them nothing and blamed them for everything. It was nearly the end of a shift, so he cut across the lovely old Jan-Wellem Bridge to the city, which would cut out a few paces and avoid the part of town where some of the more unsavoury incidents might happen. He wanted to be home, to sit outside and enjoy the last hour of sunlight before dinner.

At the centre of the span he saw an old man with a crusty beard, ill-fitting clothes and lank hair. This man, an old drunk or a lunatic, was wandering the bridge aimlessly. Then Bauer saw him step up onto the parapet and his heart sank for this would mean a report and a call to his station to describe the man and have him placed under arrest for the evening. Or, he could turn around, walk to the next bridge and turn a blind eye to the jump that was certain to come soon. Then he would have seen nothing and the report of a body downstream would be as much of a surprise to him as anyone else. More importantly, it would be out of his jurisdiction.

But then he thought again. He had not become a policeman to mark time to retirement, to watch Jewish families taken in the night, he was here to serve the people, even the ragged bottom-of-the-barrel drunks like the man on the bridge. Very well, he would go and see if the man needed any assistance, or if not, whether he needed to be arrested. As he reached the top of the rise, Bauer noticed that the man's shoes were a little out of the ordinary. These had clearly been stolen from a gentleman, so perhaps it would be an arrest after all.

'You there, on the bridge! Stand still!' I am on officer of the Ordnungspolizei. Step down from the edge, I order you!'

The man was unmoved by the shouts. He looked to the sky, then downwards. Bauer had to act now. He quickened his pace to a run, just as the man spread his arms wide, gently tipping forward. Bauer reached the man as he began to fall, grabbing at his tails, but then overbalancing on the metal guard rail. He felt the brief rush of the wind, his cap torn off as he hit the water feet first. The world was dark for a few seconds. Bauer realised his coat would weigh him down and he might drown after surviving the fall. He thought quickly, he had been trained for this very situation. As he rose upwards, he began to unbuckle the belt and to tear at the row of buttons. Once his coat was open, he simply brought his shoulders together and slid out. At the surface, he gasped and splashed around until he could get enough air to breathe normally. His cap bobbed next to him and the coat had disappeared. He could not see the dirty old man anywhere. He swam for the bank, his boots filling with water, the next danger to his safety. Then he saw the body, face down, and motionless, rolling on the gentle current.

From the bank, there came shouting and splashing as people reached the edge of the water to pull out the policeman. The old man was dragged in as well. He was alive, but not breathing. Quickly, Bauer slapped his face repeatedly, then he rolled him over and slapped his back hard between the shoulders. The man gasped, coughed and vomited on the bank. He was alive. A small crowd had gathered, and now a motor launch was coming along the river towards the bank, probably looking for the source of the commotion. The policeman jumped to his feet when he saw a superior officer alongside, shouting across.

'What is going on here? Who are you, Officer?'

'Rottmeister Bauer, Orpo, sir. I was assisting this man, sir, when we overbalanced and fell into the river.'

'You fell? From *this* bridge? Are you sure, Bauer?'

'Yes sir, I was lucky, I fell in boots first.'

'Well, I must say, you are most lucky. The other fellow? Dead I assume? Suicide? Jew?'

'Certainly an attempt at suicide, sir. He is alive. I have not discovered if he is a Jew.'

'I hope that he is not for your sake, Bauer, I would not want to think you risked your life for one of them.'

'Sir.'

'Does he have any identification?'

Bauer searched the man's pockets. 'A wallet, sir.'

'And?'

'It says KE on it. No identification papers at all. Perhaps washed away.'

'Money?'

'Two notes sir, and one coin. Not much.'

'Probably drunk it all away. Is he drunk?'

'Can't smell any drink, sir. I would say not.'

'Let us take him aboard and go to the station. No identification, worth investigating, don't you think?'

'Of course, sir, if you say so.'

'I do. Good work, Bauer, on you go.'

The old man was lifted onto the river boat and it moved away. Bauer was more uncertain than ever. The man's clothes were strange. Filthy and rotten, but not the usual bits and pieces of the street. But here he was. Bauer thought he must be a Jew, tired of running. Perhaps the kindest thing would have been to let him fall and then drown. He would have to report it, but the case now belonged to the Gestapo and the SS, the confused jurisdiction no longer a worry for Bauer.

--oOo--

The boat lurched and bumped on the Rhine, slowly winding around to the lower Dusseldorf office of the SS. Karl was aware of his surroundings, but his head was cotton wool, his back ached and a painful stab was ever present in his neck. The fall had either not killed him, or he was in a special kind of Hell.

'What is your name? And do not lie to me.'

Karl looked for the face that owned the voice.

'I said, what is your name?'

'Karl.' Briefly, Karl thought to make up a name, but it was hopeless. If he lied, it would be all the worse. 'Karl Eisner. Doctor Karl Eisner of the District Landstrasse Hospital and the Kaiserswerth Institute. I am a practitioner in infectious diseases.'

'Then you must be a Jew.'

'I am not, sir, I am the son of Professor Eisner.'

'With a Jew mother, I expect. We will soon find out.'

Karl felt himself lifted by strong hands into a dark, cool office that smelled of old tobacco. The little pile of papers on the desk was neat and the row of pens had been placed by the hands of someone who cared about appearances. He noticed his wet, stinking clothes and the thin, drawn skin underneath them.

For an hour he waited, his clothes drying on him, scratching at his skin, which was itching and raw. His neck was still in pain, his back stiffening. He was an emotional and physical mess. Exactly how the Gestapo liked it.

'So, Eisner. We have some very interesting information about you. You are a protected Jew, were married to General Langer's daughter, name of Liesel. Yes, a protected Jew. So why do you think there is an immediate arrest notice on this file? Tell me that, Herr Doctor Eisner of the Institute? Herr Doctor of nothing, I am afraid. You have been released from all responsibilities. Perhaps you already know that? It says here that you attacked Fraulein Langer, causing her to be with child twice.'

'It is a mistake. I am not a Jew, nor am I in any criminal trouble. I am the victim of a terrible mistake. A mistake of vanity from Liesel's brother.'

'That would be Herr Kurt Langer of the SS. Of course we know him, he is one of our superiors. He is the one who issued this arrest notice.'

'Then you can see, you are instruments of a family dispute. You are being used for a family vengeance upon me by my ambitious and foolish brother-in-law.'

'Feel free to accuse an officer of the SS, in the office of the SS. It is a most helpful course of action for you.'

'Why is that?'

'Because it makes it all the easier to have you sent away to a camp. Insulting an officer of the SS, family or not, is sufficient grounds to have you transported. Perhaps to Mauthausen. Do you understand that?'

'No, not really. That sounds like the crazy insecurity of a lunatic.'

The officer stood and struck Karl roughly with the back of his hand.

'Silence. You do not have the luxury of insults here in this room. I have had enough of you. Take him to the holding room. We will see exactly what is to be done with him. Contact Standartenführer Langer immediately. He is now in Berlin.'

Karl felt his shoulder jerked back and his shirt grabbed from behind. He was pushed through the grey corridor into another windowless room and left alone. But the door soon opened and a tall man in SS uniform entered.

'The Gestapo can be most cruel, but the SS can be your friend. A true German you say? Let us talk to your papers and see what they say. Here they are clear. Israel? Well now, that is not the name of an Aryan patriot is it? Is it?'

The officer slapped Karl over the head with the papers and slammed the desk with his fist. Karl had not seen his face, only heard the voice. The voice that had a distant and detached, but strangely familiar tone. He thought perhaps it was Kurt acting a part, or an old school friend now in the uniform of an enemy. But then he placed the voice and a spark of courage rose in Karl's heart. He was already a dead man and had no more to lose, he had tried to kill himself today and wanted nothing more of this lunacy.

'Be aware that I am an officer of the SS. I am Sturmbannführer Jancker. What do you have to say on the question, hm? You are not an Aryan patriot at all, are you? Are you saying you are not a Jew?'

Karl sat there in silence for a moment. Jancker picked up the papers and hit him with them again. Still Karl sat in silence. Then he looked up at him and smiled.

'So, Jancker. How is the angel of Bavaria?'

'What?' The officer jumped to his feet and roared at Karl. 'What? That is no answer to my question?'

'I said, you ignorant ass, how is the angel of Bavaria? It is not a hard fucking question. How are the beautiful legs of Frau von Adelsdorf? Do they still part like a good SS officer's wife should, eh?'

'How could you possibly know? How? What do you know? Speak or I will have you shot this minute!'

'I doubt it, not with Herr Langer on the case. Herr Langer. Do you know that I am married to his sister?'

'What, but that is impossible! How?'

'Impossible? That I'm married to Herr Langer's sister or that I know of Frau von Adelsdorf?'

'Frau von Adelsdorf of course, you fucking bastard!'

Dieter stood to strike Karl again. Karl was feeling a little amused. His death throes might hold one last flourish of joy.

'Strike me if you wish, but *you* cannot kill me.'

'I don't give a damn, you pig. Tell me *now*!'

'Youthful passion, Dieter, I had forgotten how raw it can be.'

'Oh, fuck!'

'Now, you do not know who I am. For all you know, you flatfoot, I might be the Gestapo, or fucking Heydrich himself.'

'Who are you?'

'I am trouble for you. Get me out of here, or I will sit here and shout your name and that of the Gauleiter's sister, who is married to Count von Adelsdorf. He would be the Director of Security for the whole fucking Gestapo, if I am not mistaken?'

Karl watched as conflicting expressions fought on Dieter's face. Clearly, the man had expected that he would be the one carrying out the interrogation. He would not have been expecting this shambles of a man to be cross-examining him. Finally, he addressed Karl once more.

'Are you a Jew?'

'No, I am the victim of a terrible mistake. If not a mistake, then a victim of revenge.'

'You are a protected person, yes?'

'Yes.'

'Then Langer is punishing you for marrying his sister?'

'Yes.'

'Why?'

'Because my family ran to Austria for a reason I do not know. My mother and grandmother are what you would describe as Aryan. I can only assume that the merest hint of suspicion would damage Herr Peacock's reputation.'

Dieter's face twitched, but whether it was in laughter or anger, Karl could not tell.

'Langer will kill you. I will make sure you do not speak before then.'

'How Dieter? How? Stay with me? What about the lovely Renate's legs? Or rather, what is between them? Renate von Adelsdorf. So, she would have been Renate Florian before then? Did you get her into bed then, or did you go off like a cork too early, you ass?'

'Fuck you. You do not speak of Frau von Adelsdorf in such a manner. Have you no respect?'

'Do you? What you were doing was—'

Dieter struck Karl, knocking him off the chair to the floor.

'Fuck you, Eisner!'

Dieter kicked Karl repeatedly. His nose was now bleeding and his face swelling, but Karl was laughing inside for the pain was as nothing to the cool blackness to come.

'I tell you what, Dieter. You are making my hair look a mess. How about you let me go out into the street and I will never speak of this again?'

Dieter's boot stopped. Karl heard the scraping as he left, the door closing loudly behind him. Karl eased himself up on to the chair again, the pain now growing in his wounded face and body. He began to laugh. The door opened again and Dieter entered with another man.

'This is him. He is not who he says he is. This is not Doctor Eisner.'

'Very good, sir. I will take him away immediately.'

'Do not harm him further, he is a German citizen and a friend of the Gestapo.'

'Yes, sir.'

The young sturmann looked quizzically at Karl before gently

escorting him into a car and driving him to the end of Landstrasse. He was released with a tap of the cap. Karl was laughing openly now. The driver shook his head and drove off.

--o0o--

Dieter sat down with his notes and a pen. At the top of the report he wrote:

19.20 Man in river claiming or presumed to be Karl Israel Eisner (arr. SSStF Langer). Mistaken identity. No identification on person. Investigation – that this man took the identity of Eisner, either by theft or by force. Investigation complete. No evidence of crime or cause to detain. Recommend no further action. SSStB D.O.M. Jancker.

The report was filed and the telephone call to Langer was cancelled. Dieter made his excuses and left for the day, spending the afternoon chain smoking by the river, pacing up and down.

CHAPTER TWENTY

Dusseldorf April 1939

The air was fresh and the morning sun was wonderful to feel again on her face. The time confined to bed in her unchanging room was now almost forgotten as the sweet scents of renewal flowed over Liesel as she walked in the gentle April breeze. The air had not yet the warmth of the coming spring, but the sensation of cool air and warm sunshine was invigorating and as she walked, she felt the strength returning to her. The prospect of once more being surrounded by the love of her children inspired her to recover. She ached for them and every part of her longed for their embrace, their noise, laughter and tears. How desperately she wanted them back. Her parents had felt that it was best to keep the children away from home until the Karl situation was resolved. However, in the absence of Kurt, the professor had prevailed, his words carrying considerable weight. And so the children were coming home next week. Once Liesel had eaten all that she was given, then there was no barrier to their return and perhaps the house could feel like a home again.

As she reached the end of Landstrasse, she took a long look at her home, remembering the first day she spent here as a married woman. There was a small lace cloth over the bell, which fell when she pulled the chain, now the house had a mistress to take care of it. Her loving husband had opened the door. She stepped inside and touched everything in sight, it was hers to arrange, to love and to care for. How she longed for the sound of children, leaping from room to room, singing to them in the evening and telling tall tales of the woods. How happy she had been. She thought of then and of now, the present filled with pain and loss. The children would bring comfort, but her husband was gone. She had a sunken, empty feeling that he would be forever lost. Her brother was the cause of this. She could not live without Karl and could not stay, so she had to leave this strange, dry wilderness and find peace again.

As she neared the corner where the house stood tall over the shadows of the oak trees, she saw a poor old man shuffling away. Liesel wondered if he had been cast out as a Jew, like her husband, or had simply fallen on hard times. She said a little prayer for him as he disappeared.

'May God protect you sir, as I hope he does my husband.'

CHAPTER TWENTY-ONE

Dusseldorf June 1939

General Langer had told Liesel that he thought it best to appoint a tutor for the children since attending school was now out of the question. That his daughter was being cared for by a loyal German housekeeper was pleasing to him. Liesel knew that Kurt had been instrumental in arranging regular visits to her house to ensure that all was in accordance with the propriety of the Nazi regime. The name of Eisner was no longer to be mentioned in the house. She wondered how much of all of this her father really knew, his tact was never well developed, but his sense of right had once been a powerful and guiding influence for his children.

Liesel was provided with a living allowance, which enabled her to live comfortably and provided rations sufficient for two adults and two children. However, she was not to be seen near her father's home, just in case someone were to misunderstand the situation. Until the affair of the Jew could be resolved, there could be no possibility of a return for Liesel and the children to Dusseldorf's polite society.

For Liesel, the bliss of having the children home again was indescribable. To have the sound of young voices filled with energy and hope nourished her soul and gave her an optimism so desperately lacking since Karl had left. They had seemed a little unsure when they first returned, like new kittens, wondering about the safety of their surroundings. They knew that their mother had been unwell and they seemed uncertain whether Liesel needed their absence instead of their company. She happily showed them that she needed them around her, swamping her with their stories and love. It was not long before at least part of the house was back to a normal routine. Liesel felt that a little of the fog of doubt over the family had lifted. When Karl came home, it would seem as natural and loving as it should be.

The children adored the notion of a tutor at home as they did not have to leave the house on very cold days and on sunnier days, their lessons were held in the garden. It was easy for them to fall back in at home. Liesel hoped that they missed their father. They seemed reluctant to speak of him and as is the way of children, they soon adapted to whatever was in front of them. Liesel pondered this, perhaps they had decided that if their father had gone, it was easiest to get on with their lives. On occasion, in the evenings, Liesel would talk of their father and his love for them. Their questions were innocent of the motives of the Langers and the cruel Herr Gauleiter. They just went away satisfied at how hard their father worked for his family and that his sacrifice would be worth it in the end.

Liesel immersed herself in the lives of her children. She could not bear the day otherwise. At every turn she saw the face of her husband in their young skin and her only connection to Karl was in their touch. Franz would smile and it would be Karl. Monika would shake her head at Franz and it would be Karl disapproving of the wooden toy wreckage on the floor.

She still received official letters from the office of the Race Administrator enquiring about her husband and the education of the children. He remained keen to speak with Karl if he were ever to appear, in which case he must attend immediately for an interview to clarify matters finally and fully. Liesel dreaded these letters because they showed her that the memory of the Nazi Party was long and spiteful – whether German or Jew, it was all a matter of perspective. Whatever protection Karl had officially had from the law was now erased completely by the orders of Kurt, using his friendship with the Gauleiter to force his will upon the city. It was no good replying to the letters, or even seeking further clarification since it would only provoke the already snarling wolf. Karl was officially an outcast, both wanted and unwanted. The official dissolution of his marriage and his removal from Dusseldorf were formally required to preserve Kurt's reputation and to enhance his standing in the evil machine. Liesel knew that if Kurt could not achieve this, then her own life would also soon be in danger. Many others would feel the brutality of her damaged and embittered brother as he sought to cover over this disagreeable situation with ever increasing glory and victory on the political battlefield.

--oOo--

Each day, the menacing black car would drive slowly along Landstrasse and then stop at the end of their street, facing towards the house. Unseen eyes were watching, noting and reporting. Just before the stroke of eleven each morning, it would sweep past, then at the wall it would slow to walking pace and pass their gate, continuing onwards around the gentle curve in the road. Liesel would often glimpse a second or third figure in the car. It was the Gestapo, or the SS, but she was sure it was never Kurt himself. She imagined that Kurt was now in Berlin, feeding the elite with lies and fancies for his own advancement. It was impossible to imagine this man the beloved brother of her childhood. He was nothing but a beast, with a cold eye and a cold heart. A thinking and calculating demon, sinister and rotten. Destroyed by his survival, not elevated by his death. She no longer felt any shame in thinking it would have been better for her own family if he were dead, cold in the ground along with the victims of his brutality.

But the daily routine with the car was at least predictable. The car never came to a complete stop, never lingered long enough for an occupant to be recognised. The front door was never darkened by the shadow of one of them and the men inside never spoke with anyone in the street. She never saw a figure in the shadows, nor the tell-tale glint of a lens in the light. Whatever patrols Kurt had ordered were dutifully carried out, but it seemed that his orders now received merely cursory attention from the Gestapo, with no sight or scent of Karl in the neighbourhood that the wolves could follow. Perhaps there were more important matters to attend to than the apprehension of a single protected Jew, with no crime to report and no sign of the man day after day. Liesel hoped that they might even tire of this daily ritual and stop visiting altogether.

Whether the car came or not, Liesel had tried hard to find out more about her husband's position using the well-connected person who still regularly visited her home. Herr Professor had hinted at help that had been offered to the disappearing Karl, but there was nothing more to be said and nothing new had been discovered about his whereabouts. The professor had clearly heard nothing more and seemed troubled, perhaps embarrassed if ever Liesel enquired. Troubled it seemed by guilt, rather than concern for his own safety. She had no more avenues of help available to her. Her parents were slowly receding from society, their age against them, even with their unquestioned loyalty to Kurt. Her father was now elderly and perhaps his hawkish mind was finally failing him. Her mother seemed unsure of her position and was concerned only with holding her insular world together.

There was now only one person Liesel could trust to follow leads to her husband, one who would not arouse suspicion from the wolf pack. Liesel wanted to know once and for all if Karl lived, for she now knew that he could never visit their home with the eyes of Kurt upon them all.

'Karl trusted you, didn't he? He placed us in your care on the night he disappeared.'

'You know that already, Frau Eisner. I love this family, I care for you all as if you were my own.'

Liesel placed her cold and trembling fingers on Frau Weir's arm.

'And Karl? Do you want to know what happened to Doctor Eisner?'

'But surely by now, he is… he must be—'

'Not here! He is alive. I can sense him, feel his presence out there. Perhaps it is his personality in the children, but he lives, I know it to be true.'

Liesel's voice gave the slightest clue to her own frailty and perhaps she was not entirely convinced by her own words.

'But Frau Eisner, do you really believe it?'

'I do, I have to.'

She looked deep into Frau Weir's eyes, reading the sincerity in them. These were fearful and troubled times and trust was so very hard to give.

'I want your word on something.'

'Of course, Frau Eisner.'

'Your life then?'

'Yes, willingly.'

'I want you to find him.'

The housekeeper looked doubtful. '

But we have tried, we have looked everywhere that he could ever know to go. He is not in the city of Dusseldorf or we should have spied him or he would have been arrested by those terrible men. He is not in their cursed hands or the Gauleiter and the Race Administrator would not still be writing to you. But if they cannot find him, who can?'

'I beg you. Will you try for one final time? I have been thinking, trying to put myself in his place. There is a place we have not already looked. I thought it too dangerous for him until now, but with eyes turning slowly from him, it may be possible that he goes there to sleep in safety, in a place he knows and trusts.'

'Where is this place, Liesel?'

'It is the Kaiserswerth. He is no longer allowed to work there but he knows the grounds and there is a hidden corner where we could be alone for five minutes in the day. It was special to us. It is secluded and unknown. The kitchens are nearby, for food and warmth.'

Liesel looked down and blushed a little.

'We even kissed there for the first time, after the big parade in 1918. The day that… never mind. Look, it is possible that he has visited there. Will you try?'

Frau Weir looked surprised and patted her hair with her palm.

'I will go, Liesel, although I am not so sure he would think the way you do.' Frau Weir looked out of the window for a moment. 'It is dangerous, but not as dangerous as it is for the Doctor. But I have an idea first.'

--o0o--

The next day was cooler with rain in the air, but the ground was mercifully still dry. Liesel and the housekeeper waited near the window until long after eleven, when the Gestapo car had been round for the daily visit. It had come early the day before, but today it was almost noon. As usual, it drove around the sweep of the road, slowed at the gate, with at least four eyes upon the house, watching and reporting. At last, it swept past the gate and moved away. For a moment it slowed but then drove off and without returning. Finally, the front door opened and Frau Weir quickly left.

Never had she been made to run an errand like this. She had been a housekeeper ever since her father had died. It was a good life with the Eisners, hard work sometimes, but the family were wonderful and caring employers, friends really. Recently, Liesel had come to utterly depend on her support for her very survival. She was a fierce patriot, but no friend of the Nazis. In her hands now rested the lives of a German family in deep trouble with little hope for escape.

The small omnibus route north followed the sweep of the Rhine, almost all the way out of town towards the village and hospital complex at Kaiserswerth. But the omnibus did not go all the way so a short walk would be needed, the best part of an hour perhaps, if she did not hurry and give the sense of undue haste. On her walk, she saw only two people, a man with a stepping cane and a woman with a small dog in her arms. Not likely for Gestapo or SS, since the disguise would be too obvious and the dog was only good for attracting attention. The way was most likely clear.

As she approached the institute building, she grew more doubtful that Karl would ever come here, but perhaps that was just her nerve failing her. It was so far away from the city, safe perhaps, but too far from home and family if he chose to find them at all, which he had not. If he had been foolish enough to be watching the house, then he would realise that the Gestapo had their eleven o'clock routine and would surely discover him at some point in the future. Even so, why had he not made any contact? Maybe a single note? Perhaps he really was dead, or even in custody and the letters sent to Liesel were just to put her off asking questions. He might even have been sent to one of the labour camps. Poor Doctor Eisner, a man of considerable learning cast aside like refuse to rot on the banks of the river, or in a vile alley somewhere. Surely not. But there was simply no way of knowing or finding out the terrible truth of his disappearance. She reached into her small bag and felt for the wax of the envelope.

The little note that Liesel had penned for Karl was very detailed, but hidden in words and phrases that held a deeper meaning only for the two of them. As she walked closer to the hospital, Frau Weir sought the quieter research wards. She found them easily enough, including the little space under the stairs so clearly described by Liesel. It was indeed a dry space, and high enough for a couple to stand under to steal a kiss. She smiled at the thought of young love. They did love each other – that could not be doubted, even in Karl's absence.

The little spot had matched Liesel's drawing almost exactly. Just around the corner, the ground had been disturbed a little, probably by a dog or a fox, but the little hidden space was clean except for a few dried leaves. It seemed no one had been here at all, certainly no one was living here now. But Liesel had expected this. Her husband was a clever and resourceful man, if not experienced in living the life of an outcast. The housekeeper placed the little envelope in the bracket by the wall. The note contained clues that would be meaningless to any intruder. It was a gamble, but it was more for dear Liesel's comfort that she had come on this errand than as a possible salvation for Karl. Given the stark reality of living outdoors, she doubted more than ever his ability to survive for this long, friendless and alone in the open.

--oOo--

Liesel waited at home, willing Frau Weir to return before nightfall. It was a simple journey back, but it was long as the omnibus was eternally slow and lumbering. At seven, the unmistakable figure of the housekeeper finally appeared, tired but determined. She looked hot, perhaps a little unsettled, but she was here and no one had followed her. Once inside, Frau Weir confirmed the letter was now in place, just above the little alcove behind the opening under the staircase. A person would have to be directly underneath and looking up in order to see it. It was unlikely to be disturbed, even if another couple discovered the attraction of a discreet hiding place.

The next stage of the plan was the hardest part – to wait. But for how long and to what end was unknown. It was to be a vigil, a prayer for the return of a good man to his loving home. It seemed an odd part of a plan to sit and wait, but with the Gestapo watching and the long reach of Kurt, it seemed the only safe thing to do.

CHAPTER TWENTY-TWO
Dusseldorf August 1939

For seven weeks, Liesel kept a vigil at the window, just out of plain sight from passing cars. Each time a figure she did not recognise appeared, her hopes would rise, and each time they would be dashed as the shadow passed without looking up or into the house. The tension became unbearable. Perversely, the daily visit from the black car became a comfort. They did not have Karl, so there was still hope.

But as each day passed and each night came around, brief though the hours of darkness were, dreams of harm to Karl would flood into Liesel's imagination. The children, ever loving, were now clearly frightened. They sensed the fear, the alarm and the dread of the unsaid words. It was Franz who could not bear it any longer. It was early, but light was coming in through the gaps in the blackout curtains. His footsteps came into Liesel's senses. The moving of the blanket and the coldness of Franz's feet on hers. He shook her awake, wanting to know about his father.

'Mother, I was dreaming of Father. Is he dead?'

The bluntness of his young voice chilled Liesel and roused her to alertness immediately.

'My darling, of course he is not dead. He isn't here because he has to work away for a time. I have told you this.'

Franz looked doubtful. Liesel saw this and drew him to her. He wrapped his arms around her and drifted slowly back to sleep, trembling gently.

'Darling little Franz, he is quite well, you will see. Now sleep, my little man.'

She kissed his head and drew up the blanket around him, more for comfort than for warmth for the morning was going to be warm again. At least the weather would be pleasant if Karl was out of doors or needed to move and hide. Liesel tried to sense him, but it was an empty effort. Franz turned over and over, restless. He put his head up again, turning to Liesel, who was awake but with her eyes closed.

'Will I ever see Father again? If I can't see him, please tell me.'

Liesel sat up. His feelings had not been calmed by her first words. She would have to explore the truth with her son and trust his curiosity not to fill the gaps with despair.

'Your father left because some bad men wanted to take him away. They will not hurt us or your sister. But they want to speak with your father. I know you will ask what he has done. But he is not a bad man. Your father heals the sick and cares for those who have nothing. We must take our turn to look after him now. He will return but I cannot say when.'

Franz seemed comforted and yet his face, the very face of his father, belied his fear.

'But, Mother, why do the bad men want him?'

Liesel took a deep breath. He was old enough to know some of the truth.

'It is because they think he is a Jew.'

Franz's face lit up at the name.

'I have heard this name at school. Is Father one of the greedy men who hate Germany?'

Liesel swallowed hard. She hoped that the twisted words of his fascist schoolmates could be undone with sympathy for his own father.

'That is not what the Jews are. Frau Rosemann loved you, didn't she? You thought her kind and caring. They think your father is like Frau Rosemann.'

Liesel could already hear her own words separating and dividing her own neighbours, feeling little better than the Race Administration. She wanted to move on with Franz away from this terrible subject.

'I don't like Jews!'

The bluntness in Franz's words, the product of an education that Liesel thought they had cancelled just in time, shocked her.

'That is not kind, Franz. Your father is not a Jew. It would not matter if he were. We do not know anything about the religion and the bad men are only using this lie to upset your father and make him do as they wish.'

Franz seemed satisfied with this. 'Will they kill him, Mother? They kill Jews, don't they?'

'They won't kill him because they know your father is a good man. Your father is a loving man, Franz. Now if you cannot sleep, then go and wash and dress for the day. We can go outside and read in the garden.'

Liesel saw Franz step across the bedroom. Every muscle on him was the essence of his father, every move of his arms was Karl in miniature. Would the Nazis seek to set son against father? She already knew the answer.

--oOo--

Sleep did not come easily to Liesel in August. The nights were warm and she could feel the symptoms of her illness returning. Whether it was the lasting effects of the scarlet fever, or grief at the presumed death of her husband, she did not know. The professor diagnosed extreme fatigue brought on by lack of sleep, and the hours at the window scanning the streets did not help her recovery. The joyful hours of time with her children had changed into minutes in which she felt the need to tell them constantly that their father would soon be home and not to worry about him. The need to reassure them was for her own comfort and solace, for her words only seemed to make them more anxious.

What was worse for Liesel was her financial dependence on her father. The city in the shape of the Gauleiter had frozen and confiscated all the money that Karl had invested, declaring his shares void and worthless in companies owned by Germans. The money he had on deposit was simply embezzled by the Gauleiter, the letter of confiscation noting the money as reparation for damages and charges to investigate Karl's disappearance. Liesel was a true-blood German, set apart from any investigation, but it made little difference if her husband's finances were tied. Her resentment and anger were barely contained – it was unfair and contrary to law, but what did it matter? Who would come to her aid? The income from her father was all that she could access for the household. It was both absurd and tragic, and Liesel became all the more despondent because of it.

August was glorious. The weather was hot and dry and the garden looked beautiful, now tended by her father's old gardener who was happy to earn an extra bit of income. But Liesel could get no joy or pleasure from the scents and the glory of the blooms. She no longer felt able to speak with the old man who used to show her how to pluck a rose without pricking her skin, or to open a carnation for her hair. He would not stay to talk, never wanted refreshment and would never step indoors. Liesel liked to believe it was more from a sense of propriety than of reluctance because of the Jewish issue. She knew she was only fooling herself.

But Liesel did notice that some things had changed during August. Apart from the daily routine with the black car, which no longer appeared every day, the Race Administration Office had stopped writing so frequently. Had their interest in Karl faded? Had they taken him captive?

As their interest seemed to diminish, so did her hopes for his salvation. He had been missing from home for nearly nine months. She had expected some word, some sign of his well-being, but there was no word, not even through Herr Professor, who was clearly to be trusted. It was almost certain that something had happened, or was happening now. Frau Weir had been again to the Kaiserswerth, this time only to calm Liesel and to settle the matter in her head. The letter was untouched so Liesel had nowhere else to turn. If the Gestapo had not found him, what chance had a virtually housebound woman with two children to care for? A woman who spent her days in a front-room vigil at home, no longer with the luxury of friends. She lived in a world of suspicion, driven by fear all around and always under the careful, meticulous watch of the SS, urged on most decidedly by her despicable brother.

--oOo--

Karl dared not move, this time it was not just in fear of discovery by the Gestapo. The dry little cellar was a perfect hideaway and he did not want to give it up lightly. It had once been the storage room for Herr Kohler and his jewellery business before he had been taken to a camp. But now the musty rooms were scattered with the empty boxes that he had once used to present little antique brooches, beautiful German pieces for the gentle ladies of Dusseldorf. A Dusseldorf not split along lines of politics, race or fear.

There had been a sudden stamping of feet in the street above, the voices excited and insistent, the stories were already all over the city. Something strange was happening and Karl was afraid that it was against the Jews and that someone might now come directly for him. Perhaps some informant had seen Karl descend, or perhaps someone was looking for easy money by raiding the jeweller's cellar. Perhaps it was Dusseldorf itself, one more clearing of its collective throat, a voice of hate and fear, now expelling Jews and protected Jews alike. Really, what was the difference? Although Karl was neither, he was labelled as both. He resolved to find out what was going on for he needed to know what was happening to the enemy who sought him and now hunted him to death.

Voices were shouting about Poland, something about deliverance, that Hitler had been right after all. The voices agreed that the Germans needed more room to live and land to farm. It wasn't the Jews this time, at least not only the Jews. Maybe for once, he might be able to move in the open unnoticed. No one was looking for an old man with a grey beard. The news about Poland seemed to be the cause of great joy. Karl thought about the Poles and wondered whether he might also be on the street rejoicing were he not in this situation. To his shame, he could not find the answer. Now, he only thought of those poor people being chased down the streets, hunted for slaughter to appease the same evil men who also hunted him. In his primeval state, he was a little glad that they were hunting the Polish people and not coming for him.

He wanted to be home more than anything but danger was all around and as his strength and energy failed, he feared that inattention and clumsiness would hasten his capture and death, perhaps within sight of his beloved family. He missed his wife's embrace. A little thing perhaps, but a warm human touch was everything a soul needed to revive. His children's smiles, their laughter and play were food for his very being, denied from him by an invisible force that could strike him down at any moment.

After hearing the voices, he was now certain that Kurt was not watching the house himself for he would want to be at the centre of whatever horror was happening in Poland. So he grasped his courage and climbed the little stone steps up to the street. As he climbed from the cellar, his limbs sore and stiff, he had to concentrate on each step to make sure he did not stumble or fall. The top step was a large stone, which was grooved from all the feet descending into the little jewellers. He looked down to make sure he was sure of the height and then he lifted his head, straight into the eyes of a Gestapo officer. Instantly he froze, a reflex that he cursed himself for, terrified and unable to move. The officer peered towards him, regarding his face for a second longer than was comfortable to Karl.

'Sorry, old man, I did not mean to startle you. It is good news for the Fatherland today, eh? The Führer has delivered us.'

The officer gave a smart salute and moved away.

'Heil Hitler.' Karl remembered and croaked the words, his parched mouth could do or say little more. The officer had already moved away, without so much as a suspicious glance. This disguise, unintended and unrehearsed, was working. He looked nothing like the confident doctor he had been. But as he stepped into the sunshine, his arm was tugged, spinning him around towards the Gestapo man.

'Can I offer you a ride to the square? The cathedral looks so beautiful today.'

'Thank you, that is very kind, sir, but no. I need to walk to exercise my old bones.'

'It is the smallest thing, I insist. Here, the car is just here. Let us get in and we can take an old man to the celebrations.'

Karl now thought this to be a ruse. He thought he had been recognised and that this was a way to arrest him without any fuss. He had to get away quickly.

'A very kind thought, but if I do not exercise my legs, then they will fail me. Very kind, sir, but it is such a beautiful day. How many more of these may I have left?'

The Gestapo man, now joined by one of his companions seemed satisfied at that.

'Ha, very well, old man. Enjoy the walk.'

Karl saw the black car come around the corner and panic now rose in his body. Every fibre was telling him to run and so he had to close his eyes to the sight for a second to help his fear subside. It was identical to the car that passed his house every day, nearer to noon now than eleven. Karl had worked out why the timings had changed. The car now left the offices of the Gestapo at eleven, stopping to note the new occupants of the old Jewish shops in Landstrasse. Their smashed windows had been repaired, the burn marks around the doors and frames had been painted, and the red-lettered words of fear and hate had been washed away. Aryan families were now hard at work on a new, Jew-free beginning for the street. The car came later each day, as the Race Administration Office and its unsympathetic staff worked hard to process the ever-widening stream of small faces, gaunt and sick, tired and terrified. Karl would soon be one of them, married to Liesel or not.

He wondered at the Gestapo's words, at what might be happening in the square, curious to know whether this new development in politics might ease the keen Gestapo and SS interest in him, and even free his family from the threat of arrest or worse. But all he saw were his fellow Germans now set free from the bonds and rules of society, open and united in their hatred of the Jews, of the sick, of the unseen and unwanted underclass who would only hold back the great progress of their Fatherland. In front was the white and bright flesh of the Guild of Maidens who were marching in formation through the square to cheers and applause from men and women alike. There were younger boys, perhaps thirteen years of age, in neat brown uniforms marching behind the women, smiles wide, carrying identical flags, each with the terrible mark of the swastika, blood-red and angry, leaping to bite Karl.

Doctor Eisner certainly would not have stomached this torment and Karl now knew that he and his wife would walk away from this ugly, ignorant, mob-ridden parallel existence. He no more recognised his city with these eyes than he would have done with his old ones. He had perhaps now resolved to leave Germany, with or without his family. His conscience was troubled, the bonds of trust with his homeland weakened irreparably.

He walked the square confused, troubled, and uncertain of what he should now do. The remorseless weeks of destitution, desperation and fear had broken his mind. He could still understand the signs, recognising the little changes that came upon him. More than ever, he needed the healing of his family but he was further from them than he had ever been. Would his return bring their destruction? Were they resolved to live without him? Had they made a pact with each other never to mention his name? Was his memory too painful to recollect? He had tried the other path and it was bitter and cold, empty and lonely. Now he would risk his home and his family. In his mind it would be safe today with all eyes on Poland, he would seek solace in the arms of his bride and the comfort of the children he adored. The streets were full of cheering crowds, knowing that something was going to happen, or had already happened. He could hide in plain view of the wolves.

But then he heard the news for himself. Another war had begun. There was suddenly a frantic race in the streets towards the old news dispatcher who was reading from the morning newspapers that had just arrived by train from Berlin. The radios in the city carried very little new information, but it seemed that German Army forces had moved eastwards and across the German border and into Poland. Relentlessly, the machine ground down the weak. Foreigners were arrested for questioning, the physically weak and any remaining Jews were captured and moved quickly from sight, their children running to keep up. Undesirables viewed with contempt and suspicion were eagerly collected, taken to holding cells and then to trains transporting them away from Dusseldorf. Today was a day for German rejoicing. Today was the start of a new Germany and no one was going to prevent pride in the Führer's achievements.

--oOo--

Liesel had little interest in what was going on today. She was still very tired and drawn and the children were being difficult and excitable, seeing what was happening outside. In her weakened state, Liesel barely noticed their presence, in fact noticed very little and had no incentive to take an interest in anything. She wanted to grieve, needed to feel loss and accommodate her feelings but her husband was in a place she could neither find nor leave. There was no certainty that he was dead, but no words or dreams could make her believe, not without a body to touch and mourn. This twilight of pain was far worse.

The evening was light, a new September evening fitting for the celebrations in the city. German citizens were gathering to sing and rejoice. This was to be the final act of ascension for Germany and the end of the evils of Versailles. The deliverance by their beloved Führer and hope for a Germany fit for the ancient kings. The streets emptied slowly, the wave of people moving to the squares and cafes on into the night. Occupied in their own world of ignorant bliss, filled with songs and stories, with not a thought for Polish people running and falling, nor for the death sweeping from the west with screaming bombs from above.

Karl hoped nobody noticed the shambling old man. The down-and-out in torn, stinking clothes, his beard reaching down almost to his collar, who waved in celebration as he passed the cafes. He was clearly one of them, a little unusual, but still a German in the celebrations for German people. He stepped slowly and turned into Landstrasse, his feet finding the shape of the stones, a familiar comforting shape. The house, the windows, the children, the love.

He pulled gently on the bell. The dull clank, so familiar and safe. The sound of the opening door, the solid and safe sound of home. The small feet of the housekeeper. He strained to look up into Frau Weir's eyes. He saw her cup her hands to her mouth and lean towards him, her face turning instantly to pity for the poor old stooped man. He could barely manage the words, he was choked and terrified, but he could take the separation no longer.

'Mein Gott, Mein Gott! Frau Eisner, Frau Eisner, come to the door now, you must come quickly, please! Come now!'

'What is it, what is the problem?'

Liesel looked down at the man, his hands dirty and bruised and his face sunken and sick.

'Oh, it cannot be! It cannot be. My darling? My Karl?' Liesel fell on her husband. She held him, foul or not. 'I can scarcely believe it. My darling, my husband.'

'Frau Eisner. Sorry, *Doctor* and Frau Eisner, we must get you off the street. It is not safe to be seen like this, even today.'

'Of course. You are right. Come in, come in. I will quickly close the door.'

'Oh my love, my love. Where have you been? Where did you live? We have been lost without you.'

'Frau Eisner, for now we must wash the doctor and put him to bed. He needs rest. Then some food. We can ask him these questions later. He is here, safe. I should watch the windows.'

--oOo--

Liesel saw the marks on her husband's body. Bruises littered his back and legs, his chest and his groin. He had lost a tooth, possibly two, his hair was infested and almost white. He was only forty years of age and yet he looked twice that. Hollows in his eyes and wrinkles in his skin, and yet, it might still have been worse.

She did not tell the children immediately, but they seemed to sense her change of mood. It would be good for them to have a loving mother return to them, for they also needed reassurance. That night, Liesel slept in the former guest room, not daring to disturb her husband, but she wanted to lie with him, warm and healing. The nurse inside her felt the conflict and yet she did not dare to hurt his weakened body further. But the lengthening night could not pass quickly enough. She wanted to see him desperately so he could speak to her, like he used to, with a tenderness and love hard won from the ashes of the First War.

The morning came early for Liesel. She had heard Karl cry out in the darkness. Clearly, he did not know where he was and he was afraid. He had a fever now and was delirious on top of everything else. There was nothing Liesel could do but call Herr Professor if Karl was not to die in front of her just at the point of salvation. She knew Herr Professor and trusted him for he had been deliberately indiscreet on more than one occasion. When she telephoned him with the news and her fears, the professor's answer was immediate.

The professor arrived in his own car and had no one with him this time. He was alone and unobserved, a city doctor out early visiting a patient. It was normal, predictable, expected. He tapped the glass three times and then did it again. There was no doubt who it was.

'Frau Langer. It is joyous news? He is alive and delivered to you? Let me see if I can make him well.'

'Thank you, Herr Professor. I am so grateful for his deliverance to us but I am afraid for him, please come and see him for yourself.'

'Well, let us see.'

They quickly stepped into the bedroom, Karl was on his back with rivers of sweat streaming from his body.

'I can see the fever, but he has no signs of pox or scarlet fever. What did he eat last night?'

'He has had nothing. We bathed him and he was immediately asleep. Almost in a delirium from the time he appeared.'

'Hm. It may simply be that he has eaten something disagreeable that might pass. He suffers because he is already weak. Now, I have a little something in here. He is not going to like it, but it will do him good. It might make his skin a little grey or yellow, but it is worth a try.'

'Professor, I must ask, apart from the food, is he strong enough to live?'

'Yes, Frau Eisner. But perhaps only long enough to be arrested, hm? What will you do to keep him from the grasping hands of those devils?'

'I have not altogether thought of that.'

'Well you must and quickly. They are ruthless. You may not think it, but they most certainly already have thought it and planned for it. Whatever evil you can think up, whatever torture or twist of truth you can imagine, they have already thought it and tried it to the point of perfection.'

Liesel looked at the professor with tears in her eyes. 'But surely now we have him back, there is a chance?'

'Mark me, Frau Eisner, it is no blessing that he is home. It is only a stay of execution. Good night and God bless, my dear. Call me anytime you need me. I am as assured a companion to you both as can be.'

The professor picked up his hat and looked around to see that he had not left anything behind.

'If you wish proof, I will tell you this. In the cellar of my house, you will find Herr Gerbowitz and his wife. He is a fine apothecarist. I will have him prepare the medicine for your husband and have it sent here. I will not bring it myself, since too many visits would be suspicious. But medicine following a doctor, well that is quite normal.'

Professor Scheckter patted Liesel on the shoulder and left, placing his hat on his head and keeping his face towards the floor. Karl was upstairs, still delirious, angrily calling out for the men surrounding him to leave him alone.

'I have no money... I am not fleeing. Hungry... I am hungry... looking to find something to eat.'

Liesel looked at him, then bathed him with a cold cloth. She carefully lay beside him on their bed, kissing his head gently, enjoying the feel of his skin, wet and salty on her lips. She fell asleep and woke to find the room full of the animations of her children, delighted to see their darling father returned. Karl did not wake but Liesel was certain that when Monika touched his hand, he squeezed her slender fingers and a smile came over his face.

CHAPTER TWENTY-THREE
Bazentin-Le-Petit November 1939

William sat reading the newspaper in silence. Although he had now mastered reading at full speed in French, the words he read disturbed him deeply and he would rather have had one more day of ignorance. He had seen enough of this before and now it was to come around again. The radio offered no comfort, only fear where courage had failed. The German giant slept no more. The years of secret arming, pacts and coalitions, putsch and counter-attack were now reported freely and openly. The Nazi machine had moved into gear and rampaged east. Blessed relief, William thought, that it moved east for now. Today, France was not threatened. But the French were no fools and knew it was only a matter of time before the peace between them evaporated. There would be a new battle for France, no one knew when exactly, but the grey uniforms would certainly sweep the fields of Picardie again. William was certain that he could not stomach the sight again. War would be different all these years later, but death would surely follow, riding a black charger over the countryside, taking the souls of the damned. There would be many to take.

William had read enough for one morning and joined Odile, who was holding a letter that had just arrived from England with Armandine's beautiful handwriting. Armandine had just turned nineteen and was in the good habit of writing regularly to her parents. For now, her letters were still arriving in France but perhaps the time might soon come when this would change.

Dear Papa et Maman,

I write to you again! I am sorry that it has been so long, but I have been working at two very small schools, which has occupied every moment of the day and evening, but I have now secured a teaching position at a delightful school in London where the very small girls now learn French! I could not ask for a more wonderful position. I teach for three hours every day and in the late afternoons we hold games and classes for handwriting. The war does not seem to have changed very much for us yet. Everyone here thinks that there will have to be battles, but the children are not asking us questions yet. Grandma and Grandpa Collins are so wonderful to me. They have given us both the most wonderful kindness of a home and enough love to last a lifetime!

Arthur says that you are not to worry, but he has decided to change his studies. He will write to you himself, but the Dean has encouraged him to make the changes so I suppose that it will be well for him. He seems happy enough, but of course, he never has been one for keeping us all up to date, my dearest solitary twin brother. I will try to visit him next month, perhaps as term ends for Christmas. I think Christmas might be quite dreary this year if this war begins to change us all.

I am so pleased to have come here, it is simply the best thing I have done to help me to become a teacher. It is quite funny really, speaking English and French so easily. I find myself using both even in the same sentence, especially when I talk with Arthur. It can cause quite a bit of laughter and also keeps our conversations secret, ha!

I have also found an admirer. He works in a legal firm in London. I think he is a partner actually, but I am not yet so sure of anything, I am so busy and happy. I will write again at Christmas.

All love

Armandine.

'William, she writes an enormous letter, full of lovely news and then at the very end, the *last words*, she tells us she is in love. What do you think of that?'

'I think she most certainly is in love, Odile, what else is there to say? If she is her mother's daughter, she will make a very good choice of husband and she will be a wonderful wife. My mother is watching over her, you will see.'

'Of course, I know it was the right thing to do to let them go to England, but both of them at almost the same time, was it wise?'

'They are twins, Odile. There is something in them both that joins them, an invisible thread that draws them together, a world we do not understand. They live knowing all about the other, without living in one another's pockets. She will know if Arthur needs her and Arthur likewise. Besides, they are better there than here. Have you read the papers?'

'I have not read them, but I have seen the headline. Let me have a look now that I know Armandine's news.'

William went to make tea, which he did often, enjoying making tea in France. They had some leaves left over from England, but William noticed with disappointment that their supply would not last. Armandine had her head so full of teaching and love that she might not remember to send a parcel. It was already pointless to ask anything of Arthur. His head was already full of, well, who knew what it now might be. He looked in the tea jar, only a few spoonfuls left.

'Blast it, no tea!'

But suddenly he dropped the pot, which smashed into tiny fragments on the wide stone flags. He sank quickly into his large armchair in the kitchen. Odile stood, took a deep breath and followed him into the kitchen.

'Oh, William, are you hurt?'

'Tea, Odile. I remembered the tea on the road to Montauban. I had come back from the lines and a corporal tried to move me on, thinking me a private.'

Instinctively, he placed his hand on his neck and rubbed where his uniform collars had chafed over twenty years ago.

'Watkins was dead, I wanted to go back to fight. General Cowling came to me and only with reluctance let me go on to Longueval with the Scots. That was the time I was knocked unconscious and Walter found me. Dear Walter, I wish I could write to him, but my hand never seems to make the page. I wonder if he is one of… well… one of the Nazis. I pray he is not. I trust in whatever demons are left to us that he sees clearly and is not afraid. I am sorry, I must stop doing this. Here, let me clear the floor.'

'Was it the papers? Was it the story that made you think?'

'Perhaps, but I am also very tired. Looks like no tea for me either.'

William eased himself up from the chair and looked down at the shattered remains of his favourite china teapot. Odile stroked his back as he spoke, which calmed him although he felt conscious again of the deep grooves of his wartime scars, the wounds from the trenches. His side, deeply scored from shells and bayonets and bullets. His knee, which Odile would ease with warm towels. They remained in silence for a moment before William got up to pick up the tiny pieces.

'I have made a right bloody mess of my favourite teapot. It was full of tea leaves as well, bugger! Perhaps I can fish them out.'

'William!'

'Well perhaps not then. Odile, I wonder if you would like to take a walk with me to see the crucifix at Bazentin-Le-Grand?'

'My darling, if you want to visit the cemetery, you should just say so.'

'Will you walk with me, to Flatiron Copse?'

Odile smiled and took her husband's arm. They stepped into the cool sunshine and walked down the hill, the short distance to the Contalmaison Road. As they passed the spot where Watkins was killed, William stiffened as he always did and Odile squeezed his hand more tightly, which kept him calm. The cross was upright and the grass beautifully tended, so William continued down the hill, easing back to his normal self.

'William, do you think we should go to live in England? Do you think perhaps the ghosts of this place, of that time, are too much for us to bear?'

'No Odile, they are as a companion to me, a comfort if you will. These were my men, well our men. I am in a place surrounded by eighty-thousand silent brothers. There are not many men who can say that of their home. This place is as much home as anywhere else could be. It is a comfort.'

He smiled at her.

'But I could do without the reminders when I do not expect it, they are the problem to me. To say nothing of wasting my tea leaves.'

Odile smiled back, squeezing her husband's arm again. He placed his hand on hers, she was a wonderful comfort to him.

'Well I suppose they would be with you, wherever you were, in France or England.'

'Yes, so I perhaps ought to be here, where you are happiest and where I know is home. Where I can look after them and honour them, I suppose. Our twins, born here are thriving and helping others. We have a business here and Henri will do very well from it, I am sure. He is a fool of a boy, but he is fearless and lucky. Horace would have seen what I see in him. A clever, resourceful, lucky survivor. He has his parents in him and a slice of his grandparents as well.'

'Yes, but I wonder what the future holds for him? I am worried, William, I am most truly worried for France.'

'Yes, this is a fine conversation, but there are other considerations. All this talk of staying and living here and being normal. It is probably just that, idle talk. Events in Poland and England might change all of that for us.'

William stopped and hesitated for a second. 'Can we speak in English for a moment? I want to get this right.'

Odile nodded. 'Yes, although I do not want to have this conversation, I had been hoping the worst for France would quickly pass.'

'Well, that is why I wanted you to come with me. Fresh air for me, to shake off the memories, but also to talk more seriously of the future. I do not want to live elsewhere, I do not want to leave France, but fear we may simply have to, but perhaps only for a short time. If the Germans do come again – which seems more likely as each day passes – I will most certainly be separated from you. The Germans will be suspicious and probably arrest me. Also, I am still of working age and English to boot, and it stands to reason that the British will fight for France or Belgium like they have done for Poland in a way. I think we are in more danger than we can possibly imagine.'

He watched his wife as she looked across the sweep of the road, down to the little square ditch in the ground that had once been a deep German trench.

'William, I cannot go. I endured the awful camps to be here. I fought, if that is the word, to return to this little village. To go would tear me apart, for I feared I would never return. The trenches were here, the ground was soaked in our blood and yet we are here still. Surely such a war could not return here again to be fought over this ground? France cannot resist the Germans. They would be here and we could not stop them. You mentioned the defence line along the border, would that help us?'

'The Maginot Line?' William shrugged and thought for a moment. 'If I were the Germans, I'd drive around it. They could be here in ten days if they used motor lorries and cars. There would not be battles here, at least not with guns and bullets, but France would become German, of that there can be no doubt.'

'Then what is the point? Let us stay, whatever happens. But perhaps you might need to hide if the Germans come. We can hide you William. Please don't leave.'

'Let us hope it will not come to that.'

'William, you see these things clearly as both a soldier and a civilian. Perhaps you could go to England as a civilian, out of the war? I simply cannot think. Perhaps you should make a telephone call to the Engineers?'

William looked deeply into her beautiful damp eyes, kissed her forehead tenderly and stepped back from her.

'If I made a call, it would not be to the Engineers.'

Odile's face dropped. 'Once again the Germans might part us, then?'

William then smiled gently and looked up, delicately lifting her chin with his hand.

'But I do have an idea.'

--o0o--

Henri returned home from his errands. He had spent the whole morning dreaming of the future and his mind was full of Yvette. All he could see was her hair, her bright smiling face. And of course he imagined the rest of her, smiling to himself before he almost ran off of the road in thought. He was now nearly eighteen and he had finally decided to ask Yvette to marry him.

She was twenty-one and he felt sure that what they shared was love. He felt it and he was sure of her feelings for him. Now he wanted to earn Alain's trust and consent. The nights when he brought his niece home late were never filled with anger, just a shake of the head and a warning that next time it would be different. But it never was. Perhaps Alain knew where the couple were heading and was deeply grateful that it would be to Henri that Yvette would turn for love. But Henri was unsure of his father's reaction. He would find the right moment. It just had not happened yet. As he turned to ride up the hill, he saw his mother and father walking, which was unexpected since his father was due to deliver a little machine to a workshop in Albert.

'Papa? We shall be late.'

'Oh Henri, I quite forgot. My darling, I will see you in two hours. We have a little delivery to make.'

While Henri started the engine, William took his wife by her hands, then he turned away and joined his son. Odile waved the car out of sight.

'Farewell, my lovely gentlemen. Do not get into any more trouble!'

--oOo--

Odile went to the kitchen to read the newspaper more thoroughly in the temporary silence of the house. First, she leaned down to pick up some of the remaining broken teapot that had fallen out of William's sight. It was sharp and she cut her finger. Spots of bright red blood fell upon the photograph of a swastika on the cover of the newspaper. It soaked into the paper, smudging the image of Adolf Hitler.

'Curse you, you demon! Have you learned nothing? Damn you for doing this to us again.'

She pushed away the newspaper and it fell to the floor. On top of the spots of blood fell the clear salty tears of a frightened French survivor. Odile knew what was to come. She had tried to act normally, but knew she was not convincing. They had suffered so much at the hands of the Germans and now they were coming again. How a man who had fought in the trenches could allow this to happen was quite beyond her. Her tears flowed for her husband and her children. In her own home, she felt again the insecurity of war. As if the tree roots were loose, blowing in an unseen wind. She drifted into a haunted sleep, still leaning on the kitchen table. In the distance she heard the unmistakable sound of the family car. A luxury or necessity, she never really knew which. Henri was driving as he often did. It was probably too fast as well. In her dream, they were floating, safe above the clouds.

--oOo--

Father and son had returned home much later than planned. Henri had plucked up the courage to ask his father on the journey home. He was terrified of his father's response, not because he was frightened of him, but because his father would speak sense, encouraging him to wait. But he did not want to wait and hoped for a word of encouragement because he wanted to marry his beautiful fireball sooner rather than later.

'Henri, I cannot imagine a more perfect union. You, the clever fool thinking himself fireproof and the shooting star, blazing across the Pozieres Ridge. It sounds delightful. You'll need luck and if there is one person who is lucky, it is you Henri Collins, it's you for certain. You don't need my blessing, you know your mother and I adore Yvette and her Uncle. I only wish that her father had lived to see this. He might have turned you down, boxing your ears for thinking of such a thing. But, my son, I cannot imagine that Alain will, ha! Look. Let us go and perhaps see if you can take a drink.'

'Thank you, Papa. I love her and nothing will keep us apart. There is no wind devised by man or nature that can extinguish the flame. Does that sound poetic?'

'Sounds terrible, don't write it down or the page might catch fire and a bloody good job it will be as well! Longueval, Driver, and be quick about it.'

Henri was still smiling when he closed the car doors, noting that the hinge needed oil.

--oOo--

At the Tabac, William made a ceremony of letting Henri buy him a drink. Alain would be along in a few minutes to join the impromptu celebration, a little happiness in a gathering storm. The Tabac held a little whisky for William, as well as cognac for such occasions. Tonight it would be cognac. The little tumblers were filled and William could feel a change inside. He was a father but now was about to let a fledgling go and find his own wings. He wondered what Odile would think and feel, but perhaps she already knew. He smiled at his son and lifted the glass to his lips.

'Henri, a little one before Alain gets here just to settle the nerves, eh?'

'You said Alain would not refuse me?'

'Well, you still have to ask. You wait. You have talked with him as an uncle for years, but this will be something quite different. Take a drink, my boy, and savour it. I promise that you will remember tonight for all of your life.'

Henri put the tumbler to his lips and William smiled as he winced at the fiery liquid. Alain had just come through the door and found them. Henri stood and shook Alain's hands. For nearly an hour, the conversation was all about farming, the countryside and the situation in Germany – anything but Henri and Yvette. William knew that Alain was teasing Henri and enjoying himself. It was good to see his friend happy. But Henri was red and hot, perhaps the cognac was a little too much for him to handle. William watched his son gathering his courage.

'Uncle Alain, I was hoping that you might allow me to ask Yvette to marry me.'

Alain flashed a glance to William, who looked away quickly to ensure Henri did not see his wide grin.

'Marry Yvette, Henri?'

William's smile grew wider. Alain was not a very good actor and his true feelings were quite obvious.

'Henri, of course you may ask Yvette. I would be honoured for you to marry my niece, if she says yes of course.'

Alain smiled and winked at Henri. At that, Henri took a long look at his tumbler and drained his glass. Alain pulled out three small cigars that he had brought with him. Henri looked suspiciously at his father, but William simply shrugged. Alain passed one to Henri and the second to William. None of them really smoked but this was a very special occasion. Alain took out his brother's old army waterproof lighter and lit his own cigar. He offered the flame to William who lit his cigar whilst leaning over the table. Before William could react, Alain had swept the flame to Henri, who took the lighter into his own hands. William saw the flame and his heart sank in an instant. The flame marking the target for the sniper's bullet. For a moment he wanted to shout out, sweeping the cigar from his son's lips. But he told himself that it was only superstition and he did not want to mar his son's joy, so he forced himself to forget it.

--oOo--

As Henri stepped through the door, he could see the newspaper on the floor, a little dark purple stain on the page. His mother had fallen asleep on the table, her head leaning on her hands. The door was open, and she would awaken cold and stiff. At first, Henri thought she was bleeding, but then he saw the little cotton bandage on his mother's finger. It was nothing.

'Maman, we are back, your lovely gentlemen are home.'

'Odile, my love?'

Henri watched his mother's nose wrinkle as her eyes slowly opened.

'William, you have been drinking. And smoking!'

'Yes, well Henri? Rescue me from your mother – quickly now!'

'Maman. I have some news.'

Odile sat up, looking wide awake now. 'That is wonderful Henri. It is about time you made an honest woman of Yvette.'

'Maman, how could you know?'

Odile stretched and smiled at her slightly dishevelled son.

'Henri, I have been your Maman for all of your life…'

--o0o--

William helped his wife to bed for she was very stiff from the draught coming in through the open door. William got into bed to warm Odile's cold back. She fell asleep again almost immediately, most likely because of all this worry for the future. The newspapers had predicted another war through France. It had not happened yet, but it was coming. There could really be no doubt now. The politicians were no longer talking. They were posturing with each other, facing away to their own people and not towards the enemy. It was a recipe for another terrible catastrophe. A tragedy unfolding slowly on what was the Western Front.

In the morning, William heard the door open downstairs. The little creak was always a sign William could detect. It opened slowly. Henri had answered the door to the postmaster from Longueval. Not the post boy, but Monsieur Orlan himself. This was unusual, but William knew already it was going to be bad news. He got out of bed and went straight downstairs.

'Monsieur Collins. I am sorry to disturb you but we have received a telegram for you from London. It is, as you know, impossible for such information to remain a confidence as we have to place the message for you. Do you understand, sir? So I have brought it myself. Sorry, I know it is important. Only two of us have seen it.'

'Monsieur Orlan, as you say, it is a telegram. It is in French, sir, so the sender knows full well it will be read. It is quite in order to read it. Please, won't you come in?'

'Thank you sir, I will. It is very cold this morning.'

William's mind was as fog on a cold morning. With a telegram so early in the hands of the puffing postmaster, he needed to think clearly, but he could not. He made some coffee, disappointed that tea would be impossible to prepare. Then he opened the single sheet and noted how large it actually was. The first words confirmed his worst fears.

COLWCOLLINS+SIT DEVT IN BRITN NEED FR LIAISON SOONEST STOP REQ KINDEST AGMNT TO LOC TO LDN TEMP IN FST INST STOP WILL TELEP 180039NOV22 ADVISE BY RPLY CONTACT AND AFFRM –SBSB 2111/39 MAYFAIR 72 BEST R/ADM HAWKER

'Monsieur, is the news grave?'

'Perhaps. May I trouble you about a little matter tomorrow evening?'

'Certainly, Monsieur. The telegraph office is at your disposal.'

'Thank you. Would you be kind enough to send this telegram and if you could add your office telephone number at the end.'

William scribbled a note on the reverse of his telegram.

'Please destroy the note when you have sent it. Will you do that?'

'Of course, Monsieur. The postmaster's office is in confidence. That is why I am here and not my boy.'

'Yes, I understand. Thank you. Please charge the message to the sender of this note.'

'William? What is it? What is happening?'

He looked up, hearing the voice of his wife.

'Will you excuse me, Monsieur Orlan, I must talk to my wife?'

'Certainly, goodbye. I will see you in the office tomorrow. Kind wishes to Madame Collins.'

The postmaster tapped his cap to William, patted Henri on the shoulder and stepped out into the street. It was now raining and the wind was picking up the rain and lashing it against the window.

'Perhaps, Henri, you might use that motorcycle of yours to deliver some of my telegrams! The cold does make my legs ache and Philippe's legs are too short, ha!'

Henri smiled and closed the door. A biting draught blew through the bottom. William now knew it was bringing a war.

'What was the message, William? It was a telegram?'

'Yes. Monsieur Orlan delivered it personally.'

'He did? Our twins?'

'Oh no, sorry. No, nothing to do with them. Everything to do with Germany and their aggression. Our fears are confirmed. I think London is worried that France is next.'

'You cannot be in the army, William! Your wounds! And you are too old.'

'For fighting, yes, but there is something that they want of me. I am not sure that there is much I can offer them but they want to talk to me tomorrow on the telephone in Longueval.'

Odile put her hand to her mouth.

'But you cannot be involved in any operations. You are forty-three! You were so young in the Great War and you must be too wounded to fight. What do they want of you?'

'I can speak French, I know France and the French way of doing things. Perhaps they see that as being important. The telegram addressed me as Colonel and was signed by an Admiral so I know it is a military need that I am to serve. We shall see.'

He fetched two cups of strong coffee. Odile was in no mood for it so William drank hers as well. Army habits die hard. He looked at his wife, who turned slowly towards the window.

'Will you have to leave France, William?'

'Probably not permanently, but they do want me to go to London for a little while. Possibly quite soon as well.'

Odile looked at William, her eyes misting as tears formed in little pools.

'That is decided then, they want you back and you are going?'

'Wait, Odile. It is not like that. Besides, what choice do I have?'

'But what about Henri? What about our home? What about me? What shall we do?'

'But yesterday we talked of this being a possibility, did we not?'

Odile was silent. William saw his wife distressed. A lot had changed since their walk yesterday.

'I don't know, I will just have to say no to London.'

Odile reached out to him.

'I am sorry, William. We have both tried to deny the truth for our own protection. You cannot say no. What is more, they will not allow you to.'

'Oh, Odile, I just do not know. I must go and work. The rain means I can only work in the shed today. I can get the motor car for the Tabac running again. We must do all we can for Madame's Tabac.'

William squeezed Odile's hand a little.

'I love you, William Collins.'

'Whatever happens, it will be for the protection of France and Britain. I cannot stand aside, not after everything we all went through. I will only be in the shed.'

'Go and work, my brave husband.'

CHAPTER TWENTY-FOUR
Bazentin-Le-Petit November 1939

William used Henri's motorcycle to ride to Longueval. He rode down the hill, turned left onto the Contalmaison-Longueval road and looked to where the trenches had been at the bottom of the hill. An almost unrecognisable spot now, of course, the green growth had long ago reclaimed and masked the landscape, even up at High Wood. But William knew. His mind was full of the military again and he knew that the telephone call would surely mean a part in the war to come. He rode past the junction in the road where the crucifix that had survived the incessant shelling was now full of holes and the scars of war. He rode up and over the little ridge that had sheltered his men attacking High Wood. To the left, the sweep of the ridge and the valley, a scene of death and destruction, the fall of the cavalry and the effort to take the woods in mid-September of 1916. He rode past the cemetery at Caterpillar Valley, the graves never changing, silent and peaceful. He nodded towards the cross and rode on to Longueval village. Outside of the Tabac, he stopped and left the motorcycle. He waved to two older men drinking inside. These men had looked out on Longueval from before 1914, from before the horrors of trench warfare that had torn at their village.

At the postmaster's office, William hesitated for a moment and then strode in. Whatever the call would reveal, it could not now come soon enough, he simply wanted to know. He knew he would most likely have to go to London – Odile and Henri both knew it. But he was not sure how long it would be for and how quickly he would have to prepare his affairs.

The telephone rang loudly. Monsieur Orlan picked up the large receiver and asked for the caller's name in English. He moved the receiver from his ear, passing it to William.

'William, it is Admiral Hawker. I will be next door.'

William nodded his thanks to the postmaster. Almost imperceptibly, his body stiffened as he addressed his superior officer.

'Hello sir, this is William Collins.'

'Ah, Collins, the line is good and I can hear you quite distinctly. Are you alone there or is it a shared line?'

'Quite alone, it is the postmaster's phone and he is now in the office next door.'

'Oh, Longueval? I know of that place. Delville Wood?'

'Yes sir, I can see the trees from here. And the gravestones.'

'Look, I need to be quite blunt, Collins. We are in need of a French-speaking liaison officer in London. You know the bloody Germans are in Poland. We think they will be at France next and then that means us. We have to get the French brass to think our way. Our concern is their fighting guts. They may not be up for another Verdun. Tough buggers, but they just don't have the military to face up to the type of war the Germans are waging. It has put the wind up us all, it is not their fault. Will you come and assist us with that? Just a liaison job. But we need clever thinking and French understanding. You seem to be the chap we need. It will mean coming to London by Christmas and staying for a few months. We will work out the rank and so forth, get you on the books again. What say you?'

'Why me sir, if I may ask? I am a retired colonel and wounded. If I am honest, I do not feel much like a colonel at all. I only ever had that rank in a bloody hospital. I have never really received the proper training to be a senior officer.'

'Yes, Collins, we are aware of that. But your job will be to get things done. You did it once before, no reason it won't be the same this time. We can handle the military business here. We need what is in your head, not what is in your boots or on your shoulders, old boy. What say you now?'

'I have to say yes, sir. The German activity has us all worried.'

'You think the French will fight?'

'Yes, with all their heart. With sticks and shovels against those bloody Stukas.'

'And the BEF behind them, Collins!'

'We will fight again in France sir? Is that the plan?'

'It is one of a number of possibilities that the newspapers are considering… so it must be accurate.'

'Yes, sir.' William's smile was thin and without humour. He was imagining the conversation with his family.

'Look, we will send you all the details. Be ready to leave in a week.

Understood?'

William felt his back stiffen. He was being given an order.

'Sir, yes, Admiral Hawker.'

The Admiral was already gone. The operator clicked closed the line.

'Thank you, Monsieur Orlan, I am finished.'

The postmaster returned. 'Monsieur Collins? Can I get you anything?'

'No, Monsieur. Thank you for the use of your telephone.'

'Not at all.'

'I will see you soon, I think there may be more telegrams at least.'

Orlan nodded and opened the door. William decided to ride to Delville Wood before returning home as he wanted to look at the graves there again. Such death on a large scale in such a small space. What on earth was that all about? It seemed madness twenty years on but what a sacrifice for what was so little in reality. And now it seemed it was all to come back again. Of course it would be so very different. There were tanks and aeroplanes and more motor lorries now, not carts and horses and lumbering artillery. The British had a small army, France's army was also small, but it had battleships and aeroplanes. But the Germans had gone into Poland with nearly two million men. A sweep of the hand and it was done, conquered and suppressed under the marching boots of the Nazis. William was sure it would be the same here. No last desperate stand on the Somme, nor patriotic resistance in the salients of Verdun and Ypres. The Germans would be in Paris within days – that was the reality of the situation – with the Maginot Line an unimportant relic of a long-gone age.

Those helmets in his head again, with young faces underneath them, just as eager to fight. He looked out over the mass of graves. Here was a battlefield cemetery, right in amongst what had been the trenches. So few men found and buried, most of them unknown to this day. A soldier of the Great War. He had been one and right here as well. He wondered if he would now also be a soldier of the next. He placed his hand on the first grave, cold to the touch. It was of an unknown South African soldier. The sound of the South African voices, the distinctive accent, the blood as red as his own and just as easily spilt.

'Damn you bloody bastards, not again.'

He looked down, tapped the stone gently and turned around to leave. The wind was gently rustling through the trees and the ghosts of his past were walking free in the cleared grass in front of the wood. William turned his motorcycle around and set off on the ride back home. This time, he turned right at the old windmill, riding up the gentler slope on this side of the ridge towards High Wood. He passed the cemetery where the German defensive switch line had once crossed the road, and looked out to the sweeping fields of Martinpuich where the British tanks had first rumbled over the dry, uneven ground, terrifying the enemy. Then he looked over to where he had been found by the Guards in hiding. He shook his head when he remembered the weeks of silence and fear. The cowl of war was descending over the land again, black and inescapable. He moved off, and this time he turned left down the slope and back to his home in the village. On the corner by his own house was the memorial to the nine brave men. He read the names aloud, knowing that before this war was done, there would need to be a few million more.

When he reached home, Henri met him at the gate, worry written on his face. William drew him into his shoulder, kissing his son's head gently and holding him close.

'Your mother is going to need you to be a man, Henri. She can cope, my goodness, she is a survivor, but she will need the love and comfort of her son. Can you do that for me?'

Henri squeezed his father.

'Yes, Papa. With all my heart.'

William, let him go and went inside and upstairs to where Odile was on the bed, her eyes closed but awake. He closed the door gently and told her he was leaving for London in one week.

CHAPTER TWENTY-FIVE

Bazentin-Le-Petit December 1939

The car came for William at exactly eleven. It was an old French military car that had long ago seen better days. It was dirty, and the driver was disinterested in the formalities of suitcases and etiquette. He opened the rear door and waited for William to appear. Whilst he was waiting, he managed a furtive cigarette.

'William, it is time for you to go, my love. It will not be for so long, you will see.'

'I am going, Odile, but I am not sure if this is the right thing to do.'

Odile squeezed his hand.

'My love, go and do this for our beloved France and for our children. Go on now, we will be here when you return.'

William looked doubtfully at Odile. He felt a sense of panic rise for the first time. Had he simply said yes because duty called? He had a duty here.

'Come home in the New Year and we can talk about the future. If the future is England, well so be it. You will be late.'

William stepped outside. Alain and Yvette were already outside waiting by the car. William embraced Alain as a brother, asking him to look in on Odile.

'Look in? I will visit every day. We can manage without you, you fool. Make sure you visit Arthur and Armandine, yes?'

'Yes, Alain. I will be back soon.'

Yvette promised to care for Henri. Their wedding had now been planned for July 1940. It might now have to wait.

William turned back to Odile. His beautiful, strong, wilful bride. He needed to go, but he wanted more of her before he left.

'Will you walk with me to the church, Odile?'

Alain told the driver he could wait in the house and that William would return presently but he needed a moment. The driver shrugged, sat down in the driver's seat of the car, and pulled his cap over his eyes.

At the steps to the church, almost on the exact spot where they married in 1919, William turned to his wife, taking her face gently in his hands. She lifted her hands to his, stroking the back of his hand as she always did.

'My love, each day that I am away my thoughts will be filled with you and Henri here in France, of this home and our village. My heart will carry a little of France with me so even though I am in England I will have the love of home around me. Will you remember that?'

'I will, William. I will, English boy from over the sea.'

William and Odile leaned towards one another.

'It won't be for long, Odile, I promise.'

'William, I feel that I am giving something back to Britain that had been given to me for safe keeping, something precious and fragile. And now I am handing you back to the men in uniform. Come home, William. Please return to us soon, stay not a minute longer than you have to.'

Pierre and Marie-Louise appeared at their gate opposite the church. Pierre was tapping his way to the street, waving at William. He probably knew, they all did. This land was at war again. Perhaps not yet declared, but the land was to be in dispute for certain. The rightful owners would again be subjected to harshness and brutality.

William returned to the car, the driver sat up and they quickly moved off with William waving from the rear window. He had not worn a suit in quite some time but his uniform was out of date and did not fit him anymore. Colonel Collins in 1918 was recovering from wounds and was a gaunt, hollow soul. He may not have recovered from his life on the Western Front, but his body had responded well to home cooking and the attentions of his wife, his daughter and his mother-in-law. He smiled thinly. France would be worth fighting for again, if it came down to it.

As he was being driven to Amiens to take a boat train to London, William Collins the engineer, father, friend and problem solver of Bazentin-Le-Petit in Picardie fell away, melting into the surroundings to stay here undisturbed with his silent brothers. From the depths of the battlefields came Colonel William Collins, a soldier of the Western Front. William felt the soldier rise in him again, filling his body comfortably. He cared less for the Distinguished Service Order or the Military Medal and the bar and ribbons earned before he was swept up in the blast in Belgium. He cared only for the men, the struggle, the survival and the safe return to his wife. He felt again the desire to push for peace, to hold the enemy at the gates. But this time, he realised the enemy was an altogether more sinister opponent.

At Amiens, he boarded the boat-train to Harwich, which went through Calais. His seat was in a small carriage, shared with only a handful of French-speaking military personnel. He was back in the service of his country and warming to the task already but he was none the wiser as to what use his talents might be put.

At Harwich, the train was placed on the tracks bound for London Liverpool Street. He arrived, tired but curious, and attended the Ministry building as ordered, where he was escorted quietly and efficiently into a little windowless office. For an hour he waited without any offer of water or the courtesy of an explanation. The harsh light was hot and he felt annoyed and agitated. Wrenched from his home to be treated this way. It was not right. Then the door opened.

'So sorry to keep you, Colonel Collins, I am Major Edwin Smyth. I will get some tea brought to you, bet you have not had a decent army mugful in a little while, eh?'

'No, you are quite right, Major. Anyway, pleased to meet you but can you tell me why am I here?'

'Yes, well, that's the thing. We are not yet so sure but what we need you for is coming. Sorry, let me be clearer. France is almost certainly to be invaded by the Germans, probably next summer when the weather turns. If we were to do it, we would run tanks straight into France and units around the Maginot Line, through Belgium and perhaps Holland as well, all at once. One big iron fist with a heavy punch from the air. Paris think it as well but they think talking might yet sort it out. Well we don't. Their politicians are old and wise but worried for their country and a bit old-fashioned. We understand that. So we think in all honesty that the French government is not strong enough and will collapse under a lot of German pressure. Hitler is persuasive but his tanks are decisive. You see, so far?'

'But the French are already in Germany are they not? Is there not already a move to invade?'

'We have intelligence that the German generals are unsure what to do. Hitler keeps moving his pieces around. Von Rundstedt, von Manstein, Halder. He shoves 'em here, there and everywhere. We think it will be through Belgium, wide into Holland, then with tanks through the forests in the Ardennes. We give France eight weeks. In return, France is poking the Siegfried Line, but nothing more. They may have already withdrawn.'

'So what is the plan for me? I am not a soldier.'

'Perhaps, but you were, old chap. It isn't soldiering we need, it's clever cunning and a bit of calm on the issue. We need you to plan for the arrival of the French Government – one that we approve of, naturally.'

'The what?'

'We have been instructed by the prime minister to make such preparations as necessary to receive the French Government in exile. We have not told them that yet, they would not countenance it, but we see it as an inevitability. Run before they are overrun. We think Paris will soon be in contact with us anyway. Best do it on our terms. We are already receiving the Polish and some of the Czechs. A proper cosmopolitan line going on.'

'France would operate from Whitehall?'

'Quite so, at least that bit of France that was not working with the enemy. We have received information, top secret, you understand, that in the event of the fall of France, an accommodation would be made with the enemy to save France from destruction. Sounds an almighty trifle but we can understand it, would not want the old capital to be blown to pebbles. Well, so far it is all just fine and cordial but it might not last. We are going to encourage a legitimate government to speak for the people that isn't a mouthpiece for that rascal Hitler.'

'I understand. So when do I start doing whatever it is you think I can do?'

'You already have, I suppose, sir. We have an office for you and an appointment at Gieves this afternoon for a new uniform, Colonel Collins. Sir.'

William was escorted out of the room and once again allowed to roam free. There were few orders except to plan for a government to locate in accommodations in London. This was just another problem to solve. The telephones and typewriters, that was easy enough. But it would be the hearts and minds of those left in France that would be hard. The shots had been fired and the Germans were most definitely coming. William worried that his own plans might be all too temporary. The Germans would not stop in France. They would come for Britain, to live and rule. He almost shivered at the thought. He opened the Orders of Government (Military Disposition) and began underlining familiar names. Perhaps some of these might turn out to be companions from the Great War he could call on in a time of need.

--oOo--

Christmas in London was a drab affair, wet and subdued, with the civilian population living through a phoney war. While war had been declared, it seemed that little was happening. William could see that plans were being drawn as there were some alarming scenarios on his desk. Germans would land at Pevensey, Camber, a deep port such as Hull, or at a smaller set of landings all along the coast. Plans to blow up Parliament, move to the Lake District, Wales or even to America or Canada. But the biggest plan was for an Expeditionary Force, which was in mobilisation already, on its way to France to stop whatever came over the hill. Some eight-hundred-thousand men would be deployed and there were the same numbers again if needed. It might be enough, along with the French, to halt the Germans in the north. He feared his home would again be in the line of fire, with Odile and her parents once more a line drawn on a battlefield. He hurried to the Admiralty. The operation for which he was responsible was a combined one.

He now had to undergo a four-month training programme to understand the military of 1939 and to take on a legitimate commission activated at the rank of Colonel, which for the time being was in name only. His knowledge of France and the French was invaluable, but as an army officer here and now, he was useless. He had no connections and no idea of how or where to start. That was why his first appointment was Major Smyth, as deputy military liaison to the French Government in exile.

In March 1940, the Expeditionary Force was largely in place. The temporary offices for the French Government were ready and the protocols that William and Smyth had devised for communication and decision making were tested and retested. London was ready to welcome the exiled French Government. Only the French had not realised it yet.

At the end of March, William was able to telephone Odile for the first time. His work was secret for now as the British did not want to give the impression to the French that they had already conceded France to Germany, but that was the plan for William's operation. Plan for it and it will not be a surprise when it happens.

At least Odile sounded well enough but it did not stop William worrying for his wife. She was not frail, she was strong. But the war had scarred her. She had been a nurse, wilful and proud, strong and resilient. And yet there was a place deep inside that remained troubled, hidden from view. It surfaced rarely but it kept sickness a constant companion. He saw it in her mother as well.

'When will you be coming back to France, William?'

'I cannot say, my darling, but it will perhaps be in three more months.'

He heard the silence, which told him everything he needed to know about how his wife felt.

'Oh, very well. Henri is keeping your workshop running. He has another new car to build. This will tide him and us over until you return and it is good that he is busy.'

'That is good news, Odile. Henri is a good son.'

'Oh, William, I do want you to come home. I want you to be with your family but you must also do this for France. I am not sure how I feel. I want you in both places at once and it is upsetting to think this way. Have you seen our twins?'

'It is difficult—'

'Have you seen them?'

'I am not allowed to leave the offices. What we are doing cannot really be discussed.'

'Find the time, William. Your children would enjoy seeing their father. Heaven knows we have not given them much of our time, have we?'

William could hear the harsh edge in her voice. He was not being scolded, but he was being left in no doubt that in Odile's opinion, Britain had already had its fair share of her husband. He should certainly be allowed to see his children. He could work for France and for the Collins family together, he did not have to choose.

First, he would try to see his daughter. She was not so far away from him but a world away from this work. Arthur was probably still in Cambridge although he really was no longer entirely sure of his son's studies. Arthur was like his father. Kind and thoughtful, but hopeless at communicating, never writing, never sending a telegram. William could see it and was sorry for how he must have made his own parents feel all those years ago in the Great War.

CHAPTER TWENTY-SIX

France May 1940

William rose early as the weather was so clear and bright. The sun shone through broken clouds, and the open windows brought in the scent of the Thames, a little salty air mixed in with the coolness of the river breeze. But the improving weather could bring the war closer, giving the enemy an opportunity to fight. William was planning to meet with an official from the Prime Minister's Office at eight o'clock on the Victoria Embankment. The Germans were now very likely to invade France. Perhaps the British would counter attack and then who could say what would happen? William had estimated eight weeks for France to hold out. In honesty, he did not really think it would be as long as that. He knew France would fall and there was no way to bring Odile and Henri here for the papers and orders could not now be arranged. Other priorities had taken over. But he would not leave the matter alone for long.

'Tell me, Colonel Collins, what do you think of The French prime minister? Have you met him?'

'No sir, I have not.'

'No, well, it was a long shot. We seem to be at odds with our friends over the old channel.'

'What is it this time?'

William could imagine very well the shrug, the look, the dismissal of the British as fools.

'Hm, this time indeed! Well, we have telephoned the ministers a great deal over the last few days. You see, we need to agree some messages for radio broadcasts. We have not heard from them, that's all. So, on to our business. We need to—'

The sound of fast-running footsteps stopped the conversation. The sound could only mean one thing. A young naval officer ran straight up to William, saluted smartly and looked sideways at the civilian.

'Sorry, sir. Urgent. Overnight reports are in from France, Belgium and Luxembourg. Looks like the Germans are on the move into France, sir.'

William's face darkened. It had begun again. Even though it was inevitable, it still came as a shock to hear that diplomacy had been utterly futile with the German leader. He turned to the prime minister's adviser, raising his hand to signal a parting.

'If you will excuse me, I must return immediately to my office. Shall we speak again soon?'

'Indeed, Colonel. I think we may well have the approval we need to move. Good morning to you.'

On the walk back, William could think only of Odile and Henri. He had not really planned on staying this long, but it seemed that there was a never-ending set of things to finish, with each one to be the last. He had not thought of all the dangers to them until now, until he actually heard the words confirming the invasion. Suddenly, he wanted to go home, regretting his optimism for peace, and angry that he had not acted more decisively for his family. He wanted at that very moment only to be with them. Who else here had family so deeply in peril? Should he act now to help them to escape from the Germans? For them to stay would be a mistake. He stepped into his office. The plans for the French were now in operation. He had a duty, but he was torn, he wanted only to be with his wife and son. At the door to the French Government's new accommodation in England, still empty and ghostly, William stepped forward to outline his proposal for a French Government in exile.

--oOo--

Odile and Henri had gone to stay with her parents. There had been no news from William in the nine days since the Germans had finally invaded France. They were coming from the north and the east. She had felt this fear of the unknown before, a wave of panic rising in the streets, the distress, the fear and alarm. But this time there were no French soldiers in the villages to move them or help them. The mayor had told the villagers to stay indoors and await instructions from the army. But there were none and no army came for them. Running south was hopeless because the Germans were coming. West was out of the question because they were simply moving too quickly.

Odile knew that Henri was angry and that he felt helpless and empty for he wanted to do something. But there was nothing to be done, how could there be? The French Army was not in Albert this time, other than a token reserve. She knew that the Germans were driving along the Albert to Bapaume Road again, just as they had done in 1914. Some of the villagers had driven out to see them go past. She forbade Henri from going since it might end in fighting that could get him needlessly killed.

Since the invasion, Odile's father had been sitting in almost stunned silence for three days and her mother just held onto his hand. There would be no rescue for them this time. Why would Pierre's skills be valuable now? The machines had moved on and he had been left behind. Now, he would just be another refugee, an inconvenience, and it would not serve them for him to be seen as a nuisance to the Germans.

'Are these bastards going to flatten my home again? Where is our damned army? We have been abandoned. Vive La France. Pah!'

'Pierre! Please. We have been through this once before and you know we simply must endure again.'

'Must we? How much money has France spent on defence? All those concrete blocks in the north? Where are ours? They are here again.'

Odile could see that Henri was agitated and perhaps felt less of a man being unable to do anything to help. There was no army to join this time. Only homes to hide in. She knew that he was also worried about his beloved Yvette. Odile could see their future fading, dreams shattered before they could even begin. She remembered that feeling as if it were only yesterday.

'I want to see Yvette, Maman.'

'No, Henri! Not until the Germans have passed us by, which they will.'

But it was really no use. She could see him anxious to go, desperate to see his love again, so she closed her eyes and waved him away. Henri kissed his mother and left to walk the short distance to Yvette and her uncle.

Odile saw the little door open and Yvette's slender arms reach forward and embrace Henri, drawing him inside. Once satisfied that he was safe and in good care, she returned to her parents. Pierre rose to turn on the radio. It was full of static and garbled nonsense. The Paris stations were too distant to be heard. Amiens was broadcasting but it was playing slow, mournful music. No news or anything of consequence was broadcasting.

'The radio is useless. We are on our own, my loves.'

Pierre sat down and lit his pipe. The smoke billowed for a moment and then rose to the ceiling. Odile watched the little curls evaporate, imagining the smoke and fire from the bombs that destroyed the lorry on the day they were captured in 1914. Would it be like that again?

When they finally came, the messages on the radio were hours out of date. The news was of actions long gone, which they could almost see from their windows. There were no French forces here and the British were not yet in this part of France. The Germans were not stopped this time at Albert. They simply drove through. She hoped that they would not stop and fight here again, the memories too painful for them all. Perhaps driving over these battlefields might make them think twice. But she knew that it would likely make no difference to these younger German soldiers, their heads full of tales of victory and glory.

Odile heard with horror some sporadic gunfire in the distance. Heavier, deeper and more dangerous than any shell she had heard in the Great War. Where it was or who was shooting, she could not tell, so she simply waited for the enemy to appear over the ridge once again. Just as before, waves of ants crawling over the countryside.

But it was not until the ninth day of waiting that they saw their first German. A small car, open-topped and with a motorcycle escort was driving on the old military road from Martinpuich. The car arrived at Bazentin-Le-Petit and stopped at the top of the ridge. The officer got out, holding a small camera and a pair of binoculars in his hands. Odile could see the man quite plainly as he was now standing outside her own house. She saw the officer step up to her door and knock quite politely. He waited and then began to walk around her garden. It could have been the postmaster or the telegraph boy, it seemed so innocent.

'I must go and speak to this man. It might be about William. He seems to be interested in talking. He has not kicked down our door.'

'No, Odile. Don't be so foolish, why would you do such a thing?'

'Because it is my home. We have worked so hard to have a home.'

'But his is a German! They are the enemy.'

'I know, but he does not have a gun and is not going to arrest anyone, is he?'

Odile opened the door of her parents' house slowly. As she did so, she could sense other eyes looking upon her from behind closed doors. She walked past Alain's house but no one was at those windows. The German officer saw Odile and strode down the street to greet her, a broad smile across his face.

'Ah hallo, hallo! Madame, I'm in your city for viewing seeings.'

'Your French is terrible, let us speak in German.'

'You do? My goodness, your German is excellent. How is it that you speak German so very well?'

'I was a nurse in a German military hospital and I also tended German victims of the Spanish influenza.'

'Oh, I see. I see.'

Odile knew that such a story would disarm an honourable soldier. This man seemed decent enough.

'Well, I have come to look at the battlefield from the last war. My father was here in this village. He was wounded in a place called Delville Wood. I presume that you know it?'

'I do. Is that all you are here for?'

'Yes, yes. Look, I am not an infant. I know this is difficult, especially here, in this place. This region is important to Germany as well. We lost many thousands of men here. Yes, I understand that we were the ones coming into France. I am only looking to see where my father was wounded. I mean no trouble.'

'Tell me, what is going to happen here?'

'Oh, Madame, I do not know. But I expect the district will have a commandant and he will tell you all what is to be done. I have to say, I do not think your French Army is going to rescue you. I mean no harm. I am just here to see this place. Please show me the way to Delville Wood.'

Odile gave the officer directions and turned away to return to her father's house.

'Madame, if France falls, we can live together in peace I think?'

Odile did not turn around. She carried on walking, needing nothing more from this German officer. As she moved along the street, each door in turn opened a fraction. She could hear the whispers, sensing a desire to know what had happened. Was it William? What was going on? She reached her father's house, entered and sat on a chair at the big kitchen table, breathing out heavily.

'Once again, our war is just beginning.'

CHRIS CHERRY

CHAPTER TWENTY-SEVEN
Cambridge England 1941

Arthur hurried down the corridor, already late for the tutorial, puffing, with a red face and his books tumbling behind him. Turning left, he could see his tutor waiting at the door, impatience written across his face.

'Something keep you, young Collins? Something more important than the restoration of the new world?'

'I'm sorry. My bicycle has a puncture and the chain came off. I did not know how to repair it, so I carried it on my shoulder. Very sorry.'

'Not much of a cycle mechanic, eh? Found the trip over from Cavendish to Downing a bit too much, eh? From the dishevelled state of your attire and the bicycle bits in your pocket, it looks like the change could not come soon enough.'

For the next three hours, Arthur and his tutor dissected and examined, questioned and argued. Arthur immediately felt a warm energy rise through him and out through his words. Words that flowed like a river that was sure of its course. His arguments were constructed, rotated and examined in his mind the instant before articulation. Afterwards, his tutor had suggested that Arthur remain behind and share a sherry with him and two older students. The two men arrived and were warmly introduced. The conversation moved around Europe and the Middle East, but soon turned to America and the possibility that America might not participate in the war at all. Bombs had fallen on Cambridge on and off since 1940. This year, the Germans had dropped incendiaries, trying to start fires in the streets they believed to be full of the plotters of Hitler's downfall.

Arthur found the conversation stimulating but ultimately pointless. It was words in the air, fuelled by sherry. He had long ago mastered the art of sipping, just touching his lips with the liquid, making a single glass last the evening. The others were further along and Arthur felt it was time to leave, he had a lot of catching up to do and no time to waste. As he left the little room, Arthur reflected on his tutor's reason for keeping him behind for sherry. It had been to put a proposal to him. Arthur had already accepted in his mind, but wanted to take a day to think about it. Before he gave his response, he felt he needed to gather a little more evidence for his decision. He stepped over the road to his little rooms. Once inside, he took down a large leather-bound volume from the shelf above his bed. He opened the book to the chapter he wanted and read. When he turned over the page, he knew he was gripped and resolved to meet his tutor again the very next day.

--oOo--

At a little before seven, Arthur was dressed and downstairs, pacing the corridor until it was polite and acceptable to charge into the little rooms occupied by Roger Crawley. By seven-fifteen, he could wait no longer. He almost ran across the road and into the college, the halls towering in front of him, eight-hundred years of history soaked into the walls. But this particular period of history was dangerous, for here was a troubled world, with weapons to bring buildings down to their very foundations. His footsteps echoing on the stairs must have alerted his tutor since Crawley opened the door just as Arthur arrived.

'I presume it must be a yes then, Arthur?'

'Yes. It is a yes.'

'Well, do come in then. There is someone I think you ought to meet later today. I will arrange for your absence from lectures. Let us go and eat breakfast. I think this day is going to be a wonderful one for both of us.'

Arthur, smiling broadly, accompanied Crawley down the stairs and out into the grounds. As they walked, Crawley began again with politics and thoughts on the conduct of the war.

'Apparently, Herr Hitler is confident that he can break the Russians by Christmas this year. I suppose, whilst he is occupied on that, he will leave us alone. Their soft underbelly is exposed and I would imagine a chance to break through from the Balkans, or Italy. What do you think, Collins?'

'I think that whatever happens, we cannot win the war without America. Britain is strong and brave but we simply do not have enough men, steel or coal to do this alone. The Russians are unpredictable. They fight, they give ground, they repel and they concede. The country is simply too vast to defend and too vast to capture. At some point, there must surely be an agreement and then Hitler will come for us.'

'Well, that would certainly be an interesting proposition.'

Arthur felt his face harden and his eyes narrow, remembering his family in France and the occupation. He had spoken with Armandine, and whilst they themselves were both safe in England, they wanted the Germans out of their beloved France.

'An interesting proposition? Does that mean that you agree with Hitler?'

'About the Russians? Yes. But he should be stopped at all costs, of course.'

Arthur's brow relaxed again.

'Right, tea. Eggs, Arthur?'

'Yes please.'

Arthur ate quietly. Crawley was talking more of America, but Arthur was less interested in the politics. What interested him was the resolution. How this might end and how the last man standing would claim a victory of moral right over the vanquished. He felt the fire that had started in him begin to flame brighter until he could wait no more.

'When do we leave?'

'I can make the necessary arrangements today. Perhaps at the end of next month? Give you time to prepare. Time to write that little piece I have been waiting on for a month, hm?'

'Yes, of course.'

Crawley leaned over to Arthur, lowering his head and his voice.

'You do want this, don't you?'

'Yes, more than anything. Why?'

'You seem very distracted. Is anything wrong?'

'No, I am keen to get on. I'm just thinking about what is left for me to do.'

'Well, you have now got a lot of reading to do. Still, I am confident you can manage all of that.'

'Yes.' Arthur finished his tea and stood to leave. 'Look, perhaps I had better go to my lecture this morning. It might help to calm my mind. Give me time to think about all of this. But it is terribly exciting.'

'You know, a little Russian and German would not do you any harm…'

The voices nearby were silenced and the metallic clang of a dropped spoon was the only sound that could be heard. Crawley laughed.

'You never know when you might need to use them.'

Arthur gave Crawley a thin smile and turned to leave.

Crawley looked down at his half-finished eggs.

'Shame to waste these, even if they are half powdered milk.'

He picked up his fork and took a mouthful. Then he reached into his pocket and took out the single sheet of handwritten notes and looked at the title. Two words at the top of the page, in large script. *Superior Orders.*

'Hm, the last excuse of the damned.'

--oOo--

The lecture bored Arthur. His mind was already detached and had moved ahead of his body across the borders, he was scribbling furiously but not about the subject of the lecture. He had also decided that it was high time he visited his sister and felt a strong urge to contact her in London. Where his twin sister was concerned, Arthur never questioned his feelings as their connection was simply too strong and beyond any scientific understanding.

His mind also drifted across the sea to France. He had chosen, at the same time as his sister, to get to know the birthplace of their father. They had a strong connection to England and felt British as well as French. Both were fluent in both languages, although their English was shaped by their father and his occasional awkwardness with words, reverting to the language of the army when things became complicated. Even so, they had chosen to follow studies in England and their grandparents were only too pleased to help. Arthur felt remiss not to have seen them at all in the last nine months. He resolved to visit them also, and before saying goodbye to England, he would call in on them. Immediately, he felt better just thinking of his connections to England.

Crawley had proposed to him something quite unimagined up until now. The world had seen the birth of a League of Nations. A clever but ultimately futile attempt to unite the fractured states of Europe and beyond. Bonds of friendship from the ashes of the First World War. But this was altogether more ambitious. The Americans were not even involved and yet here they were, conceiving a future for the world in which the menace of war was already over and the punishment for such evil was impossible to escape.

This was going to be an important adventure. Sometime in the future, those responsible for the intelligent reasoning would be in the light of the public gaze. But there was one detail that he did not have the power to control. The philosophy to which he must now turn his mind and attention for all of this to succeed. The philosophy embodied by one man, a man of power, if not powerful. Adolf Hitler.

CHAPTER TWENTY-EIGHT
Eastern Poland March 1941

His orders had come through the night before. He had opened the sealed envelope with an eagerness, keen to learn his role in the operation to come. The words were simple and he read them with relish over and over until he could remember them exactly, word for word. After reading the single sheet of paper, he took out a small cigar lighter and lit the corner of the paper, turning it round in his fingers as the flame consumed the thin waxy note. This was going to be a major invasion and Kurt knew that he had a very significant part to play, exactly as he had wanted it and exactly how he had requested it.

For the next two months he would have to encourage and train his men to kill without mercy as that was to be their assignment now. But for Kurt, the best part was not only the killing, but doing it openly and brutally in front of the civilian population so that they could see the power of the enemy attacking them. If this was vicious and quick, perhaps Russia would quickly bend to the will of the Nazi machine.

Kurt knew that he needed this. He had grown so much over the last ten years and he had long ago reconciled himself to this life of brutality and self-sacrifice for his Fatherland. He had seen Germany grow and emerge from the shackles of Versailles. All that mattered to him now was Germany and his Führer. He often whispered the oath to himself over and again. *To the Führer, to Hitler, to the Fatherland.* For him, this would mean glory, perhaps coming to the notice of his own Commander Heydrich, who knew him but did not yet know what Kurt was truly capable of becoming.

Kurt walked back to the wooden-walled office that was his temporary quarters. The Einsatzgruppe, which he was now to lead, had been given the task of following the regular army into Russia later in the year. His job would be simple. Suppress any and all resistance quickly and without mercy. There were no rules for him other than do it brutally and quickly, target the leaders and report success the same day.

He looked out of the large window, which overlooked a brook and a meadow beyond. It immediately reminded him a little of France and for a fleeting moment Odile came into his mind, running up the hill towards him, her hair about her shoulders. Of course, his mind was fixed on a girl of eighteen, she would be forty by now if she was alive at all and she would look quite different. No doubt he could pass her in the street without recognising her and she would pass him by just the same.

He thought deeply and with a pained sadness about those early months in 1919 when he went to look for her. What a foolish and stupid boy he had been. Kurt let a thin smile cross his lips at the thought of chasing a train to Switzerland to find a dead nurse who wasn't Odile. He remembered the only other possible sighting, a fleeting recognition of a pretty girl in a nurse's uniform on her way to Koln railhead to meet some non-existent patients. That trail was not even worth consideration for it was probably a genuine journey made by a real nurse bringing home the wounded who could not care for themselves. The trail was long ago cold and he had been forced to let her go. For all of the years since, he had kept a special place for her deep inside of him. Perhaps that was the real Kurt deep inside, now crusted by evil and the deeds he had done in the name of power.

Every girl since, every woman encouraged to take an SS officer to bed for the Fatherland, was compared to Odile. That girl with the wonderful open face, beautiful eyes and a gentle touch. None of them could compare, which was perhaps why he never married. He had been offered plenty of women and his rank and position required him to take women as often as possible but none stuck to him. They rolled off like water on wax paper. Only Odile ever touched him and how completely she had seized his soul.

He shook off the memory and turned back to the deep pile of administrative papers on his desk. He had no time for memories, there was other work to be done. But as he poured himself a little coffee, he was distracted by her again, her memory not letting him go. It took him back to Cambrai and the afternoon in the rain when he had truly bared his soul to Odile and she had rejected him so completely. Of course he was the enemy, he realised that, but he had thought for a time that he might form a loving union with her. Perhaps it was that moment, over any other in the months that followed, that had placed him here, SS-Oberführer Langer of the new death squad Einsatzgruppe Russia-West. Perhaps Kurt was always destined to be here and being buried in Avocourt had driven him to live a life in the service of Germany. But it was always to the memory of Odile, to his first and truest love, that he turned in moments like these. The years of struggle rising in the Sturmabteilung, the move to Munich and the heady seduction of the Schutzstaffel, the brief years in the Gestapo, searching out the undesirable enemies of Germany. He had relished it all, but it was not who he truly was, a mere rat catcher. He was a grand soldier, riding to glory on a golden chariot. Perhaps then, perhaps at that final moment of jubilation and glorious triumph, Odile would step forward to claim him, to take him from that place and to love little Kurt Langer, a boy who loved a girl.

His golden chariot was now here and his orders delivered the opportunity to make an indelible mark for the Fatherland. There would be no stopping him now, nothing would be allowed to get in his way. For the Russians, the message was simple, Kurt Langer was coming.

CHAPTER TWENTY-NINE
Western Russia July 1941

The road was dusty, but Kurt did not mind. He was advancing at great speed through the woods and fields of Western Russia, the sun and the wind in his face. Here was the opportunity. The army had advanced, leaving behind the angry and the bewildered, the defiant and the vengeful. This was good for him because it would make the day so much more meaningful and just for his cause. He tapped the driver, signalling a desire for more speed, to push faster through the lines of vehicles, the onrushing Germans and the burning remnants of the Russian forces. He passed the dead bodies of comrades and enemy alike, civilians here and there, half naked and dazed, wandering aimlessly without a home or a friend in sight. The German soldiers were advancing on the women and as for the men, they welcomed them with their rifles and bayonets. At the head of the line, Kurt was flagged down and stopped in a cloud of dust whipped up by the wind following the vehicle.

Kurt stepped down from his armoured position, his face now covered in the dust of a conquered Western Russia. He had just witnessed a perfect bombing run from the Stuka dive bombers that he had requested from the Luftwaffe. The picture now in front of him was one of near total devastation. The town was ablaze, buildings crumbling and falling before his eyes or being destroyed with tanks as he watched. Russian citizens running about without order or direction, some being shot as they did so. The roads and paths were crawling with the German Army as they entered the town, pushing aside the carts and barrows of the population who were desperately trying to escape. Some of the women were being pulled from the lines and pushed into vehicles and the children were kicked into ditches. Kurt was not commanding this action but approved wholeheartedly of what he was witnessing. His work was yet to begin. The army could continue towards Smolensk, but Kurt would stay here for now as his Einsatzgruppe moved up from behind the army advance.

In the evening, as night drew in slowly upon the scene, the flames in the city had died down enough for him to enter the outskirts with his men. He ordered every house to be emptied, the local political commissars and members of the district committees were to be brought to him and any citizen resisting should be shot immediately.

'Who are these men coming along the street?'

'It is the local party committee, sir, there are four that refuse to leave.'

'Is that all there is?'

'We are still clearing the commissars' offices. I think there will be more.'

'See to it for this isn't enough for a proper demonstration.'

'Yes sir, there are also fifty Jewish families in this part of the town, what shall we do with them?'

'Excellent. Bring them here.'

The first four figures, terrified and stumbling, were brought in front of Kurt. He took a deep breath and entered the character of the SS Oberführer, stepping down theatrically from the armoured vehicle that had brought him into the town. Then he turned to the squad leader who had been responsible for emptying the streets.

'Bruno, are there any civilians left here?'

'Only a few, they have been driven out and north by the army.'

'Bring them as well, I want some witnesses.'

'Very good, sir.'

Kurt waited to see if any more men from the commissars' office were joining them but none appeared.

'Speak German?'

The figure hanging from the arms of a soldier looked up at Kurt and spat at him and a bloody clot landed on Kurt's cheek. He wiped it on the back of his hand and looked at it for a moment.

'Perhaps not. Well, it is of no consequence. We were not to have a conversation anyway.'

He took out his pistol and aimed it at the man's head.

'Where are the others? There are more of you rats here, I can smell your foulness.'

The man just shook his head. Kurt moved the pistol over the man's heart, touching his skin. The Russian winced and looked set to scream but Kurt pulled the trigger and the man slumped, his heart stopped by a bullet from Kurt's gun. Next to him, the other three men gasped and began chattering wildly in Russian. The soldiers holding them grabbed their hair and turned their terrified faces towards Kurt.

'You, more? Where?'

'No, German beast. We already count as dead.'

'You speak German?'

'I was always told to know enemies and you, sir, are enemy.'

'Perhaps I may have a use for you?'

'What? To fuck your sister, eh?'

Kurt hit the man with his stick, pulled his chin up to meet his gaze, kicked him hard until he grunted, then squeezed the trigger of his pistol into the man's petrified face.

'I am bored of this, Bruno, have these other men hanged in the street. This one with no face, have him hanged upside down and stuff his fucking balls in his pockets.'

As Kurt looked up he saw three more men, clearly terrified after witnessing what had just happened. They were kicking and scratching at the dirt, trying to escape. The soldiers holding them were much stronger and they simply carved tracks in the ground, like railway lines. There was no escape from the hands of the Einsatzgruppen.

'Any of you bastards speak German?'

'Yes, I do. But what of it? You will only kill us, there is nothing else you can do.'

'What is your role in the committee?'

'I write the official record of meetings and take the actions forward. It is only orders.'

'Can you sing?'

'Can I what?'

'Can you sing? I think perhaps not if you are deaf...'

'Yes, I can sing. I have been a member of—'

'Shut up, I asked if you could sing, not to give me your life story.'

'But why?'

'You go to Smolensk and tell them that we are coming for them. There is no point in running, we will find you all and send you to whatever Hell you believe in with your balls in your pockets. See? Do you hear me?'

'Yes. What do I tell them?'

'You tell them about this. Exactly what you see now.'

Kurt stepped forward, taking the second man by the hair and throwing him to the floor. The soldier holding the third pushed him on top, holding him down. Kurt wiped his pistol and shot both men with a single bullet. The one at the bottom did not die but screamed in pain, unable to move for the dead weight on top of him. Soon enough, he would die of suffocation or blood loss.

'No sense in wasting bullets. Make this man watch until that body is dead and then let him see that man have his balls cut off. Then let him go with a note to be escorted unhindered to Smolensk. Where are the Jews?'

Kurt looked up when there was no answer.

'I said, where are the Jews?'

'Sir, they are being taken together to the field at Birisov-Ladiv.'

'How many?'

'It's nearly four-hundred sir.'

'Where are my commandos?'

'Just arriving here now, they are going directly there to meet you.'

'Good. Let's go. Make sure this commissar watches. You understand?'

'Of course, sir.'

The soldier took out a clean-bladed knife and advanced on the body with no face. The terrified commissar was sick on the roadway. His head was jerked up roughly to watch the gruesome butchery at first hand.

Kurt stepped back onto his armoured vehicle for the short drive to the village of Birisov and waved his fingers for the vehicle to move away. There were a few spots of bright red blood on his uniform that had already soaked in and stained. He would have his kit cleaned for he did not want filthy blood on his uniform. A surge of authority flowed through him as he began to prepare himself.

At the edge of the village, a number of motorcycles and vehicles were already gathered. To the left, already on their knees, were about four-hundred Russian people from the town, known to be Jewish. Their names and details had already been recorded and Kurt was handed the list to review. He selected four of the names and asked for them to be brought to him, wanting to know if any of them spoke German. None were identified as being able to or willing to admit to speaking German. But Kurt thought that fear would make them understand.

'Friedrich, tell these four in Russian that I want to know if these people are all Jewish.'

'Yes, sir.'

The soldier turned to the four terrified bodies crouched on the floor.

'You. Tell me, and tell me truthfully, are they all Jewish here?'

'No officer, sir, none of them are Jewish. We are all just innocent people of Russia. We mean no harm to Germany. We are not your enemy. The Russian system is the enemy. We are starving and poor.'

Friedrich turned to Kurt, 'They say they are not Jewish but just poor and the usual rubbish.'

'Hm, tell him if he identifies Jews, he will be allowed to live. We will give him food and the thanks of the German people. He will not be harmed.'

The soldier turned again and addressed the man in Russian.

'You tell us the truth and Germany will be thankful to you and we will offer you protection and food, you can live in peace and with goodwill.'

The man's eyes dropped to the floor and then he slowly turned towards the crowd.

'My wife also, officer, sir?'

Kurt tapped his stick impatiently on his leg.

'Your wife as well.'

'Very good. Yes, Jewish, all of them. There are twenty more in the cellar of the big house. Please, sir, my wife.'

'Herr Oberführer, he is asking for his wife.'

'Fetch her.'

The woman was pulled by her arm from the pack of terrified people. The shouts of horror and hate rose as the soldier dragged the woman along the row of frightened faces.

'Friedrich, make sure they are all dead, will you? Make sure this man here is a witness to it all.'

'Yes, sir.'

'And when they are dead, shoot these two last and put them on top but shoot her first.'

'Sir.'

'Bruno?'

'Yes, Herr Oberführer?'

'Find the twenty in the big house, whatever that is.'

'Of course, sir. What do I do with them?'

'Make sure whatever doors they went in through are locked and then burn the house. Post guards to make sure none escape.'

'Oh, and Bruno?'

'Yes, sir?'

'When that is done, find some women, clean ones. Our men have earned some reward for today.'

'Of course, sir.'

Kurt took down a small wooden footstool from the armoured car and placed it so that he could see the execution of the Jewish citizens. He felt nothing for them, did not care for their lives or that they had families, they were just obstructions to his glory and that of Germany. To him, they were just in his way like something blocking a pathway that could be kicked aside, a job, and an order to carry out. His conscience was not troubled in the slightest by his enjoyable work but it was hot. He shouted over to the group of Germans carrying out his order.

'This is taking too long, Friedrich, don't we have a machine gun here?'

'No sir, but one is coming this afternoon.'

'Well get more men and get this over with, the screams are putting my nerves on edge. Besides, I am hungry.'

Kurt watched until the last of the group were dead, some shot with a pistol to make sure. He stood to see the last man on the pile and then he turned away towards the big house, which was clearly built in the times of the indulgent and opulent early Romanov Empire. Outside, he saw his men surround the building whilst others poured fuel into a chute before setting fire to it. The fuel flashed a white flame and then began to burn with a thick black smoke. He could hear faint movements below but no sounds of people.

'Are they in there?'

'Yes, sir. There must be fifty at least.'

'Are the doors sealed and guarded?'

'Yes, sir, we have already shot one runner.'

Kurt watched the house catch fire and burn openly in the breeze. Rain was coming but today it was dry, the house would burn well, a symbol of the power of the German will. This would go down well with his superiors. He hoped for a day when he would have few superiors and he would have command of a great force for the betterment of Europe.

'We have found some women, sir. Russians of course, but they seem clean enough. What shall I do now?'

'Get the men, they have three hours and then we move on. Did the commissar leave yet?'

'Yes sir, he is trembling and mumbling nonsense. They may not believe him.'

'Never mind, they will know we are here soon enough. Let us eat, I am hungry.'

CHAPTER THIRTY
Bazentin-Le-Petit 1941

'Do you see, Madame Collins, we can make a difference, even from under the eyes of the Germans?'

'I do, but we have to be careful, we do not even know who we can truly trust.'

Odile's eyes dropped.

'Madame, we have come to you just because of what happened in the last war. No one doubts your patriotism but your credentials in Germany must count for something that might wrong-foot the Germans for long enough. You have come as a recommended citizen, will you think about it, I mean seriously think?'

'I give you my word, Monsieur. I have no love for the Germans but we are without power and hope. Whatever salvation and liberation may come our way, it will come from outside of France. The south is lost to us, the north is still frightened. We are weak and only the voice of de Gaulle speaks to us. My husband you see... Well, I will give you my answer tomorrow, I promise.'

The man placed both palms on Odile's kitchen table and rose to leave. As night drew in, Odile stepped outside into the street, moving quickly to the side of her house that looked out over the road to Martinpuich and across to High Wood. In the distance, the small row of lights of Pozieres blinked. Her visitor had asked her to become the leader of the northern leg of the Resistance route for the escape of Allied airmen shot down over Belgium and Germany. She probably owed it to the thousands of bodies buried here, undisturbed silent witnesses, guarding the ridge eternally. She was more than capable of leading the silent and secret movement of men south from Lille to Bordeaux or Bayonne. The trains were still publicly operated, with guards for sure, but with clever deception, planning and fearless execution, the war could be fought in the shadows. She knew all about that. How could she refuse? It would be dangerous, who knew who could truly be trusted? But the war was here, it had chosen to involve her once again and she would not turn her back on France. With resolve and thoughts only of her family, she retired to bed, content that she would lead the fight against the enemy again, once again in secret. Thoughts of the camps from 1914 came to her, strengthening her nerve to the fight ahead. She wiped her brow and turned over to sleep, her head full of the sights and sounds of the camps from the Great War.

Meetings took place above a little cafe in Albert. She looked around the room. Some of the members were friends and neighbours who wanted to make a difference and who had been taken into the circle of the Resistance, such as it was in Albert. Others were strangers to Odile but their courage was in no doubt. She looked at the girl on her right keeping coded notes for the group. A charming and bright girl, Delphine Fournier, but one given to illness. Often she would suffer from chest chills after late nights. Still, although she was not the strongest girl in the world, she was very clever. Her meticulous records helped her to plan runs as she had knowledge of train times, routes and who would be working the barriers and guarding the trains. The group needed friends in the railways and Delphine had notes on all of them. Only three people could decipher the code – Delphine, Odile and Monsieur Reynaud, who owned the cafe and had his ear to the ground when Germans came to call.

They talked again of the plan to move men from the German border into Belgium, to Antwerp, Ghent or Brussels. From there, they would take trains or bicycles south. Some would go to Brest and be picked up. Others would move south to Paris into the anonymity of crowds, before being escorted by members of the escape group south towards Bordeaux and Bayonne. From there, the next group would take them over the northern Pyrenees into Spain, or the southern route through Pau or east and south from Toulouse. Often the suspicion of the Germans would determine the route so plans were loosely made and easily adapted.

The café owner cleared his throat and addressed Odile.

'Madame, we all know this is delicate but we have today accepted Henri into the *Sunshine Road.*'

Odile was unable to prevent it. To stop him would have split her family. Henri wanted to help and he needed to feel part of the struggle against the enemy.

'Monsieur Reynaud, when I was his age I fought and resisted. How can I refuse him today? It is dangerous, but dangerous is our lot and we must accept it.'

'Very well. We will take Henri and train him to run the line from Lille. He will work with our most experienced runner, Aurelie Dubonnet. Her runner name is Fifi. Aurelie's father is an honest and noble soldier and she is as courageous and as clever as he. She is also young, no more than twenty-five. The German soldiers look at her and notice her. But she is also clever at concealing her looks. She can teach Henri how to stand out and disappear almost in the same breath. Her own father did not recognise her when she first started running. He said she would pass for a woman of twice her age. Henri will be in the most capable and loyal hands. There will be no reason to doubt that theirs will be a successful partnership. In all honesty, there is very little danger if everyone remembers their training and does not lose their head. You now have the instructions for communicating and we must begin immediately. The British bomb Koln by night and there are already many pilots to move. Good night, Madame.'

As Odile left the *Sunshine Road*, she felt the old fears from Cambrai and the camps return. Once again needing to out-think the Germans, but this time the uniforms hid a darker soul, a purpose more sinister than the soldiers of 1914. These men used cunning, trickery and deception, hiding amongst their own people. Tempting the honest with fear, driving protection through collaboration. Monsieur Reynaud was wrong, there was a great deal of danger and now she had allowed her son to become part of it. But secretly she wanted it as well. She wanted the Germans here not a minute longer and Henri was in no more danger on a train from Lille than he would be sitting in the front room of their home. The Germans could come for him at any minute of any day. He was young and fit. When they accounted his presence, he would be taken from them and sent to Germany or Poland or goodness knows where.

As she walked in the cool evening to where Henri was waiting for her, she thought through the plans for the runners and the *Sunshine Road*. When she saw Henri, she realised that he would be very good indeed. Strong, quick to think and learn and most of all, he was lucky. More than once he should have come to trouble but trouble never stalked him. She did not yet know Aurelie but thought that both of them were going to have an adventure. Born of necessity and danger, of course, but it was for the liberation of France. She saw him each evening listening to de Gaulle on the radio, imagining his own father at the right hand of the French general. Odile could not refuse him. Had he been another's son, she would have welcomed him into the group and breathed a sigh of relief that fortune had smiled on the Resistance.

CHAPTER THIRTY-ONE
London and France 1942

William had seen enough for one day – he was not a politician and had never intended to be one. He had set up the machinery for a French Government at Carlton Gardens, setting up a disguised communications centre in a busy bar in Soho. Then he had managed a small network of agents to feed information to and from the Germans in France and had helped to write the speeches that General de Gaulle gave almost every evening, broadcasting in plain French from the British Broadcasting Corporation radio studios.

The general could be insufferable and sometimes William could almost forget who the real enemy was. But he seemed to appreciate William's deep understanding of France and the French, and William suspected that it was only knowledge of his family in France that kept the general from turning on him. He often told William that he liked him, that he liked his style, his ability to anticipate needs. But he had voiced strong reservations at the plans for an underground resistance and military action by civilians to decapitate the German machine. The general felt that without training, weapons and co-ordination, it would only anger the enemy into condemning men, women and children to die. William knew that he had to speak up.

'Did you not hear what I said in June 1940, Collins? Did you not feel the power of the French collective breath? The damned Vichy is sucking the will from our citizens and the Germans are murdering our Jews.'

'I did, sir, and I do understand. But just rising up simply puts all our heads up above the parapet to be shot at one by one. Better one great co-ordinated move than piecemeal acts of defiance that cause retaliation. Do you see that, sir?'

General de Gaulle waved his hand vaguely towards William.

'Of course, but it would be better if our British friends gave us what we needed. I ask each and every day. Now, I must read these reports, Collins. Thank you.'

The general, clearly irritated, retreated behind a copy of the intelligence reports from the Vichy region in southern France. William knew these were never pleasant reading and the photographs of French police talking and smiling with German officers clearly disgusted de Gaulle.

So here he now was, outside on a park bench, overlooking the green space of Westminster, where kings and queens had passed down the centuries. At least the Germans were not coming here in the near future – the Royal Air Force had prevented that catastrophe. William missed Odile more than ever and wanted to get her out of France, most likely it would need to be in secret. But she would not leave. Yes, they were both torn in all directions, stay or go, take a risk or be safe. In truth, neither France nor England were safe. At least in France the German occupation was settled and Odile could live in relative safety and comfort, of a sort. At least, safer than Cambrai had been. Hungry, yes. Free, no. But the risk was lower and the citizens could endure this time.

But something else kept her there, something deeper than love or honour or duty. She insisted that William stay in London, fighting for the Free French cause. She understood it, despising the Vichy capitulation, Petain more than any of them. Often, she told him *Do not come home until it is done, William.* So there he was. The telephone calls begging him to come home had changed. Although she seemed calm it was hard for them all. What hurt most was simply being apart from his wife after all they had endured to be together. Each time he embraced her, he felt the connection to the past and hope for the future. Each time she touched his scars they were both reminded of the past, making them ever more determined for the future.

But today he felt elated as he was to see Armandine. He had not seen her since his arrival in England, a fact that his daughter reminded him of often. At first it was a gentle tease but now it was more insistent. William worried that she must feel cut off from her roots with her mother and one brother in occupied France and her father working secretly in London. He had not been allowed a pass to pay her a visit, but wanted to see her to give her the security that only a father can provide to his daughter.

Armandine was currently teaching French in a small town in the Lake District, having been evacuated with the children during the Blitz. But now that the threat of bombing was receding her attachment was ending. She was due to start teaching English to the young French refugees in a town just north of London. General de Gaulle had offered to host a surprise reception at his home in Hertfordshire. William had to laugh at the gruff, bullish and typically Gallic general who appeared to want nothing more than to give a traditional English garden party. That afternoon, William would take the train to Berkhamstead to make the arrangements, the general would be there the next day and Armandine would arrive the day after. William was glad of the excuse to get him out of the office so that repairs could be carried out. The office had been hit by the Luftwaffe and the General enjoyed defiantly poking his head out of the hole in the roof and waving a French flag above his head. Even Mr Churchill had asked him to refrain – the telegram from Downing Street had made William laugh so loud that he thought he might be sacked on the spot.

GENERAL RE YOUR ASSERTION TO BE
THE REINCARNATION OF J OF ARC STOP
REMEMBER WE HAD TO BURN THE LAST ONE STOP

--oOo--

William departed for the railway station a little before two in the afternoon. Armandine's train was early and all he could see amongst the disembarking crowd was a tall and elegant young woman. His little daughter was now twenty-two and engaged to a partner in a legal practice in London. He saw Odile in her eyes and he recognised himself in her face. She was here, his much-missed daughter. How he wished that Odile was here with Arthur and Henri. Where was Arthur? What was he doing? For that matter, what was Odile doing? He had heard so very little from his wife for some time now. He was not worried but just felt a little lonely.

'Oh, Papa! You look so well and handsome in your uniform.'

'Ha, well welcome to Hertfordshire, you look quite the grown up.'

'Papa, I am twenty-two, not twelve.'

'Yes, sorry. I feel very old now!'

'Well, I am so excited to be here to see you. Come, let us go and have tea. I have some ration coupons saved up just for today.'

She reached her father and leaned to kiss him.

'Armandine, my love. I have made arrangements for tea. Keep your coupons for your own use. They most likely would not stretch to this.'

She dipped her head quizzically. 'Well, Papa. I am intrigued. Come, let us speak French for a few moments in honour of our home.'

'Yes, of course. Tell me one thing, I must ask. Have you had word at all from your brother?'

'I must admit I have not spoken with him in nearly a year. But do not worry. Our little hermit crab is quite well, I would certainly know if it were otherwise. He does not write, does not telephone, but his master has my number in London and the number of the legal practice that Michael is in, so if there were a problem we would know. You know him, Papa, he ploughs his own furrow.'

'He does. Well, here is the car. Do get in, my love.'

'Papa? This car has flags. This is a government car. Is this allowed?'

William smiled at his daughter and nodded.

'What a wonderful retirement job it is for you as well.'

William laughed. He could hear his wife in Armandine's voice and it made him happy.

At Rodinghead, the car turned off the small country road into a wide driveway. A uniformed French officer stepped forward, opening the door for the new arrival.

'Papa, where is this?'

'You will see, my love.'

In the entrance hall, the housekeeper took Armandine's bag and coat and she looked more intrigued than ever. Then the door opened and the general stepped into the hallway, ready to kiss his guest in welcome. Armandine turned to her father and smiled as she was taken into the main drawing room.

'Mademoiselle Collins, welcome to a little bit of France in England, or perhaps I mean a little bit of England in France?'

'Well, General de Gaulle, sir, it is an honour to meet you!'

'Mademoiselle Collins, the honour is mine. Come, let us have English tea. Colonel Collins, will you join us for tea?'

--oOo--

After tea, the general took William into the garden while Armandine spent time with Madame de Gaulle and their three children.

'Colonel Collins, I am facing considerable pressure from within France. Those cowardly fools in Vichy shout loudly and the Americans are listening to them. Mr Churchill is an ally I think, but I think he finds me difficult, obtuse perhaps and rather too uncontrollable. You know why I need to be visible, the French citizens need to hear a voice of France that they cannot have for themselves. Do you see William?'

'I do General, I truly do. Perhaps you should speak again with Mr Churchill?'

'Perhaps, but I need a speech to unite all of France. To expose the Vichy for what they are, collaborators and capitulates, curse them. I perhaps will need to speak again of honour and of loyalty and of the values of the French. This must come from me and soon I think.'

'I wonder if we could seek approval from the Prime Minister to discuss the appointment of the new ambassador to France?'

'You read my mind William, or anticipate my needs. Whichever it is, I will not complain.'

'I will go and speak with Duff Cooper. His Grenadiers pulled me out of a hole on the Somme battlefield. I think he may just be the politician we need.'

'Yes Colonel, I would like you to help me persuade your Prime Minister and the king to appoint Mr Cooper to be the ambassador to France for his support would be greatly appreciated. A have a secret weapon! Ha, my rivals for the advocacy of France do not have you to help them. I am rightly convinced of success. Besides, Mr Cooper is also a thorn in the side of the Germans. You know he is on their list for execution if they were to invade?'

'Yes, sir. Of course, you and I are also on that list. What do they know that we do not?'

De Gaulle laughed. 'I have a very good feeling that you and I will be very great allies.'

CHAPTER THIRTY-TWO
France 1942

Odile was careful not to be seen. Although Bazentin-Le-Petit itself was quiet and out of the sight lines for the Germans, Albert was not. But she had to go to Albert today as the meeting place was never outside of the town since it was easier to disperse and hide in a town – in the country, there was simply nowhere else to go and hide, too few people, too little cover. Odile understood that but it did not make the meetings any easier. They were to gather and discuss the next part of the plan to establish the repatriation route for British and American airmen from Lille to Bordeaux. The little group had to be careful as the Germans watched, from a distance perhaps, but they would look for patterns of behaviour and weaknesses and then use it against them. They would seek ways to infiltrate, to intimidate and to crush brutally without warning.

The January weather was very cold and only a few souls braved the icy wind to move around the town meaning that any movements would be noticed by the wrong people. Odile took her place at the front of the group. As their head, she had to make sure that their loyalty was always assured. Any suspicion or doubt had to be investigated. Her own son was the member tasked with these investigations and she was the only one who knew that. In the year since she established the little line of communication to Lille, they had moved over fifty men back to England without attracting the slightest suspicion of the Germans. The group was tightly knit, quite deliberately so, with everyone well known to each other, fearful of detection and more so of strangers. She looked around the group. Six familiar faces, four women and two men. The men were older, unlikely to be targeted for work or labour, or to appear subversive to the Germans. They looked quiet and useless to German eyes. The women were younger. They had to be as these women were the runners, taking and moving men from Lille to the edge of Bordeaux or Bayonne, handing men on to the next stage of their journey to Gibraltar. By now, they could pick up a man in Lille and he could be in Gibraltar in under five days.

Odile liked her cover name. She had chosen Dodo, because that was all she could say of her own name when she first learned to talk. Henri was given his by Madame Dumon, Charlemagne. Odile had mixed feelings at her son being the King of the Franks, knowing that Charlemagne was as terrifying to the Germans as to the French. His seat was in Aachen, a town that Odile remembered all too well and not with fondness.

At the end of the meeting the group were careful to disappear slowly, cautiously and without arousing suspicion. Odile waited behind to leave last with Henri. He had a small box of vegetables as a cover for his movement. They had the correct papers and the bill for the goods, duly signed by the greengrocer.

'Henri, you must leave with Fifi tomorrow morning. Take your motorcycle and lock it away when you reach Amiens. The bills for travel are all at the house. Take care, my love. You were back in three days last time. I must urge you to do the same this time.'

Henri leaned in to his mother and kissed her. Odile held him tightly, afraid the cargo was more dangerous this time, then she let him go with his box of vegetables. He walked across the square, past the Basilica and on towards the Bapaume Road. Odile watched him carefully as he left, watching for the slightest movement in the streets. She loved her son dearly and knew that he needed to do this. Henri was their third child, but the one who embodied William the most. He had learned so much in his short life and he was resourceful, clever and – as his father told him often – lucky.

At the corner, Henri disappeared from view. It was now time for Odile to return home. She quickly found her bicycle and began to ride away. A German soldier on the corner of the square simply waved to her. She nodded politely but said nothing, which was the expected behaviour. He could have stopped her but he did not. Odile had seen him before and hoped he saw her as just a woman going about her business.

Tonight, Odile was not returning to Bazentin and had arranged to stay with her Uncle Olivier in La Boisselle. Olivier still kept ducks and many of Pierre's machines but he had lost his sight in his older age. He never went out but his heightened sense of hearing was perfect in this little safe house. There were outbuildings, sheds and cellars, which were perfect hideaways for anyone in need. Odile was going this evening to prepare the Inn, which was the Resistance name given to the little cellars that were used to house the airmen. More British and Canadian soldiers buried deep in the ground at La Boisselle. Odile wanted to make sure that the rooms were dry and free from rats, as well as dark enough outside when the little lights were on. The Germans were very good at hunting down the Resistance out here. There were not many members and it was very difficult to hold secrets for such a long time. People could accidentally say something to the wrong person and the whole world could come apart, so suspicion ran like a fire through tinder. Satisfied it was safe and ready, she sat down and made supper for her uncle.

'A little broth from the vegetables that Henri was carrying earlier, Uncle.'

The old man inhaled and smiled. 'How I love onions and turnip – they are the best of all.'

Odile laughed. 'Well, that is very fortunate!'

'Ah, Odile, how I love to hear you in the house – you are always kind and appreciative.'

Odile laughed. 'To say nothing of being family, of course, Uncle!'

'Ah, yes, of course. Family. Any added safety and security is welcome in these times.'

'So how are you faring, Uncle?

'I am very well, thank you. Now how are your mother and father, Odile?'

'Ah, they are old and tired, you may not even realise how much they have aged.'

'Well look at me, my little duck. Old, bald and blind. Your father got the lucky cards in life, eh?'

'Well, if he did, then he is a very bad card player.'

'Don't let him hear you say that. He will say you are never too old.'

'Oh, Uncle Olivier. How I do love to come here. I miss the days before the Germans came back.'

The mood turned quiet for a moment. All that could be heard was the sound of spoons against the supper dishes.

'Odile, there will be a day when all of this foolishness is done. Until then, we keep on going. Is your boy off and running again?'

'He is. We think three days… it might be more difficult this time, of course.'

'Try not to worry, Odile, Henri has youth and luck on his side.'

She patted her uncle's shoulder. 'I hope so, Uncle, I hope so.'

Odile's work for this run was finished. She had set up this run, planned it and sent everyone out for their jobs and now it was up to her little *Sunshine Road* group to bring home their precious cargo.

--o0o--

By the time Odile had reached La Boisselle, Henri was well on his way to Amiens, his vegetable box simply left outside some lucky citizen's door. Now he was on his motorcycle and speeding along the smallest roads with his lights off. He knew the roads well, the distances and the timing. Henri had practised this route often in the daytime, and while that meant using precious fuel, he had to know his way in the dark. Fifi would be waiting for him at Amiens. They would take the train together towards Lille, using their own papers. That was important, there must be some truth to the deceptions or they simply could not work.

It took Henri just over two hours to reach Amiens using the route that he had practised. He was allowed to travel by train as there were no travel restrictions in place in this part of France. Carefully, he locked the motorcycle in a little wooden shed owned by another member near the station in Amiens. Fifi was already at the station. To his tired and straining eyes, she looked beautiful. As part of her own disguise, she always made a particular effort to look attractive and noticeable on the journey north. That way, in plain sight, she always drew the attention to her and away from whatever companions she was travelling with.

Like his mother, Aurelie Dubonnet spoke excellent German, having previously worked as an interpreter for the French Army, which was a considerable advantage. Henri enjoyed his trips with Fifi, for she was beautiful, although a little older. Sometimes he felt like a boy around her but he loved Yvette and always tried to think hard about her when he was on a run with Fifi, she could be quite intoxicating, even for a boy already in love.

The train was very late, which added a great deal of tension to the journey. It meant more time standing around, which invited opportunities for questions from the Germans, and even idle questions designed only to pass the time could be destructive since their stories must match perfectly. But Henri knew he was on safe ground with Fifi since both of them knew their jobs and how to do them. Any deliberate attempt to avoid the German's attentions could be more suspicious than standing around in the open. Henri instinctively preferred the shadows but Fifi was not that kind of woman.

'So how long have you been in France, handsome?'

'I'm sorry?'

'You heard me, General. How long have you been in France?'

'I am sorry, but I am not allowed to say, of course.'

'Oh, come now, you are not going to be shy with me?'

Henri tried to gesture to Fifi, but she deliberately avoided his gaze. His palms were damp and his shirt was wet, which now made him look suspicious, when all had been perfectly normal before Fifi got going.

'Shy? No, but I am on duty. You are a, well a…'

'Blonde with attitude? How is my German?'

'It is very good. But why, well, why are you here?'

'Going to see my Aunt in Lille. She fell over, you know. Silly old lady.'

'I see. Well, I hope that all is well with her.'

'Thank you, your name is?'

'Gunther, but I am not a general, ha!'

'Well I am pleased to meet you, Gunther.'

Fifi, took the cigarette that was offered to her and accepted the light. She stood staring at Gunther for a moment or two, then tapped his arm and turned away. She did not immediately return to Henri. Another soldier tapped his cap as she passed and a third invited her into the station bar for a drink with a group of German soldiers. She disappeared inside and was gone for fifteen minutes. When she finally came out, still smiling and smoking, she found her way towards Henri.

'We are safe now to Lille. These soldiers are on our train. They are simply moving in rotation back to their quarter and have no interest in us. I have their names and units.'

'Fifi! This is surely asking for trouble?'

'No, Henri. This is planning for success. Not one of them is even remotely looking at us to challenge us about our journey. They are like kittens at the milk bowl.'

'Well, please, enough for now, is that agreed?'

'Until Lille, yes. From there, it might be harder.'

Fifi was right. The train journey was indeed uneventful. Two further cigarettes were offered and accepted and the conversation was pleasant if unimaginative, with nothing important in their words and nothing given away. Henri heard himself being cast as Fifi's baby brother, 'just in case any naughty soldiers try to take advantage of his big sister.' Henri had to hold back a laugh at that one. Fifi was outrageous, but it worked because she knew exactly what she was doing.

At Lille, they made their way to the Citadel and the Parc d'Azure. Here, their contact, Merlin, would escort them to the cellars of a very reputable wine merchant to the French and Germans. The wine bottles were always perfect covers. The bottle stacks acted as baffles to any sound and the glass reflected light in all directions, averting any attention from accidental lights as well as breaking up the shapes of people moving and hiding. But the Germans also knew this ruse and so wine merchants were routinely raided for evidence of any occupation. This cellar had been raided the previous week, but the three airmen had been safely in the roof beams where the Germans had not bothered to look.

Henri stepped down into the cellar to look at his companions for the run to Bordeaux. He knew that there would be two, but the plan was now for three. The travel documents would need changing and it was never a good idea to do this in a rush.

'Merlin, you are a fool. You did not tell us there were three of them.'

'We sent a message with the last run for Dodo. Did she get it?'

'No, what message?'

'We have two Canadians and an Englishman. Turns out he is wounded though. Not so badly, limps with a stick. We can dress him up to look old.'

'I don't suppose the Canadians speak French?'

'No.'

'We understood there were two and none of them wounded.'

'What do you think, Charlemagne?'

Henri rubbed his neck and took a step back.

'Fuck it, what choice do any of us have?'

'None. They were all aircrew on a bomber that crashed in Ulmegeden on the border. The other crew were killed, with one still a prisoner.'

'Well, let us hope they fare better than their comrades. We had better brief them.'

Henri and Merlin looked over the false identification papers that had been carefully prepared, noting what changes would be needed. Their comrade in the German Administration of French Affairs Office in Lens had stolen blanks and copied the stamps perfectly. There were two spares and one could be used here. They were genuine and the false stamp looked so convincing they were confident it would work. At the border of Spain, they would take them back to be used again by the next crew of airmen.

The plan was deliberately simple. A train from Lille to Amiens or Cambrai and then on to the Paris Express. This was the most dangerous element, because this train was popular with Germans and always full. An hour or two of idle chatter could lead to mistakes and Henri did not like mistakes. Risks yes, mistakes no. The positive part of this journey was that most of the Germans were taking leave and looking for relaxation – Fifi's speciality – not paperwork. The last thing that the Germans wanted was a prisoner capture wasting their precious weekend passes, which they would not get back.

At Lille station, the group had to disperse, with Henri taking one of the Canadians and Fifi taking the other Canadian and the wounded Englishman. Hopefully, her special charm might deflect attention from the nervous-looking airmen who still moved more like able-bodied military men than infirm grandfathers wounded at Verdun. They had to stop striding around and shuffle a little as if the world had to be endured and not enjoyed, or they would be captured and probably not survive. Each man also swallowed a small piece of cordite since it greyed the skin temporarily and upset the stomach, providing real discomfort and forcing them to walk slowly and with difficulty.

At the platform, Fifi disappeared to go and change her appearance. She returned with no makeup and wearing a plain wig. Just enough of a change to deflect attention from her natural hair colour so she could avoid the soldiers' attentions completely. No one would imagine this to be the same flirtatious and dangerous woman. This way, she could now move more freely, a different disguise for a different purpose, unattractive and unenticing to the soldiery.

The train from Lille to Amiens turned out to be quieter than the train coming in to Lille, which meant Henri's luck was holding. But since none of the airmen spoke any French, there was a risk that they might stand out more if they were detained in conversation just to pass the time. If they were stopped by Germans, then Fifi would have to do all of the talking. A quieter platform meant you would stand out more, but there might be fewer soldiers to question your travel. It was the weekly gamble of the *Sunshine Road.* This time they were lucky. A quiet carriage with each man asleep in a different compartment. From here, the train would take four hours to reach Paris, with five scheduled stops. Each stop brought the possibility of attention from the feared Gestapo or the military intelligence men of the Abwehr. If missing airmen were brought to their attention, they would surely search the train.

The journey was hot and monotonous. The sounds of the engine, the rattle of the tracks and the hypnotic rocking of the carriage were comforting and alarming as each change in sound could spell danger. But as each minute passed, the closer they came to the relative anonymity of Paris and then a train to Bordeaux. The outer edges of wartime Paris could not come soon enough.

Outside the carriage, the gently rolling countryside finally began to give way to rows of houses and the smell of the city. Just before the train arrived in Paris, Henri and Fifi gently nudged the airmen so that they would wake without alarm. As each man woke up, he was reminded to remove his coat and drape it over his right arm and to carry a newspaper in his left hand. That way, if he were lost, he could be spotted even if his face was not visible. Each one identical, but in the boiling mass of people in Paris, visible enough to a watchful trained eye. Fifi and Charlemagne now returned to the roles they relished, but ones where their expertise had come through bitter experience.

At the platform in Paris, in a sweep of smoke and steam, Henri and Fifi stepped off the train in advance of their little party. Henri stepped quickly to the end of the platform where the German guards were lazily checking identification papers, almost in a dream-like repetitive process of question and answer. Henri wanted to listen to the questions and the answers that drew the least response. The Germans were usually unimaginative and the questions were banal and routine.

'Identification papers. Who are you?'

'Robert Maillard.'

'Where are you going today?'

'I am visiting my mother in hospital.'

'What is wrong with her?'

'She is just old.'

'Very well.'

'What is the reason for your journey to Paris?'

'I am travelling back to Bayonne to see my sister who is having a baby soon.'

'Did you board in Lille?'

'No sir, Lens.'

The repetitive questions for passengers from a train starting in the north were expected and usual, but the Germans changed their questions routinely. Could they get enough French into the airmen on the platform to avoid any suspicion? They had to try.

'Fifi, it is just destination today, purpose of visit and boarding station. Nothing about the weather or the times of trains. It is the same question over and over.'

'We must be quick, whilst the platform is still busy. Which of the Germans is the quickest?'

'The SS officer is certainly the slowest, the others all seem disinterested and miserable.'

'We will go to the two on the right by the wall, furthest from the SS man. The barrier is also widest there.'

'You go first, Fifi and I will go last, just in case.'

This was always the most dangerous part of the transfer across Paris. Always better moving in the brightly lit view of the Germans than skulking in the shadows, where suspicion always followed. Fifi approached the barrier with her genuine identification papers and a wide-open smile. She lifted her heel a little and turned her knee towards the officer. He looked away from her card to her leg, smiling almost absent-mindedly at his good fortune. He passed the card back to her without a word, just an idle stare at the little leg she had allowed him. It seemed all too easy. A Canadian went next, the first looking directly into the eye of the officer. Not a flicker from either man, he was waved through without a word. The second Canadian stepped up and handed over his card before he was asked a question in the usual bored manner.

'Are you in a hurry, then? Where are you going?'

'I am going to view my sister, who is ill.'

'What was that?'

Henri instinctively took a pace forward, placing himself now directly behind the Canadian. His eyes darted to the machine pistol on the shoulder of the German. The second soldier had one as well. The SS man had his back to both, with just a pistol. If he had to, he could move on him in an instant. He was poised and ready to move.

'I am going to see my sister, who is ill.'

'Where did you board the train? Lille was it?'

'Lille.'

The guard looked at him for a second or two. His face gave the slightest air of suspicion, his eyes narrowed a tiny fraction. Henri knew that fractions were all that were needed, but the guard said nothing more. Slowly, he passed back the identification papers, nodding for the airman to move along. The airman took the papers slowly, and his face gave a slight crease and a twitch as he took them.

Damn it! Henri said to himself, certain it was loud enough to be heard even though the words were in his head. *Why did he have to look at him? View? He must have noticed.*

Taking the initiative, Henri went next, wanting to engage the German in conversation, keeping the focus away from the airman who was now rapidly disappearing around the platform in a sea of brown coats and on into anonymity.

'Busy train today?'

'What? Who cares? Where did you board the train?'

'Lille, like most people here.'

'Shut up, just answer my questions.'

'Sorry, I am excited to see my sister in Paris. I have not seen her in three months.'

'What is her name?'

'Marianne Leglantier.'

'So, married then?'

'Yes, to a fat balding fool who is hopeless at cards! I'm hoping to teach the man a lesson.'

Henri reasoned that the little French these men used did not extend this far.

'Hm. Move on.'

Henri moved quickly ahead of the airman who had passed through the barrier without a word. It was nearly perfect, but not quite. Henri was troubled. He moved quickly forward, not daring to look back, sensing that something had happened at the barrier when he looked at Fifi.

'What happened?'

Henri could read Fifi's face, she was watching a movement behind him.

'The guard has moved into the office. We had better hurry.'

'Come on, we must move now. Split up into two groups again. See you at the Gare de l'Ouest. Let us meet on the Place de Rennes, where the train crashed, one hour from now.'

'One hour.'

Henri was feeling hot and angry. One word, one tiny word and the guard had spotted it. He dared not look at the faces of the two men with him. The nature of the job meant he did not care who they were, he just had to get them safely to Bordeaux or Bayonne. He could sense the Canadian wanted to talk so he moved faster to avoid the need for conversation. Henri took them through a long sweeping route out and around the city towards Montparnasse and the Place de Rennes. He wanted to take up some time, perhaps to avoid the extra guards that might be placed in the stations if the alarm had already been raised. And he also wanted to see if anyone had started to follow them.

The Gestapo were sometimes deliberately visible in a uniform of their very own. Some wore the sinister Homburg, others a black leather coat and gloves, mostly for effect. It spoke volumes about them before they ever got close to you. But out here in the streets it was different. They blended, melting into the grey foam of humanity this way and that, avoiding eye contact. But they saw everything and Henri knew it. He cursed under his breath at the stupid Canadian. His nerve failed a little and he started to second guess their movements, which made him take an unplanned wider and longer turn. But he realised he was doing it and quickly gathered his thoughts again – perhaps it was this skill that meant he was still alive. Quick wits and quick feet and lucky. He smiled. Dodo would be proud of her youngest son, running airmen through Paris on their way to Spain and liberty. From there to return to the air to drop bombs on the heartlands of the Nazi industrial west. Henri stood up straighter. He had found his inner strength again. Silently, he thanked his mother for that gift. At the Rue de Rennes, Henri found the street mostly deserted. Should they proceed now or wait for more people to pass by? They were already going to be late. Fifi would be at the Place de Rennes already, under the window that was obliterated when a train came though years before, smashing into the paving stones below, killing an innocent French woman. Henri hoped that no French woman would die here today.

--oOo--

Fifi was uneasy. So far, nothing had happened. But the Gestapo were long ago masters of an art that the French underground were just learning as they went along. Fifi had found herself a Resistance operative. The Gestapo men had chosen this life, groomed to perfection, their skills sharpened by years of Nazi fanaticism in Germany. Fifi shook the thought from her head. She was no amateur, she was every bit the match for the Gestapo. This was her country and she could melt away.

She now stood looking anxiously across the Place de Rennes in the direction she felt sure that Henri would appear from, the airman at her side making idle conversation. He was shabbily dressed and she had again taken on the outward personality of Fifi, wanting to be noticed. The plainly dressed woman at the barrier had been anonymous. Here was a film star. The two could never be confused, except if she had been seen moving easily between them.

With a shudder, her experienced eye spotted two men dressed in ordinary clothes, but moving with an assured swiftness that was not at all French. Here were men from one of the special units in the Nazi machine. She suspected that they were agents of the Abwehr, the military intelligence branch, or Gestapo in plainer clothes. Abwehr officers were only interested in the capture of military secrets and it was possible that these airmen might know something. The men moved across the square, never looking towards Fifi, but their sweep took them in an arc to within just a few steps of Fifi's position. They could arrest her here, they could simply walk up and take them away, but the men did not move. They waited. Cigarettes were lit, smoked and stubbed out on the stones. Within fifteen minutes, a little pile of stubs had formed at their feet. Smoking used as cover for observation, Fifi assumed. To her, they stood out as plain as day. To the throng of frightened Parisians, they were just shapeless figures to be negotiated around on their way to somewhere safer.

She had to find Henri and tell him of the danger. But what could she say? She told the airman to move into the station, to pass the guard only in a line of people, to push into the middle if he had to, but always to make sure that people were behind, wanting to get through, angry at the impertinent man in front. Look late, but not hurried. Eyes down, even when spoken to, for that was most usual. She hated leaving the airman for they might never find each other again.

'Keep your coat and newspaper just as we planned. It is the way we do it in *this* group, not the way everyone does it, so you will not be noticed, except by us looking out for you. Look for my return. Come to me as a friend, kiss me and take my arm when I return, but never look at a German uniform, not even for a second.'

'Yes, Mademoiselle, thank you. See you on the other side.'

'Speak French, you fool!'

The very moment that the airman was around the curve and out of sight, the two men moved from their pile of stubs towards Fifi, taking her gently by the arm. The airman was long gone.

'Please do not make a scene, Mademoiselle. Stay calm and quiet and no one need be hurt. You must come with us, now, we insist.'

'Who are you? What business do you have in detaining me?'

'Do not speak again, look directly ahead and keep walking. We ask the questions and you do not.'

Fifi heard the German accent in their French words. Not cultured, but functional. These men had trained for this moment and she had nowhere to go and no possibility of alerting Henri. She did not look to where her airman had moved to avoid the arrest. He was alone now, from here he had no possibility of sanctuary, since the contacts did not know him and he did not know where to find them. It was now only a matter of time before the Gestapo had him in their grasp. She was moved firmly to a waiting car. Inside it, she was flanked by the two men who spoke to one another and to the driver in German. At the corner of the Place de Rennes, she saw another man in a leather coat tap his hat as the car passed. They were not Abwehr, they were Gestapo. Her heart sank. Nobody in her network knew she was here. She might never be seen again and now knew that she could be tortured for information. Had she been given the chance, she would have taken a pistol to herself, rather than betray her comrades. The car moved into the streets around the station. Despite her fear, she noticed that they were unusually busy for the time of year.

--oOo--

Henri arrived at the Place de Rennes, now sure that they had not been followed. The airmen flanking him looked normal enough. Rough unshaven faces, tired from travel and weary from captivity. They knew to follow exactly everything that Henri asked of them, without question, at least until they reached Bayonne on their way to Spain. He scanned the entire square and looked to where the train had crashed, to the exact spot that they had agreed. Nothing, even though he had been certain that Fifi would arrive first. She had to be here. But the square was deserted. He dared not wait any longer. The last train to Bayonne was due to leave in forty minutes. It might take that long to get through the German inspectors, even with luck, perfect French and papers to match.

Henri knew that his face was going to give him away for he could feel the heat in his skin, and the sweat on his forehead and on his nose. He had to move now. Without a word, he pointed towards the barrier and in French asked his companions for a cigarette for the journey. As they came together, Henri whispered in English.

'Fifi is not here. It may have been dangerous to stand here, I do not know. They may have gone already for safety. The time for her to be here has already passed. We must go.'

The two airmen nodded in agreement and the three men moved towards the barrier to the platform. The little wooden gate was open but flanked by two Germans in ordinary uniforms. These men were not Gestapo, or SS or any of the organisations trained to spot their movements. These were foot soldiers whose duty was to control the crowds. As before, the airmen went first. Henri did not move ahead to listen first, there was simply no time and the place was too crowded. The men would have to fend for themselves, which meant that the levels of danger rose sharply. Fifi was on his mind now, no longer the safe passage of the airmen.

Henri was deeply worried for Fifi was very good at this and he was terrified that she had been captured and even killed. A pain in his stomach took him by surprise at this thought, so he thought instead of her hair and her smile, her easy manner charming the Germans into little puppy dogs, hers to command. He was sure that he would see Fifi on the train and she would tell him of the suspicious movements in the crowd that had forced her to abandon their meeting. As they got close to the first guard, Henri could hear the German order to hand over identification papers.

'Papers.'

'Here.'

The first airman was through. It was clear that neither he nor the German spoke any French at all.

'You there. Where are you going?'

'Excuse me?'

'Bordeaux, Bayonne or Pau?'

'Ah, Bayonne. My sister.'

'Move on.'

The second man was through. A question in German, answered in terrible French. It was certain that the French around could hear this exchange and he hoped that none favoured the Vichy south and would choose to speak up. He scanned the people around and no one looked up.

'Papers. Where are you going?'

'Bayonne, my brother is there and I am visiting my sister, who is ill. Well, pregnant really.'

'Move on.'

Henri reached the platform. The train had not yet arrived, but already he could see the mix of German soldiers and civilians moving on the concourse. This was a dangerous moment. They had no route of escape and if caught now, there was no possibility of alerting Fifi.

--oOo--

The car rounded the large circus along and past Les Invalides. The swastika-adorned flags fluttered in front of the Ecole Militaire. Fifi was being drawn into the administration of German-controlled Paris, a journey with no exit or possibility of a final reprieve. There was no point in trying to be charming to these two. They were simply not interested.

Then the car stopped suddenly in the middle of the street. At either end, a uniformed German soldier stepped out seemingly from nowhere to block the road. The men turned to look at Fifi. One of them looked down at her legs then back to her face. He moved a little closer, his face moving to meet hers. She felt like spitting at him, or biting his nose, anything but this. But she felt the grip of the other man on her arm, holding her back, forcing her face to face with the Gestapo.

--oOo--

The train was delayed, but at least this meant that everyone else was also agitated and annoyed, so they did not look so out of place hiding in plain sight. Henri moved to the platform edge to see if the train was approaching, almost listening to the sound of the rails to see if he could hear the train wheels. Nothing. He turned again down the line and then back to the airmen. It was only a second, but they were gone.

Damn it! Where are they? A wave of panic rose inside him. He was now alone, fearful of the fate of his charges and still worried about Fifi who was clearly not here on the platforms. Suddenly, this operation had become a disaster. He had to think fast or it might become his undoing as well, so he stepped back into the shade of the ticket office to give himself a chance to think and a slightly higher vantage point. Newspaper. Coat over the arm. But there were no coats and papers together.

Have you forgotten the rules, you fools? You stupid, fools. You've killed us all. Henri was only talking to himself, but he knew that his face must betray his feelings.

'You! Get down from there and come over here immediately.'

Damn it! Henri stepped down and towards the officer who had commanded him in German. As he stepped across the parting crowd, he sensed another man now moving alongside him. He was wearing gloves. His heart sank. He knew where this man was from. As they approached the uniformed officer, the man with the gloves spoke in German that was too fast for Henri to comprehend. A hand was placed over his arm and he was turned into the ticket office, through and out into a waiting car. The airmen were nowhere to be seen. He was pushed gently into the back seat, the chattering of the crowd and the harshness of the German language to his ears only adding to his panic. He had to remain calm. But here he was, an amateur fighter amongst the trained professionals. They had undoubtedly had years of practice at this, fine-tuned skills practised on their own people. He only had his wits and some loyal companions, who right now, were nowhere to be seen.

--oOo--

Fifi felt herself pressed back in the seat. The face moving closer to hers. The mouth of the man moved to touch her cheek, brushing her skin lightly. She felt panic rise and nausea build inside her. She would prefer death to this public humiliation. His hand moved onto her body. It was only a matter of time before he touched her breasts or plunged his hand between her legs. Her arm was pinned, her face gently but firmly held back. The driver began to laugh to himself, no doubt sensing what was coming. The man's hand rested on her shoulder as his mouth reached her ear. She felt him draw breath, his mouth was that close. Then he spoke to her, in the smallest whisper, in excellent French.

'Listen to me. Don't move, not even your eyes.'

The man kissed her earlobe gently, moving closer still.

'When we get out, let me push you to the wall and then inside. I will not hurt you. You will see. It will be painless. If you understand, sigh gently.'

Fifi's mind was a whirl of emotion. She could not decide if this man meant for her to be safe or not. But there were no other options. At least on her feet, she might have a chance. Here, she was pinned, exposed and missing. The man kissed her neck and his hand briefly hovered over her breast. She nearly cried out, but managed to sigh instead. The second man released Fifi's arm and she felt the tug to get out the car. Her shoe came loose and she stumbled onto the pavement.

'Hey, Max, leave a little for us, eh?'

Fifi felt herself being pushed towards the wall, then spun around, her face towards the German. He turned, barking at the other men. A door next to them opened, an inky blackness greeting Fifi. The guards in the street moved aside and the car then moved off. She could not understand the words being spoken, but she knew that her troubles were only just beginning.

--oOo--

Henri was watching everything, the movement of the men in the car with him, the easy control of their hands and bodies. They were lean and well-treated. These men moved people around for a living. They were in control of their movements, their senses alert and quick to respond. In one sense, Henri envied them, but he feared them more. He was going to be difficult with them for he wanted to give nothing away. The conversation was in German. As they passed soldiers, other officers and men, they were saluted, passing orders and conversation between themselves. The barriers at the Rue Malmedy were immediately raised. With horror, Henri realised that he was being taken into the ancient buildings of Les Invalides. The car was then parked close to the wall so that Henri could not escape around an opening car door. A large wooden portal opened up, the darkened interior giving no clue as to the building's current purpose.

Henri was moved into a small room in total darkness. He sensed a presence but could not understand it. But then there was a change in the air, a certain scent in his nose. It was Fifi. He feared his senses were deceiving him by making him imagine her here. He now knew that he desired her, quite in what way he could not understand, but he wanted her here with him now. The scent grew more real, he was certain it was her in this room. But then there was a voice. It spoke perfect French with a hint of a German accent.

'I am very sorry for bringing you here like this but we had no choice. Your runner at the station. Such a small mistake, almost perfect, but the soldier alerted the Gestapo, so we had to move immediately.'

Henri felt unable to reply. His mind was a tumble of thoughts. Would agreeing condemn him? Was this a mind trick? If he said anything, it might mean he was shot on the spot. The walls were thick enough. And for that matter, why were the lights still out? At that moment, a blinding flash of light flooded the room. Henri was as shocked as he had ever been in his young life and it was now all too clear to him what had happened.

CHAPTER THIRTY-THREE

Dusseldorf March 1942

Liesel looked at the photograph of her husband with what looked like a totally different woman on her wedding day. The round face, the open smile and free spirit in her were distant memories. The Liesel of today was haunted, troubled and afraid.

For two years, the Eisners had feared arrest or at least questioning. Her brother had mysteriously disappeared, the black cars no longer prowled outside each day and nobody came to see them – no friends or neighbours. Worst of all, her parents had virtually abandoned them. Perhaps they knew that it was their own son who hunted Karl with a craven passion for his own advancement in the Nazi world. Perhaps they did not appreciate that little detail. But Karl had now not been outside in almost a year. His body had withered with his spirit in the darkness of their own home.

Each day Liesel watched the cars that passed by her home, looking for the tell-tale signs of the Gestapo or the SS. But perhaps they had lost interest in the Eisners. Lost interest or lost orders. Perhaps the only impetus of this investigation was the order of Kurt Langer, who might now be engaged in some other horror, distracted or removed from the Dusseldorf political turmoil. Things simply had to change, or her husband would fade forever from her, as a flower dies in the darkness.

Liesel felt a tear emerge from the corner of her eye at the picture of the woman who was so full of life only twenty years ago, full of hope for the future with her doctor and the prospect of a family, full of laughter and love. Already she had made the huge sacrifice of sending her children back to her parents, for their own safety, claiming that she was too weak to care for them and praying that neither of them would speak of Karl's presence. Today, she would end this imprisonment. She would see if Karl was hunted still, or whether the law had prevailed and he would no longer be arrested on sight.

'My darling, I will be gone for this morning. Please be careful not to be seen at the window. Why not go and read in your study for the time I am out? I have brought you the latest journal and put it in there for you.'

'I have begged you not to go Liesel, but you do not listen.'

'Karl, please go and read. This is something I must do. I will try and bring you something fresh to eat.'

Liesel decided to leave without another word on the subject so she quickly put on her coat and hat, and left. None of her outdoor clothes fitted her thin and drawn body. It seemed a giant had crept in and swapped clothes with her. Still, perhaps she could hide undetected beneath the layer of heavy cloth.

--oOo--

Karl watched from the back of the bedroom, just seeing a glimpse of his wife as she scurried off as if she were the one under suspicion. His beautiful bride looked small and hidden from the world, her neck thin and seemingly barely able to hold up her head. He remembered the charming, confident and talented nurse who had tumbled into his life in October 1918. The perfect white uniform and the scolding she was given by his own father over the identification card. Clever Liesel. Yes, clever, beautiful Liesel. Perhaps there was hope for them, deep inside of her. A surge of excitement suddenly coursed through him. They should escape Germany! If Odile in France could do it in 1918, then why should they not try it in 1942? The world was just as dangerous, but it had to be better than this miserable humiliating existence. Were they strong enough? But then he felt ashamed. He had forgotten about Franz and Monika. Monika was growing up fast, she was now a young woman and this was no life for her. And he knew that Franz was angry and confused. His son's friends were full of passion for the army and the Fatherland and he could not understand why it was not possible for him to be part of it. He was considered an Aryan, a true German, but the mark of his father held a shadow over him. A shadow he could not run from, however hard he tried.

Karl turned away from the window. Just as he did so, he noticed a man standing on the opposite side of the street. He wore a faded leather coat against the wind and a wide-brimmed hat, and he was watching the Eisner home with interest. The man lit a cigarette and moved a step closer, watching intently, smoking cigarette after cigarette. He did not try to hide in the shadows. Here was a man confident of his authority. Karl realised that he was Gestapo and that they were still interested in the Eisners, himself in particular.

The man moved yet closer and Karl could see that he was now looking along the wall of his house, the very place that Karl himself had hidden when Kurt was at the window. There was a sound at the back, something had fallen and broken. It sounded like a window. The man took another step forward, leaning his head to get a better view. Karl realised that someone else was now inside his home and that he would become trapped upstairs if he did not move.

Quickly, he went to the tiny rear stairs and down to the back of the scullery. He knew he could get down to the cellar if the unwelcome visitor went inside the house and didn't notice the slim entrance to the cellar steps, with the little door added so that the children would not fall into the cellar. The door did not move, but more sounds came from within. The distinctive sounds of voices became clearer. Someone was calling his name.

'Herr Doctor Eisner? Herr Eisner? Eisner? We would like a word with you. We now know you to be here. It will make it very much worse for you of course, if you do not come with us. Eisner? We know you can hear us. We simply wish to ask you some questions. Herr Eisner? Eisner? Come now, Doctor we know you are here.'

Karl sensed the voice had moved into the house itself so he dared to test the small door that lead to the cellar steps. To his dismay, it was either locked from the outside or jammed and to force it would bring the intruders straight to him. But he was trapped anyway, so decided to push gently. With a little force it gave way and opened with only a slight jolting sound. He moved down to the hidden pit in the store room that lead down to the secret surgery his father had built years before. The door to the surgery was almost impossible to find for anyone who did not know it was there. With relief, he made it down to the secret surgery and locked the hidden door from the inside.

There was a little dirty window in the cellar room that looked out at garden level where it was concealed by a flower pot and a wooden frame. It was too small for an adult to climb through. The door that had previously been used by visiting patients had been covered by a wooden fence nailed between two wooden posts. It could be removed, but it would require tools and time, which would at least give Karl time to pick up a hammer or a shovel to use as a weapon.

But no one came around or down. The voice eventually faded and Karl hoped that the man had been satisfied that the house was empty and had left. He dared not return to the surface just yet. Liesel would guess something had happened and come down for him when she had returned from whatever investigations she was undertaking. He would wait in the safety of silence.

After what must have been two hours, Liesel did return, tapping on the little outside window gently with her boot. She called down to him from above.

'Karl, oh that is a relief! It was the Gestapo that came here. There were five of them. I saw their car drive away. They have been through all of our possessions and have taken away some documents. I do not know which ones yet, but the pile of papers has been disturbed. Stay there, my love, do not move for the moment. I will bring you food and blankets and come down to you. Be strong, they have not found you and will not find you. I must make sure that they have not returned or chosen to watch us closely outside.'

But then came the sound of men's voices and several SS officers and men with rifles approached Liesel in the garden. She was gently restrained by a young German soldier who seemed unsure of himself.

'Please, Frau Eisner, or should I say Fraulein Langer? Do not try to run.'

'Take your hands off me, soldier, I am a German citizen. You have no right to detain me.'

'Please, just stand there then. There are many officers of the Gestapo here in any case.'

The soldier nodded towards two men slowly moving into the garden. Rain began to fall and Liesel felt the air chill around her, making her shiver. The first man approached Liesel and nodded to her, tapping his hat.

'Fraulein, we are in search of your former husband, the man known as Doctor Eisner.'

'He is still my husband and a doctor, and he is not here. Anyway, what business do you have with him?'

'I am sorry, but I am not at liberty to say.'

'Well I can tell you. *Your* Gauleiter has declared him a Jew. He isn't, not that it should matter in the slightest. But he is married to me and I am a German citizen, the daughter of a decorated General of the Prussian Guard. So far, I fail to see your business here. I order you to leave immediately.'

The man raised two hands in a calming gesture towards Liesel.

'Don't you try to stop me speaking in my own home! I am a German, my husband is an upstanding German and you are not only mistaken, but you are offending me by standing there.'

'Fraulein Langer, I am afraid that your information is incorrect. Your former husband—'

'Former? He *is* my husband. I was given away to him by my father, a general. The attendant to my husband was my brother, who is a colonel in the SS. As I said, leave. If you address me again, you will call me Frau Eisner. You insult me if you call me by any other name.'

The Gestapo men looked to one another and conferred quietly.

'Frau Eisner, or more correctly, Fraulein Langer, your marriage has been declared void by the office of *our* Gauleiter. As a result, you are no longer married. In fact, officially, you never have been married. Karl Eisner is now a fugitive of the Fatherland, a protected Jew but one now wanted for arrest. We hope he is not being hidden here on these premises. The ownership of this house has been officially and legally turned over to the city of Dusseldorf and is now under the kind protection of the office of the Gauleiter. The Gauleiter himself has kindly consented to your continued residence here on the condition that you turn over to him the person named Karl Eisner.'

Liesel was shocked. The cold harshness and brutal degeneracy of her life with Karl into so few words, delivered without even a flicker of understanding or empathy from a fellow German. It was if marrying Karl was a crime itself.

'Do you understand, Fraulein Langer?'

'Stop calling me Fraulein Langer. Besides, if that were true, then what does that make my children, born of an Aryan German woman?'

'We do not have that information, but I would conclude that the Gauleiter is satisfied that they become wards of Dusseldorf as the bastard children of a German citizen. Perhaps they may be placed in the custody of your father, the decorated general you are so keen to promote.'

Liesel wanted to cry, to shout and to deny their words. But she would not give them the satisfaction.

'Please leave. My husband is not at home. In fact, you have driven him away. You watch this house, you know he is not here.'

The men turned to leave. At the gate, one of them turned back to Liesel.

'Be assured that if we discover him here, the Gauleiter cannot confirm his ability to protect you from... let us call them... the others.'

Once they had gone, Liesel was careful to enter the house through the wide rear garden door. The door was not overlooked and it would not be possible to see into the house from any vantage point around. Her father and Kurt had already made sure of that for their own protection. But the side and front were visible, and so would the little window be from the road. She had been lucky. Perhaps they thought she was gardening or picking herbs from the little frame over the window.

Once inside, she closed the door and locked it. She went to the front door and locked that. On the little table, she saw a single sheet of paper, folded neatly. On it were just a few words, smudged by what looked like a drop of water or a tear.

Frau Eisner.

I am sorry, but I am afraid of the Gestapo and the SS. I cannot stay. I love you all and adore the children, but without them, you have no real need of me. I must look after my own mother, who is frailer now as each day of this war passes. She is afraid of the bombs that drop as well.

I wish you all luck.
Marthe Weir

Not a word to her face, this was another cold hand on her heart. She put down the housekeeper's note, which blew from the table and floated to the floor. Liesel sat on the stairs for a moment to compose herself. The shock of the Gestapo and the news of Frau Weir's departure together took away her strength for the moment. In silence, she took deep breaths. She had to keep going, to keep moving, to get her family away from this waking nightmare. With a final deep breath, she stood and moved back to the little store to call down to Karl.

'My darling, I am going out for a few moments. I will be home soon. Please keep away from the windows and remain in your study.'

She moved down the little steps to her husband.

'Stop calling it that, it is nothing but a freezing prison cell.'

Karl drew his wife to him and kissed her but she pulled away.

'It is like that, is it?'

'Nothing is like anything. I have to leave now, Karl.'

Liesel almost ran to the telegraph office on the corner of Landstrasse and Wilhelmstrasse. The little postmaster smiled at her. He knew nothing of anything and greeted her as he had always done. His discretion was well known and Liesel knew he was no Nazi sympathiser. She did not have any money on her but she knew that this was not ordinarily a problem.

'May I beg of you to send a telegram immediately?'

'For you, Frau Eisner, I would walk the telegram there myself. Is it to your sister in France again?'

'Yes, please, the same place.'

'Write it down and I will send it immediately. Let me set up the machine. Three lines at this time of day would work best. Is that enough?'

'Thank you.'

'Better be quick, perhaps the bombing might begin again. You never know.'

Liesel had decided to risk everything here and now. They were at the end of the line. Kurt had truly and cruelly forsaken her and was now in a deadly pursuit of her husband to further his own Nazi career. Her father was ignoring the facts that were staring him in the face and her mother was too frightened to offer any assistance. They were without friends, family and hope. Their children had been wrested from them, what was left to lose? Perhaps it was rash but she hoped her instinct was right. The Gestapo had been in their house, they were now watching their every move again, and something was clearly different. A change, a movement that could not be reversed. Someone was again interested in them and they had to get out of Germany, away from this evil of the Nazis.

CHAPTER THIRTY-FOUR
Paris 1942

Henri blinked in the dazzling light. Across from the little table was Fifi, her face ice white and her eyes closed against the hot bulbs and the glare reflecting from the white walls. Next to Henri was an unfamiliar man in a new leather coat, the smell of the hide was almost intoxicating, as was the aroma of good American tobacco. Henri wanted to call to Fifi but he thought he should not. There was a second, younger man sitting next to her who was wearing a new coat that looked several sizes too big for him. Perhaps he was a new recruit.

'You are in the care... shall we say... of the Abwehr Southern Paris Office. I take it you know what the Abwehr is? You should, when you are attempting to transport escaped prisoners of war. Dear me, how amateur you are. You *are* amateurs, are you not?'

Henri said nothing. The silence was unbroken for minutes before another sound was made. Fear rose in him. There seemed no obvious escape route here and no one else knew that they were here.

'Herr Rausch, would you be kind enough to leave us for a moment? I think I would like some time with these young people to, let me see, acquaint myself with their stories.'

'Yes, Herr Wagner.'

The younger man stood, stared at Fifi and then left, locking the door behind him. Henri scanned the room. There was nothing except the dazzling lights, the table, the chairs and Fifi. He saw fear in her eyes and resignation in her movement, she looked so frightened and he just wanted to hold her close.

'Henri, it says here. But I do not think this is your real name is it? Rollin? No, no, no. I know who you are. The question is of course, do you know who I am?'

'Some Abwehr ass who can't tie his own shoelaces. How old are you?

Twenty? What the fuck do you know?'

Wagner held up his hand.

'I know a great deal more than you think, Monsieur, a great deal more. For now, let me speak with the beautiful young lady who charms the army and slides into a clever disguise. It was almost good, Fraulein. So, you are Mademoiselle Dubonnet?'

Fifi looked up. 'I don't know anyone by that name, it certainly is not me.'

'So you are not the Aurelie Dubonnet who has been running pilots from Lille to Bayonne for a year?'

Fifi jerked, her eyes wide. 'I… I have no idea what you mean.'

'If you do not, then very well. But who was that man you pushed to the barrier? A man who we arrested. It seems his French is a little basic for a Frenchman. Perhaps he drinks himself into a stupor or perhaps he is an Englishman? Canadian? Australian? American? How am I doing, Herr Collin?'

Wagner did not move his gaze to Henri as he addressed him, he stared straight at Fifi. Henri wondered how he knew so much. How did he know? Who was feeding him information? There must be a break in the chain of secrecy in his mother's line. It would lead to his mother and she would be shot. His beloved mother, who had suffered so much would simply die at the end of a pistol round. But killing this man would do nothing, he would have to fight to the top of this pile to discover the truth.

'I asked you a question, Herr Collin. How am I doing? Am I right?'

'I simply have no idea – Herr Wagner, was it? A fine upstanding Aryan name, I see. Well, fuck you.'

'Now, now, Henri. Let us have a conversation. You and I are both men of the world. What should I do to this pretty tigress we have in our presence, hm?'

'Touch her and I will kill you.'

'I do not think that you will. You know there are fifty men outside? It will not be long before they return.'

Wagner leaned in towards Henri and took out his notebook and a pen. He opened the book in the middle at a blank page, then flattened the book on the table.

'Write down the names of the three pilots that you were to transport to Gibraltar. Here, do it now.'

Wagner passed the notebook to Henri. To Henri's surprise, the page was not blank. It contained words, in French.

This room has a secret microphone. The Abwehr can hear every word you and I say.

Do not show any reaction to my next question.

I am a friend in wolf's clothing

'Good, thank you. Now perhaps I should help myself to the lovely Fraulein Dubonnet for my troubles. Do you want to hold her down for me, Collin, ha?'

Henri was unsure of his next move. Going along might be exactly what this man wanted. Perhaps it was simply a trap. He had heard of this tactic before. Indeed, he was most certainly in with the wolves and the clothing matched. He looked up at Fifi. She was stony faced, her lips almost invisible. What would she do? How would she react? He could not sit here and do nothing now that he was walking with the enemy, being drawn in by their charm and seduction. The years of Nazi domination in Germany had fine-tuned their skills in to an art form.

And what of himself? A boy turned into a man because of a war. A clever boy, but this was an altogether more sinister proposition. He looked again at the words. *I am a friend in wolf's clothing.* Where was his choice? He would be condemned as an enemy of the Nazis, no longer a mere citizen to be tolerated and suffered to live. Once he had acted against the regime, that meant prison or even death. They would not care – they killed their own for less. He wanted more time, he needed to speak with Dodo, he felt like a little boy again, seeking out his mother to comfort a wound.

'If you insist, Herr Wagner. What do you want me to do?'

Wagner stood, scraping the table. He banged his fist on it two or three times and then pulled Henri and Fifi up by their arms. Henri looked across and saw Fifi looking terrified and beaten for the first time since he had met her. He felt his own confidence fail. Her charm and self-assurance inspired him and drove him onwards, perhaps to the point of recklessness. But today they had been careful and still the military police had found them. He wished that Fifi knew what he knew about this man – for if there was the slightest chance that this man would be sympathetic to them, she might regain her composure and work this particular problem. Wagner pulled them to the door, banging on it loudly with his boot. A young Abwehr officer opened the door, taking Fifi by the arm.

'Please take these prisoners to the cottage. I will join you in a few minutes. Let me get my notebook.'

Fifi blinked in the daylight but Henri kept his eyes shut. He tried to think but his head was a fog of confusion and conflict, thinking of the rows of the dead all over his homeland. They came courageously to liberate and die for his country. Now he must do the same. He knew where he was, for this was one of the most famous buildings in all of France. Would the Germans also know of the tunnels? He thought of breaking free. The Abwehr had pistols, but would they use them inside? Could he and Fifi communicate a plan? She looked defeated but perhaps she was scheming in her mind and her plan would soon be revealed.

Once again, they were put in the car, with Wagner at the front directing the driver to the cottage. To Henri, that sounded anything but charming and he imagined torture and brutality, their chances would not improve in that place. The car moved towards the beautiful Seine, shimmering in the light, but he could not enjoy its fresh air or cool waters through the glass window. So close to liberty, but a world away in the custody of the Nazis. Wagner spoke then, interrupting Henri's thoughts.

'I need you both to listen carefully. We are officers in the Abwehr, but we are so much more than that, certainly as far as you are concerned. I could have you shot or sent to a forced labour camp so you never see your families again. Do you understand that?'

'There is much that I do not understand here, Herr Wagner.'

Henri decided to try to find out more before throwing in his lot with this German.

'Perhaps, but this war is a complicated business. The politics, the borders, the cultures. In the east it is easy. Here in the west, well, it is more fluid, shall we say?'

Fifi looked up from the floor and Henri wondered if she now had an inkling of what was really being said. She gently nudged Henri, who looked up, an almost imperceptible widening of the eyes between them.

'Many years ago, I discovered a terrible secret. As a matter of fact, it was a scandal. You might ask, for example, why my French is so good. You may ask indeed, for that might be something for you to cling to as you slide down this particular rope.'

Wagner looked out of the window and indicated that the driver should turn left to avoid an oncoming SS car.

'As I said, I discovered a secret. But it was not so much the secret that shook me, it was the pain and suffering of my mother, driven to the position that she found herself in. Do you follow me?'

Henri and Fifi shook their heads. Something was not right with this German officer, but Henri could not unlock what was being said.

'No, well perhaps I should dare to tell you more. The cottage we are going to is a secret location, but in fact there are two. The first is operated by the SS and the Gestapo, with whom I have a cordial and co-operative relationship as an officer of considerable talent. It is to that first location that the Abwehr believe us now to be going. But there is also a second cottage, a small house above the Moulin tunnels. You know of these tunnels, perhaps?'

Henri nodded, familiar with the Moulin tunnels, which had been built by the citizens of Paris fearing first the revolutionaries and then Napoleon. He dared not hope for too much in case this man was not all he seemed, for it might yet be a trap to trick them into betraying their comrades. But this Wagner knew their names. He knew Aurelie Dubonnet and Henri Collins, even if he hadn't pronounced it properly. Someone was talking, but talking to a friend in wolf's clothing.

'Good. Well it is to this location that we are going. Two poor young people, innocent of everything, will be taken to the SS cottage and roughed up a little and then released without charge, an honest case of mistaken identity. It happens. But before *we* arrive I must know that you truly understand what I am revealing to you. Perhaps you fear an Abwehr trap so that you condemn your friends to death at the hands of the SS? Well I need you to understand more of your situation. We are nearly there now.'

Henri looked around. They were driving towards the Rue Montmartre, a part of the city where relationships between Germans and Parisians were more complicated.

'Henri, your network was infiltrated by a German agent six months ago. Who it was, I cannot reveal, for I honestly do not know that myself. But we know you are controlled from northern France, and not Lille or Lens. Where exactly, I do not know and do not yet wish to know. But you are running to Bayonne or Bordeaux. There you hand your captives to the Spanish Line and they run to Gibraltar.'

Henri did not move or speak, afraid of what he might give away with the slightest movement or sound.

'You need not respond, I know I am right. But ask yourself this. If we knew, why did we not act? Why did we not arrest your friends and break the chain? Well, that is where I come in. I am your friend in wolf's clothing.'

Henri nodded and Fifi glared at him. No wonder, for Fifi must now suspect Henri. Wagner had asked him to write something, but Henri had written nothing. She must wonder whether her friend was one of them, a double agent. Finally, she turned her face away from Henri and addressed Wagner.

'Herr Wagner. You refer to a terrible secret, a scandal, what does this have to do with you being an Abwehr officer with sympathies to the French?'

'Well, if you want me to finally convince you of who I am, before we reach the Moulin Cottage, let me tell you a little of my life. My mother is a true German patriot, she loved her Country and at the time, admired the Kaiser as a God in human form. The man I was brought up to believe was my father, was a fine man of high standing in Koln. He was an officer of heavy cavalry, the photographs of him in uniform were magnificent. When I was young, it was the photographs of that man that filled my dreams. But it was years later that I discovered a truth. A truth that shocked me deeply.' Wagner looked down for moment, Fifi saw his body soften for a second. Henri could see it as well.

'A truth hidden to this day from the Germans, for my mother is still alive. The man in that uniform died in Ambleve in 1914. A casualty of the very early days of the last war. My mother loved him, grieved for him and survived his passing. But healing was another thing. You see, I was not born until 1919. Do you understand what I am saying? The man who *was* my father died in 1914. The man in my mother's life who *is* my father was an English man, living in hiding in Koln. It was to him that she turned for affection, to fill the void of her existence. She had grief and need for comfort and solace and he gave her the strength to live on and to love again. To love the little baby born of this union.' Fifi leaned forwards, almost wanting to comfort the German in the front seat. Wagner looked up again and turned slightly towards Henri and Fifi. His eyes were red and damp.

'When the Germans discovered him in hiding, he was taken as a spy, but of course he was no such thing. They dragged him alive behind a horse and cart, kicking him and shooting at him with pistols to frighten him. My mother told me that they stripped him naked and whipped him. For what reasons only those animals could know. When they had finished, they tied him to the wheel of a cart and whipped the horses until they ran in terror, the poor man spinning on the wheel in agony. Again they shot at him and mercifully he was killed. My father simply shot in the street, like a rat. My mother looked on, she saw, she remembered and of course she can never forget. She has never really recovered. She had grown to love this man, who gave her comfort.'

Henri gently placed a hand on Wagner's shoulder, for now he chose to believe the man.

'He allowed my mother to mourn the man in Ambleve, without a thought for personal improvement. The pity was, it was just days before the end of that war, when the English occupied the city. She had left to visit the man in the grave in Ambleve, to grieve him and to honour him. But for some reason, she had missed the train. When she returned, the Germans were inside her home, tearing books from the walls, tossing her life upside down for the man who was my father. So, I too can never forgive.'

Wagner looked down and took out a handkerchief.

'But the Germans were rounded up and the whole matter was forgotten. When I was born, no-one questioned my mother. She moved to another part of Koln and as I grew, the date of my birth never seemed to matter. But I felt no more German inside or out as Winston Churchill.'

Fifi now placed a hand on his arm. If this was a lie, his wet and trembling face did not betray it. She believed him. She saw the wetness in his tears, the gentleness in his description of his mother.

'But you are in the Abwehr? They would surely investigate your family?'

'As a part of well-respected German family, I could have been anyone. My age is a lie, making me eligible for the SS. I wanted to oppose the Nazis and the Abwehr, well known as an organisation able to tear itself apart from within, seemed the obvious choice. I felt I could help undiscovered, undetected.'

'So what of us, Wagner?'

Henri was blunt, not quite ready to believe the man in the front seat, but craving his story to be true.

'I am going to return you to Lille with the authority to travel. The three pilots were intercepted and taken to Pau where they will be left by the roadside to be picked up by your companions. They will be in Spain by tomorrow evening, you have my word.'

'How do we know that you can be trusted, and that this is not just a cruel bluff?'

'Mademoiselle Dubonnet. At the barrier, one of your pilots revealed his identity with a simple mistake in French. The barrier officer came and reported this in all sincerity to me. He did not know that I would come to help you. Monsieur Collin, you were very good and would have escaped, you also Mademoiselle. But the Germans are trained to hear everything and they did, so I was forced to act. The genuine Abwehr need to be handled carefully, so I had to give the impression of interrogation. Fraulein, I apologise for the discourtesy, but the Abwehr are men of illiteracy and degeneracy.'

Fifi looked down but Wagner continued.

'So here we are. I am extending a hand of comradeship to a French man and woman. Will you accept?'

Henri looked up at Fifi. Her face was blank, she shrugged almost imperceptibly. He reasoned that they had no choice since the airmen were gone, and their mission was over. He tried another tack.

'What is the story of the driver?'

'Well Monsieur, he is a German, a member of the Abwehr and an excellent driver. What you do not know is that he is also a member of the Special Operations Executive.'

Henri and Fifi looked blankly at each other.

'Espionage and sabotage on behalf of the British.'

This puzzled Henri but he felt that trust was worth a try since they had no option.

'We accept, Herr Wagner. But you must understand that trust is earned and not given. I will tell you nothing of our comrades and we will not betray our country.'

CHAPTER THIRTY-FIVE
Bazentin-Le-Petit March 1942

Odile sat alone in her kitchen, looking over the road to Martinpuich, the little land originally dug by the Germans in the Great War. With sadness, she remembered the camp again, still feeling the soreness of her hands, burnt by the strong chemicals of the latrines. She saw her mother being pushed from soldier to soldier – she would have been about the same age as Odile was now. Each day she would try to remember the face of her husband and her children as she rested alone. When Henri was on a run, it was almost unbearable. She wanted him to stay at home, but he was too much like his parents. This way, she could control the danger, or so she liked to think.

There was a loud knock at the door but it was a familiar rhythm, the postmaster. Still red and out of breath as always, he gladly took the offered glass of water and finished it in a single mouthful. He offered a little brown envelope, then nodded politely and left, whistling as he went down the lane. Odile watched him go, noticing that he turned and bowed his head as he passed the military cemetery. She locked the door and opened the telegram, angry with Henri, who should never have sent a telegram. As she opened the envelope, she saw the familiar code for Dusseldorf and sat down, trembling slightly, hardly daring to read what was written.

Dearest sister. DDF is lost to us and in danger.
Need help. Most urgent to recreate the story of Oct 1918.
Will need four cards this time, to make up a pack.
Cannot wait to see you.

The sheet dropped from Odile's hand and she saw a rainstorm coming in the darkening sky. Liesel was in grave danger. Perhaps it was

Kurt – revenge perhaps – and Odile knew what he was capable of doing, even to his own sister. For Liesel to ask such a dangerous thing of her meant the situation in Germany was desperate. Clearly, Dusseldorf was no longer safe for Liesel and her family so she must do something. There was only one thing that she could realistically do. She thought it over and over, each time coming to the same final conclusion. After some time, she switched on the little radio, waiting for the broadcast from General de Gaulle. She liked to think that William was watching the general speak the words he had written as he made the broadcast in a little studio all that distance away over the sea.

--oOo--

Henri and Fifi returned to Lille, hardly speaking or looking at one another. At Amiens, Henri wanted to leave the train and go directly home, but Fifi shook her head.

'Henri, we cannot just ignore what has happened. The Abwehr and therefore the Gestapo know about us now. We are no longer under cover. We have to report this today.'

'I know, but it will be the end of it. The end of our *Sunshine Road* group.'

'Not if we trust Wagner.'

'Do you?'

'I think so. Look, if the airmen get to Spain, we can trust him right?'

'Of course not. Three airmen are nothing to gain our trust and favour, they are a very small price to pay in return for our guard coming down and revealing our operation. Call it a small loss for a bigger gain.'

Fifi's shoulders slumped. 'I suppose we will be excluded from the group now, for fear of leading the Germans to it.'

'Yes I think so. But of course there is a bigger question. Who do you think it is?'

'I am afraid even to think about it. I thought I knew everyone. They may all think it is me, a double deception.'

'I know it is not you, Fifi. I saw your face in the interrogation. You are not that good an actress.'

They both smiled thinly. She moved a little closer to Henri.

'What I do not really see, Fifi, is this story about his Prussian father and the Englishman. The tears as well. A nice touch.'

'Well they convinced me. I am sure the story is true and he wants to be one of us. Do you think that would be possible?'

'Only if we were the only two ever to know about it. Besides, this card he gave us. If it is his real name, it exposes him to investigation. Name, code word and address. If this were left on a train?'

'But he gave it to us. It was a mark of trust. We should see.'

At Lille, the two were greeted warmly. A coded message had arrived with news that the airmen were already on a boat from Gibraltar bound for Southampton. Charlemagne and Fifi had done it again. Already there were two more to run. But it was not yet their turn to run the line again. They quickly returned to the small house in Lille, near the citadel that hosted the *Sunshine Road* operatives in its northern quarters.

'Was there anything else in the message?'

Henri tried to act as if nothing out of the ordinary had happened.

'No, just the normal code white. Why?'

'Well, the airmen's French was terrible. I'm glad that they made it from Bayonne.'

'Pau wasn't it?'

'Well, yes, of course. Yes, Pau.'

Henri looked uneasy and turned to Aurelie.

She stepped forward. 'The Abwehr know of our existence.'

The three Lille operatives looked at one another in disbelief.

'What did you just say? The fucking Abwehr?'

'Yes. But it is not quite as it seems. Let me explain.'

'You better had.'

Henri could see one of the Lille operatives moving his hand slowly to his coat pocket, but for now he did nothing else.

'Look. We were followed. But it was not some clumsy error on our part. They already knew. Whatever we did, they knew. One of the pilots made a small mistake, but it was more than that. The man who arrested us is one of us.'

'Abwehr? One of us? You fools! You've led the bloody Nazis here. How could you do this?'

'Wait. Look. He gave himself away. More than just a tease for bait. He has put himself in real danger and I think we should trust him.'

'Well we don't. The Germans are lying and deceitful. This is a trick and you two bloody naive idiots have condemned us.'

'I don't think so.'

'Look Aurelie, I have known you for years and I trusted you. But this Abwehr arrest and release – it just does not happen. They want you and they have followed you. Watch now, they will come for us with machine guns. You fools.'

'I really don't think they will. In fact, I think the opposite will be true. I think this meeting will make our work much easier. Will you trust me for now?'

Two of the operatives put their hands up in resignation and one of them spoke.

'For now, yes we will. But you must watch this man. Watch everything. This could still be an elaborate trap. We must be cautious, even more cautious than usual.'

'Very well. We should go and speak with Dodo.'

Henri turned to Fifi. The train back to Amiens was due out in ten minutes.

'Fifi, you should come back to Albert. My mother would love to meet you.'

'And I should love to meet Madame Dodo.'

--o0o--

Darkness had already reclaimed the ridge when the little cart arrived. Henri had left his motorcycle in Amiens since he was now travelling with Fifi. The horse's hooves rattled the road and the little lamp created a mysterious and eerie scene for the return of the *Sunshine Road* runners. Henri leapt down from the cart, holding out his hand for Fifi. She took it, and Henri found it warm and comforting. As she stepped down, he could not help noticing her slender legs. But it was no good to think of such things and he looked towards the door at the little light that was left on whenever he was away. He took Fifi's arm and drew her down from the cart in the dark. She leaned on his arm to avoid the mud, his arms were around her shoulders and she looked into his eyes and smiled. Henri was so busy looking at Fifi, that he did not notice that a front door just along the road had opened by the tiniest fraction.

'Maman, there is something that you must hear from our journey to Paris. You must sit and listen.'

'Paris?'

'Yes. Please let us tell you before you come to a decision.'

Odile sat forward. 'Oh? This is most unusual.'

'In Paris, we met up with officers of the Abwehr.'

Odile stood up from the table, her composure lost for a moment. 'The *Abwehr*?'

'Yes, but the officer is friendly to our cause. He has a secret, and by sharing it with us, he exposed enough to get him arrested by his own officers.'

'The Abwehr? That cannot be. If it was the Abwehr, you would not be here now? It must have been the Paris underground, perhaps fearful of your presence. They must have taken you off the street for fear of exposing *their* operations.'

'Does the Paris Resistance operate from offices in Les Invalides?'

'Of course not. Why?'

'Because that was where we were taken. He spoke to us then let us go with travel documents to Lille, and here we are.'

'My God. It was the Abwehr! What does he want?'

'To help us.'

'You believe him?'

'Aurelie does. I must say, he was most convincing.'

Odile sat down again while Henri detailed everything about Wagner and his story.

'Well, Henri, such a story might signal the truth. But who can really be sure in such uncertain times? We need more proof. Information.'

'He knows all about us, Maman. Our names and where we live.'

'He does?'

'Yes, he addressed me as Henri Collin. That's nearly exactly right. He perhaps assumed it was a French spelling. And Aurelie, he addressed her as Mademoiselle Dubonnet.'

'We must close the line. *Sunshine Road* must cease to exist. We could have the Gestapo here at any moment.'

'But Madame Collins, if we were known and his intent was to expose us, would the Gestapo not *already* be here? Would we not already be dead?'

'He might be trying to lure us in a little more first.'

Henri nodded. 'Yes Maman, we had thought of that. But we think he is sincere. We could trust him a little. Here, he gave us a card.'

Odile took it and smiled before handing it back.

'Perhaps he is convincing. Perhaps what I need to tell you might be the very best way of proving his intentions without compromising the line. For now, Henri, perhaps you should both sleep? You look exhausted.'

Henri was tired and went to bed, while Aurelie was installed in Armandine's room. In the morning they would talk more of Herr Wagner and the Abwehr. For now, he would get some welcome, if haunted, sleep.

--oOo--

Odile did not sleep for the memories of the Great War danced around her kitchen and in her mind. The name Wagner had brought back memories of her escape. It was all too much to take in on the very night that she had received such desperate news from Liesel. Now it would be Odile's turn to repay the debt to help her German sister. She must come up with a plan that would not involve hairpins and permits. This time, she would have to use something eminently more precious and valuable to her. She would have to send her son.

--oOo--

In the morning, Henri awoke to the sound of breakfast being prepared. He had not felt so safe since before the war. The cycles of danger and security wore him out but he was determined that the Germans should be overthrown and that peace would return to France. He looked out and saw the graves of the fallen, which had always made such a deep impression on him. When he went down to breakfast, he descended the wide stairs to find Aurelie in conversation with his mother.

'Henri, here, come and have fresh bread. We have some fresh milk as well.'

'Thank you. What is it that occupies you both so much?'

'Henri, please sit down. I need you to do something for me. Something that you may find strange or impossible. But it is something that we must do. This might also be a chance to see if your Herr Wagner can be trusted without exposing the whole line. I need you to go to Germany to bring to safety my sister and her family.'

CHAPTER THIRTY-SIX

London March 1942

William was secretly greatly enjoying his new relationship with de Gaulle. The man was difficult, prone to ridiculously overblown speeches on the radio, ignoring William's carefully crafted words in favour of his own brand of political posturing and brinkmanship, even with his allies. His messages to France on the BBC were strewn with promises of action, which William knew were very far from the truth, even if they were heartfelt and well received by the beleaguered citizens of the north of France. But beneath it all the general's voice held together the communities of hope and opportunity. The British and American Governments were forever writing to William, instructing him to scold the general and to take more control of his words. William had to chuckle at some of the messages from Downing Street, written with such formality and pomposity. William wanted the general's words to flow free from the heart. Of all the Allied officers circling the little offices in Carlton Gardens, William understood the French way of life. The general was not always easy, but William knew that Mr Churchill liked him and the French would grow to see him as their force for liberation.

William now rarely left the office to visit the sights of wartime London. He was pleased that Armandine was so settled in England, safely away from the German bombings and the attentions of the American forces in England. Her growing love for her young lawyer was both pleasing and worrying for a father, though. He did so want to hear news of Arthur, but his eldest son's movements were as secretive as his own and he supposed that no news was most likely just that, no news.

The short walk through the Westminster sunshine was always refreshing, but the March winds were cold. His side ached and his troublesome knee was always sore in the evenings. He often used it as a clock, one that told him to return to his small apartment rooms. As he opened the door to his rooms, he saw a little envelope on the floor. It was a message from the Foreign Office, containing official notification of messages received from known French citizens working for de Gaulle in the north, away from the hated Vichy regime. It seemed strange that it had been delivered here and not to Carlton Gardens but once he'd read it he saw why the kind clerks had delivered it here. It was from his Dodo.

William, my love, you are well and making quite a reputation for yourself in London.
Pleased A well and no news of AHP – what else can we expect from a son of ours.
H had a near miss in Paris, but have another purpose.
Must bring Eisns to France. Please help with plan.
Your loving wife OC

William's mind raced. They both owed Liesel so much for what she had done for Odile. But to bring a German family into France? Why? What terrible thing had happened that the Eisners could not help themselves? Whatever could be happening in Germany for the daughter of a respected Dusseldorf general to be asking for help? Back in France, William had already checked up the name Eisner when Liesel's telegram had arrived signed Sarah. There were records of refugees from Russia dating back over fifty years, showing trails of Jewish migrations into the Tyrol and the Vienna regions of Austria. Distasteful as it was, William tried hard to put his head into the mind of a Nazi. The law in Germany at least seemed clear. A wife of a Jew was not considered Jewish unless her mother was a Jew. The husband of an Aryan German was protected, Jewish or not.

William could not see what might necessitate such a rapid escape from Germany. Except for one thing, which he wanted to dismiss. Kurt could surely help his sister whatever her predicament. He was older than William, from a respectable family. He must surely have connections. It could only mean one thing. The Kurt from 1918 was no different in 1942. He was still a bastard. One who was now driving his own sister to risk the lives of her family. One with more power and influence than the boy of 1918? He did not know Kurt and never wanted to. But he sensed his hand here.

He immediately asked for any information on a Kurt Langer, held anywhere in the military intelligence records. But there was nothing. The only tiny crumb of a clue came in a short note, informing William that in the period immediately after the last war, a Kurt Langer in Dusseldorf had joined the Freikorps, quickly gaining a reputation for extreme brutality. He had then transferred to the Sturmabteilung but had left for reasons unknown, bringing about a move away from Dusseldorf. William decided that Kurt must still be in the Nazi hierarchy, as it would be difficult to leave. He noted that the source of this information was an informer in Dusseldorf, but who it was or why they had kept this information, he did not know.

He felt obliged to help, if only because his wife was asking him to. William knew that Odile was active in leading a small part of a larger Resistance line, taking airmen from the Belgian and German borders to England. He also knew that a small anti-Nazi group operated in Germany – there were some papers about this group in his office. Perhaps if he could put them all together he could possibly find a way to smuggle a family out of Germany.

William spent the evening thinking and sketching on a map what might work to bring Liesel to France. In fact, she should come to England and be placed under his own protection. She was German, so it would be difficult, but not impossible. It would be dangerous if the British discovered the truth and the French would be furious with him. It was a real risk but William felt that he had one more risk left in his deteriorating body. The question was, would the risk be worth it? Then he thought of his Odile, beaten and bruised at the hands of the monstrous Kurt. If not for Liesel, he would not have his family so he decided that Liesel and her family were absolutely worth it.

CHAPTER THIRTY-SEVEN

France July 1942

The little room above the old estaminet was perfect for the meetings of the *Sunshine Road*. Up until this week, Odile had kept the truth about Henri and Aurelie from the remaining members, choosing not to mention the strange meeting with the German, Wagner. For this to work, she needed their co-operation and she had decided to be truthful, which would risk their anger and disapproval. From the time Henri returned in March, there had been four other movements to Bayonne and none of them had been intercepted or prevented. No one had been arrested or detained and not one member had even been questioned as they moved around France. She could only take comfort from this, but as always, remained suspicious of an extended hand of friendship from the Germans, especially from the Abwehr. Even the French knew how they operated hand in hand with the SS and Gestapo.

She had received several messages from William in London. Most contained small elements of instruction hidden within messages of family news and life in London. All were bland on first reading, or irrelevant to a casual observer. But they both knew that observers were never casual and any one of them might be interested in their operations, suspicious of their actions, or ready to strike.

Over the months since Liesel had begged for help, opportunities to act had come and gone. Any part of the plan that was not perfect meant that the whole expedition had to be cancelled. But finally, a chance had come and it had to be taken now.

The group sat ready to listen to the plan and Odile tried to be calm so she could speak clearly. Their mission was to recover a larger than usual group of pilots and airmen from two Halifax bombers that were shot down on their return from bombing Stuttgart. The first had suffered a rudder problem and it had moved south and west into northern France and the second had engines damaged by anti-aircraft weapons returning north of Metz. The pilots were quickly picked up by the local Free French and taken into hiding. Their aircraft had been set ablaze, with pig carcasses cut up and thrown inside along with parts of their uniforms. The runners would travel by rail to Reims and then split into two groups, one bound for Metz and the other travelling to Nancy. The group in Nancy would prepare for the return journey and the group in Metz would go on towards the village of Thionville, where the aircraft had crash landed.

Odile was clear about everything, who would travel, who their contacts would be and how they would use the friendly railway network to manage a safe return. But she left out one little detail of the operation, one stone would remain unturned for the runners of the *Sunshine Road*. Charlemagne and Fifi were not needed for this operation and as far as the others were concerned, they were extras. They would meet the rest of the group in Reims, ready to move to Metz and Thionville.

'Charlemagne and Fifi will travel directly to Paris from Amiens. Their documents will be left with Marcel. He is on the night trains all of this week and will make sure that the Germans are distracted with other business. Hugo and Demoiselle will be in the Metz team. The train to Reims is now short and direct. Bluebell and Daisy, you will be on the Nancy team. Henri and Aurelie will meet you in Reims.'

As expected, Odile was asked every question about the run. Nothing had been left to chance and everyone knew their place. But the question came at the end. Odile took a deep breath.

'Madame Collins, why will Charlemagne and Fifi not be travelling with us directly to Metz? What is the purpose of a third group going to Paris? It risks the mission, if you do not mind me saying.'

'Of course you can ask. I am sending Henri and Aurelie to Paris first with a message that will be for the office of the Free French in London. I cannot send it by telegraph and it will be quickest to send it with our youngest members. Are there any other questions?'

'No, Madame, but I must say that I am not happy about this at all.'

Odile sensed the air of tension, especially about the clear and unexpected deviations to their regular routine. Train travel was easy. The Resistance had operatives in all of the railway lines and the movement of French people with proper identification was unrestricted in most circumstances. This meant that the run there should be simple. Getting the men back would prove more difficult, of course, but certainly not impossible.

The distance was short and the weather was good. But Odile knew one detail that the others did not. Henri's real mission meant he would have to be in Germany on the night of the thirty-first of July. On that night, the British had promised a diversion of almost unimaginable scale to enable the rescue of Liesel and Karl. Only they called it a strategic bombing mission on the Ruhr industrial steelworks in Dusseldorf.

The group dispersed as usual, each night taking a different route away from the meeting, always wary and watchful. There was very little German interest in the town as a rule. But this was Albert, which was important to the Germans for its history if not its strategic importance. German units wanted to come here, just for a time, to stand in the place of their fathers, who fought and died on the battlefields just a few short kilometres away from the town.

--oOo--

Henri had sensed a coolness with Yvette, an imperceptible change in their relationship. He could not quite understand what exactly had changed, but something most certainly had. Surely it could not be Fifi, because she had only visited his home twice and his mother was always present. But perhaps Yvette had misunderstood Aurelie's presence for she did not know that Henri was an operative of a small Resistance group and may have imagined Fifi to be her rival in love. But Fifi was a woman, not a girl, and he was still really a boy. Maybe it was just their relationship changing. There seemed to be no tenderness now in her touch, no charm in her words. He looked at Fifi. He was not in love with her, so why would Yvette imagine that he was? Since he could say nothing of his activities, he had to accept her coolness, which only seemed to make things worse. Still, he had a job to do and he would have to put Yvette out of his mind for now.

At La Boisselle, Henri and Fifi packed a small bag of clothes. They decided to take their bicycles to Albert again, leaving them at the little store near the basilica. From there, a cart would take them to Amiens, a pair of simple travellers going to Paris to see family. Always family. The rest of the group would travel that evening, farm workers moving around with the seasons.

--oOo--

Once the runners had left, Odile's work was done, but she wanted to be certain – one last detail had to be just right. Liesel had to be at the railway station on the stroke of ten for this to be possible. They had a chance – it was perhaps only a one hour chance, but it was a chance. William had been so clever and now it was up to Henri – her son, the jewel that she risked for the care of her sister in Germany. She was gambling his life for the salvation of theirs and she prayed for their lives, to whatever God was left after all of her years of pain.

--o0o--

Fifi squeezed up to Henri, placing her hand on his shoulder, her mouth leaning to his ear.

'Henri, I am cold. Will you hold me a moment to warm me?'

'Of course, Fifi. There is a blanket here, it is a little soiled but it does not smell.'

'No, just your coat and your arms, thank you. I will feel less like an old lady.'

'Well how old are you, Aurelie, or am I not allowed to ask?'

'You can ask, but I will not tell. Older than you, but not as old as your mother.'

'Ha! Are you ready for this?'

'I don't know, Henri. But as Fifi and Charlemagne, we have a chance.'

'The Abwehr found us pretty easily did they not?'

'I have thought about it often, Henri. I cannot place who might have alerted the Germans in Paris. Perhaps it was someone in Lille for we do not know them very well, do we? Perhaps one of them told someone accidentally who then told someone who told the Abwehr. You know how this works.'

'I suppose so but do you think Wagner can be trusted?'

'Well, our little mission is totally dependent on him, we cannot succeed without him so we shall soon find out. At least this way, we do not expose our whole line.'

'A friend in wolf's clothing he said? A friend. But I still do not see why he is so driven. So what, his father was English? So is mine. It seems a bit too far-fetched to be real. We may well be walking into a trap.'

'But you remember your father's plan? The border to Dusseldorf is impossible without German help. We must have a German ally. No chance is no chance. With him, well we will know…'

Henri shrugged a grudging agreement and wrapped his coat against Fifi. His face was pressed into her hair and he felt warm against her. Perhaps this was love and what he felt for Yvette was only affection, or the beginning of what might have been love. But he had a shared experience with Aurelie, a history that was full of danger and risk. It was a powerful sensation. Perhaps her desire for warmth was a signal to him. He decided that it was time to find out and placed his hand on her chin, raising it gently so her eyes met his.

'What is it Henri? Do you see at last?'

'I see, Aurelie.'

He leaned in and kissed her. Aurelie's hand slipped behind his head, drawing him in deeper and Henri was happy to fall, since this woman held his life in her hands anyway.

--oOo--

Once again at Amiens, cold but dry, they both returned to the job at hand. Immediately, Henri went to check on his motorcycle, which was still locked and secure in the little shed. He might need it in the future to get away from here.

Inside the station, Henri and Fifi fell into their routine. The permits to travel were in order, and the ticket master did not even look up when passing them the envelopes. So far, it was going well. The train arrived early, taking on a little more coal for the uphill part of the short journey to Paris. Their train was going directly to the city and the later trains were directed to Reims and then on to Dijon. They all seemed to be expected and the arrangements were secure. Henri and Fifi joined the carriage and settled into a small bench away from the other passengers. Henri was desperate to kiss Fifi again, his feelings for her clarifying, but he chose to remain careful and in control of his feelings.

Their tickets were inspected on the train, which was always the best way. Any German soldiers travelling were disinterested and occupied in other things. The train guard for this journey was unknown to them both, but he just glanced at their tickets and nodded in acknowledgement.

Henri was uncertain still about Herr Wagner and it played on his mind – and most likely also on his face. He had seemed sincere, but an elaborate hoax was still a possibility that Henri seriously entertained. Fifi seemed more confident and she had cheerfully told Henri that she could easily read a man's intentions. The telegram and reply to and from Herr Wagner seemed simple and brief enough. They asked to meet and he had readily agreed, and if he was surprised at the specific time and date, he did not object. There would be little time to set up an Abwehr trap, so perhaps he realised that he was being tested.

At Paris, Fifi and Henri had no problems at all with the soldiers on the barrier. They asked the same dull questions and spoke the same terrible French, the few words they recognised played back to them by everybody regardless of what they were going to do in Paris. Those lines with soldiers who insisted upon speaking German were avoided or ignored, so their lines were the shortest. Fifi and Henri chose the longest line, with the most annoyed guard, who was clearly doing more than his fair share. This time, there was no car waiting for them, so they walked across the city to the large open spaces, just like any other couple in love.

At the Café de Flore on the Boulevard Saint Germain, they spotted Wagner seated at a table and sat at the table next to him.

'Herr Wagner, we need some documents and permits for travel

into…

Germany. A permit to a large city near the border.'

'Tell me why. Is this a test?'

Fifi looked to Henri, who shrugged.

'Partly, Herr Wagner, but we do need permits to enter Germany, passage for at least two into Dusseldorf and permits for…'

Henri hesitated. To go further would mean no coming back from this brink. He thought of his mother, of home, of the unseen and unknown family they were to rescue. They had names and a photograph. Showing Herr Wagner the photograph would seal all of their fates, perhaps even his.

'Go on…'

'For a family of four, their name is Eisner. We do not know them, but they are important to us. Our mission is to bring them out of Germany and back to Amiens.'

Wagner looked thoughtful. 'Are they Jewish? They sound Jewish.'

'We do not think that they are. The woman is the daughter of a general from the Prussian Guard.'

'But the name Eisner is possibly Jewish, is that their problem?'

Henri had to nod in agreement. 'It might be.'

'But the husband of such a high-standing German citizen would be protected from arrest, at least for now. Perhaps it is something else, is he a traitor or plotting to kill the Führer?'

Henri shrugged but said nothing.

'I need to know what forms of identification and permits I might need. Germans coming into France is unusual. Perhaps they might be visiting Vichy. When do you need the effects?'

'Tomorrow.'

'*Tomorrow*? That is not nearly enough time. It is almost impossible.'

'But not totally impossible. Time enough, yet not time enough to alert your Abwehr and Gestapo colleagues.'

'Very well. But if it is not perfect, then you may fail.'

'It is a chance we must take. Where shall we meet?'

'Very well. I will meet you at seven in the evening on the Rue de Reine, at the Café Timochet.'

'Why there? What is so special there?'

'Do you not know of it?'

'No. Why there?'

'Because it is where the Northern Paris Resistance meet. Until tomorrow then.'

'Until tomorrow then.'

--oOo--

That left an evening in Paris to savour and Henri felt an awkwardness now that a threshold had been crossed. He had kissed Aurelie, but what should he now do? What was now expected of him? And, what is more, what should be his thoughts for Yvette? He felt ashamed but excited at the same time. But the matter was resolved by Fifi who took his arm and slid her hand into his. She was warm and soft to the touch, a softness he craved in a time of anxiety. They walked along the Seine towards the Ile de la Cite and Notre Dame. The little cafés outside were busy, if less lively than they might have been before the war. Here and there were German-only bars and bistros where the officers and men were strictly segregated. The French had the poorer fare in their own country. It was strange to Henri, here amongst the enemy, walking free and unhindered. Any one of them could ask for papers and identification, any one of them could have him arrested, but somehow it was tranquil despite the occupiers. Fifi pointed to a little café, away from the road to the bridge so they sat and drank chicory coffee in the light breeze. Henri did not enjoy the coffee, but enjoyed the company, suddenly noticing Fifi in a new and intoxicating way, seeing the feminine quality to her movements and realising the power of her presence on all men around her.

'I'm told that I could pass for Hedy Lamarr. What do you think, Henri?'

'I do not know who she is.'

'You don't? I can't believe it. She is only the most beautiful woman in the whole world. Have you not seen *Ziegfeld Girl*? I saw it here last year.'

'I am not a cinema sort of person.'

'Well *I* can see the resemblance, so now you know.'

Henri laughed. 'Well, I am certain that she is only the *second* most beautiful woman in the world.'

Aurelie blushed a little.

'Aurelie, we should perhaps seek out the rooms we have for this evening. The runners' house is on the south side of the Quartier Latin. By the way, do you know the Café Timochet? I do not.'

'Yes, of course I do.'

'Let us go along and see where this takes us. We shall soon know from the papers that he gives us.'

'Or doesn't. Come on, let's walk through some more of Paris.'

Henri tried to make it an idle stroll, to the casual observer, they might just be two young lovers enjoying one another's company in the Paris evening. Of the two, Henri might attract suspicion, being a young and healthy male in Paris, he might be suspected of being up to no good. But

Aurelie would turn heads, drawing attention to her wherever she went.

At the little door to their rooms, they were greeted warmly but quickly taken off the street and into a large dormitory where five others were sleeping. Everyone slept in the clothes they wore in case of alarm. There would be a change of clothes in the morning if they wished, but with no guarantees on the quality and the fitting, of course.

--oOo--

Odile was alone again in the house she treasured. It had been built by her clever husband and father on the old foundations of her grandmother's house. The old house had been destroyed completely by shellfire during the war, but William had made sure the house stood on the foundations of Odile's family history. The new house was much bigger, with outbuildings and a store for the motorcycle. Odile had imagined having a large family, perhaps six children, but they had been blessed with three and she adored them. But tonight she was alone. It was always like this on a run. The lamp outside was lit day and night when Henri was away. She could get in touch with William, Armandine and even Arthur at a push. But when Henri was away, there could be no contact.

A knock at the door made her jump, for it was unusual since it was nearly dark. Odile called through the door and a little voice confirmed that it was Yvette. Odile knew she wanted to talk about Henri, but Odile did not want to discuss his absence with someone who was not a runner.

'Good evening, Yvette. How is your uncle? Do come in, the fire is lit and it is warm.'

'Thank you, Madame Collins. Uncle Alain is very well. He said he will bring wood and a tray of vegetables to you tomorrow. I think he feels more obliged with, well, with Henri away again. How long will he be away for do you think?'

'Well that did not take many words to ask, now did it? You have barely sat down and already we are talking about Henri!'

Odile smiled and placed her hands on Yvette's shoulders. She ran her hands through her long red hair in a very motherly way.

'I think I will need to make up some egg milk for your hair, my love. It is quite dry with that awful soap we have to use.'

'Thank you. I am never quite sure what to do, I never had a mother to learn from. Uncle Alain just washes his hair in the pig trough!'

They both laughed and Odile sat down next to Yvette.

'Henri is away, Yvette, working for his father. He will be making several trips in search of engine parts and machine oils. He will be home soon, I think. Perhaps in the next few days. I am never sure. He will be quite keen to see you when he returns, I am sure of it.'

Yvette brightened visibly. 'Do you think? I wonder if he perhaps is not so keen now that we have become engaged. I was wanting to ask... never mind.'

'She is the daughter of a customer of ours, from Peronne, if you really want to know. So you need not worry.'

'Oh, who? Oh, I was not worried.'

Odile enjoyed the company if not the subject. She wanted to move Yvette away from the delicate subject of Aurelie and her visit to their home. It had been a risk that night, of course, but the news was very important.

'So, have you thought about your uncle's ideas for the Tabac in Longueval? I know he was thinking of purchasing the land and the premises. Do you think you could run the Tabac the way that Madame used to? It would be an honour to be the mistress, you know. I could see you being the centre of the village. A pretty young girl like you would have the place lively and full every day.'

'Er, well, yes. I think it would be very good. I know I can make it a business for the family. But perhaps not with a war and not, well, not yet, with everything that is going on. I would hope to be... goodness... even saying it makes me feel so old! I would hope to be married before I did it. It would be right and proper.'

'Yes it would. Now, will you have something to eat with me? Perhaps you could go back and ask your uncle to supper?'

'That would be most kind, thank you. He has a little cheese from Albert. I will go and fetch it.'

When the door closed, Odile leaned on it and wept. The secrecy and the resistance she could cope with, but it was the lies to loved ones, the corruption of all of their children's youth and the constant threat of discovery. Henri was forever a moment from death. She knew that feeling and wished none of it for her children. Her older children were at least safe in England, safe from the harshness of the *Sunshine Road.* Yvette troubled Odile. She was a kind and gentle girl, but foolish and rash, as well as being delightfully open and fresh. She could never be a part of the group of runners, but here she was knocking on the door, asking about the boy she loved and had become engaged to. Did that give her a right to his secrets? It was interrogation by a friend, but it was one pair of eyes too many. Could Odile risk breaking the girl's heart for the sake of the line?

--o0o--

Henri could not sleep. The room was airless and hot. So he spent the hours before dawn just looking at Aurelie as she slept. Fifi, the cleverest of the runners had evaded and diverted the Germans on countless occasions. She had willingly agreed to help his mother and a family she did not know, to pluck a German family from the heart of the Reich without a visible motive. Yet she agreed without a murmur. The plan agreed with his father was bold and perhaps reckless. He had not solved the one problem the journey presented. But here was Fifi. She had the answer. It was a risk, but he trusted her instinct. Her lips moved, almost as a kiss to his longing, her chest rising and falling and her hair laid out on the dirty pillow. Henri would have to try hard to concentrate, so he lay back. He tried to think of Yvette who seemed a girl next to Fifi. Perhaps Fifi was no more than twenty-five, but she seemed out of reach for Henri.

Now he realised what his father had meant when he spoke of enduring love. When it happened, it was unmistakable, a branding iron on the soul. Henri now believed that in Aurelie, he had found the key to unlock his heart. So he lay back again to replay in his mind their kisses. Sweet, soft and deep. He felt almost sick and knew he should try to sleep if he was to stay alive in such dangerous circumstances. Finally, resolved to succumb to the night, he rolled over and forced his eyes shut. He was awoken some time later by loud and insistent shouting. The sounds came from outside, but no one was bursting through the doors into the now light room.

'The Germans are taking the Jews again! Look, there are three men and the lorry already has twenty inside. It is men, older ones it looks like. I can see the SS man over by the trees. The bastards! Those men are dead for sure. They will not be able to work.'

'Why don't we go outside and shoot the pigs?'

'It might be kinder to go and shoot the Jews instead. Don't be a fool. We kill five here and a hundred will find us and kill a hundred of us. We can do nothing. But we can try and stop them taking more.'

Henri was now at the window, rubbing sleep from his eyes, wide awake in the way the Resistance had to be. He saw the first lorry moving off. It looked a pitiful sight, men taken away as cattle to a slaughterhouse. The lorry bumped and rolled with the faint cries of the men almost drowned by the roar of the engine. In a moment they were gone. Henri knew, as the men themselves must know, that they would never return.

'Mauthausen is about to receive some more guests. It will be a short stay.'

'You think those men can be worked to death? No, you are right, they are going to be killed. You will never see them again.'

Aurelie was now also awake and busy changing her appearance. She chose dark trousers and a large blouse. Her coat was a size too large and she wore a little scarf and wig that disguised her hair. The fabulous looks from yesterday had been transformed into a very different woman today.

'Are you ready to leave, Henri?'

'Yes. Let us have coffee here and then move away.'

Once on the street, the young and carefree lovers from last night became the shuffling invisible citizens of an oppressed Paris lower class. They could move almost unseen along the streets, this time not taking in the sight of the Seine, the beauty of the Left Bank or the bustle of Montmartre. Instead, they walked a while until they found a small café. They crossed the road and Fifi went to sit in the centre tables by the entrance, but the waiter politely but firmly directed them to an outside table.

'It is a beautiful clear morning today! Why not take in a little of the air? I will bring you some coffee and a little something on the house. Would that be agreeable?'

'Yes,' said Henri, a little irked at not being allowed to sit at a table of his choice. Fifi saw his reaction and slid her hand into his. His stomach dropped to the floor and the feelings that he'd had under control raced away with him again. The coffee arrived. It was very good, not a hint of the awful cheap chicory coffee. Better than they had seen in some time in fact and no Germans in sight. The café was very well provisioned. Someone with money and influence prospered here.

They spent the day talking through the next part of their journey. From here they must take another train to Metz, through the still scarred battlefields of Verdun and the Argonne. At Metz, they would find their companions and make the move on to Thionville, where the pilots were being sheltered, hidden and protected, for the time being. They did not know exactly how many, since that was for the other team to know. But with the number of French involved, there might well be five or six to evacuate to Gibraltar.

But they would not be concerned with Gibraltar and the pilots. Their mission was much further north, into the deep darkness of Nazi Germany. Henri and Fifi went over William's plan once again. How they would move north, how they could navigate in the darkness and how they should avoid the Germans. But this was where William had come up short, pointing out to them that there was no way to fly Germans out without alerting the SS or Gestapo. German transports around and into Vichy happened regularly, but there was always a trail of papers and many questions asked. They had no luxury of chance. They had no option. An overland theft in the darkness of the four inexperienced and doubtless frightened travellers. Henri considered their chances slim. His mother had known that and yet here they were. He held Fifi's hands tightly.

'Thank you again for coming on this run. It was not for you to incur an obligation to my mother.'

'Your mother is the one woman in all of France that I look up to. I am here for her and for you, my Henri.'

She leaned to him and kissed him. This time, it was most politely, if slightly longer than was customary.

That evening, they found their way to the agreed café a little before seven. Fifi had hidden in an alley nearby and removed her outer clothes, coat and wig. Underneath, the Fifi for the bright lights emerged. They entered and headed for one of the centre tables, but the waiter intercepted them.

'Here, let me show you to a table out of the wind. Why not sit just here. There will be a little meeting of the art society over there, so I will take an order now from you. Can I fetch you something to drink?'

'Champagne for me, please.'

'Wine.'

Henri was very anxious and tried to suppress the urge to run. He was in a hornets nest for sure, but he reasoned if he escaped tonight, then there would be many more nights of this before too long. At seven, Wagner arrived, nodding towards them. He kept his hat on his head until he reached the shade of the table, then sat with his back to the street. Clearly, he felt safe, but not unobserved.

'Good evening. We must not be seen here too long. There have been problems with your papers. I needed more time. I have permits and identification papers, but without the travel permissions, your people cannot use a railway to move to Koln or Stuttgart. I cannot get these until tomorrow at the earliest. Even then it may appear suspicious.'

'What does that mean?'

'It means, Monsieur, that if you go into Germany without a German, you may as well put a pistol to your own head and fire.'

'Then that is it. We go home?'

'We do nothing of the sort, sir. We can get into Germany, but you must take me with you.'

Henri stood up, red-faced and furious. 'We will do no such thing. This is a trap!'

Fifi pulled him back.

'Sit down and be quiet, Henri, you never know who is watching. One more like that and there will be no need for you to have a pistol. You will have a choice of fifty in your face, courtesy of the SS.'

Henri's anger subsided. It was an anger borne of fear rather than mistrust. The plan was unravelling. Wagner watched him closely and then continued.

'We go to Metz and then take possession of a car. Whose and from where, well that is up to you. We drive to Koblenz at night, stop, rest during the day and then move north to Koln and then Dusseldorf. We take fuel from the streets and eat whatever we can. You will travel under the seats in the rear and I will drive. At Dusseldorf, the plan you have arranged with the German family must take place exactly when you have agreed. There is no possibility of rail travel at all. The name will be on the record and even if the SS or Gestapo are not actively looking, there is a chance that someone somewhere may idly check. Then it will be over.'

'They know what to do. I only hope that the note to them was understood. We wait only two hours and then we leave, with or without them.'

'What train are we taking?'

'It leaves Paris in forty minutes.'

'For what purpose are you travelling by train?'

'The Abwehr travel without a reason. No one will check and if they do, the trail leads back to my office and a dead end. I answer to no one for my investigations. It has been made so for each of us in the intelligence offices.'

'Then let us drink up and go.'

'Agreed.'

Herr Wagner left first, keeping his hat low over his face. Henri had the inner doubt still of his true motives but chose to say nothing, reasoning that Wagner was seeking advancement and a clever deception would seal his reputation as a hunter of intelligence.

--oOo--

At the station, the platforms were quiet but not deserted. The guards were unusually polite and friendly. Normally, this would be a cause for alertness and concern, but the tickets were in order and the reasons for their late-night travel were plausible enough. On the train, Wagner travelled with the German passengers. Henri went through the plan in his mind. They were to meet the Metz team in Reims. But the changes with Herr Wagner put them directly to Metz. The orders for the runners in this situation were clear. Do not wait – the best thing was always to continue and be cautious. There were always ways around problems, which is why more than one team was assigned. The others would be worried, but their fears would be allayed in Metz.

The train arrived in Metz to the deserted platforms of an early morning. No guards, no checks on papers and no one around. Clearly nobody had telephoned ahead with a warning and it appeared the Germans suspected nothing out of the ordinary this evening.

At a little cottage on the Hayange Road, Henri found their contact waiting. He brought in Fifi, but told Wagner to wait outside, hidden from view. He was Abwehr after all, and unknown to this group. Henri reasoned that he was now alone, with little possibility of contacting anyone. But if this group knew what was in the bushes – whether it was a friend or a wolf in wolf's clothing, it would mean death for someone, most likely Wagner.

As night drew on into the early hours, the last train arrived in Metz. They could hear it approach from the cottage. Within half an hour, the remaining members of the team had arrived and looked relieved to see Charlemagne and Fifi. The plan was still operational. They decided to sleep for two hours and then move to Thionville to make contact with the group protecting the pilots. They would take bicycles as it was only a few kilometres. The road ran alongside the river, so seeing and moving in the dark should be easy enough.

'We will not be coming directly to Thionville.'

Fifi's words reverberated like a grenade in a tin.

'What? Why not? Are you not well?'

'Henri and I have a second operation. We cannot explain here but we will meet in Nancy for the return in a few days.'

'Was it Dodo?'

'Yes. This operation is hers.'

Hugo and Demoiselle looked at each other.

'It is better this way. We can protect one another better. You cycle to Thionville and we will find ourselves a car.'

Once outside, it became clear that the night would be warm but moonless. Finding a car would be easy enough, stealing it should be just as easy for someone who understood machines as Henri did. The real problem came with driving in the dark. They might attract attention, but out here it was quiet. They just might be lucky.

Henri and Fifi made the short walk back into the quiet streets of Metz. There was very little German activity here, as it was seen as a peaceful region, and Metz was very close to the German border anyway, so who would start a fight here? Henri scoured the roads trying to find a car suitable for carrying six people at night through hostile lands. He thought he knew what he wanted, and just hoped he would be lucky enough to find one. For an hour he dipped in and out of the shadows. Some cars seemed right, but because of the shortage of petrol, had not been started in months. He was hot and weary from exertion in and under the cars. One had seemed perfect, but it was registered to the German Army. The familiar lettering of the enemy deflated Henri's spirits.

'It is no use, Aurelie, there are no suitable cars in Metz. I am looking for something long and larger than most, to carry six. It is no use. The war and petrol shortages have robbed us of an opportunity.'

'Perhaps we are looking in the wrong place, Henri? If it is a larger car, should we not look in the part of town where the richer families live? Perhaps they will have one?'

'Well, it is worth the effort. Do you know where to look?'

'No. But this is not a large town.'

The darkness soon gave way to the first rays of the early morning. At this time of year, the night was still short. Henri supposed he only had an hour left before sunrise. At the Rue de St Germain he saw it. A Citroen Traction Avant. It looked as though it had been used as a family car. The tyres were clean so it was still being driven. He looked in the window and with a swift movement he had the door open, a dull click followed by the hinge yielding to his gentle movement. Aurelie placed her arm on his shoulder and squeezed. In the little storage box he found a neat pad of stamped petrol coupons. The numbers were continuous and almost unused. This was great fortune for the car thieves. They would be able to purchase fuel in France, perhaps even carry some into Germany. The car was large and had room enough to hide passengers if needed.

Henri decided not to start the engine right here. The electrical starter needed a little attention and he did not have the light to see and clean the contacts. Fifi sat inside and he pushed the car forward, rolling it gently over the little ridge and down the slope into the central district. If they were spotted now, it would mean certain arrest, Abwehr help or none. But all seemed quiet.

At the bottom of the hill, Henri pushed the starter. It worked and the engine began to run. It sounded perfect, quiet, clean and well-maintained. This might be good enough. Henri remembered where the German car was parked and returned to remove the registration plates. There would no doubt be reprisals, but it was unlikely that they would be serious, perhaps the theft would be blamed on young boys hunting for souvenirs. His only worry was the discovery of the missing car before they were out of the region. The clock was now ticking and they had to keep moving.

At the cottage, Wagner was ready. His little case contained the documents required to travel in and out of Germany. He chose to drive with Fifi sitting next to him, looking every bit the French fancy of a young Abwehr officer. Henri hid under a blanket in front of the rear seat. The wide bench had a small indentation he could lie in, almost unobserved. At least it made his shape look less human. So the little group left. There would be no turning back now until they reached Dusseldorf.

At the border town of Monchy, they were able to acquire some petrol, enough to fill the tank almost. They had hoped for more, but Herr Wagner of the Abwehr would be able to secure more without too much trouble. Henri fitted the army registration plates. He was slightly concerned that they were Wehrmacht plates and not Abwehr. But Wagner assured him that the border guards would not be concerned once his identification was known. Vehicles were moved around and as long as paperwork was in place, it should not be a problem.

CHAPTER THIRTY-EIGHT
France July 1942

At the border with Germany, a small hut connected to a single pole barrier prevented access to the Fatherland. The pole extended into the hut, so it could be lazily opened by the guard from inside without him ever leaving or getting wet in the rain. He glanced at Wagner's credentials and waved him through. They were in Germany with barely a blink of an eye.

'I told him that I was bringing my little mistress for a weekend of entertainment. He wasn't even bothered enough to look in. But there will be more checks. Stay calm and out of sight and I think I can get us to Dusseldorf.'

'Henri, how many times do you think we will need to take on more petrol?'

'Twice before Dusseldorf. Do you have any petrol papers, Herr Wagner?'

'No, we will not need any. I can requisition petrol with my Abwehr credentials. You are in Germany now.'

Henri smiled thinly. Yes, they were in Germany.

--o0o--

At Bitburg, they decided to stop for rest, to allow Herr Wagner to secure more petrol for their journey north. With an extra can on board, they would be able to continue north towards Koblenz. This was a safer road, faster and wider than the road to Aachen. At Koblenz, a German patrol stopped Wagner to look at the car, but in truth it was to get a view of Fifi. She moved to Wagner and with the gentlest twist of her hips, she leaned over and kissed him. In French she asked him to hurry up as she was tired. Henri lay motionless and out of sight, not daring to move a muscle. He was wondering how they were going to do this with four in the back and began to doubt the plan.

At Koln, they decided to stop for two days, to ensure that the meeting with the Eisners would go to plan. There was a very specific alignment of events and they needed to be exactly on time and not early or late to their task. Neither Fifi nor Henri knew exactly why, but his father had been very specific in his note. Last day of July in Dusseldorf. Look for early morning, but before the dawn. Henri now realised how their movements could be covered so they could escape unseen and unnoticed. As they bumped into the heart of German industrial production, a smile came over Henri's face.

--oOo--

The bell rang. At least whoever it was had been courteous before entering. It was the telegraph officer from the station. An urgent telegram had been sent from Munich but the coding was unfamiliar. Liesel tore it open. It was finally what she had been waiting for.

Dearest sister! Greetings from Munich. Will be home soon to collect you for our little holiday.

Pack a bag dearest and wait for me at cousin Lotte in Hellerhof. I will be arriving before first rounds 31 of this month.

This will be fun!

This was it, the final message. They had to leave tomorrow evening and find their way to Hellerhof in the south of Dusseldorf. She had to put into action her plan for the children. With her mother now almost completely estranged, Liesel would simply have to act and keep moving, with no time to think or to try conversation with her family. Perhaps through fear of Kurt, Liesel's mother had forsaken her own daughter and cared for Franz and Monika as her own. There would be little point in reasoning with her, Kurt's influence was just too great and the long arm of the SS stretched deep into the heart of the Langer family, tearing out the loving soul and leaving a cold empty shell behind.

So Liesel visited the home she grew up in as if it were a stranger's house. But despite the history, she still longed to see the room she had spent hours in and the memory of her time with Odile was still precious to her. It was Odile who gave her the confidence to go on, to live and to love her husband. At the door, her father's nurse recognised her immediately but hesitated.

'Fraulein, it is good to see you. May I enquire as to your visit?'

'Frau Eisner, you fool of a woman. This is my family home and I need tell you nothing of my visit. Now step aside and let me enter.'

'But the court? Well, you are not allowed to see the children. Not whilst, well, whilst you are married to a Jew.'

Liesel furiously stepped over the threshold, pushing aside the nurse. But she regained her composure, addressing the nurse without turning around.

'Where is my mother?'

'She is resting in her room. I must wake her. Please remain here.'

Liesel ignored her and moved up the stairs quickly and with the memory of the house in her own soul.

'Just step aside, I will speak with her.'

The nurse turned to answer, but there were loud thumps on the floor from inside one of the bedrooms. Then she saw the door open and Franz's face appeared.

'Mother! Oh, Mother! How wonderful it is to see you. Are you now well again?'

Franz tumbled into her arms and Liesel held him with all of her strength and love. He was a strong boy, but thinner and more drawn than he should be. She breathed in deeply, holding back the tears. Monika was now also at her door, dressed in an exercise outfit. Liesel gasped. Her daughter was being made to get fit to be a German mother, but she was barely sixteen.

'Mother? Have you come to take us?'

'Yes, but we cannot simply leave. I must speak with your grandmother. Wait here for just a moment.'

Liesel stood outside the door to her mother's upstairs room. She knocked and entered immediately. The room was dark. Perhaps her mother was unwell, or deeply saddened by how troubled her life had become.

'That is you, Liesel? My only daughter. I know why you are here. You know it is not safe. You cannot simply take the children. You risk them and you risk us.'

'We are in danger from our own flesh and blood, Mother. Kurt is the only one placing this family in danger. You know Karl is no more Jewish that I am.'

'Liesel! You cannot say that! The court and the Gauleiter have agreed.'

'Agreed only with Kurt. This foolishness has gone far enough and is at an end. I am taking my children. As a free Aryan woman, no court has forbidden me from seeing my children and I do not expect you to try to stop me.'

Frau Langer rose from the armchair and moved to block the door.

'But I can forbid you. You are my daughter and all you will do is kill your family. You know we loved your husband as our own son. But he is your husband no more. He has been declared a Jew and there is nothing else we can say on the matter. Your father—'

'Who can barely remember who he is anymore, have you thought of that? Step aside, Mother. I am taking my children.'

Frau Langer slapped Liesel's face, Liesel stepped back in shock. Frau Langer now raised her own hand to her mouth and sank to her knees, holding out her arms to Liesel.

'Oh, Liesel, my dearest daughter. Forgive me. I am so afraid. I scurry about my own house with my head down, for fear of something or someone striking me down. That cannot be how it is for you and my grandchildren.'

Liesel embraced her mother who was shaking and weeping, tears dripping from her nose and her cheek. She fell onto the bed, her head down. Liesel noticed how frail she suddenly looked, as if the spirit had gone from her in the instant she had struck her daughter. But whatever now happened, Liesel had to leave, she had to choose her children. No daughter should have to make this choice.

'Your father will not know they have gone. His nurse is also loyal to us. She is the daughter of a man who served with your father in the army. I will ask her not to speak to anyone. But Kurt will find you. So go quickly and do not look back. As you leave, my life will be over, I know that. I have given my life for you, Liesel, in a way that leaves me contented and at rest. You can never come back, do you understand?'

Liesel looked at her mother. Right at the end, she had understood. Perhaps Liesel had relieved her of the burden to make up her mind and act decisively for the children. The children kissed their grandmother goodbye. She had been harsh with them, but not unkind. But it seemed to Liesel that there was a coldness to them, as if they would not let the world inside. She knew that they would never see their grandmother again. It was a last goodbye. Liesel ushered them out and turned to leave.

'There will be a day of judgement, Liesel and I doubt both my children will be living when the reckoning is done. I pray that I will not be there to witness it.'

Liesel took one more look at her mother, then left the room. She clicked the door shut, took a deep breath and moved the children to the stairs. The nurse was hovering on the landing.

'Fraulein Langer, I could not avoid hearing. My father owes your father a great deal. No word of your departure will come from my lips, I promise. I do not know how I will explain the children's disappearance, but no one will know the truth from me.'

'We must leave.' Liesel turned to the children. 'Quickly darlings, do not gather any belongings. We will travel with only the clothes we stand in.'

'What do you mean, Mother? What about my wooden toy soldier?'

'Leave it. You will see, my love, you will see.'

--oOo--

On the street, Liesel felt safer as all three of them were legitimate German citizens. Nothing prevented Liesel from seeing her children. It was Karl, it was always Karl who was the difficulty in their plan. Protecting him would be the biggest worry for the days ahead. When they returned home it was getting dark, which meant no prying eyes, but someone could be upon them unseen and unprepared. Liesel watched at the window, Karl rested in his secret study with his children by his side.

'Franz, do you understand what is happening to us?'

'I don't understand at all. You are our father and yet you are shut away here. Other boys talk of Jews and fighting in the war. I just agree with them, but they come to me and beat me, calling me a Jewish animal and a sub-human. I see only me, the same boy I have always been.'

'Our home is not safe, Franz. For reasons that will make no sense, we have to leave.'

'But where are we going?'

'I am not certain, but out of Germany, that is certain.'

'We will come back?'

'I do not know. Perhaps not until this war is over. If Germany wins the war, we will never return, I think that much is certain.'

'So we want Germany to *lose* the war?'

'Yes, but it is more the Nazis, not Germany. Not everyone in Germany is a Nazi. Their view on the world is like seeing through a warped looking glass.'

The door to the little room opened and Liesel lowered a plate of bread and cheese with cups of milk.

'It is all we have and it might be the last food we have for some time. We should also sleep down here tonight in case my mother has had to give up the truth to someone. Perhaps the Gestapo watch us and are simply waiting for us to move.'

--oOo--

The morning was spent watching the road intently for any movement, or for any car or person lurking in the shadows. But there was nothing all day. Liesel imagined that they might be safe until they moved and at the very point of moving towards safety, they would be pulled into the machine and consumed.

Hellerhof was in the south of Dusseldorf. As a family, they might not attract attention, just a normal Aryan couple and their children out for a walk. It was a Friday, but not all schools were open for children in the summer. Many were holding classes for young people on German citizenship, but seeing their attire, any passer-by would see that the children were loyal subjects of their Führer and had already spent much of the summer at a camp. The father might be convalescing perhaps, since he did look so unwell. Liesel and Karl dressed in their finest clothes, to try to give an appearance of normality. Franz dressed in the uniform of the Hitler Youth and Monika was told to wear the blouse and necktie of the young German maidens, the *Bund Deutscher Madel.* Karl could barely make the walk. Liesel knew that he was afraid of every move, but he would just have to be strong and imagine that each car that passed would just be someone going about their business and that none would be Gestapo or SS.

This one last walk from Dusseldorf was a final act of defiance to her brother. Her family would leave with their heads held as high as they could manage, and they would never return to Dusseldorf if she had anything to do with it. The love for her parents had been eaten away by the actions of her inhuman brother, who was now lost to the Nazis and never wanted back. All who mattered to her in Dusseldorf were with her now – her husband and children. She held their hands and moved on, smiling as they passed strangers in the street, wishing them a good morning.

Liesel knew that they had to reach the final meeting point by no later than two in the morning. She wanted them to get there early and keep watch. If they did that, then they might see if they were being followed. Six hours would be more than enough and the children could suffer hunger and boredom that long. The prize for their stoicism would be so much more than the little hardship endured. By six in the evening, without incident, but hot and thirsty and with weary feet, they reached the quiet square where they would wait to see if they had been followed.

--o0o--

The road from Koln to Dusseldorf had been bombed many times by the British and the Americans. In particular, the British had targeted the Ruhr and the Rhine lands. The army controlled movements on the road, taking priority over any other transport. On this section, even an Abwehr officer could not simply take his French fancy for a ride so both Fifi and Henri would need to be out of sight. They moved the rear seat up and back, so it was almost folded, then curled into the space that was left, with dark blankets on top of the seat to cover their forms. It would not pass a detailed inspection for a moment, but if Herr Wagner could get through without a problem with his genuine Abwehr credentials, then it might be possible to succeed.

Dusseldorf was almost on the horizon and it looked as though a giant foot had stepped on it. The bombing had damaged many taller buildings and the construction of new replacement buildings was proceeding at full speed. This was the centre of industrial production, the very machinery of the war effort came from here and there were checkpoints at most road crossings. Herr Wagner's story and identification were accepted at each one. No German soldier questioned the Abwehr. Perhaps one or two might have wondered about the requisitioned car with Wehrmacht plates, but such things were not so unusual.

'I am not sure where we need to drive to now? Do you have the note with the directions?'

From the rear, Fifi took out the little coded scrap of paper and read the four words in the first line.

'South of river left.'

Herr Wagner drove until he reached the Rhine, wide and magnificent, sweeping through the city, unchanging and unstoppable. There was only one road on the south of the river, which banked around a low hill and down to the level of the river itself. They saw a small sign for the Hellerhof railway station that was closed due to bombing. It was now almost dark and none of them knew exactly where to go. Dodo had specified that Cousin Lotte lived on the Bergasse, a large street lined with big trees and little parks. It was here that the meeting would happen. It was away from the city and more importantly away from the factories and steelworks.

Once in the district, Henri got out of the car and went around by foot. He held in his hand identification papers for a dead Hitler Youth member, killed whilst putting out fires in Dusseldorf a year ago. But again here, it was quiet and peaceful. For now. He looked down at his foot on German soil. He smiled to himself. They were on their way. Finally, he found the street, the sign was obscured by a tree, but it was most definitely the right place. The avenue was quiet and the little square and park were dark and unseen from the road. He ran back to find the car and gave Wagner and Fifi the good news.

--o0o--

Liesel was watching from behind a wall. The street was otherwise deserted. Then suddenly from the end came a figure. Crouched down and running low to the ground. It had to be them. If it was, then this was

Henri, Odile's youngest son. Her first human connection with Odile since she ran from Dusseldorf in 1918. She had sent her precious son to rescue her and here he was! She leaned down to Karl, who also put his head over the wall.

'It must be him, Liesel. The little baby in the photograph is our only friend in Germany. How are we supposed to make contact?'

'You go out and smoke a cigarette. You stamp it out four times, that's four of us. Go do it now.'

Liesel watched the man she hoped was Henri disappear. A few moments later, a couple appeared. Perhaps just a couple returning home.

'Stay down, Karl, there is a couple coming. Wait! It is him again, this time with a woman. He has a companion. Go Karl, and smoke that cigarette.'

Karl stepped out of the shadows and coughed slightly as he lit his cigarette. When he dropped it, he stepped on it four times, then turned back behind the wall. Liesel watched as the woman took the man by the arm and led him across the road. At the wall, the woman pressed the man against the bricks and began kissing him. Liesel closed her eyes. Perhaps they had been mistaken. The woman was speaking to the man now and Liesel listened carefully.

'Oh my darling, call me your little Liesel, Karl. Call to me. Kiss me now, my love.'

Liesel turned to Karl. 'Did you hear our names? This has to be them. Perhaps once more to be sure.'

'Karl, let me see your lovely face. Show your Liesel how handsome you are.'

Liesel lifted her head slowly.

'Liesel?'

'Yes. We are here. Is that you, Henri?'

Liesel smiled to see the boy panting and reeling from the kiss. His first meeting with his aunt and he was smeared in lipstick.

'It is, Aunt Liesel.' He blushed. 'We have a car here. Where are the children?'

'They are also here, around the corner.'

'Good then let us get into the car. We will explain the plan. You have not brought any items with you?'

'No.'

Henri went around the wall to see the couple hiding in the shadows. Liesel smiled and embraced him.

'How is your dearest mother?'

'She was well when I last saw her. We shall see her again and you can look for yourself. Come on.'

The family of four emerged from behind the wall and stepped towards the car. Wagner got out and moved the seats so that Liesel and Karl could sit on the very rear seat. Liesel looked at Wagner, who addressed her in perfect German. This man was German! This voice was trained by the Nazi machine. Her nerve failed her slightly and she watched Karl take a step back.

'May I ask who you are?'

'My name is Maximilian Wagner, Frau Eisner, Max. In the car I will tell you more. We do not want to risk creating a scene out here.'

Liesel's eyes narrowed. For a brief moment she was afraid. But he was with Henri Collins and she knew all about him. If they were together it must be well. Odile would not have planned this otherwise.

'I must get my children.'

Wagner nodded and tapped his hat. Liesel returned with the children and the four of them sat in the back of the car. It was a squeeze but it was possible. Henri and the woman stood with Wagner outside the car.

'So this is it then, Fifi. I will take the car to the waiting point. You have a train to catch.'

'Well you can give me a lift to the station, surely?'

'You would have to sit on my knee in the front.'

'I think I could suffer for the reward.'

Herr Wagner stepped forward, his palms down. He looked agitated.

'Seven in a car? It looks odd. If we see any Germans, we are as good as dead and I mean all of us, me included.'

'It is only to the railway station. It is now open again, the road was marked if you remember.'

'Yes, but it will be guarded, do you not see?'

'Yes. Look, we have to try. Will you try?'

'Very well. We should go now to the waiting point. It is nearly time.' Wagner drove slowly away from the street. Liesel needed to know the story of Herr Wagner. Here was a connected German clearly, with an educated Koln accent.

'Sir, you were going to tell me your story?'

'As we are now all clearly conspirators in this escape I should tell you that I am an officer of the Abwehr in Paris. My role is to locate and interrogate pilots that have been shot down, to try and extract militarily important information. But I am also a friend in wolf's clothing. You should not fear me, I intend to help you, not have you arrested. I have been with these two since Paris and risked a great deal personally. I have even provided you with travel documents, if the need arises.'

Liesel looked at the documents. They seemed in order and genuine. For now, with her husband by her side, she was prepared to go along with it. There was so much she wanted to know about Henri and his family, but for now, that would have to wait. Liesel's French and Henri's German were not good enough for a conversation. Not yet.

The car stopped again by the river, facing south. William had been quite precise about the location, suggesting south of the river, on the Koln road, some three or four kilometres at least from the city. But it was up to them to decide exactly where to stop, out of sight, waiting for the right moment. They chose a secluded location so they could decide what to do next and observe any movements of vehicles on the road.

'Fifi, you and Herr Wagner should take the train to Koln and then to Paris. The car is large, but so many passengers will attract attention. You have the right documents and if you cling to the arm of Herr Wagner, there will be no problem with the German authorities.'

'But Henri, we agreed to stay together, whatever happened! Why the change?'

'I just don't think we can all make it, not in one car, even though it is big enough. I thought we would be safe, but seeing the number of us now in this car, I am not so sure. Even if the children ride in the very back. It just seems so risky. We did not know what car we would get, so we always had to be flexible here. You know we did.'

'Yes, but it is big enough. Herr Wagner will have no problems with the guards. You will see. Have strength.'

Henri smiled. 'Very well. But let us keep it as an alternative. What time is it?'

'Nearly midnight.'

Liesel looked at her children, they had the eyes of terrified, trapped deer, awaiting their fate. For now, the shock of their departure had not yet subsided and for now at least, the children were obedient and quiet, and she hoped they would soon sleep.

'What time do you think, well, when do you think it will start?'

'I expect it will be around two. We should be undisturbed here. I have checked and we cannot be seen from the road. We will need petrol soon, which is my biggest worry. The route of the bombing will be south and then west, with the wind. We will see them overhead only after they have dropped their bombs, if they get it right.'

--oOo--

One hundred miles away, over the rolling uplands of the German borderlands, thousands of men were preparing to attack the steelworks and factories of the Rhine. Lancasters, Wellingtons, Halifaxes and others were streaming eastward, high above the ground. The relentless roar of their engines taking them mile by mile and minute by minute closer to the target of Dusseldorf. The raid would be the biggest of the war up until now, almost one thousand bombers aiming to drop their deadly cargo on the industrial heartland of the Reich. William had taken advantage of the planned raid by arranging for the Eisners to run while the bombing created a diversion.

William knew that each bomb aimer would be sitting and lying in the chilled space in their aircraft, regarding their maps over and over, until the target was imprinted in their minds. For fifty of the aircraft, the little fork of the Rhine, shaped like a warped trident would be their target for tonight. If they could drop their bombs on the north east of the bridge, then they would hit a small factory making tools for engines, but in doing so, they also risked destroying the three streets of the wealthy district in which the Langers and the Eisners lived. He prayed that his son and his friends understood what he had told them in code, so they would stay clear of the planned targets and surrounding areas. Otherwise, he could be sending them to a death filled with frightening terror from above.

In London, William looked at his watch. He telephoned bomber command and, after some difficulty, discovered that the mission was proceeding as planned and the weather proving perfect, with every chance of success. He wanted to telephone Odile, but decided that this would be a risk to security, even in coded language, or in casual conversation. He thought of his little Henri, of his older son in Trinity Hall, Cambridge and of his daughter in the Lake District. The little school she was teaching in was safe from the reach of the German bombers – for now at least. General de Gaulle had shown no real interest in the bombing actions for this evening, but when he left for the night he had placed a little bottle of Cognac on Williams's desk with a small note.

Colonel Collins. I hope the night brings you all that you wish for.
Charles

--o0o--

Odile sat at the kitchen table, her bread and cheese untouched. She knew that the place she had been taken to in 1916 and escaped from in 1918 was going to be attacked in a single massive operation by the British Bomber Command. Her son was among the masses of people under the path of the bombers and she prayed he would be lucky. But not just her son, her friends and even the mysterious Herr Wagner were also under the path of the bombers. Odile smiled. Wagner, now there was a name she remembered. She thought back to that morning on the train, so very long ago, taking on the identity of Maria Wagner during her own escape from Dusseldorf. She hoped it was a sign that her sister would find her way safely to France.

--oOo--

'Fifi, as soon as it starts, we should begin to move south. The road to the west down to Stuttgart is going to be impossible. Herr Wagner, please remember to keep to the right fork and keep the river close to your right until we exit the big bend, perhaps a mile away. After that, we should use the roads.'

Wagner and Fifi nodded.

'The note was clear. Keep to the road towards Koln, but turn right at Wiesdorf towards Ehrfstadt. From there it is straight to France.'

At a little before one-fifty, the deep roar of a waking giant was heard all around. The rhythmical rolling of aircraft engines was now unmistakable. In the distance, there came the wail of sirens and the sky became lit by what seemed like hundreds of lights – long beams scanning the heavens for their targets. Then the ground below erupted in convulsions – raindrops on a pond. Fireballs reached skywards – mushrooms of heat and flying objects. Death and destruction were in Dusseldorf tonight.

From their position south of the river, the occupants of the car looked on as the city whirled to destruction at the hands of the aeroplanes overhead. They saw one plane begin to fall from the sky, tumbling earthwards, its tail on fire. Fire broke away from it, perhaps an engine falling away, then it struck the ground and a little puff of yellow flame erupted.

'Serve the bastards right, fucking Nazis.' Henri spat out of the window.

Liesel saw the flame and was sorry for whoever was underneath the explosion.

--oOo--

Frau Langer stepped towards the window, looking out over her garden, in bloom from the summer sun and the gentle care of the gardener. Even in times of war, she wanted life to continue as before. But she was now heartbroken. The garden gave her little comfort. Her grandchildren and daughter were now gone forever. Her husband was just an empty shell – the man of her dreams, the proud officer, just a distant memory for both of them. Her son, what could she imagine of him that made her proud to have raised the man? She could think of little, which made her hurt deep inside. Her body had created this man and he would bring eternal shame and pain to the house, she felt it deep inside.

She turned back to her bed, craving the safety of the blankets. Once more hoping that the night would bring relief from her anguish and that there would be no dawn for the Langers. She checked the door was locked and that no one could enter. Satisfied, she climbed between the cool sheets. The open window let in the calming scents of the garden, which helped to steady her nerves and to welcome the temporary relief that sleep might bring. She awoke to the sound of sirens. Herr Langer was shouting to his nurse, instructing her to leave for the public shelter, taking Frau Langer with her.

'But sir, we cannot leave you here.'

'I will not be leaving my home. If I am to die, I will die at home. Go quickly, the bombs are coming quickly and there is little time left to run.'

'Herr Langer, I will go down to the cellar with Frau Langer. Please come with me, please, sir.'

'This is my home. I will not be hounded out by the English.'

The nurse moved towards Frau Langer's room. The door was locked. She knocked but there was no answer. As she turned towards the stairs to find the spare key, the stairs disappeared from under her and she fell through the hole as the two sides of the house fell away. The entire floor of the house collapsed, folding into the cellars, and the roof now fell onto the foundations. The gas lamp outside ignited the storage tanks and the front wall exploded as if kicked by a giant. The debris below was lifted upwards in one movement and was then set down again with a heavy crash.

--oOo--

On the corner of Landstrasse, a black car appeared. A new order had been received to check again for the missing Jew known as Karl Israel Eisner. The Gauleiter had agreed with the report received that the man was now a convicted rapist, having taken Liesel Langer repeatedly against her will, resulting in two children. He was to be arrested and taken to the central district for detention and questioning by the SS. This was an order that had no expiration and was to be pursued until successfully obeyed.

Inside the car, the red end of a cigarette was all that could be seen of the occupant, its plume of smoke escaping upwards. The occupant had been instructed to ignore any sirens and alarms since the cover of bombing provided an opportunity for a rat to escape. Not tonight. The car door opened, the occupant got out and tossed down the cigarette. With a single twist of the boot, the light was out. The man looked up and adjusted his hat. His uniform was of the SS, a sign for everyone to beware. He took a step forward just as a blinding white flash appeared before his eyes, sending him backward with the force of a speeding train. His dead body fell towards the ground as explosions erupted all around, from the river to the end of the square, where the telegraph office had stood. The papers inside were now ablaze, little sheaves of paper fluttering, sending hot sparkling embers over other houses, setting them on fire.

The west end of Landstrasse was obliterated almost in an instant. The house that had belonged to the Eisner family was now nothing but a crater, the only part of the house untouched was the little statue on the fountain at the end of the garden. It slid forward at an angle, as the water slowly stopped flowing down into the hole that had been the lawn. An instant later, a large metallic object fell at speed into the crater, throwing up bricks and wooden furniture. The aircraft engine rolled down the pile, settling in the cellars of the house, exposing the little secret surgery and hideaway undiscovered by the Gestapo.

--oOo--

'Remember Wiesdorf and look for the fork. It may not have a sign now or just a military one, watch out for the road after the big bend. This must be it.'

'Have we gone far enough?'

Wagner was worried that the bend was not big enough to be the big sweep of the Rhine in the south. At that moment, in front of them, the road began to erupt in spouts of smoke and yellow flame. Wagner steered the car around the first explosion, the road surface now littered with lumps of solid stone and earth. The car slid from the road and continued through grass. Another explosion ahead, Wagner tried to turn away, but the grass took away the car's grip and it lurched straight forward, stopping on a small earth hill. There was no time to wait around and look, Henri and Karl got out and pushed the heavy car until the wheels at the front gripped again. The car surged towards the road. Out of breath, Karl and Henri got back in and Wagner did not wait a moment longer. Behind them, another bomb fell. The tool factory had been missed by at least two bombers and the road to safety was now under attack by the very men who had unknowingly created an opportunity for the little party of runners to leave Dusseldorf.

With forty kilometres still to go to reach Koln, the petrol tank seemed desperately empty. In Germany, Wagner could obtain petrol, but only if he knew where to look for it. There were no roadside stations here. Even if there were, the bombing would mean the pumps were turned off and the tanks sealed. After driving in the near dark for forty minutes, a little stream of light came towards them. It was another car, almost certainly a German military car, but it was too late to get off the road and the oncoming car slowed.

'Ha! You there? What are you doing so late at night?'

'Who are you?'

Wagner decided to fight a question with another question. These were just damn army recruits and he was the Abwehr.

'Who are we? Did we not just ask you—?'

'Abwehr, now fuck off.'

'Abwehr? Why? What rank?'

'Here are my credentials. Look, and then be off with you.'

Wagner got out of the car and the two soldiers got out warily, but leaving their weapons behind. Wagner gave them his identification.

'Very good sir. Good night, Herr Sturmbannführer Wagner.'

As they turned to leave, one of them bowed his head to look into the car and smiled at the two women.

'Perhaps young Herr Sturmbannführer Wagner is going to be a very lucky man tonight!'

Wagner narrowed his eyes, but decided to say no more, keen to get going again. He was unhappy that he had been identified by name, and that the two women had been seen. It might go somewhere and get recorded. He had no business on the road from Dusseldorf to Koln. Wagner was a common enough name in Germany and he hoped it would soon be forgotten. But he was not truly convinced, knowing that German soldiers seldom forgot any detail in case it might become important later.

Liesel leaned over the seat to the rear and squeezed her children's hands.

'Monika darling, will you hold your brother, he is very cold. I will hold your hand.'

Henri smiled broadly. 'Liesel, this is all going to be fine, we will soon be in France and once we are there, we can disappear into the countryside.'

At the road to Wiesdorf, Wagner found the fork, took the right over a small bridge and onto the other bank of the Rhine. From here, they would leave the river behind and navigate by small roads and villages, one after another. At first light, a little after four, they stopped in a farmyard, hiding the car near an empty shed. They could deal with a farmer, that would be simple enough. Liesel and Fifi went in search of food and Henri briefed Karl on the plan for the rest of the journey into France.

'We cannot take the train here, Karl, but in France arrangements are in place for us to board a train from Nancy. The station there is friendly and our team will be waiting.'

Karl nodded but remained silent and Henri continued.

'Karl, we need to be strong and silent at the border. Wagner will do all the talking but, Abwehr or not, his presence will be suspicious. Fifi and Liesel might draw interest away and that might be enough for us to find a way. But we might have to kill the guards and escape in haste. Do you think the children can be quiet enough?'

'I will talk to them, Henri. We knew this would be dangerous but they are not children really. They have already seen much and they both know that this means survival for all of us, they truly do.'

Four loaves of bread were lifted from the farmhouse, along with a bottle of clean water from the pump. They would be missed and the alarm could be raised, but the runners hoped to be long gone by then.

--oOo--

'If I may say, Herr Wagner, you did handle those two soldiers most expertly, Abwehr or not.'

'It is what I do, Henri. I seek out the intelligence in the military. I looked and they had none.'

Henri smiled through a mouthful of bread and Fifi nudged him.

'He did not find any in you either.'

They had moved on to a deserted-looking farm, with an old shed that would provide some shelter. Should they be disturbed, they would simply pretend to be lost. Henri sat with the two children, they had been quiet all day but he worried that even the slightest noise from them might give them all away. He had to find a way to make sure they kept out of the way and alive.

'Monika, when we drive to the border, we will have to keep as quiet as possible, whatever you hear or whatever happens. You will have to grow up quickly, you know that our very lives can depend on this.'

Karl sat with them, placing his hand on Monika's arm as he did so.

'My darling, what do you think we could do about your brother? Can you keep him calm and quiet?'

'I will try, Father, but if we are frightened, we don't know how we might act. I am certainly afraid.'

Karl drew his daughter to him and kissed her forehead.

'We all are, my love, we all are. But we have to be strong this one more time. For your old father.'

Henri beckoned Franz, determined to lighten the boy's mood. 'Franz?'

'Yes, sir?'

How formal the boy dressed in the uniform of Hitler's boys' club.

'Sir? How polite, young man. I need to give you an order. I order you to keep quiet for three days. Can you do that?'

Franz looked doubtfully at this father. 'I will try.'

'If you do, then I will give you a medal.'

Karl smiled at his son and then at Henri. 'A medal, Franz. How about that?'

Franz stared at the floor, then looked up at Henri. 'I will try, sir.'

Henri smiled and poked Franz gently. 'You spoke! What about my order?'

Karl took his son in his arms, and smiled. 'No medal for you, young man – disobeying orders!'

'Oh, Father!' Franz laughed and sat with his sister.

'But seriously, we will need you to lie in perfect silence at the border, whatever happens. It is most important.'

Both children nodded and Monika looked at Henri and smiled.

As it was only August, the evening took a long time to turn into night. They took turns to sleep, but they remained undetected. The cool evening brought the opportunity to drive a little further away in the cramped car and nearer to safety.

--oOo--

They passed through and around Ehrfstadt, Zulpich, Rommersheim and Bitburg. The roads were not deserted, but other cars innocently enough used the roads, allowing them to hide in the open at night. Wagner decided that they could not make a border crossing at night, so they stopped at Bitburg, ready to plan how they might cross into France – whether through a barrier, around it on foot, or using the car off of the roads. Henri walked to the back of the car to find the children.

'Franz? Are you taking good care of your sister?'

'Yes, sir, we are quiet. We have not said a word.'

'I know, I am so proud of you both. We are nearly in France. Stay quiet for me. It is nearly time to cross.'

CHAPTER THIRTY-NINE
Czechoslovakia 1942

The telephone rang loudly in an office in the heart of the castle in Prague. Once used by the kings of Bohemia, it was the largest castle ever built. Kurt had been on duty since first light. His current and most pleasing posting put him at the centre of the security services and near to its chief, Reinhard Heydrich. The call informed Kurt that SS-Obergruppenführer Heydrich was ready to depart from Panenské Březany to come to the office. Kurt would be ready for the chief, who would be as pompous and miserable as ever, a man who was rarely in a good mood.

He looked out of the window. Kurt longed again for the glory of Berlin. Here, he was near the top of the Nazi tree, but he was distant from the real glory in Berlin. At least with this posting, he was guaranteed an important promotion at the end of it in August 1942. His preparations for Heydrich were simple enough – security briefing. Intelligence from all around the region had been collated by Kurt's junior officers and he had filtered the important information. He was ready, and sat waiting at his desk for the bell summoning him to the chief's office. He waited, but nothing happened. That was odd, it was only a short journey, perhaps twenty minutes. Suddenly, Kurt's own aide rushed in.

'Sorry, sir. Please come quick! The chief has been shot, well hit with a grenade! You are to leave for the Bulovka Hospital immediately.'

'Is he in there?'

'No, he was shot outside of it.'

'Damn it!'

Kurt rushed off and into his own car. It sped towards the site of Heydrich's shooting, where Kurt found the chief's car empty and no one around. A small number of people had helped the wounded chief into a delivery van, which had gone back to the hospital. Inside, Kurt found the chief being operated on, having summoned the personal physician of his superior, Himmler himself. Kurt decided to move the office here, with the staff and administrators setting up in a room nearby, ready to begin the investigation.

For seven long days they waited, on some days the chief's condition improved, on others it deteriorated. Kurt remained in the hospital room the whole time, fearful of a second attempt to complete the assassination. On the day that Heydrich died, Kurt received a direct order from Himmler to reform his Einsatzgruppe and to apply a collective responsibility warning to the village of Ležáky.

Kurt was angry. Once again his chances of advancement had been stifled by the actions of these people. Perhaps somehow, the blame for the attack would fall to him. Had there been any intelligence on a possible attack? Should he have known? In written orders before he left, he distanced himself from Heydrich's personal protection squad, preferring to write about arrangements to execute Himmler's orders. Within three days, his unit had arrived and he put on his familiar field uniform, which lifted his spirits. He then drove off in search of the village to avenge Heydrich and in doing so, show himself to be the hero of Ležáky.

By the time Kurt arrived, his advance units had already gathered some of the townspeople into the street. Each house had been forcibly entered, the occupants pulled out onto the streets, the children pushed back inside at gunpoint. The men and women were herded into the tiny square under the shade of the modest chapel. The women were tearing at the German uniforms, desperate to get back to their children. The men were angry and powerless to intervene. A large lorry arrived, which took away some of the older children and the very youngest. It would be bound for Chelmno, where the SS were testing new mobile vans to remove unwanted populations. When the lorry arrived, the soldiers moved aside, allowing the townspeople to see of the loading of their children – a cruelty that Heydrich himself would have appreciated. As the lorry moved away, the people fell silent and the only sound was the crunching of the gearbox and the scratching of tyres on stone. The sound faded away to silence.

Kurt issued orders to three officers at his side. Quickly, his men moved to fetch cans of petrol and dry brushwood. At random, they opened doors and pushed in piles of wood, tossing petrol liberally on the thresholds. Behind them, soldiers tossed rags soaked in petrol into the doorways. The dry houses caught fire immediately, the cracking of timbers and the sounds of falling masonry soon filled the empty air with a menacing roar, heralding the arrival of the final act of cruelty.

The German soldiers now looked towards Kurt. He looked around the scene, at the utterly powerless and frightened townspeople. Women were on their knees, vomiting on the ground. The men were pale. If any dared speak, a harsh blow with a rifle silenced them. Kurt knew he had a choice but Berlin called to him and if he could not advance by status, he would do so through reputation. He looked at the people lined up against the wall of the chapel, their faces now empty and subjugated. He turned to his officers, and they turned as one, firing on those lined up, and the town of Ležáky died.

As he tried to leave, two women ran to him, begging mercy for their departed children, falling to their knees, tearful and pleading. One woman was immediately pulled away, her skirt was torn from her and her flesh was exposed, then she was pushed into a car and taken away. The second had her hand on Kurt's boot. He went to kick her away but as he looked down to her, he saw her face and it stopped him cold.

The dirty, torn clothes and the bright eyes were just the same as his Odile, from the camps of 1915. It was her, here in a long-forsaken village far from anywhere. The face was round and beautiful, and he recognised the fear, desperation and dependence on his mercy. He froze, unable to move. In the car, he saw the other woman with five of his men surrounding her, taking turns with her body and grabbing her breasts. He looked down again. This must not happen to this woman, she would be spared the humiliation. He took out his pistol and with trembling hands looked into her eyes. She cried out in anguish. But Kurt knew this was preferable to the alternative. He shot her and she fell to the ground, dead.

When he looked up again, he saw the other woman now on the ground, naked and bleeding, trying to grab the rags of her clothes. More of his men were coming upon her, ready to take their turn. He looked down again. The woman at his feet was now at peace, spared the awful agony of such a public spectacle. He took out a handkerchief from his pocket and placed it over the dead woman's face. With it came the little square that had once belonged to Odile. He could not let thoughts of her come to him in this place of misery and death, already the dead woman's face had cut him deeply. He quickly replaced the little scrap of cotton and looked up again. Kurt ordered his men to burn the town, but to leave the women alone, just to kill them. He called over to his trusted second-in-command, bringing him to his side.

'Bruno, the woman at my feet, have her covered and buried will you?'

If Bruno was surprised at the order, he said nothing.

'Of course sir. I will see that it is done.'

Kurt nodded, patted Bruno on the shoulder and turned away. He glanced back at the woman who lay dead on the floor in front of him and then towards the still-moving body of the naked woman in the grass. A single shot rang out, silencing her cries of pain and agony.

Shaken, he left the town behind, now intent on avenging his chief. In his mind, it would be more to prove his loyalty and to enhance his reputation than out of any genuine respect for Heydrich. He knew that Hitler would be watching personally, the stories of the aftermath whispered to him by the awful Himmler. Kurt had no respect for this man, who ingratiated himself into the heart of power through the slime-laden wriggling of a snail. But he would ride to Berlin on a golden chariot, the spoils of his war, dragged behind in blood-soaked glory, the red and white trails set off by the glint of the sun on the hot metal.

Kurt redoubled his efforts to investigate the assassination of his chief. By the end of July, likely conspirators had been rounded up and shot, Kurt just missing out on the final gun fight in Prague, but successfully arresting the British agent responsible for planning the entire operation. He enjoyed the sport of interrogation and he knew he was skilled at it. But this was still rat catching, a reprisal for Heydrich admittedly, but it was individuals, not countries. The advancement of the Reich would need bigger operations and grander plans, and that could only happen from Berlin.

But first, he must turn again to the one rat he had still to catch, the fucking Jew Eisner. The fools in Dusseldorf had been sloppy with his orders. Just because he was in another country did not mean his order was not still valid. He still held a Dusseldorf Gestapo and SS rank. He would have to attend to it again. Although Karl had disappeared, he had been successfully denounced as a Jewish rapist who had taken his sister repeatedly in a sinister act of cowardice under the noses of the innocent Langers. Their marriage had been dissolved and the document torn to pieces by the Gauleiter himself. But Karl was still alive since there had been no body. There had been some arrests on suspicion, but none were Karl. When he was finished here, he would have to conclude his business in Dusseldorf as swiftly and discreetly as possible. While Karl Israel Eisner lived, the shadow of shame would prevent the light of Germany from shining on his face, however fast he ran to escape the creeping shadow.

CHAPTER FORTY
Dusseldorf 31 July 1942

Kurt arranged a flight to Koln and then a staff car to Dusseldorf. If he landed in Dusseldorf, someone might talk and in any case, many of the airfields had been bombed by the British and the Americans. In Koln he had many friends. In Dusseldorf there were many tongues to wag.

He landed at three in the morning, the quietest time to arrive. The aeroplane was diverted to an alternative landing strip as there was yet another bombing raid on Koln and Dusseldorf. The car and driver were already on the grass when his plane landed. Kurt was inside in just a few seconds. His driver was unfamiliar, but covered in dust and dirt from the drive though the bombing. They would have to drive from Koln to Dusseldorf indirectly as the bombs had closed some of the roads. This meant taking the Ossendorf road to avoid any chance of being caught up in any further air raids. They passed only two other vehicles, both military and clearly neither were planning on hanging around for very long with the threat of more instant death from above.

Once at the dusty and damaged SS building in Dusseldorf, Kurt was greeted by a scene of confusion as conflicting reports had come in after the bombing that night. The enemy had successfully attacked the steelworks and factories along the Ruhr and Rhine, but the central target had clearly been Dusseldorf. Immediately, Kurt enquired about reports from the streets of his family, but there was no new information yet. Bombing there would have been most unlikely, he was told, as it was too far from the vehicle and armament factory even for the British. While he was relieved for his parents, he was a little disappointed as he had secretly hoped a bomb had fallen on Karl, driving the man into the centre of the earth, leaving the rest of the street undamaged and allowing him to return to Berlin a resurgent hero of Heydrich's vengeance.

'Ah, Oberführer Langer! It is good to see you.'

'Good evening, Wolz. May I enquire as to your progress with the arrest of the fugitive rapist Eisner?'

Wolz looked around him. The office was a chaotic scene of papers and the coming and going of men gathering reports from all around the city. In the distance was the flaming red glow of the steelworks and the industrial zone ablaze from the firebombing. He turned back to Langer.

'Well, sir, we have placed a man outside his house almost every day for weeks, but so far as we can tell, there is nothing. Not a sign of him at all. We are expecting a report soon—'

'No! Take me to Landstrasse in your car so that I can see for myself. I have had quite enough of this dithering and incompetent hesitation. I want him arrested immediately.'

'But sir, the bombing last night—'

'What of it? Would not a bombing raid be a perfect opportunity for a fugitive to disappear?'

'Well, yes sir, certainly. But do you think that likely?'

'The man is a cowardly rat. He is capable of anything.'

'Very good, sir. My car is here. It has new thicker tyres in case there is damage to the roads. We will be there in just a few minutes.'

'I know where I live, Wolz.'

'Of course, sir.'

The car moved off, turning first towards the river then over the little bridge by the small cinema, which had been showing two new films of German success on the Eastern Front. Kurt wondered whether any of his operations would be featured. He would enquire later. At Duisbergstrasse, he was met with a scene of complete devastation. There were three huge craters stretching right across the road and water was pouring into the holes. Kurt was now fearful for his own family. Before he moved on to Eisner, he wanted to be sure of his parents who were very near to this spot.

'Turn around and take the next right. Quickly!'

The car roared around and sped off, making the turn and forcing Kurt almost sideways as it did so.

'Faster, man!'

The driver tried to move faster, but the road was littered with tiny holes making progress slower.

'And right again and then stop at the end of the road.'

'Sir, look, it is blocked. There are young SS firemen there now, see? It looks like it was a big fire.'

Kurt's eyes snapped immediately to the scene. He stepped out of the car. Almost at a run, he found his way to the end of his street, the wide road littered with debris from what must have been several huge explosions.

'No further. Not one step more!'

Kurt turned with his eyes ablaze at the impertinence of a lowly boy fireman.

'Do you know who I am?'

'Yes sir, a senior officer. But my order stands above all others.'

'What? Why, you impertinent child?'

'Because there is an unexploded bomb in the middle of that house, sir. There is a team now setting it to blow and looking for survivors. But there won't be any.'

Kurt looked up. He knew instinctively that it was his father's house, or a hole where his family home used to stand. He leaned on the tender to steady himself, his eyes now damp, blurring the terrible scene. But he had to see what was left of his home one more time so he wiped his eyes and moved to go forward.

'As I say, sir, you cannot go through. They are going to detonate any second now.'

'Were there people inside? It was my house.'

'They can't investigate until the bomb is safe, sir. They listened for hours but nothing came from inside. They used little microphones sir, very clever, but no sounds at all. They can detect breathing, but nothing. No one is alive, sir. Very sorry, if someone you knew was inside, sir.'

Kurt placed his hand on the boy's shoulder, softening to the boy's kindness and bravery, in standing up to him. He now took a step back, looking at the scene for one last time. As he watched, the debris convulsed, as if taking one more deep breath and then blew hard. Timbers lifted, split and then fell. Kurt knew in his heart that his parents must have been at home inside, or else they would be here watching the scene. It was now quite clear that they had died in the bombing. He thought of Liesel, softening to her a little, just for a moment. She would be devastated. Suddenly he thought of her children. They were pure German. Might they have also been here?

'When the occupants are identified, I want you to report to me personally, do you understand?'

'Yes sir. Oberführer?'

'Langer. Go to the SS office and report there. Speak to no one but me, even if you have to wait all day.'

'Yes, sir.'

Kurt went back to his car and sat back. The boy looked towards him as he went, then turned back to the fires and lifted his hose a little higher.

At the south east end of Landstrasse, all seemed quiet. There was no fire here, but beyond, the houses were ablaze, the fire devastating the rest of the street. But this corner, a desolation of rubble, was quiet. In the destruction, Kurt recognised a British-made Merlin engine, which had fallen from a Lancaster bomber perhaps, a small strip of the propeller still attached. He looked at the damage. It was near total and nothing inside could be recognised with certainty.

Liesel's house was gone, completely destroyed, and even the bricks had split in the heat of the fire. The Gestapo reports had placed her in this house tonight, at least just before dark.

Kurt stepped towards the house, its garden in ruins. He had actually quite liked the garden and this house and had planned to develop it when he returned for a little extra income. It was, after all, now officially his. The furniture and effects were destroyed, just pieces of charred wood now strewn around. The ground underneath was barely visible. If bodies were here, then they would surely have been seen from the thorough inspection from the SS and Gestapo. But he saw none, there were none. He had lost his parents last night and had expected to see the body of his dead sister here this morning. But the body he wanted most of all was missing and unaccounted for. He clenched his fists and his new leather gloves creaked with the strain. The rat had fled the scene, the lucky Jew had run from the death shroud over his own home.

He continued to look through the debris, angrily kicking aside ornaments and charred sticks of wood and rubble but found nothing but burnt clothing and the remains of a mattress. There was no sign of the children at all. Perhaps they were indeed dead, their little bodies lying in the hole of the Langer house. Perhaps they all were, Liesel included. They would all be dead. But no, not Karl, who was either here or still at large.

As he turned to see the front of the house, a little patch of white wall beneath the floor caught his eye. This was a cellar room. Kurt had not seen this on the plan of the house and had no inkling of its existence. There were no cellars on this side of the house, else he would have seen them. This was a room of which he had no knowledge. Perhaps the rat was here.

'Wolz, come and help me move debris from this room. Quickly man! It is a hidden cellar. Perhaps they are here, alive or dead.'

'The timbers are wet sir, the cellar looks to be flooded.'

'Damn it! You bastard, Eisner.'

'Sir?'

'Nothing, Wolz. This was a secret room, but there is nobody here. Look there, a blanket and some clothing floating, but no bodies. They either escaped from here, or were not here at all. Either way, they are not dead. Will you request an urgent search of my parents' house? Now?'

'Sir.'

Wolz went to the car and within fifteen minutes a response had come back.

'Herr Langer. Report has found two bodies. An elderly man and a younger woman.'

Kurt's eyes lifted. Perhaps this was Liesel. A cruelty of fate killed only his family. No word of his mother. She was old and could not be easily mistaken.

'A housekeeper perhaps? A nurse for your father? There is evidence of a uniform and not regular clothing.'

His heart sank. It was his father's nurse. The loyal German woman had stayed with him through the bombing. He would send money to her family. His mother would be dead somewhere in the rubble. If his father was there, then his mother would be there also. They had just not found her yet. But no children, no Liesel and no Eisner, although he had not expected him to be in that house.

'Take me back to the office, Wolz. I have seen enough of this.'

'Most unusual sir, for them to get the bombing this wrong. The factory is perhaps three kilometres away. It isn't an exact skill, but if I am honest, the river is a very good marker. Perhaps the Royal Air Force rely on untrained boys now. That must be a good sign.'

Kurt ignored the comment, he was looking at the reflections of red glowing, rippling flames in the front windscreen. His inheritance and foundation in Dusseldorf was gone.

'What reports have come in from tonight, apart from the bombing? Any movements of transports, anything unusual or unexpected?'

'None sir. No transports, and trains stopped at two when the raid was known to be coming, roads were closed at about the same time. The only thing we have is a report of an Abwehr officer on the road near the Rheindorf checkpoint. Apparently the two soldiers only reported it because the car had army identification plates and the officer was extremely rude. They were just going to say hello and beg a cigarette.'

'Abwehr? That useless load of horse-shit eating, corruption-riddled drunks. Did they get a name?'

'Yes sir, a Sturmbannführer Wagner.'

'From Dusseldorf?'

'We have not yet investigated. We were not going to, given everything else that has been happening tonight it seemed to be of low importance.'

'Strange to see Abwehr, is it not?'

'Unusual, sir. We will see where he is from and take it from there.'

Kurt stepped outside, not able to grieve for his parents and needing to hold together his mind and his body. He would be allowed seven days compassionate leave, which he would take but he would use the time to find more of the truth about Eisner. Something remained that the hopeless fools here had been unable to uncover.

'Herr Langer? Ah, here you are, sir. From Abwehr in Berlin. Admiral Canaris has ordered all requests between SS and Abwehr to go through his office. Something about a review of operations? Anyway, this is what the office has reported on all Abwehr officers named Wagner.'

Kurt scanned the list, which told him nothing. Wagners all over Germany, the east, the west, overseas and endeavouring to operate in Spain, Portugal and Greece. There was nothing here. He put down the note. Then he thought of a different tack.

'Wolz, one more question. There are sixty Wagners here. Take out the ones in the east, overseas and in Berlin. That leaves us with six names. Can you find out where they are from? Look for perhaps Dusseldorf, Koln and Stuttgart to start with. Family connections and such. How quickly can you find an answer?'

'I will call immediately, but sir, may I ask why?'

'Call it my old Gestapo intuition, Wolz. Remove the doubt, examine all angles. One of the threads in the pile is true. It may not be this one, but eliminating it would be helpful.'

Wolz left and Kurt returned to his thoughts. He looked again at the dying flames, the little plumes of water from the fire tenders were barely visible. The fires were still not under control. Suddenly came hurried footsteps.

'Sir, there is only one Wagner in the Abwehr who is an officer from one of the three cities. He is from Koln and known to be a loyal and resourceful officer. Well respected, but he is currently based in Paris, interrogating escaping prisoners of war.'

Kurt's eyes flashed to Wolz. 'Paris?'

'Yes, sir. The Paris office have also reported him missing, well absent, three days ago. He was following a promising lead apparently, so nothing necessarily unusual in his being absent. He was following a young French boy and an older woman who were detained and then released. Looked like a pretty low-level search for downed pilots, who may perhaps have known about this raid tonight. It could be that this Wagner was here checking whether the intelligence was reliable. Seems it was, looking at the destruction.'

Kurt's enthusiasm dimmed slightly. It was an entirely plausible reason to come and check whether the intelligence was true. The Abwehr were full of holes, but some of their officers were actually quite good. This man Wagner may well be one of those.

'Bring the two soldiers to me will you, just for the record.'

'Of course, sir.'

Wolz's voice, Kurt detected, contained the very slightest note of irritation. Perhaps he was annoyed at the repeated request for piecemeal information about what was clearly an unimportant detail of the otherwise chaotic record of the night's events. Just before six in the morning, the two young soldiers were brought before Langer.

'You drove towards Dusseldorf, you say it was somewhere between two-thirty and three this morning. Is that correct?'

The two nodded, seemingly terrified of their own officers.

'Yes, sir.'

'Sir.'

Kurt looked up at them both. They looked honest and terrified enough. Good, they might remember something important.

'Then you saw a French car, a Citroen was it? It was stopping at the side of the road. Then describe for me now, in your own words, what happened next. Do not leave out the slightest detail. Let me judge what is important. Understood?'

'Sir. We stopped and then both got out because it was a car with army plates, HW sir, Wehrmacht. We were just going to ask for a cigarette, but also to have a look at the car, which must have been requisitioned in France. Nice car, sir. I am an enthusiast of the big ones.'

'Details, boy, not anecdotes.'

'Of course, sir. Anyway, I asked what the officer was doing so late at night. But instead of replying, he asked me who we were. That seemed a bit odd until he said he was Abwehr. Well, that made a difference. So I asked for his card and he gave it. A Sturmbannführer Wagner.'

'What did he say to you then?'

'Beg pardon, sir, but he told us to fuck off.'

'Did you not think that was odd?'

'He was Abwehr, sir, we did not even dare to question. Perhaps he was on an operation. There was an air raid.'

'Hm. Anything else? Think man, think.'

'No sir. Although he did have two women in the car.'

Kurt's whole body began to tingle. He only hoped these two woodentops would remember something of their appearance. Liesel was very attractive, even as an older woman. They would remember her.

'Describe them, think very closely. What did you see?'

'One was perhaps twenty-five or thirty. Pretty woman. Looked a bit like Hedy Lamarr, sir. If that helps.'

It didn't. That made her too young and although his sister was beautiful, she did not look like Hedy Lamarr.

'The other woman, maybe as old as fifty.'

Again, Kurt was disappointed. That was certainly too old.

'She looked like she could have used a good dinner. But still, she had nice eyes and a lovely smile.'

Kurt thought. Perhaps, just perhaps. He maintained his interest a moment longer.

'Think back, man.'

He did not want to feed this man the answer, nor frighten him so much that he could not think, otherwise it would all be meaningless.

'Without this seeming a ridiculous question, could you see any resemblance between the face of the woman who was not Hedy Lamarr and my own face?'

Both men looked doubtful at first. But one closed his eyes and tilted his head for a few moments.

'Yes sir, in fact, I am certain.'

But Kurt was already out of the door.

'What the fuck was that all about?'

'Fuck knows.'

Wolz advanced on the two men.

'Tell no one anything of this and all will be well. Come. Let us see if we can find you some decent American cigarettes and a little something to eat. We have some good schnapps here as well. Just the thing to start the day with, eh?'

CHAPTER FORTY-ONE
Germany 1 August 1942

Henri thought through their current situation. Here they were, four runners and three operatives by a roadside outside of Bitburg in Germany on the afternoon of the first day of August in 1942. They had a French car with German Army plates. They all had legitimate German identification, correctly issued and were permitted to travel anywhere inside Germany. They looked quite suspicious, but their travel papers were all in order. What they did not have were permits to travel into France. His father had proposed that they cross through the countryside in groups of two with the car crossing with just one person. But Henri doubted the possibility of success. The poor German family all looked tired and terrified, which was sure giveaway and they would be assumed to be Jewish. Fifi and Wagner could travel in the car without any problems as the little French fancy would not be questioned. But the five of them might be more difficult. The border region was not well defended, but the ground was still disputed and Karl was sought by the Nazis. A legitimate crossing would create a trail leading the authorities to them quite quickly. It kept coming back to that one problem, that Karl was wanted by the SS, at a high enough level to warrant an alert to Berlin. That meant that he was the one to separate and to plan for since he was the key to their possible downfall. He went to sit with Wagner in the sun while the car and its other occupants remained hidden from the road in a blind roadway that led to a disused railway shed.

'Wagner, I am worried that the children might not be able to stay quiet and safe in the back of the car.'

'Henri, I would give them more credit. Monika is frightened, but she trusts you already, goodness knows why, ha! But they have seen enough in their young lives, they know this is the only hope for the whole family staying alive. Franz is the same. He is clearly unsure why he is running, but he loves his parents and obeys them without question. Use Karl, trust me, Franz will do what his father orders.'

'Very well. Do you think that we can make a single crossing? Perhaps there are alternatives.'

'What do you have in mind?'

'We could go west through Luxembourg City to Belgium?'

'Long journey, Henri, and Luxembourg is a complicated place to be found. Because it is so fragile, there are more Germans there than in the south. We should go through Germany into France.'

'How about splitting the men and women, then?'

'Why?'

'Go through once, then come back and do it again?'

Wagner shook his head. 'No. The car gives it away.'

'We could get a second car, just for a short time, or change its appearance?'

'But the registration plate will be listed as missing in France. One telephone call and it is all over.'

Henri looked down and thought for a while. 'Do you have a gun, Wagner?'

'No.'

'We could steal one and then kill the border guards.'

'Are you mad?'

'No. Look, we take a weapon, get to the border. You play the role with Fifi and we all hide in the rear. We could practise. If it goes wrong, we kill the four or five guards.'

'You think to kill five guards without one of them getting a shot back? You think that likely or even possible?'

'I suppose not. But wait. Why don't we storm the crossing first, unseen and unexpected and then just drive through?'

Wagner sat up. 'Henri, there is a crossing at Perl on the river. It is for military horses and motorcycles only. They won't have anything like the presence they have at the road crossings because it is too tight a squeeze for cars and lorries.'

'But worth thinking about? Well then?'

'Yes, you French scoundrel, it might be our best chance.'

At nightfall, Henri loaded the car in such a way as to give him every chance of moving to a position where he could fire a weapon, if he managed to get one. Fifi and Henri sat in the rear with Liesel in the front – Henri considering it best to have another German speaker up front with Wagner. The two children and Karl were in the luggage bay at the back, they would be uncomfortable, but hidden from view. The car looked from the outside as if great concrete blocks had been loaded in the back. It would only pass a casual glance and that was why Wagner was now so important for this part of the operation. The secret family had to remain hidden from the eyes of the guards and Wagner would have to do all of the talking if they were to have a chance. But a narrow horse crossing and a big car, well that would be something to deal with when they got there.

They drove out of the secluded road and then took the road south from Bitburg towards the French border at Perl. Henri despaired at the countryside. Normally, he would consider it to be beautiful, the hills providing splendid views of the frontier, but hills to a fully laden car were a menace, potentially a deadly one. He could hear Monika talking quietly to her brother in the rear.

'Franz, you are trembling and so cold. Here, hold my hand. Father is here also.'

'I am here, Franz, my son. Things will be well.'

The road surface was good enough, and it would take about three hours to reach Perl in the dark, taking the gradient into consideration. There were three border crossing points along the Moselle River, and Henri prayed that one of them would work for them. When the car became short of petrol, they stopped at the base of the Schloss Berg so they could use Wagner's valid permits. Wagner calmly chatted with the attendant. Once the coupon was signed, Wagner got back in the car.

'Well that was easy enough. I have written over the name on the coupon, so it will be hard to read and remember. Now for the border. Henri, are you sure you know what you want to do? The plan is all yours from now, my friend.'

Henri shrugged, he was confident of everything and nothing.

'This is the only thing we are not so very sure of.'

As the car drew away, Henri turned to see the attendant at the petrol station picking up the telephone. His stomach plummeted and he closed his eyes. Could the attendant have suspected something? Could he be phoning the Gestapo at this very moment? He did not want to cause panic in the car, so he decided to keep his observation to himself for now.

The drop towards France meant that the car could now move a little faster. When the crossing point finally appeared out of the dark, there was only one sleeping guard visible. But as they approached, another guard appeared with a machine gun on his shoulder.

'Damn it, you said this was a horse crossing, Wagner!'

'It was, Henri, I don't know what this is, but this is not just a horse crossing anymore.'

'Slow the car. I am going to try to distract them.'

The car slowed and Henri rolled out, the bright headlights providing cover while he crossed to the shelter of a tree line near the guards' hut. Wagner drew slowly up to the crossing point, with Liesel in the front and Fifi pretending to be asleep in the rear.

Franz murmured, perhaps woken from his sleep by the change in the car's movement but Monika whispered to him.

'No, Franz, Ssh. Keep quiet, whatever happens.'

Liesel spoke without turning her head.

'Children, please be quiet from now. We are almost there.'

There was the faintest shuffling in the back and the car rocked gently.

'Children, you must be still, you must not move!'

When he reached the guard, Wagner spoke first, almost lazily disinterested by the presence of the border guard.

'I am Sturmbannführer Wagner, Abwehr. Here is my identity.'

The guard handed him back his identification, but did not move his gaze from Wagner.

'Where are you going, sir?'

'I am returning to Paris after visiting Koln today. I was worried that my mother was ill.'

'Koln? The bombings?'

'Yes, that is why I am driving at night. The British bomb the cities by night and the Americans bomb everything else in the daytime, eh?'

The guard laughed. 'They do. So, sir, who are the women?' He looked into the car.

'This woman here is my sister. I am taking her to see Paris. I know it is a little unusual, but I do want her to see the sights. Us poor Abwehr don't see much leave.'

'And the woman in the back?'

'She is my… well… my friend.' Wagner nodded towards Liesel.

The guard winked. 'I see. What is in the luggage compartment?'

'Just a case, nothing else. My sister and… friend do not travel light, you know.'

'Open it and show me.'

'Why would you want to see suitcases of dresses, ha?'

'The military and authorities cross at Saarbrücken. Your permit should say that. This crossing is local only. So, show me the luggage, sir.'

Wagner saw the guard's grip on his gun tighten and his finger move towards the trigger. He stepped out of the car slowly, moving towards the rear. He did not know whether to open it or not. He placed his hand on the rear to open the wide door. As he did so, the guard moved in to look, then his body suddenly crumpled with a blow to his neck from Henri.

No one moved. The other guard did not make any move towards them. He must have been still blinded by the car's headlights and reassured by the quiet conversation.

'Keep talking, Wagner, as if nothing changed.'

Henri tried to move the body away and Wagner kept talking about Germany and music and anything he could think of to sound casual and normal, with Karl joining in with chat and laughter. Henri quickly dragged the body of the guard to the side of the road, under the dazzling cover of the headlights. He took the gun and the pistol from the body.

'Hey, Hans, come on, I want to get some sleep, eh?'

'Wagner, stay behind the car and let the next guard come.'

'Well now, what do we have here? Pretty lady eh? You are not supposed to be doing this at this time are you? Mind telling me who *you* are?'

It crossed Wagner's mind that Liesel might very well point out that her brother was in the SS and Gestapo and if he laid a finger on her, Kurt would drown him in his own liquid entrails.

'I am a German citizen, you have no right to speak to me like that!'

'Papers, then. Let's do it the hard way.'

Liesel handed him her identification.

'Frau Liesel Eisner. Pretty name, Liesel.'

With horror, Wagner realised that she had given the guard her real identification and not the fake one he had given her. The fool was supposed to leave her real identity behind her.

'Well, Frau Eisner, I have a cousin called L—'

A hammer blow to his face broke his jaw and cleaved his skull and he fell dead, Henri making sure with a small knife. Two guards dead and the little group were all still alive. The crossing was clear for now.

Wagner got back in the car. 'Is everyone unhurt?' He scanned the car to see if everyone was unharmed, 'Franz, Monika? How are you?'

'We are here, sir. My sister is quite well, as am I.'

Wagner smiled at the formality of Franz's reply. He assumed that this was his way of coping with the fear.

'That is good. Now help your sister with the next part of our journey into France. Quickly turn around so that you are not in the same position and sit as close to the middle of the car as possible. But keep your heads down.'

Henri sat on the front on the engine above the headlights, directing Wagner to steer left and right to make sure that the wide wheels remained on the little track over the narrow bridge. It was close, but it was possible with care. So they drove through, slowly and calmly, past the bodies of the two dead guards. There was no point in wasting time moving them since the authorities would see this scene soon enough. On the other side, the bridge dropped sharply to a narrow roadway and they had now entered France. The drive to Nancy would be much easier now they had a French speaker and a member of the Abwehr in France. Wagner just hoped that the local French fighters gave them a chance to identify themselves without attacking this car with its army registration plates. Henri would have to look for a chance to change them back to something civilian.

CHAPTER FORTY-TWO

German-French Border 1 August 1942

Kurt was in his car alone as he dared not risk his driver discovering the truth about his sister and her damned husband. He set off from Dusseldorf and drove at full speed towards the point where the soldiers had met with Wagner and his sister. He knew this road well, but had to look out for the holes and debris from last night's bombing. Wolz had been right, the British had been a long way off their targets, which meant one less bomb on a factory, but he wished the bomb that had hit his parents' house had fallen here instead.

He knew he was looking for a French Citroen Avant, possibly with HW plates. The combination was unusual, since it was a very recognisable and beautiful car, and more likely to be noticed and remembered. That must be a mistake that Karl had made, choosing a car for show, the arrogant bastard. Kurt drove to Koln railway station first, looking for the car somewhere nearby. They must have taken a train from here to the border – he would have done that and he reasoned so would any sensible man. Here, he was on old familiar ground for he knew where to find timetables, guards and dispatchers. But there were no trains on the evening of the thirty-first of July bound for France and nobody fitting the description of Liesel, the children or Karl had been seen boarding any train with a man from the Abwehr. While there were Abwehr around, they were normally alone or with other officers. It was no use. Either they had separated or he had missed them. It was not possible to be specific about their movements because he simply did not know the details.

He drove further south and enquired at various points along the road to Saarbrücken, where the military and other vehicles can cross into France. But there was nothing unusual and certainly no French-built cars that day. He decided to wait. It was possible he had overtaken them somewhere, or they had taken a different route and had not yet reached this crossing. They simply had to cross here. So he decided to wait. His uniform and imposing presence must have terrified the young border guards as every car was now meticulously searched, even when the guards and travellers were familiar with one another. No one asked him why a senior officer of the SS was resting at a border crossing with no driver or armed escort. And no one dared to challenge him, which Kurt knew they should have done.

But just after midnight, the army desk at the border crossings were put on alert. Something had happened at Perl. Information was sparse, but it seemed that the crossing point was no longer replying to regular communications and the guards had not reported for duty changes at eleven. They would be tired and hungry, so it was unlikely that this was an oversight or mistake. Kurt grabbed the report and jumped into his car. He knew where Perl was and it would take him just under two hours to reach it.

During the journey, he became angry and resentful that the damned Jew had managed to get the better of him. Kurt wanted revenge now – it was no longer just face for him, or status, Karl must suffer and he had some ideas on what he might do to him when he found him. He used his time on the road to plan Eisner's torture. Kurt knew that Eisner was no rapist or even a Jew for that matter. But the little sheet of paper with the Gauleiter said differently and that was all that mattered. Karl Eisner beware, Kurt Langer is coming for you – you can run if you wish, but the end will be the same. Kurt liked the sport, his quarry would be worth the chase and Kurt was good at the chase.

As he approached Perl, he saw three cars and a lorry full of armed troops. The two dead bodies had been moved to the side of the road. One broken neck and one broken skull. It seemed a professional execution, which he doubted Karl would be capable of carrying out. The Abwehr man was certainly a traitor and he must be masterminding this escape. Why, Kurt could not yet understand, but he knew that Karl was here somewhere.

'Hauptmann, what clues are there?'

'There is only one clue, sir. A strange one, since it seems genuine, but very much out of place. It is an identification card, which I will have brought to you.'

Kurt's attention was now focused eagerly on the young soldier running towards them carrying something small and flat in his hand. He could not run quickly enough for Kurt. The soldier ran straight up to Kurt, saluted smartly and handed over the card almost ceremonially. On the card, was the unmistakable name and face of his sister.

CHAPTER FORTY-THREE

France August 1942

The car arrived at the railway station in Nancy. No one was talking. Henri was annoyed that they had left an unmissable trail of bodies at the crossing, which would pinpoint their destination and direction. And he imagined Liesel, Fifi and Karl still shocked at seeing such violent deaths at close quarters. Fortunately, the children had been out of sight. Still, they had got this far and it was almost an easy run home now.

The agreed meeting point was deserted. The other *Sunshine Road* operatives had apparently moved on from Nancy, perhaps they had been disturbed. But the tickets and permits they held would be sufficient for a run to Paris and the safety of the crowd. Even so, Henri did not want to risk his luck further and suggested that Wagner return to Paris, having been unsuccessful in his pursuit of Henri and Fifi.

'That would be the right strategy, Henri, and I agree. I will return tonight. From here, you should have no further problems. The family story should be accepted and you have many friends on this route to Paris. The children will provide excellent cover for your movements.'

Henri nodded. 'Herr Wagner, I am sorry if I misjudged you. Truly, you have been one of the bravest men I have ever met. We owe you so very much.'

'Well, you are only about twelve, Henri. How many men could you have met anyway?'

The two men laughed and embraced. Wagner kissed Fifi gently, as if kissing a precious jewel.

'My dear, France's future is in good hands if it produces such fine women as you. Look after him, he is a lively firework, likely to get us in more trouble yet.'

He moved to the Eisners and smiled. 'Herr, I'm sorry, Herr Doctor and Frau Eisner. Welcome to France. Good luck. I am afraid we have not had the chance to become acquainted and it is for the best, I suppose. I am no traitor to Germany, but there are better ways than this to live. Auf Wiedersehen and adieu!'

'Herr Wagner, thank you. My family owes you a great deal. But please be careful. My brother has shown he can be a dangerous and vengeful enemy. Please treat any contact with extreme caution. Do you promise me?'

Wagner nodded, waved over his shoulder, got into the car and drove off. Until the train was due, they would rest in the little house as the family were tired and sore from the journey. The children had been so quiet but now their bodies ached and they needed to be able to move in the open. Henri went out and found some bread and wine to dampen their hunger, but there was not much to be found.

The train from Nancy to Paris would leave at five in the evening, which gave them almost the day to rest and hide. They all had perfectly genuine and valid identification and Henri suggested that if they were to be stopped by the Germans, then they should speak in German, but do so in a way that sounded French. It was better than trying to do it the other way around. The Germans on inspection duties were not usually tuned into the dialects of their surroundings. He asked the Eisners to destroy their German identification papers. Karl took out three papers.

'I will gladly burn these. I never want to see Germany again. I am sorry, but there is nothing left there for me now. Liesel, let us add yours to this little pile of shame.'

Liesel put her hand into her dress pocket and her face turned pale.

'Oh no! Mein Gott! It is not here. Perhaps it is on the floor of the car?'

'Let us hope so, Frau Eisner, but we have no way of contacting Wagner to find out. Please think. When was the last time that you certainly knew you had it?'

Henri tried to appear calm, but inside he was a boiling mass of anger and terror. This could bring the Germans right to the front door.

'Oh no! I gave it to the guard at the border in Perl. As he took it, he was… The guard had it in his hand. In my shock, I did not seek its return. My identification paper is with the body.'

Colour flooded Henri's face. 'You did what? Why did you not give him the identity we gave to you? Oh my God! No!'

Henri looked at Fifi, who had put her hand to her mouth.

'Fifi! We must leave, now! When is the next train to anywhere?'

'I don't know. I will go now and find out.'

Fifi ran into the boiling heat of the street to the train station and returned, breathless.

'Henri, the next train is to Lyon in less than one hour.'

'Then we must go to Lyon first. We can take a train to Paris from there. Quickly, we must go through the barrier now.'

'I am so sorry, I have been so stupid. I only wanted to have something that had my own name on, Liesel Eisner. I was being sentimental and I have endangered us all through my carelessness. Kurt or the authorities will know we are moving to France.'

Fifi approached the distraught woman. 'Come, Frau Eisner, we have to go now, we must disappear.'

When they approached the barrier, they were fortunate for it was clear and neither German soldiers nor French guards were inspecting tickets. The platform was quiet and deserted. They were the only ones there. Four refugees and two Resistance operatives from the *Sunshine Road*.

CHAPTER FORTY-FOUR
France August 1942

Kurt had tried to fight back grief for his dead parents. But now, as he drove south towards the occupied territories in northern France, he had some time on his hands and he found them moving into his thoughts. He remembered when he was a young boy, climbing all over his father and hugging his mother tightly whenever he hurt himself. He remembered his silly baby sister, always crying or running away whenever he tried to play with her. But he also remembered the adoring looks from her as she grew, the ever-present companion around the house, holding on to his every word, trailing behind him, smiling at him whenever he turned around. Her tears as he left for the war and the softness of her touch when he first came home alive. But these were mere memories, no more solid than smoke. They could be forgotten and hidden. He shuffled his body in the seat, lifted his chin higher and drove on, trying to calculate which way his sister had fled.

Although the French car could now disappear in France itself, Kurt reasoned the fastest way out would be a train to Paris, so he drove to Metz. At the station in Metz, he was met with blank faces. The Paris train had left almost empty, carrying only some older people and soldiers. No car matching his description or carrying army plates was anywhere in sight. Nothing out of the ordinary anywhere at all. He decided to try alternative routes. What about Lyon or Nancy? Again, nothing. This was a quiet place and a quiet route. The fugitives most definitely did not board a train here.

He decided to drive to Nancy instead. There was more risk further south but it also provided a direct route to Paris. Nancy was also a quiet station, but someone might have seen something and it was worth the effort of driving there to see for himself before the trail went cold. When he arrived at the station, the Paris train had yet to depart and he was invited to wait in the office.

'Do you recall seeing a car at all? It would be a big French Citroen Avant, the Traction Avant. It may have had HW on the registration plate. Think, man! It is important.'

'No, sir, nothing like that. There was a big car earlier, not sure what type it was. Full of people, looked like they were the family of the officer with them.'

Kurt grabbed the man by the lapels and shook him.

'Officer? German? Was he Abwehr?'

'He might have been, yes.'

'Who was with him? A couple perhaps, children?'

'Yes, perhaps five or six people.'

'Five or six? How long ago?'

'The family all got on the train for Lyon. The officer drove off… south maybe.'

'When is the next train to Lyon?'

'Tomorrow morning. But the Lyon train will stop for an hour in Chaumont to take on coal and water.' He glanced at the clock. 'If you drive quickly, you have seventy minutes—'

Kurt left the shaken man at the station and ran to his car. So they had left for Lyon. Kurt reasoned that the man in the car must be Wagner and he was not coming back for a train today. They had either split up or had decided to meet later. It was worth the risk to make a wrong turn and lose the trail. Wagner could wait, he knew him and would find him later.

He drove as fast as the car would allow, heading south and west. There were not too many choices for roads and he decided to stay on the major routes. He glanced at a poor quality map once or twice, risking a crash or worse. Finally, he saw in the valley the spider-like shape of Chaumont from the height at Andelot. The railway line was not in sight, but he would find the station easily enough since they were normally in the central areas of these small border towns.

Kurt spotted a local policeman on a bicycle and ordered him to accompany him to the station. The station was on the side of town that Kurt had approached from and soon enough the red and white gates came into view. A train was in the station, with steam and smoke puffing rhythmically as it built up a new head of steam. There was not much time. Ignoring the station's signs, Kurt drove straight to the loading area and jumped out of the car. Chaumont was a quiet station. He barged through a small group of people and the German guard snapped his head up, saluting smartly as the officer passed.

The train was stationary, but clearly preparing to move off very shortly. He scanned the carriages one after another, but there was very little to see inside. Just as the train began to move, he tried the doors on the last carriage, keeping a walking pace alongside the moving train. Henri's face suddenly appeared to Kurt at the open window of the door and he slammed the carriage door shut. Kurt saw alarm in his face and concluded that it must be one of them. Then a woman's face appeared as the pair of them struggled to hold the door firmly shut. Kurt screamed out, extending his palm towards Henri's straining face. As the train gathered a little more speed, Kurt walked faster, his hand closing in on his quarry. Running out of platform, Kurt lunged at the man, his fingers stretching to grab him. As Kurt closed his fingers, his nails raked down Henri's face, drawing blood. Kurt fell back at the end of the platform and the little train puffed away into the distance. Furious, Kurt looked up, not knowing for sure whether it was the group he sought or not.

--o0o--

Henri took a deep breath and then finally dared to release the door. It had been too close. If the officer was pursuing them, then it would be an easy enough task to find the route and follow them all the way.

'Who the fuck was that?' Fifi let go of the door. 'Whoever he was, he really wanted something. Do you know him?'

'No. He had on an SS uniform. A senior officer, but I do not know what rank, looked like a two-leaf design on his neck. Thank God we kept the Eisners out of that madman's sight. Look, let us say nothing, it would only terrify them to know that someone knew we were here. We must be extra vigilant at Lyon, right?'

Fifi nodded. 'Then first let me clean that blood from your face. I will go and find a little water.'

--o0o--

Kurt was helped up from the platform by a kindly French woman. He looked at her blankly, but tapped his cap at her, not wanting to draw any more attention to himself. He wanted no one to remember his visit here while he was on compassionate leave so he went back to his car to think. It would be impossible to beat the train to Lyon. So instead of following the railway west and then south, he turned northwest towards Troyes. Kurt decided that he might even enjoy the champagne country on the way if the weather remained warm. He was sorely tempted to go north to find Odile and a surge of excitement almost made him turn towards her. But he had no time, not yet anyway. Besides, he was not even sure she was alive and if she was, whether he would recognise her.

CHAPTER FORTY-FIVE
Paris August 1942

Wagner was furious. The Eisner woman had given her identity away. Perhaps it would be nothing, but it could be everything. He thought back. The ties linking him to the journey through Germany were non-existent. His only meeting was with the two woodentops on the road and they would never remember him and besides, who would even ask? Still, he would have to be cautious and so he decided not to drive the stolen car any further. He looked for the southern train routes to Paris and found the perfect station at Melun to leave the car. The Citroen was tainted, but it had been a great friend on their journey and he was almost sad to leave it. He removed the registration plates and tossed them into the Seine in a canvas bag filled with small stones. The bag sank immediately. He left the Citroen with regret and took the train into Paris.

The train journey was uneventful, but he thought of the journey he had just been part of, the race through Germany. He thought of the beautiful Fifi and the beautiful woman trapped inside Liesel, hidden and crushed by the terrifying life she had led in Dusseldorf. As far as he was concerned, they were now safe, with little danger to them inside France, providing they were careful. They were bound for the relative safety of Lyon and then onwards to Paris, to be safe in the hands of the *Sunshine Road*.

When the train pulled into the city, he got off, instinctively scanning the surroundings for danger. But here, he was considered the danger, an officer of the Abwehr. That night he slept lightly after deciding that he was not going to submit a report, but would simply describe an excursion to hunt intelligence from downed pilots to protect German cities. That would be enough as he did not normally need to submit any further information. They would accept that without question, even if they were disappointed that there were no arrests and no new intelligence, except about a raid that had already happened.

In the morning, he dressed quickly, eager to get the morning discussions out of the way and to get onto something different from the trip to Germany. If he was first into the office by seven, then all the better. He arrived on foot, entering through the main entrance of Les Invalides, where he was surprised by the secretary.

'Herr Wagner! Welcome back. Did you have a successful visit?'

'Yes and no. I have intelligence, but no prisoners. That is the way sometimes.'

'Then the head of three section will need to see you, to extract what you know.'

'Yes, I understand.'

At his office, he opened the door. He was indeed the first officer to arrive on this fine August morning. After placing his cap on the desk, he went to find his favourite crystal glass to pour himself some water, only to find himself facing a tall, smartly dressed SS officer. When their eyes met, the SS officer gave him a friendly smile and gestured towards a vacant chair.

'Please, Wagner, have a seat.'

Wagner was unfamiliar with the man and his friendly manner unnerved him. This was not the way it worked in his own office. At twenty-three years of age he felt outmanned.

'Do I know you? Is that even a genuine SS uniform?'

The man smiled again.

'Well, let us find out. Besides, I am the one with a gun.'

Wagner shuddered as he had not noticed the gun. He now realised that the escape from Germany had not been as clean as he had hoped.

'How did you find me?'

'Let us say that some men have clear memories of suspicious men with cars full of older women. You were a fool to get involved with my sister.'

'Your what? Your sister? But I do not know you. Your sister?'

'I am SS Oberführer Kurt Langer. My unit is the Einsatzgruppen Russia-West. Do you know them at all?'

Wagner felt faint. He was out of his depth with this man – a senior officer from one of the death squads. He was someone who killed and enjoyed it. It probably did not matter to him whether the victim was German or not. He realised that at the age of twenty-three, his life was at an end.

'Then who is your sister? I do not know a Fraulein, er Langer?'

'You might like to dispense with the acting, Wagner. It is pitiful and liable to make me want to kill you sooner. My father named her Liesel, but of course, you already know that.'

Wagner felt his world drop through his stomach, his end was nearing. But he had a last act to play out, he had to keep the runners' destination and escape plans secret. The next question would certainly be whether he had seen or helped Karl to escape. He remained silent.

'Of course the name Liesel is familiar to you, and so you must also know of Karl Eisner. Or more correctly, Karl Israel Eisner. I am quite certain you would remember him.'

Wagner stood in silence, his legs weakening.

'Well then, let me put it to you like this. I am an officer of the SS and one who has just dealt with the assassins of Heydrich – you know of him and that terrible affair, of course – I was with him the day he died. Yet here I am in Paris, having followed your little party from Dusseldorf. I have followed you, Wagner. You see what I am saying? Clearly, what you have done is so important that I have left behind nationally important priorities to come to *you* in your shitty and meaningless Abwehr existence. You are but a worm.'

Wagner continued his silence.

'A worm who has placed my sister in the hands of a fucking Jew!'

'A what… but… a Jew? It cannot be! I was rescuing a…'

Wagner's voice fell away. In realising that he now had only moments left, his nerve was failing him and he struggled to maintain his act.

'If you continue to lie, I will visit your mother in her lonely old age and have her hanged upside down, with her guts poured out over the streets of Koln. Or perhaps I might recreate the miracle of your birth in 1919. A four-year pregnancy? Now that is a miracle!'

Wagner wanted to lunge at Langer, to tear out his very heart. But he realised that he did not have one. All that he would find inside the SS man would be icy stone. He nodded in terror, gripped in the evil spell of this terrible man.

'Now then. The group you brought from Germany was on a train for Lyon. From there, where were they to go?'

Wagner hesitated, thinking of his beloved mother, already forsaken by her husband, her lover, and now by her son. He made peace with her in his mind as he saw the barrel of Kurt's pistol.

'They were to go by train to Toulouse, rest there a day and then drive to Pau. Then at Pau they were to be met by agents of the Spanish Resistance and driven over the border to Pamplona. From there, they would be taken by night to Gibraltar. After that, I can only assume they would travel to England.'

Wagner tried hard to remember each step of the lie, to make sure Kurt considered it plausible. On the surface, it sounded convincing.

'Pamplona, then Gibraltar? How long?'

'They will be in Gibraltar in three more days. They sail on or around the fifth of August.'

'Very well.'

With that, Kurt turned and left. Wagner was shocked to be still alive, having expected nothing more than death by a single gunshot to his skull. But he was still alive and breathing. He picked up the telephone to the Abwehr office in Bayonne and alerted them to a group of runners fitting the descriptions of his little Dusseldorf party who might be moving to Spain through Pau or Toulouse. The Bayonne office should be alert from now until the fifth. If an officer called Langer should enquire about them, then he should be afforded every courtesy and escorted all the way to the border.

CHAPTER FORTY-SIX
France August 1942

The train finally arrived in Lyon, hours late but safely and without any German interest or incident. The *Sunshine Road* did not have any friendly operatives on this particular route, so they had to get across to the west of France as quickly as possible. To do this they could take a car and drive due west to Clermont-Ferrand, Limoges and then down to Bordeaux, or go north to Poitiers, or they could take a train to Paris and then another to Nantes. They had many good choices and if they did not know which route they would choose, then neither would any SS or Gestapo coming after them. From the final train stop they could drive to Brest to take the aeroplane that William had arranged for their final escape to England. The train would be the best option since it would give them much more control of the situation.

The trains from Lyon to Paris and from Paris to Nantes were usually well guarded since both routes were known to be used by escaping Jews and enemy combatants. However, the Paris crowds provided excellent cover and Henri was certain they had left unnoticed on the journey to Nantes. Henri and Fifi sat together, and the Eisner family, travelling as the Dumonts, were in the carriage next door. They could be seen through the double reflection of the carriage window. Everything looked normal and safe.

'Aurelie, do you think that when we get to Brest, we might talk of... well... us? We have once again suffered much together and I have quite forgotten where we had reached in our relationship. What do you say?'

He smiled at her, and she smiled back, stroking his face.

'As you say, Henri, when we get to Brest. For now, let us just be close.'

She leaned over and kissed him. As he responded, she placed his hand on her body.

At Nantes, in the late morning of the fourth of August, the train juddered to a sudden screeching halt. The unexpected jolt woke Henri and to his horror, the Eisners were no longer in the adjoining carriage. Henri leapt up from his seat and rushed to the carriage door. To his enormous relief, he saw Karl and the children looking out of the window and smiling. The train had come upon some escaped cattle that were proving difficult to catch. The red-faced and sweating farmer was leaping here and there trying to take control of the animals. A German officer was barking at him to get control or he would shoot his herd. For thirty minutes, the chase of farmer and cattle went on to howls of laughter from the children. Just once, they spoke to one another in German. Karl silenced them immediately, and they returned to their carriage in silence. Henri breathed again. Scolded and quiet was better than happy and careless.

Finally, the train moved off and within minutes arrived into the station at Nantes. There were about forty German Army soldiers on the platform, most likely waiting to embark for leave in Paris. This was normally a good sign as soldiers going on leave cared not for small details. Their minds would be focused on the glitz of Paris and the train was already late.

The Eisners got off the train first. The German on the gate asked them in poor French where they were going. Liesel replied in very poor German and the guard smiled at her in a friendly manner, perhaps appreciating her attempt to speak his own language. He waved them all through, even patting Franz on the head as he passed.

'Danke,' said Franz, smiling back at the guard.

The German soldier grabbed his arm and asked him in German if he spoke any more words. Liesel quickly moved to her son's side before he was able to reply.

'Not really. We have only taught him a few German words, so he can travel on the trains to see his family.'

The soldier nodded and looked to the next passenger.

Henri breathed again. Franz had nearly exploded their entire story with one word, perfectly delivered. Children were a risk, but up until now, the children had been impeccably behaved, given the most distressing of circumstances.

Nantes to Brest would involve a short car journey and then bicycles. Local members of Dodo's group had left the car in a friendly farmer's shed just outside of Nantes. They drove slowly with a full tank of petrol to the village of Guipavas, just outside of Brest. From there, they took bicycles and rode from to the airstrip at Gouesnou. This airstrip had been chosen as it was sheltered and slightly hidden by a low hill. The Germans patrolled here, but not very often since there were no aeroplanes kept here. Instead, the Germans left it up to the local police to patrol the movements. The Kommandant knew that the police would hear aeroplanes coming and could then watch them as they landed, intercepting any illegal traffic on arrival. What the Gestapo did not know was that the policeman here did indeed watch for every landing and was happily present to wave them off again, usually with a flask of something warming and a note for General de Gaulle.

When the runners finally arrived at the village, they were red faced and out of breath. They put the bicycles in the shelter of a field of late summer hay. Franz had remained entirely silent since his blunder at the station and Monika was now stuck firmly to Henri's side, like a limpet. This worried Henri since it might deflect his attention from the mission. Monika was of an age where such attachments can be troublesome. It was almost the end of the mission, but it was not over just yet. Nearly home, but not quite in London. Tiredness here and now could still defeat them and they had to keep going for just a little longer and Henri needed to keep up their spirits.

They were to wait until dark, sometime around nine-thirty. Then they would be whistled forward by the local Resistance and shepherded onto the aeroplane, which would arrive a little after ten-thirty. If it did not appear by eleven, then it would not come at all and there would be another attempt on the following night. When the aeroplane arrived, they would be aboard and gone in only moments and that moment was nearly upon them.

Everyone stood quietly, listening in the darkness for the sounds of the engine. Henri did not know what aeroplane was coming for them, but he imagined it would be bigger than usual with so many passengers to carry. Almost exactly at the appointed time came the distant sound of a little propeller engine, growing louder and more insistent, its rhythmical rumbling comforting and uplifting. Around them all was the blackness of the night, no lights and no other sounds. A little after ten-fifteen, a small bank of lights was quickly lit to guide the aeroplane onto the little grass strip.

Karl turned to Henri and Fifi. 'How can I ever thank you both? Words are of no use. My family and I owe our very lives to you. When this is over, we will not forget you.'

Liesel smiled at them. 'Darling Henri, you cannot know the bond between my own soul and that of your mother. I cannot explain it in words and certainly not here and now. But believe this. To me, you are family and I will love you always and forever.'

Liesel took his arms and kissed him on each cheek, drawing him to her for a moment. Next, she kissed Fifi, taking the younger woman's face in her hands for a moment. They all turned to watch the aeroplane touch down. It quickly turned around and the little door at the rear opened.

'Quickly, now, all of you.'

Two armed men grabbed the children first. Monika kept looking back at Henri, waving but saying nothing. He waved back, wondering how they would get over this ordeal. Once the children were aboard, Karl stepped up and helped his wife into the aircraft. The engines roared and the little plane was up and away into the warm night, less than four minutes after touching down in France. Within seconds, the lights were out and the Resistance men had melted away. Henri and Fifi were alone in silence, with a sudden end to the long days of running into and away from Germany. He looked at her, a smile of relief that turned into nervous laughter, growing louder. The tension of the last few days finally broken. With a flourish he took her hand, dancing around her in a giant circle.

'Now, shall we talk about us?'

Aurelie looked at Henri intently for a moment.

'No. I have a better idea.'

She took Henri's arm and led him slowly into a thick patch of soft hay. She pulled him towards her and then unbuttoned her long blouse, guiding his face onto her bared breasts and his hands to her yielding body.

--oOo--

High above the English Channel, Liesel turned to Karl, took him by the arm and kissed him lovingly. For the first time in nearly four years, Karl was a free man, one who might yet be Doctor Karl Eisner again. The delusion that was the Nazi regime in Germany might yet prevail and take over their lives again. But for now, they could enjoy this relief, and the chance to live again as normal people, out in the open, speaking and being seen. And even if it were all to change, at least they had this one precious chance to appreciate their blessings for a time. Monika and Franz were buried between their parents and the four of them fell asleep. The Australian pilot looked around at the peaceful sleeping family and smiled to his co-pilot.

'Martin, let us give these good people a smooth ride home.'

'Got that, Bill, I'm on it. Look, if we don't, you that know de Gaulle himself will shoot us, mate.'

CHAPTER FORTY-SEVEN
Paris 6 August 1942

Kurt arrived in Toulouse early on the sixth of August. He had a meeting at six with the local Gestapo agents to receive answers to his very specific questions. He wanted the answers verbally, with nothing in writing and no trace of the conversation anywhere in the south of France.

'Good morning, Herr Oberführer, I fear the answers I have for you will be of little use, especially since we have both come so early for disappointment.'

'Let me decide that. What news on the family I described to you?'

'Nothing came through Pau or Bayonne in the last four days. We only had eleven people on the trains and we followed every one of them. None were the right age or at the right departure points. Even if we had given a wide range for the age, most were men in their sixties and the women were either young girls or grandmothers. I am sorry, but we have seen nothing. If they came here by train or car, we would have seen them. Anywhere from Toulouse to Bayonne, Bordeaux to Pamplona.'

Kurt tapped his nose. There was now only one more course of action.

'Thank you. Please extend my thanks to your team of agents for being so diligent.'

'Of course, sir.'

--o0o--

It was a cloudy morning in Paris. The morning crowds were smaller than usual as the Parisian summer shortages were beginning to bite and resentment towards the Germans continued to grow. The Abwehr officers in the whole city were now busier than ever, but Paris was still a quiet posting and enjoyable if you knew where to go for the evening.

On his drive into the office of the Abwehr in Les Invalides, Wagner had decided to request a posting to the eastern office in Czechoslovakia. Prague was also a beautiful city and the weather was a little warmer for more of the year. Yes, he thought he could do very well helping the citizens to hide from the fucking Nazis. He was smiling to himself as he turned towards the Ecole Militaire. Without warning, a car sped at him from the side and smashed with enormous force into the driver's door, where the bodywork was weakest. Wagner's car spun around and slid into a wall. The other car drove off at speed towards the river. Two old women had witnessed the whole scene, but scurried into the nearest café, perhaps fearful of Nazi reprisals at a Resistance attack on the Abwehr. But two soldiers ran from the Ecole Militaire to the stricken car.

'Mein Gott! It is no use, he has been cleaved almost in two. Look, his neck is broken.'

'At least he did not suffer, his death must have been mercifully quick.'

--oOo--

Kurt's aeroplane landed in Berlin, and he was immediately handed a small envelope with the word *Paris* on the front. He opened it slowly, wanting to savour the photograph it contained. With some pride, he looked at the mess of man and machine. The accompanying note stated that the Resistance would be blamed for the assassination of a middle-ranking Abwehr officer. He smiled when he read of the concrete block, which had been placed in front of the engine. That was an especially clever addition, a violent and brutal touch for the assassin, which had certainly had the desired effect. This supposed Resistance attack afforded the SS an opportunity to clear the ghettos, kill the citizens and hasten German domination of the public squares. Certainly, he had the authority to take action in response to the killing of a German officer, but the man was a traitor. Still, that made it all the more satisfying when he slid the photograph back into the envelope and placed it in the military post with a Koln address neatly written on the front. With the envelope now bound for an ageing widow in Germany, he picked up his cap and stepped out of the office, ready to descend upon the Paris morning.

CHAPTER FORTY-EIGHT

England August 1942

'Can you see them yet? Hello, Albert? Mate, can you see them yet?'

'Nothing, but I can definitely hear them. They are coming at us all right.'

'Shout when you see them. Here's some tea.'

'Thanks. Hang on, got them. About fifteen miles out. Looking spot on for us.'

'Right, I will get on the radio. I don't think this is really de Gaulle, it is more likely a load of bloody cobblers.'

'Westbury, this is Shoreham. Have Helga in sight. Repeat, have Helga in sight. Over.'

'Shoreham, Westbury. Roger that. Over.'

'Will advise when embarked to London. Over.'

'Must advise that Falcon is pleased. Out.'

'Fuck me, Albert! It is bloody de Gaulle. Whoever these blokes are, it's important enough to bother the Frenchies.'

'I understand they're German, mate.'

'Fuck off they are! Bloody Germans under the protection of France, coming to England? That isn't true.'

'Well, we will soon find out, they're nearly here. Right on we go.'

The two old men stumbled and shuffled from their little observation point on the banks of the River Adur in Sussex. They stepped smartly over the little footbridge down to Shoreham Airfield. Inside, they put the lights on and then the kettle.

'Well, if they *are* Germans, they can't be proper Germans. These people are guests and to be given every courtesy. Orders from London.'

'Well, that's all that matters then.'

The little aeroplane touched down and within a few seconds it was alongside the white terminal building. The door opened and out stepped a man, a young boy and a young girl. All three looked tired and confused. A woman stepped down next and when her feet touched the ground she collapsed in tears, her hands sweeping over the ground. The girl went and hugged her mother. The two old men watched the scene, then went to greet the family, although the German family did not speak English and the two old men did not speak any German. A German interpreter was to meet them on the train at Shoreham Airport Station in just a few minutes. But they would at least try to be welcoming in the meantime.

'Welcome to England! Whatever you people have been through, it must have been a bad business.'

'Thank you sir. Thanking you'.

'Well you are out of it now and I might have a little something to cheer you all up.'

'Yes, thanking you'.

'Er, please, this way? We have hot tea and a muffin. Muffin? You understand?'

The man nodded.

'Ja, tea, drinks of Gods.'

They all laughed. The girl had some milk and the boy accepted a little bottle of American soda. He looked shocked at the bubbles and everyone laughed at the look of surprise on the boy's face. The woman warmed her hands around a cup of tea, but she did not drink it. The man drank a cup, swiftly followed by another. He turned to the men and smiled broadly. They all ate the muffins hungrily, as if food was a new experience for all of them.

The train would take them on to London. At Haywards Heath, they would be met by a member of the French Government as well as a member of the British Foreign Office. They had all been cleared to enter the island, but they might be able to tell the authorities something of use. A Colonel Collins was going to meet the family at the little station in Windermere. The journey north would take all of the next day, so they could catch up on sleep on the train.

--o0o--

The family were given tickets, not permits, and the guards smiled at them as they passed and did not demand to know about them or their journey. The station guard in London gave the children some Dundee cake from a round tin. They were escorted, simply because they were German and they might be overheard by fellow travellers. Franz, after being silent and hidden for five days, talked and talked, pausing only to swing from the luggage racks.

Liesel smiled at Karl. Her husband was liberated and about to start a new life in a new home free of Jew slurs. Although Karl was not a Jew, Liesel now truly understood the fear and horror of Europe, only fifty kilometres away over the sea.

On the journey, they passed through beautiful countryside. Safe, without guns and shootings and Jewish arrests. The danger they had left behind seemed almost absurd here, and the persecution they had suffered became almost meaningless in the hazy sunshine of a British summer. They had said no to Hitler and now they would be safe in England. Liesel turned her mind to meeting William, husband of her beloved sister. She was also very much looking forward to seeing Odile again after so many years.

The train rumbled on towards the Lake District, and the rolling green hills and fresh air refreshed her soul. Liesel had only seen photographs of William but she recognised him immediately. He had dressed in civilian clothing for this meeting, perhaps not wanting to frighten the children with yet more military men. When Liesel saw his smile and open arms, she threw herself into his arms. Karl followed behind, also entering William's embrace.

'William, I cannot tell you how much we owe to you. Your beautiful boy is quite well and he is also in love with the girl, Aurelie, I think!'

'That is good to know, but her name is Yvette. Pretty, with red hair?'

'Oh no, this is a Resistance girl, Aurelie, or Fifi her code name. Looks like Hedy Lamarr.'

William's eyes lit up. 'That's my Henri.'

They all laughed. William gave Franz a cricket ball and Monika a book of English poetry.

'I don't know what else to give you, the Lake District has spectacular hills, but it's very quiet.'

'God's country, William. A place to rest.'

The three adults talked more of the journey, of Henri and Aurelie and the mysterious Wagner.

'I know very little about this Wagner, perhaps because I was reluctant to trust a man from the Abwehr. But Henri and Fifi seemed convinced beyond any doubt. It seems they were right so I'll see what I can find out about him.'

When the train arrived in the Lake District, a car with French flags took the party on to Keswick, the little town under the protection of the brooding peaks of Skiddaw and Blencathra. Once there, William introduced the Eisners to Armandine and her new husband-to-be, Michael. William explained that Michael was looking at the legal aspects of Karl and Liesel being in England since it was important that the authorities understood their position and the unique interest of the French Government.

The short drive to Armandine's accommodation took them through the beauty of the Derwentwater lakeside. At the little village of Portinscale, they turned off the road and into a large stone-walled yard. The cottage was made up of three lettings. Armandine had the smaller, the larger had now been secured for the Eisners and the third stood empty, Armandine hoped that perhaps her own mother might make some use of it in the future. Michael had advised them that Karl was not yet allowed to practise medicine, as there were still complications with his German citizenship, but in a few weeks he might be able to work with certain restrictions. The children were to be given a tutor for the time being, a good and trusted friend of Armandine's.

William stayed with the Eisners for a day to guide them and help them to settle. They talked of Odile, Dusseldorf and the wars, and late in the evening, they spoke of Kurt. The man who had imprisoned his own beloved wife and who had set out to destroy the Eisners. It was clear to William that these people could not feel truly free while Kurt lived.

--oOo--

When the time came for William to leave, Armandine promised to care for the Eisners. William advised her not to talk too widely of their appearance in England. Nobody could predict Kurt's response if he discovered this truth. No doubt the man would be vigilant for any signs or news on that front.

William travelled back to London with Michael. He was planning a weekend in Richmond to catch up on paperwork and to recreate the peace of the Lakes in London. The distraction of conversation was pleasant. Michael was intelligent, practical and generous and William looked forward to passing Armandine's hand to him in 1944, if the war was over by then. He wrote a short telegram for Odile, telling her of the safe arrival of the Eisners.

Soon, he was busy assisting General de Gaulle who was planning a visit to Scotland to meet with the Free French and the diplomatic team of the Algerians. The general was concerned that the Vichy Government were being increasingly seen as the legitimate leaders of France. Renewed proclamations for his execution as a traitor were being broadcast to the whole of France. William was writing a speech to help him take back the political ground. There would be two versions. An English version containing nuances that the Americans would appreciate and a French version that could be finessed for his people. De Gaulle wanted France back and he often told William that he wanted the leaders of the Vichy regime hanged by their thumbs. Clearly, the man was worried for the French, fearing a full German occupation of the whole country, which would put an end to some of the operations of the Free French in France. When de Gaulle left for Scotland, he stuck his head into William's office.

'Colonel Collins, make this your best effort yet. See you in a week.'

William packed his bag and took a taxi cab to Richmond to the relative solitude of the cottage used by the Foreign Office for entertaining. He settled back with his secretary and dictated the first draft of the de Gaulle speech. It made him smile because he was about to write a broadcast to his adopted country urging them to rise up against the tyranny of the Nazis when the time was right.

CHAPTER FORTY-NINE
Paris 1942

Henri and Aurelie had fallen asleep in each other's arms in the seclusion and warmth of the night. He woke at around four-thirty with his arms still around the beautiful naked body of his lover. He wondered how they were to get home from here. It would be a long walk back even to Brest and he was too tired to use a bicycle. Perhaps his sleeping companion would have an idea. The local Resistance had long since disappeared and Henri did not know who they were, which was normal. The first rays of daybreak were still nearly an hour away, but he could not sleep, so he stroked Aurelie's body with a little strand of ticklish hay. She just moved closer to him and he felt her gentle breathing on his chest.

Then, from a distance he saw headlights – a dim spot at first, but quickly growing into a pair of clear beams that were moving directly towards them, a car coming into view. Behind the car was a single beam, perhaps a motorcycle travelling in escort. When the motorcycle came into view, Henri thought it had a sidecar containing a man with a machine gun. He could not see more as the natural light was not good and the headlights were bright. The car might turn right towards the village. If it did not turn soon, then its only destination would be the little airstrip. They were very well hidden but if there was a search with a dog then they would be quickly discovered. Perhaps he ought to wake Aurelie. His Fifi should have the chance to defend herself. The lights did not waver, but kept coming straight for them. Henri did not take his eyes off them as he gently rocked Aurelie awake.

'Darling Fifi, I think we have company. Don't sit up, but wake up, my love.'

'Hm? Are they Germans?'

'Must be. They have guns.'

'How many?'

'Five or six. A car and a motorcycle.'

'Have they seen us?'

'No. They won't either unless they search the area. If they do, then they will know about us anyway.'

In silence, Henri gathered Fifi's clothing and she dressed herself, ready to move quickly if the need arose. She took Henri's hand, squeezing it, neither one of them taking their eyes off the lights coming directly for them. The car appeared at the little gate to the airstrip. In front were two Germans in helmets. In the rear were two of the Resistance men from last night. Henri wondered whether the two men were under arrest, or whether they were helping the Germans. The two men had heard the names Charlemagne and Fifi and they knew the name of the escaping family as Dumont. But the family was long gone and the two men could not know the Dumonts' real identity, the name that could give them away to Kurt. He felt reassured. Whatever trail this was, it could not lead to them, and most certainly not to his mother and the *Sunshine Road*.

The car stopped in the middle of the airstrip. The two Resistance men got out, shoved by the Germans. These Frenchmen were clearly not collaborators. Their real identities were now known and they had been exposed. Henri could hear that a conversation was taking place, but he could not make out any of the words. The men were being barked at in rapid German, with little or no response allowed by the men. Even when the leader of the Germans raised a pistol, flourishing it angrily in their faces, they said very little and moved not one muscle in either defiance or compliance.

Henri watched the motorcycle rider walk up to the two men, smashing them in the knees with a large wooden club, causing them both to scream and fall on to the floor. The Germans were in conversation with one another as the two men writhed in pain. The man dressed in a leather coat and a steel helmet leaned down to speak with them. He shook his head and then flourished the pistol again, shooting each man once in the leg, causing them to roll over and shout loudly. He barked at them again. Then Henri heard a handful of words, shouted loudly and clearly.

'Bastogne. Rue de Paris.'

Henri knew what this meant. This was a coded alarm message. If caught and interrogated, the code word Bastogne was used to put the Germans off the scent. It would send them to an entirely false escape operation in Belgium, which looked genuine but was just an empty shell without real operatives. But it also meant that information had been given or revealed that could destroy a real operation. Hearing it meant that the line was exposed and that the *Sunshine Road* should be shut down immediately. Henri squeezed Aurelie's hand. They had to get home quickly if they were going to alert Dodo to the risks.

'Bastogne, you German bastards. Vive La France!'

The sidecar was turned to face the two men and a sweep of gunfire silenced their voices. The Germans got back into their vehicles and drove off without looking back. There had been no betrayal by the French men. And there had been no search by the Germans.

'Aurelie, should we bury them?'

'And reveal ourselves to the Germans? No, we must leave them to the local men to bury. They were their comrades. Let us just thank them for their loyalty and go. Come on Henri, whilst there is still a little darkness left.'

Henri and Aurelie moved to where the bicycles had been dropped. But they were gone. Taken and hidden by the Resistance, no doubt. When they reached the village, it was still quiet, so no alarm had yet been raised – that dreadful realisation would come later in the day. They found some bicycles in a small street and took them. The ride towards Brest would take perhaps three or four hours, but it would be too risky to steal a car so early and without weapons. Both had their papers and if they could get to Brest, then the *Sunshine Road* operatives could issue them with permits to travel. They just had to hope they got there unnoticed.

Henri thought about the woman riding just behind him and wondered whether he could be enough for her. After all, he was only a boy, some eight years her junior. But he was a fearless fighter in the Resistance and he hoped that would be enough for her to love him. He loved her. It would mean telling Yvette. He cared for Yvette deeply, but his chosen life had taken him away from his first love and would not let him return.

The two rode on to Brest, stopping occasionally to rest, always alert to any movements, but absent-mindedly holding hands. When Brest eventually emerged from the early morning light, the port and town were clearly visible, with the wide expanse of the sea behind. The railway station was already open and trains were moving in the sidings near to the waterfront. They left their bicycles and walked to the empty ticket office. The rear of the office had a row of pegs. On it were the stationmaster's coat and the grey coats of the Wehrmacht. Germans were patrolling here, so they had better be careful.

They waited at the window for a few minutes, but the stationmaster did not appear. This was odd, very odd. They rounded the corner to discover that he was in deep conversation with the German officer, waving his arms animatedly, trying to make his point. The conversation was in French and the German officer spoke excellent French, but most of his words were instructing the stationmaster to speak in German, the mandatory language of transport in France.

'But Herr Keller, we do not have anyone by that name who works here. Please believe me, we are not trying to obstruct the Germans, but I have never heard of him.'

'Not true, Bourdin. Not true. I think that you are lying to me, perhaps? Snaking your way out of trouble. We have the other three, we just need to speak with your man. Now if you please. You understand my insistence?'

'Yes, yes. But I do not know of such a person. Yes, he may have a false name, but the name you have given me is mysterious and unknown. Please. I cannot be more honest with you.'

'Very well. Let us say that I believe you. But if I discover later that you have lied to me, you know what will happen.'

Bourdin's shoulders sank.

'Yes I know, but I am not lying to you.'

The German slapped Bourdin affably on the shoulder.

'Good, so let us have some of your delicious coffee, which you also know nothing about.'

The two men approached the rear door to the ticket office. Henri's confidence drained. Their transaction would be in full sight of the Germans. What would he say? Too late, the train to Paris would be here very shortly.

'Good morning, Monsieur. Two to Paris, please.'

Henri looked at Bourdin, who was seated in front of him and then he looked up to the German, who was pouring coffee for two, but perhaps still listening.

'Yes, Monsieur. Two. One for you and one for Mademoiselle, is it?'

'Yes Monsieur. For the next train.'

'What is the journey, if I may ask?'

'It is to visit my Aunt Sophie, she is visiting us from Bastogne. She has been unwell.'

Bourdin's face did not register any change. But Henri knew that he would have recognised the message, knowing that here was a Resistance operative travelling to Paris. Even so, he must have felt considerable disappointment at hearing the word Bastogne, even if he managed not to show it. Henri watched him take two tickets from a drawer. On one, he quickly put a little circle with a dot in the centre but he left the other blank.

'Train in twenty-five minutes. Stay together, Paris can be a bit crowded you know.'

'Thank you, Monsieur.'

Henri took the tickets, placing them straight into his pocket. On the platform, they were not asked for identification. The German soldiers must have seen them at the desk, knowing that their superior was inside. On the platform, Henri held Aurelie. They were close and were growing closer. Henri was drawn to her, enjoying the sweet perfume of her love and he could still smell her body on himself. Finally, the train rumbled in from the sidings, fully steamed and ready to leave. The German soldier opened the door for Aurelie, tapping his helmet as she boarded.

'Bonjour, Mademoiselle.'

Aurelie smiled, placed her hand on her chin, and looked down. Henri was impressed at her act of shyness.

'Danke, my handsome soldier.'

The soldier smiled at her. He then got on the train behind her, pushing Henri out of the way as he did so. Henri did not react since the soldier's attentions would mean their journey to Paris would be undisturbed. When the train pulled out and began its long journey to Paris, the soldier insisted on sitting with Aurelie, turning his back to Henri, who was unconcerned. This was unplanned, but unimportant. In Paris, the soldier would have duties, he could not just wander the streets alone. The little time here on the train was of no matter. If they had been on a run, this would have been part of the plan.

The German soldier spoke little French, so the conversation was dull and unrevealing. But as the journey wore on, Henri became increasingly disturbed by the soldier's attentions. He had his arm on Aurelie, almost pinning her to the seat. Her voice was calm and she kept talking to him, but the man kept moving closer, touching her leg and stroking her arm. His rifle was on his shoulder, and there was nothing Henri could do alone. Aurelie was not in the character of Fifi. She was tired and unwashed, perhaps in no state to entertain the attentions of a German but he persisted. Henri knew he must do something, even if that something was to do nothing.

He wanted to strike the man, to take his rifle and smash him with it. But there were other soldiers here on the train and he would be dead before he managed to do it. Aurelie was on her own. His Fifi would have to manage the man alone until they got to Paris. Perhaps she would reject him and slap him. His comrades would tease him and insult him. Or maybe they would insult her, making him lose interest. Henri thought to himself that if the opportunity arose, he would kill the man in Paris.

Mercifully, after three hours of tedious fumbling and miserable jokes, the German fell asleep. His arm was around Aurelie's shoulder and his hand was on her bare leg. She gently slid away from him and Henri followed her to a new carriage. Two other Germans grinned at her broadly. Henri felt he needed to be careful here and use their weakness against them if he had the chance.

When they arrived at Paris, the sleeping soldier woke up and followed them along the platform, calling to Aurelie, insisting she return and accompany him for a drink. She pretended to ignore him and carried on with Henri, gripping his arm. Henri squeezed her close so that if the man approached, he could not grab her and separate them. They approached the barrier and the guard barked at them.

'Papers. Papers? Come on.'

Henri took out his little card and the tickets. The guard looked at them, but did not react.

'Go through.'

He moved aside and Henri and Aurelie moved through. As the pursuing German soldier approached, the barrier guard raised his hand, preventing him from following. Henri and Liesel were now once more in Paris. Behind them, a man in a hat stepped out of an office. He pulled his hat down over his eyes, picked up a newspaper and folded a coat neatly over his arm.

The two lovers quickly moved into the afternoon crowds. It was safer that way. They would meet at the station for the train to Amiens at five if they were separated, Henri knew that this was a routine as comfortable and as easy as making breakfast. They planned to get washed as they did not want to attract attention for the wrong reasons. The German soldier had not been put off, but their dishevelled state might draw unwanted attention in Paris.

Aurelie had suggested bringing Fifi to life again, but she did not have her wig and her clothes were dirty. They set off to find a certain dress shop and after a quick conversation, the friendly owner disappeared to find some suitable clothing and a little makeup. When Aurelie emerged from the little washroom, Henri smiled. She looked wonderful, her hair under a hat, in a clean dress, and with her face made up a little. She wasn't totally Fifi, but she was close enough.

Henri went into the Hotel Moulin where the tailor had a little collection of worn suits for this very purpose. Whilst none were quite the right size, he made little adjustments to make the suit look more normal. Henri waxed his hair and took advantage of the shaving and shoe department to turn himself from a vagrant into a smart young man, but not smart enough to convince the Germans that he should be on the next labour conscription train to Poland.

At a quarter-to-five, they linked arms, and walked confidently into the railway station, once again Fifi and Charlemagne, the lovers. Fifi went to the barrier first, with Henri behind. Henri passed her a ticket and kept one for himself. Fifi was waved through the barrier, but as Henri stepped up, a little wooden rail was drawn across, preventing him from passing through.

'The train is full.'

'But it is practically empty!'

'Who was asking you? Now shut up or fuck off.'

'When is the next train?'

'For you? Tomorrow.'

'But we are travelling together!'

'Not any more. Move away.'

Henri looked at Fifi over the barrier. He waved her onto the train. As she stepped into the carriage, he could see she was now alone and she looked afraid. This had never happened before and something was terribly wrong. A couple would never be parted and it was clear the train was not full. Someone, somewhere had informed on them.

On impulse, perhaps fuelled by his new desire for Aurelie, Henri made a run for the low wooden wall separating the platform from the concourse. In one leap he was over, running for the train. Even as he did it, he knew his impulsive action was rash and that the situation could unravel quickly. As he ran for the train, angling towards Fifi's carriage, the platform vibrated to the sudden and shocking sound of a machine gun. The air split like tearing paper. People behind the wall ducked as chips of stone flashed around the barrier.

Henri's body was forced sideways from the repeated impact of the bullets. He fell with his arms stretched towards the carriage door. A pool of blood quickly formed around him, a little cloud of concrete dust settling on him like a shroud. The volume of smoke billowing from the train increased as it began to pull away, the smoke catching under the roof and rolling down to the platform, covering Henri completely.

The man in the hat at the front of the platform looked around for a moment, pushed his hat a little further down his brow, adjusted the coat over his arm and turned to leave, tapping the paper on his leg as he went. A smile came over his face. He turned away, lit a cigarette, stepped into the crowd and disappeared.

--oOo--

As the train pulled out, Fifi watched soldiers step forward to remove the dead body of her darling Henri. But the track curved away and she could see no more of him or the station. Dry-eyed, shocked and consumed with sorrow, she could think only of Henri. On the train were two Gestapo agents, pacing up and down, clearly searching for someone. As they passed Fifi, one of them tapped his hat, smiling.

'Good day, Frau Lamarr.'

Fifi smiled and looked shy, and the agents passed on without another word. She had survived. The journey to Amiens was hot and desolate. She dared not weep for fear of revealing her true identity. But she was also worried. Because the Gestapo knew of Henri, it meant that something had fallen into the lap of the Germans. But who or what it might be was impossible to know. The *Sunshine Road* was a tight group but you could never know, never truly trust. Somewhere, someone had talked, innocently or for personal gain. And Henri was dead. Her lover, the boy she had made a man was gone. She did not know how to begin to tell Dodo of the death of her third and youngest child. She could not tell Odile that he was killed by machine gun fire racing to her on a platform in Paris in front of a hundred shocked and terrified people.

The train rattled on in silence. The passengers, having also witnessed the death of Henri, were perhaps too grief-stricken to make conversation. Or perhaps they were just relieved that they were not the target of the Germans' attention. At Amiens, Aurelie was met by Hugo and Daisy and she finally collapsed in tears as she explained the absence of Charlemagne.

Hugo shook his head. 'How are we going to tell Dodo? I cannot imagine her grief.'

Daisy placed her hand on Fifi's arm. 'We just have to tell her. Somehow.'

--o0o--

The car drew up outside of the house on the top of the hill in Bazentin-Le-Petit and the three occupants got out and walked into the house. The little light in the kitchen was lit, followed by the light in the bedroom. A few moments later it went out again. Fifi and Daisy tidied the kitchen, putting everything back in its place whilst Hugo lit a fire to warm the house, as the evening was cool. Hugo and Daisy then left, quietly closing the door behind them. Fifi sat in the kitchen, now letting her grief and love pour out over the large family table. In the corner was a little scratched carving, made by a child.

Henri Collins age 8

She ran her hands over it and imagined him growing up here in the village. Every day and every night, with the love, care and devotion of his mother. She could not let go of thoughts that his death was her fault, perhaps she had enticed him to love her, making him act on impulse – an impulse that had cost him his life. The torment burned her deeply, a scar on her soul that could not be healed. She slept in the chair, leaning on the table.

In the morning, she awoke to a cold hand on her shoulder. It was Odile. Aurelie stood, her face swollen and reddened and embraced Odile as a mother, as the mother of the boy she had loved, for Odile was her last connection to him. They stood together, holding one another, silent in their anguish.

CHRIS CHERRY

CHAPTER FIFTY
Richmond England 1942

Saturday morning was the best time for William to write. Rogers came in at eight and made them both a breakfast of dried egg and a little milk to soften the taste. He had saved his bacon ration and added a rasher to each plate to William's joy. A huge mug of army tea was put in front of William and this time, he toasted the Scots from Longueval.

As he read and redrafted the speech, he took on the persona of de Gaulle, wanting to make the speech feel as though it were the general's own words. No doubt the impossible man would change everything and he could imagine de Gaulle simply tossing it over his shoulder and making it up as he went along.

By the time the blackout blinds went up, William had finally finished the speech, the copy and the translation. Next, he wanted to pen a proper letter to Odile that would be sent as a telegram, along with a short radio message to his beloved Dodo, as well as a coded note in due course. Rogers and William ate dinner together, with Rogers bringing out one final treat, the little bottle of cognac the general had passed him for the occasion.

'Sir, with the General's compliments. He told me to tell you, sir, that despite him being a grizzly old man, his gratitude to you for your service and love of France would be rewarded when the time was right. But for now – his words sir – get the bloody speech right or he will see where they hid Madame Guillotine.'

Both men roared with laughter.

'You know, Rogers, I rather think I would like to see my wife. What say you to helping me cook up a little flight plan to bring my wife and son over here for the duration? I must warn you, we might need to kidnap them. They won't come willingly with all their duties on the Resistance front.'

'I know sir, still worth a shot, eh? Why not just get her here for a few months, could she do a bit from over here? She isn't a runner, nor a safe house is she?'

'No, you're right. I'll try to persuade her.'

'Well, put it to her, sir. I know she is keen to see it out and fight and all that. But surely she has done her bit?'

'Well, I can't go to her. Look, let's sleep on it, eh? Goodnight, Rogers'

'Goodnight, sir. Oh sir, Colonel Smyth is coming over at ten tomorrow.'

'Ah good. It will be good to run the speech past the old man.'

They both smiled and the door closed softly. William sat by the little lamp, it was all he dared to have with the blackout curtains up, not wanting a stray aeroplane to disturb this moment. He wanted Odile to come to him in London and he was going to have one more attempt to persuade her to come.

My Darling Odile,

Well, we don't write too much to one another now, do we? Perhaps I should pop this note under the shelf in the little tool shed in Martinpuich as we used to do? Well, I say tool shed, it's a bloody big barn now, after the rebuilding. But imagine it now, my love. Imagine that you stepped in out of the rain to our little space. You look down and to your delight, I have left you a secret note. Clean, fresh paper and a dirty thumbprint (sorry).

We survived, didn't we? We went through terrible times. I don't suppose you will ever tell me the whole truth and I ought not to ask. I know you kept yourself for me, but it was hard. You had to survive and you did, bless you. I spent nights in the pit of Hell, where my only solace was the thought of you (dare I say it now after twenty years of marriage) lying next to me, looking into my eyes. And then the wonderful day we found one another again, in the warm heat of the summer on the ridge. Our wedding, Cowling and the horses, our wedding night, where I gave you the one last thing that I held sacred. Yours to keep and you have it still. My heart, devoted and true, the one part of me the trenches never got. They got everything else, my faith, my trust and my belief. But you have been there for me. Our darling twins, the bliss of their birth (well for me anyway!) and the sudden impulse to love. Little Henri. Little! Funny how we always call him little when he is anything but. What joys they were as babies and what treasures they are.

Which brings me to you. Without you, all of this could never be, would never have been. France and England called us and we moved from one to another, trying to make it right, to do the honourable and patriotic thing. But now, is it not clearer? With your sister here, could you not see how it would be if you were here safe with Henri? You could do what you need to here and be safe from the awful hardships and dangers.

Think about it, my love. I know I am not good at writing to you like this. My heart has been hardened by machine-gun fire and the mine in Belgium. But I hope you see where I am trying to steer. Come to me, and bring Henri. We can find a way to make you safe. Anyway, these are the words of a rambling fool! Come to England, darling wife, and lay next to me again so I can warm your back and watch over you in the safety of England and our love.

Your William (Imbecile)
London 8 August 42

William folded the letter neatly and placed it in one of his blue and black envelopes for personal letters. It would need to be processed and then sent according to the agreed system of letters for French citizens outside of the gaze of the Germans. He sat back, hoping that the words from his heart would be understood and give Odile cause to consider coming here.

But he was tired now and his mind was filled with the memories that he had just stirred. He would retire to bed, but first he would take one last sip of the wonderful cognac from the General. All by himself, he toasted almost everyone he knew, just to make the cognac last a little longer. William's head jerked so he rested it on his desk, willing sleep to come quickly. The little cognac glass in his hand fell to the floor and smashed.

--oOo--

In the morning, Rogers came to wake William. He knocked, entered and stepped inside. One minute later, he placed a call to Scotland asking that the General be woken urgently. Shortly after speaking to General de Gaulle, a telegram arrived from France. It was marked immediate with the instruction that Colonel Collins should read it upon receipt.

CHAPTER FIFTY-ONE
Bazentin-Le-Petit 1942

There was a loud knock. Madame Fournier answered. Odile was at the door.

'Madame Collins, come in please. I am so desperately sorry to hear about Henri's accident for he was such a lovely young man. But what brings you here at this hour?'

'Madame, I am here on a most delicate matter. I need to speak with Delphine most urgently.'

'I am sorry, Madame, but Delphine is not at home. She left three days ago and I have not heard from her. I thought that she was with your family?'

'We have not met as a group for two weeks. Where did she say she was going?'

'I think she said she was on an errand, but to leave a light on, as it were.'

Odile nodded, knowing that this was the code message for *Sunshine Road* members leaving on a run.

'When did she leave exactly, Madame? Please, it is most important.'

'She left at about ten-thirty.'

This would be to catch the noon train to Paris, so Delphine had needed to run to Paris for something.

'Did she seem excited? Keen to leave? Anything out of the ordinary? Please, Madame, please try and remember.'

'No, Madame, nothing. She was probably quiet and a little down, but it was most likely that she was tired.'

'Thank you, Madame, and I do hope that you see her again soon.'

Odile had her answer. Somebody or someone had let slip something important to silly Delphine. Odile thought back to the number of times the girl was ill. And she remembered something that Henri had said to her almost in passing. *Maman, Delphine is ill again. It does seem strange that she is ill so often on a Thursday. She told me it is because we are all out so late on a Wednesday that it chills her chest.* Odile thought on this. She had not spotted the pattern, but Henri had. He had seen her illness after meetings as something more important or sinister perhaps. But it did not add up. Delphine was not a *Sunshine Road* runner for she was never well enough. But Delphine was missing. Something was wrong.

Odile walked towards home, convinced that Delphine was involved, now realising that she had half-suspected it from the time that Henri reported her strangeness, but she had just passed it off as part of being frail. Delphine was missing. Who did she know? What could she know? With a terrible shock, everything fell into place. It was Yvette. Poor Yvette must have poured out her broken heart to her friend Delphine about Aurelie staying at their house. Yvette had put Henri and Aurelie together and had unwittingly condemned her son to die.

All that was left now was to understand what Delphine had done. She knew some of the group's plans, but not enough to endanger anyone. But putting Aurelie into the mixing bowl was enough for someone to make the deadly connection. She returned to the Fournier house.

'I'm sorry, Madame Fournier. I must ask you more questions. Delphine is not with my family but I would like to find her, of course. This may be delicate to ask, but did she have any other friends? Perhaps a man?'

'Madame! Certainly not. Delphine is only seventeen. The only boy she knows is the Barbon boy, who delivers her library books from Albert.'

Odile's heart sank. She stepped to Madame Fournier and took her hands in hers.

'I do so hope that she comes home soon. We will look out for her.'

Deep down, Odile now knew that Delphine was already dead. Used by the Gestapo to find out information about the *Sunshine Road*. The Barbon boy had been identified as a collaborator and had been slowly pushed away from the community in Albert. He had been given occasional information that was incorrect and which would reveal, when investigated, where it had come from. Whatever Delphine had been told by Yvette, she had passed on to this boy and Henri had died because of it. Once again, Odile turned towards home, but this time, she would call in on Yvette first.

'Madame Collins, I was not expecting you. Please come in.'

Yvette was at her table, the wooden surface damp from a glass of water and a flood of tears.

'I cannot sleep, I cannot eat, and I cannot find the desire to live without Henri. I loved him so much and would have made him so happy.'

Odile moved to her.

'I know, Yvette, you don't know how sorry I am that you loved him so much.'

She kissed her forehead and left, satisfied that Yvette was sincere and blameless for the death of Henri. If Odile could help it, Yvette would be forever unaware of her part in his loss.

CHRIS CHERRY

CHAPTER FIFTY-TWO
Bazentin-Le-Petit Autumn 1942

The summer sun had given way to the watery haze of autumn. From her bedroom window, looking out over the blood-soaked approaches to High Wood, Odile could not help but worry for her beloved France. The occupation was hardening, the Germans seemed ready to move into southern France and more soldiers were present around the towns and villages. She had seen enough here. Now nothing was left of her life and she decided not to stay.

William had died and her last memory was kissing him on the steps of the church where they were married in 1919. In this little bedroom, she had first seen his naked body and the terrible scars from the Great War, the wounds that had now taken him long before his time. In this home, she had given birth to their twins and to Henri, with all the laughter and the sadness brought by her family. Now there was only the deepening illness of her father and the frail dotage of her mother. She had struggled so hard to return here. But what about the fight by William's comrades to win back this land? Would leaving be a betrayal? Or would it simply be handing on the torch to another generation so they could fight for this land? If it was worth fighting for then they would prevail. It could no longer be her fight. She decided to rest her soul and step aside for others to stand on the wall and defend France.

Odile went downstairs and out of the front door into the refreshing cool of the early morning. She thought of the little boy who had run down these lanes, forever shouting and falling over into the fields. The young man riding his bicycle and then his beloved motorcycle. The smiles and then the tears when he grazed his knees or sprained his ankles. And the love in his eyes when he regarded his father, looking up to him as a towering God. She walked past Alain's house. Poor Yvette, now heartbroken and thin, a gaunt ghost wandering the lands. Henri was not a perfect boy, but perhaps in another time, things may have turned out so very differently. So many young ones robbed of innocence and hope. She passed her childhood home, gazing at the grassy spot where she had built cars with her father and where William had come to live. She could hear the echoes of their voices, light in spirit and in peace. She walked to the cemetery to the fallen, with the white stones for those brave men who stood up to the invader. On the hill was the little cross to Horace Watkins and the spot where the trenches had been dug, now ploughed over and farmed again. She turned into the sunken lane, hearing the voices of troops gathering for a fight. Fear, humour, jokes and orders. It washed over her, a fading echo of harmony.

--oOo--

By the time Odile had made her travel arrangements, she had reconciled herself to the future. She stepped onto a little cart that would take her to Amiens and her own journey on the *Sunshine Road* to England. For Odile, travelling by train would be easy. She had no luggage, save a few photographs of her family. A woman of her age with the right identification and tickets would have the fewest problems of any traveller. Besides, she had survived a perilous train journey once before when she fled Dusseldorf. She could still remember the workings of the German soldier's mind, the fears and contradictions, the precision and the duty. As each stage of the journey passed, she left a little more of herself behind. Looking back, the village was quite well protected by the thousands of dead young men lying under the surface of the ridge.

Her journey through France took her from Amiens to Bayonne, along the route of the *Sunshine Road*. Odile had officially retired as Dodo and handed over the leadership of the group. At Bayonne, a small boat would take her in the darkness of the autumn evening to meet *HMS St Vincent*. This ship was sailing to Portsmouth and the captain had been instructed to accommodate a guest at the specific request of the French Government in London. Once on board, Odile took in the breeze, savouring every second of the fresh air, knowing how much freedom had already cost her family.

CHAPTER FIFTY-THREE
England 1942

After two days of sailing to avoid detection, the ship docked at Plymouth. Odile looked down at the quayside and recognised immediately the elegant form of her daughter. She could see how much of William was in her face, which gladdened her heart. There was a man in the uniform of the Navy standing very close to her. That must surely be Michael, Armandine's new husband. As she stepped from the gangway, her daughter came to her, holding out her arms.

'Oh, my darling daughter, my little Armandine. I cannot begin to tell you how much I have missed you and have wanted to see you.'

'Oh, Maman, I love you and have missed you too. Oh, Maman, how I miss Papa. I miss my father.'

Odile could hold back the tears no longer and both women simply held each other, unable to speak. Finally, Odile remembered Michael, who had been left standing awkwardly. She held out her hand to him.

'Armandine, my love, you must introduce me to your husband.'

'Maman, this is my beloved husband, Michael.'

'Madame Collins, I have so very much looked forward to meeting you.'

'And I you.' Odile embraced him and kissed him once on each cheek. 'Such a handsome young man.'

Michael smiled. 'We can take the car to the train station, Madame, and then I must leave you.'

'Oh, so soon?'

'Maman, Michael has been posted to London to work at the Admiralty as a legal interpreter – but we will see him again in three weeks. We will travel north by train to meet a very special person.'

As the train departed, Armandine took her mother's hand.

'Maman, Father was so proud to be working for France in London. It gave him something, but I was never sure quite what.'

'My love, your father and I promised never to talk of what happened to us both in the Great War and I must honour that promise. But he fought for all of us and love kept him alive when by rights he should have died. He loved France because he loved us. Love. It kept him alive.'

'I do so wish you would tell us what happened in the Great War, it might—'

'No, my darling. It is done and in the past, all of it.' Odile squeezed her daughter's hand. 'Now tell me, when was the last time that you saw Arthur?'

'Oh, now there is a mystery, Maman! I received a letter from him but it was such a bland letter. He left Trinity Hall and then it all goes a bit secretive. I assumed he was working in intelligence, but even Father could find out nothing. He is safe, though, I would feel it otherwise... Oh, Maman, I wish Henri were here with us. I miss him so much.'

Odile squeezed her daughter's hand. 'So do I, Armandine. So do I.'

She took a shuddering breath and looked out of the window and for the next hour, the two women sat in silence.

'So tell me about Liesel's children, Monika and Franz. Are they being treated well at school?'

'Well, they did get picked on and called names. Their accents are very strong and the other children didn't believe for a second that they were Dutch. It has been hard for them, but they are strong.'

After a change at Preston, they finally arrived at Windermere, where the sun slipped weakly behind the white clouds, casting a chill over the land as the year turned. A car was waiting to take them home. Odile sat silently in the car, preparing for the reunion with her sister, and simply held onto Armandine's warm hand. Although Odile was only forty-five years old, she felt years older, worn by two wars and family tragedies.

At the cottages, the driver opened the door to the car and Odile stepped into the weak sunshine. A young boy and a young woman waited at the door.

'Armandine! Aunt Odile! Please come inside!'

Smiling, Odile followed them indoors where she saw Doctor Karl Eisner, his eyes wet. She embraced him tightly, his tears falling on her hair as he held her. She placed her hand on Karl's face.

'I can see that Liesel chose well, Doctor Eisner, for you have not changed one little bit. You are the very image of Herr Professor. Your father was always kind to me, if a little strict.'

They both laughed and he took her arm and led her into the drawing room, before quietly closing the door and leaving. By the fireplace, stood

Liesel. Odile crossed the room and embraced the woman she considered to be her sister, the years melting away. Once alone, they looked at one another in silence, save for the tears and the apologies for weeping so openly. Liesel guided Odile to a wide seat and they sat down, hands clasped firmly together.

'Odile, I am so very sorry for Henri. If I had known he would come and that this would happen, I would never have asked for your help. You must know that.'

'Liesel, you would have died at the hands of the Nazis and none of you would be here today. Henri died doing what he wanted to do for France. We must celebrate him and remember his bravery. Do not be sad, for we will never forget his love and devotion.'

Liesel squeezed Odile's hands still tighter.

'William came to see us occasionally. Odile, my goodness, he loved you. You were his life. You were lucky to find each other. I am only sorry that things became so difficult.'

Odile nodded. 'He was my life too. Now, tell me about your Doctor Eisner. How is he?'

'Karl has a surgery again! It is a beautiful cottage by the River Derwent. He is so proud when he leaves each day. He is so proud whenever he writes his name. For the first time in years, he does not look over his shoulder each time he turns a corner. And he simply cannot get enough tea!'

Odile laughed now. 'Ah, it does my heart so much good to hear that.'

She paused and looked at her sister. There was one more man between them who needed to be mentioned. Odile took a deep breath and spoke.

'Liesel, I have to ask about your brother.'

'Odile. My brother is a monster moulded from the ashes of the First War by the hand of evil. Let us never mention him. I have no brother.'

'Very well.' Then Odile smiled. 'Tell me, Liesel, do you still have *them*?'

Now Liesel smiled. From her pocket she removed an embossed silver hair pin and a torn piece of card.

'Here they are. I have the photograph of your beautiful family as well. See?'

Odile looked at the happy photograph taken three weeks after Henri was born. How fortunes and lives had changed.

--oOo--

Odile remained with Armandine for four months, until the French Government and the British agreed William's pension arrangements. The property in France would remain in the family, perhaps for visits when the war was over. Odile visited William's parents and together they went to scatter his ashes over the dunes next to the sea. William's father took the little jar of ashes first and in turn they laid their English boy to rest.

William had survived the horrors of the Western Front and the nightmare of the Germans in France again. His final act was to write the speech given by de Gaulle to the French promising his return to govern on French soil. General de Gaulle himself had presented Odile with the Legion of Honour for her husband with the eternal gratitude of France. Odile gave it to William's mother, who promised to give it back when the time came. The wind blew William's ashes out over the dunes, then up and away. They all stood for a moment in the breeze, silent, remembering.

On the train back to the Lake District, Odile found herself thinking of her William and her boy Henri. She had not really been able to grieve their loss. William had been the world and the stars to her. They had lived where other had died. She had been strong and true to him in the Great War and he had been just as resolute, fighting for their love and fighting to find her through the fear and the bullets. But the War had taken so much from him that he was not strong enough to live long with her. Three beautiful children, poor Henri snatched from her arms by the wolf. How she missed Henri. His open face, smiling with a love light for all to see and share. It was no good, he was gone and the little light was out. Her third light had been taken and was not coming back. Through her eyes, glassy with tears, she could see them all. As the train rumbled ever onwards, pushing out for the north, the tears flowed for her husband and her son, for now it was time to mourn their loss. She never went back to live on the Bazentin Ridge.

CHAPTER FIFTY-FOUR
Berlin May 1945

The walls were thick, but the sounds of shelling were as loud as if there were no walls at all. Kurt had heard this sound before, he had been shelled and trapped and he was not going to allow it to happen again. If he was captured by the Russians, he would not just be executed, he would be subjected to almost unimaginable horrors before death. Word must have spread along the Russian Front about the work of the Einsatzgruppen and Kurt Langer's name would be all over their paperwork. Whatever happened to his beloved Führer now, Kurt resolved not to be captured by the Russians.

'What do you mean the Panzers are delayed? Does that mean they are coming or not? What? How? Who authorized that? Did he? Why would he do that? That bunker is cut off so how could he be sure that the tanks are... yes, I understand. We will hold as long as we can, but it is only a matter of hours...'

'So we stay and get captured, sir?'

'No, Bruno, it seems we have been ordered to stay and die at the hands of these Russian peasants. Well I am not doing that. Remember Ullrich? He has the plan for our escape. We take a car west and then south. The rest is up to him. We must go now, the Panzers are not coming.'

'But the Führer—'

'He is lost to us and we are lost to him. He cannot now escape, he is too far towards the Russians. If he is alive, they will hang him by his balls, they really will. It would be a blessing if Goebbels shoots him first.'

'So we are just going to abandon Berlin?'

'What would you have me do with eleven men? Stand and fight? There are thousands of Russians here now, and the Americans are nearly here. It's over. We stay, we die!'

'Then I stay for my Führer.'

'Don't do this, Bruno. I could order you to come with me.'

'Then I would be obliged to disobey an order of my superior.'

'Bruno, think of Ingrid and Anke!'

'I am, sir, I am. I must stay and fight for the Fatherland!'

'You fight for peace?'

'If I must, but I cannot abandon my post. My place is with my Führer.'

'Where is your Führer now, hm? Is he by your side?'

'He would be, he is here with me. Germany is here with me. If you go, you will be nothing more than a deserter.'

'Bruno! How dare you use that insubordinate tone with me? Friend or not, I hereby order you to accompany me out of Berlin!'

Bruno stood stiffly, clicking his heels together in the old tradition of the Bavarian Regiments.

'Sir, I respectfully ask you to withdraw the order, to release me from my duty and post me to the Berlin garrison!'

Kurt looked down, his anger subsiding.

'Bruno, there is no Berlin garrison. It is a myth. There are only a handful of us left. Look at us, in command of little more than our own pistols. Not much of a garrison.'

'Look, I will escort you to the outskirts and then return. If you are going, then it must be now.'

Kurt and Bruno stepped down from the little observation point.

'We have to break out, I think west is the only way.'

'Generalleutnant Weidling is planning a mass breakout tonight, perhaps you could be part of it, Kurt?'

--oOo--

Kurt found his way to the almost total ruin of Generalleutnant Weidling's quarters in the west of Berlin. Orders had come from Hitler to attempt a breakout.

'Helmuth, may I request to be a part of the operation tonight?'

'Kurt Langer? Mein Gott, I thought you had been captured. Go west. Take Bruno with you. Push for the Charlottenbrucke, or at least cross the River Havel any way that you can. If captured, then God protect you because I will not be able to!'

'Thank you, Weidling.'

The night could not come quickly enough. The shelling on the city was relentless and with each burst, more of the Berlin he knew and loved fell away, the dream of Germania lost, the hopes of a thousand-year Reich evaporating in a cloud of grey dust.

'Take off your uniform, Bruno. Burn it.'

'Is that an order?'

'It is the order of Generalleutnant Weidling, my friend knows what he is doing.'

'If we are captured, then what?'

'We are poor Germans bewildered by the shelling, I suppose.'

At eleven, the night was upon them and the small group of the garrison moved off. Some turned north and some south but none went east, where the bulk of the Red Army were upon the city. Kurt and Bruno's group were ordered west through the Tiergarten, towards the Charlottenbrucke bridge over the Havel and on towards the American and British lines in the distance.

As they set off, they first walked the empty, shelled and burning streets of the west side of Berlin. Shells were falling, Russian shells that whined as they came over and burst with a crash, lifting people off their feet with the vibration of impact. There were no bullets here, but shells were the deadliest weapon in a street fight, sending splinters and masonry falling all around, promising instant death.

The darkness shielded the worst of the destruction. There were dead bodies littering the streets, silent soft obstacles, which they carefully stepped around. These were not peasants and undesirables. Here were the citizens and defenders of Berlin. Behind Kurt, his loyal subordinate followed. Far from basking in the light of a glorious Germany, they were now just running in the dark.

'Why can't we have a car? No one would hear it in this shelling.'

'I know, but there is no fuel, Weidling has sent the rest back with the Panzers. If they cannot use it, then no one can.'

The sky was ablaze with red flames and the bursting of shells on the city. Berlin was now lying in state, with the death of the Nazi Party burning before them. At the Tiergarten, the beautiful gardens were ruined, holes blown in the ground and no animals in sight. Here, the garrison spread out, taking up their arms, ready to face the Russians encircling the city.

Kurt reached the bridge. In front of him, the small garrison was over and into Spandau. This part of West Berlin was still quiet, except for some occasional shelling. Most was aimed at the centre of the city. Perhaps the Russians would be surprised at the appearance of a small garrison of men.

When no shooting could be heard, Kurt and his group stepped up onto the bridge. They were vulnerable on the bridge, but there was no escape other than over. They hurried across and down into the district of Spandau. Still moving west, they encountered a small number of Russians on a corner, smoking and cleaning their rifles, ready for an attack on the centre. They could be avoided, so Kurt kept moving forward, not disturbing them. A firefight here would be death, they still had too far to travel.

An almost untouched building had a wide-open door. They paused to gather their thoughts, Kurt deciding that they should simply continue west. They had no intelligence on Soviet movements and positions and they would have to learn as they went. Kurt decided that they would continue for another two kilometres and then if needed, fight their way through to the Americans. They had to get to the Americans at all costs.

At the end of the street was a Russian tank sitting as a silent sentinel. Its gun was cool and silent, pointing along the street. Kurt was sure it would be poised and ready, but it was not possible to hear whether the engine was running or not. They had to take the chance. Just in front of the tank, four Russian soldiers sat talking, without any weapons.

The garrison split into two groups, left and right. The group on the left sat quietly about twenty metres short of the tank, still undetected. At once, the second group was upon the Russians, punching, kicking and striking with their weapons. But there was still no shooting because that would make too much noise. Kurt and Bruno then made their own move, straight past the tank and past the small house in which some Russians were singing and laughing. Once past the tank, the street stretched out for them, north-west to the American soldiers they knew had to be there.

Kurt decided to run until he could run no more. With each step he tried to shed the Nazi cloak that enveloped him, his dream was still for a strong Germany, but he now realised that Hitler's power was gone. For now, it was only survival. Live to fight another day. Rise again from the ashes of the past. Perhaps even a Fourth Reich…

'Halt, identify yourselves. Who are you?'

Kurt was sure that this was a British voice. He answered in English.

'I am Rolf Meinz, my general and I are at the mercy of what men?'

'General? That's damn funny. We're Americans, part of the Ninth Army.'

'What will you do with me?'

'Process you, find out who y'are and get you the hell outta here.'

Kurt looked down at his boots. At least it wasn't the Russians. At least he was protected by a law of some description. The alternative was just too awful to contemplate. He decided that he should come clean and save the punishment of being found out a liar.

'My name is SS-Gruppenführer Kurt Langer and I formally surrender to you. I am not armed and I am at your mercy.'

'A what? A Gruppenführer? Hey Mikey, Gruppenführer, that's a brass hat, yeah?'

'Yeah, a Generalissimo, if he ain't lying.'

'Well okay, Generalissimo Langer, you're coming with me.'

'Hey, we got another one, says his name is Bruno but he don't speak English.'

'Well Langer, who is your friend?'

Kurt looked across at Bruno, whose head was bowed.

'He is Bruno Spier, SS-Brigadeführer, another generalissimo.'

'Shit buddy, two top brass in one night. Got any more of your asshole Nazis, Langer?'

'The rest are soldat and sturmann assholes.'

CHRIS CHERRY

CHAPTER FIFTY-FIVE
Nuremberg, The Palace of Justice 1948

The young clerk almost ran from the courthouse to the little administrative building. In his hand was the notice from the judges to the Chief Prosecutor, instructing him to reconvene his team as soon as possible. A decision had finally been reached on each of the charges for every one of the defendants.

'This is it, Art, this is the moment we have been waiting for.'

'I know, Ben, I am ashamed to say that I have been waiting with eagerness for this very moment. It is for my brother, you see.'

An immaculately dressed general emerged from the building. He too was young, having only turned forty the previous February. He put on his cap and smiled at his prosecution team.

'Gentlemen, it is your time today. We have put these men before the mercy of a court. A courtesy, by the way, they did not afford their many victims. Let us go and hear what justice feels like. Go and feel history being written in every word of the judgements. Go on now.'

'After you, Ben.'

Art stepped aside, allowing his senior to pass by and enter the court first. The general gently tugged Art by the arm and turned him around to face him.

'Art, this has been one hell of a trial. I could not be more proud of you. In fact, I have a little surprise for you. I had your wife and mother brought here today. I had them invited and dammit they came to see you in your moment of triumph. You know those six are going to hang?'

'I see, sir, thank you.'

Art stepped smartly away from the general. Indeed it was a special day, these men were guilty of some of the most horrible crimes imaginable. But his dear mother, should she see this spectacle? Still, it was his proudest moment and prosecuting murderers was what he had come to do. He reached the coolness of the anteroom and entered the court. Ben was already inside the courtroom, standing with his hands on his briefcase.

The two men shook hands at the table and sat, awaiting the appearance of the defendants. The six men had defended themselves, perhaps an extreme arrogance, perhaps cleverly showing a vulnerability that the court would have to take into account. Over the last six-and-a-half months of cross-examination, they had tried to justify the crimes that they had doubtless committed, explaining away their orders, willingly carried out for the Fatherland and the Führer. They had remained calm, controlled and in command. It had been their way, their training. They could not have risen to the high ranks of the Gestapo or the vicious and pitiless Einsatzgruppen, without coping expertly with pressure.

The door opened and the court hushed. The watching galleries were full and the sounds of the creaking timbers grew louder as every single person leaned forward to get a view of the six accused, certain that they would be found guilty. The evidence was too awful for any other verdict.

They entered in silence, as they had done each and every other day of the trial. Perhaps looking more tired, thinner and with greyer complexions than on the first day, but still immaculately dressed, upright and defiant. The calmness and coolness had been unnerving, almost terrifying, especially when the evidence of their crimes was laid out in front of them.

Then the three judges entered, Judge Musmanno, Judge Speight and Judge Dixon. They seated themselves, taking time to compose the final scene of the trial, the final act of justice upon the six accused. Still the men refused to look at the judges. Still they looked sternly ahead, lost in their own thoughts. Art hoped that their thoughts were full of nightmares and remorse. Seeing them again hardened his thoughts towards them, once more he was a lawyer. He looked up to the gallery. There was no sign of his wife or his mother. Perhaps his mother had been unwell this morning. She had been unwell from time to time recently.

Judge Musmanno made his opening statements before finally turning to the accused.

'Will the defendants please rise to hear the judgements of the court?' The calm authority in the voice expected obedience. The defendants were unmoved.

'The accused will stand to hear the judgement of the court.'

One of the six shifted uneasily, but all remained seated, staring at the floor in front of them.

'Very well. If you are not prepared to stand, I will deliver the verdicts to you seated, but I will note your lack of co-operation with the court.'

The little gallery door opened almost silently. Art heard the noise and looked up. He smiled to himself as he saw Marion, his beautiful American wife enter, and behind her, his mother. He watched them scan the room until Marion pointed him out. She smiled to him, then sat at the front where seats had been reserved, her smile fading upon seeing the six men sitting there. The judge gathered his papers, the rehearsed delivery of the judgements was imminent. The court hushed to silence.

'I will begin reading the judgements of this Court upon the accused for the indictments as read to this Military Tribunal. Firstly, defendant Kurt Langer – the court has considered…'

There was a gasp from the gallery. It was Art's mother. She stood and cried out.

'Mon Dieu, it cannot be. It simply *cannot* be.' She quickly turned around away from the scene below. She pushed her way up and out of the gallery. The commotion above caused the judge to bang his gavel loudly on his desk in a futile attempt to restore some order in the court.

The oldest defendant, now also deeply shocked upon hearing that voice, looked directly up into the gallery, his former calmness and composure gone for the moment. His eyes filled with tears, the sounds of his sobs coming from his very boots. The years of devotion to the Nazis, the years inflicting pain and suffering in the SS, the yearning for power and glory for Germany falling off him as he shed the iron exterior, like a discarded overcoat after the rain. He spoke quietly to himself, looking up as the woman left the gallery.

'Do you hate me still?' The Judge's eyes blazed fire at this disruption to proceedings

'Silence. This is outrageous. The defendant will be restrained. Officers?' Kurt repeated the words quietly to himself.

'My Odile!'

Odile had by this time reached the top step of the gallery and now stood, reaching out for the handle to the door. She hesitated for a moment, her hand hovering over the handle. She could see her hands trembling a little. She took a long deep breath, she could feel all eyes of the gallery and the court below upon her. She turned the handle, the door opened and she was gone, without looking back.

In the dock below Kurt now stood, staring at the closed door, tears openly flowing down his cheeks. His knees weakened and he was firmly pushed back on to the bench, but his gaze did not leave the door. After a moment, his strength finally failed and his head dropped to the floor, the blurred image of his boots washed with tears he could not stop. He dissolved into himself. The cool exterior of the Nazi officer was gone forever, all that was left was a poor, insecure boy, still in love with a French girl. Nothing more could hurt him now.

Art looked on in amazement. He had half risen to his feet, but Ben put his hand on his shoulder and drew him back in to his seat. He looked again at the gallery above, now in uproar after the scene. The press men were writing furiously. He saw the back of his wife as she too disappeared through the door, rushing to comfort his mother.

The judge was still banging his gavel loudly, trying to get control of the Courtroom.

'The Court will be silent for the verdicts or I will be forced to clear the Court and adjourn.'

The noise slowly died down, five other defendants now ashen faced, agitated at the terrible scene before them. None looked to their right at the last man on the row, their former Gruppenfuhrer, their leader and their unifying force during this trial. He was the man who had killed freely in the name of the Fatherland. He was sobbing into his own lap, his hands shielding his face, his leadership dissolved in the pool of salty tears.

'The Court has considered the evidence put before it by the prosecution and finds the defendant, Kurt Langer, formerly of the Sturmabteilung, the Gestapo and the Einsatzgruppen Russia West, guilty of all charges and indictments of crimes against humanity, war crimes and of superintending murder on a massive scale. In the exemplar case of the murder of four-hundred Russian Jews in Birisov-Ladiv, you are also found guilty of the indictment of a crime against peace.'

--o0o--

The five other verdicts were read with the Court in silence, except for the quiet words of Kurt Langer, spoken only to himself.

Art looked at Langer and the others as they were finally led away. They had certainly deserved to be found guilty, their crimes undeniable and unimaginable. The last to leave was Langer, who did not turn to look as he had done when he first entered the Court. He was led away by three officers, the door closing behind him with a loud and decided clank.

Arthur looked down at his hands. He now was trembling. He wanted to see his mother urgently. He wanted to know how she knew Kurt Langer and how it was he knew nothing of him. What of his father? Did he know? What secrets had they all held? His poor parents and that awful conflict all those years ago, unspoken and unknown.

He picked up the small pile of papers and placed them into his briefcase. He looked at the little embroidered lettering that his mother has pressed onto the leather strap – A.H.P.C.

He felt Ben's hand on his arm. He was saying something, but Art could not hear. He thought only of his mother and Langer. He knew her. He *knew* her.

Art picked up his briefcase, closing the little brass clasp slowly, resting on the top. The briefcase that had condemned Kurt Langer to hang.

--oOo--

Outside he found his mother, still upset, but when she saw Arthur, she stepped towards him, with her arms outstretched. She spoke quickly in French, so that others around could not understand the words between them.

Odile had not cared to follow the trials in Germany from the quiet safety of the English countryside. Her invitation to the Court was quite by surprise. She had not asked to know who was on trial, she simply wanted to see her eldest son in the Court.

'Perhaps it was wrong of me to come to the Court to see you and these men. I am so proud of you for being so strong and bringing these men to justice. I only hope that I have not brought shame upon you. We could not have foreseen this.'

'Of course not mother, but how do you know this man? I have prosecuted him and he has perpetrated some of the worst crimes in history and you *know* him?' She placed her palm gently on his face. He was also the very image of his father.

'I do Arthur. But your father and I swore never to tell the secrets of our suffering in the last war. I cannot tell you now, but please know this. If this man has been brought to justice and what has happened today does not change that, then I am contented and I hope that you are as well'.

Arthur looked at his mother, he had so many questions. Her face was loving but resolved. He would not find the answers here and chose simply to let the curtain finally fall on the story of Kurt Langer.

--oOo--

Now back in his cell, the sounds of the courtroom resounded in Kurt's ears, along with the briefest vision of his Odile. He stared at the plain grey wall, remembering his time in Cambrai. Even now, he could still feel the softness of Odile's touch on his face. And he could still feel her shy, unwilling kiss – an unwillingness that he had put down to her innocence.

If only she would have stayed in Dusseldorf, they would have had a life together and she would have loved him for the boy he was. He almost cried out when he remembered that heart-breaking day. A day that was now burned on his mind. That terrible day when he came home from the

First War and she was gone. The one he had truly loved was gone. Until today.

With a jolt, the cell door clanked open and through his damp eyes Kurt saw the guard enter. The officer reached towards him, and placed a firm grip his shoulder. It was time. He held up his hand, weak now and unsteady. The fire was out.

CHAPTER FIFTY-SIX
Paris 14 July 1984

Odile walked carefully towards the gate of the park, where a young woman collided with her.

'Sorry dear. You should look where you are going, especially at your age.'

Odile did not look up or respond, but carried on.

'Suit yourself!'

The sounds of the children faded as Odile moved towards the stone memorial. Once there, she looked for the inscription and stood in front of it. Out of her tiny handbag, she took a single sheet of paper, gripping it tightly in the breeze. When she put on her glasses, the list of names on the sheet of paper came clearly into focus. She wanted to read her little note in the quiet of the morning.

Where do I start, the one who God in His mercy has left behind? If I omit a name through failing mind and frail hands, I beg forgiveness. To my treasured Liesel, as much a sister as if you were my own blood. To Karl and your father, for showing kindness and compassion to a foreign girl in hard times. To Herr Wagner, a friend in wolf's clothing, a helping hand from the other side. To my darling Arthur, taken from us too soon, my love, and my Henri, the little light put out by a force of evil and torment. My own mother and father, stoic and proud, defiant and loving.

To my beloved William, my own boy from over the sea. You came to find me, to love me and for that you are mine alone in my heart and my body. I miss you each day. I see you each morning in my waking moments. Henri is at your side. My loving Arthur is in a tree reading.

This is my penitence for letting you all go. To wander in search of peace that I can never find. My loves, for the glory of France and for the sacrifices you made, one and all. I shall not be able to come next year, this may be the last time that I can come to see you. Adieu.

Odile folded the paper, leaned forward and kissed the top of the memorial stone, which was dedicated to those who gave their lives in the defence of France. She turned away and walked slowly out of the park, closing the gate behind her.

Made in the USA
Charleston, SC
26 November 2014